The exciting, original story of a group of men and women brought together by the whirling fates of Europe—waiting on the Mexican border to take the high-way of hope to the U. S. A.

Hold Back the Dawn

by

KETTI FRINGS

The characters in this novel are refugees of a type Ellis Island never saw: aristocrats and intellectuals, the gay and cynical, the pampered and the poverty-stricken, white-collar immigrants waiting at America's back-door for quota numbers they don't even know they'll get.

Here, at the Colonia Gomez in Tijuana, only four hours away from Los Angeles live:

Klaus Eckert, whose lovely American wife, Jennifer, drives down from Hollywood every week-end; Lankowski, Polish pianist and his wife Irmgard, whose lover had deserted her; Emil Klabec, who was once one of the wealthiest men in Czechoslovakia, and his desperately efficient wife; the Old Man and the Kid, strange pair; and finally the irrepressible bounding Tibor Szolinay — a big handsome bundle of bad news.

Set against a background of bull-ring and adobe hut, against the background of beckoning security across the California border, this is a pre-eminently readable novel of tragedy and comedy and current history all mixed together.

Hold Back the Dawn

Hold Back the Dawn

KETTI FRINGS

DUELL, SLOAN AND PEARCE
NEW YORK

*In some parts of the world
there is a saying—that
Man is made up of three parts:
Body, Soul, and Papers.*

Hold Back the Dawn

1

TIJUANA in the bright light of a busy Sunday afternoon is an old whore come to life again. But see her on an average weekday, or late Sunday night, when the crowds are no longer there, and you see what a dreary piece she really is. As the life in the town wanes northward back to the United States the old bag sags, and as she sags, is sad, because of the days that used to be.

Tijuana remembers: The days before 1935 when Agua Caliente was open, when the crowds came and stayed a weekend, a month. When champagne flowed and a little ball went spinning. Three miles beyond Tijuana, and all Tijuana worked there . . . spun balls, shuffled cards, served drinks, threw out drunks, swept the rooms, cleaned the swimming pool, danced, pranced, cooked, poured and whored for the pleasure-seeking, money-spending people from all over the world who came to try their luck at Caliente.

Cárdenas took the gambling away, robbed Tijuana of its life-stream. Tijuana dried up, aged. She paints and powders still on occasions, but underneath she's a dead hussy.

You don't see that at first, when you first cross the border. You've driven south along Highway 101 . . . from San Diego, only seventeen miles away—or from further

3

north, from Oceanside, Laguna, Santa Ana, Long Beach, from Los Angeles or Hollywood. You come in long miles of cars today because today is a Sunday in summer, and today are the bull fights at Tijuana.

You drive in line across the border, past the Mexican Immigration Building, on the right as you enter, and follow the stream of cars to the bridge, into the Tijuana town. Today the town is a jumbled sound track . . . hawkers hawking, horns blowing, donkeys braying, children shrieking. Today is Sunday, and the tourists are coming! Thousands of cars, thousands of Americans. Get 'em, sell 'em, bleed 'em, while you can, Tijuana. Mexican cigarettes at five cents a pack. Tortillas, enchiladas, tamales. Tamales *caliente*. Buy a scarf, señorita. Buy a basket. Buy some perfume, cheap from Europe . . . no duty, lady! This is a free zone, Baja California. Buy some pottery, buy some silver, buy some Mexican jade. Buy some English woolens . . . forty dollars in America, here only twenty. Cheap because no duty. Buy, buy, buy. Buy and spend so Tijuana can live.

Here you, tourist, get up on this donkey cart, against a painted backdrop of cactus. Have your picture taken for a quarter. The photographer will lend you sombreros and serapes, to doll yourself up . . . send the picture back home to the folks . . . let them know you've been to Mexico. They'll think you have; so will you—though Tijuana is only Baja California, and Baja California is only a part of Mexico, a territory, as Alaska is part of the United States. Tijuana is not Mexico. Mexico is wonderful, beautiful, romantic, picturesque. Tijuana is dowdy, dreary, forlorn, a border town, treated badly by the United States,

4

treated badly by Mexico. It's the Siberia of Mexico, Mexico's land of forgotten people.

You see strolling guitarists, gay for the day, red, green and yellow serapes over their shoulders. You hear spritely Mexican tunes, see a few Mexicans in charro outfits showing off on capering horses. At first glance it does seem like color and romance. But look behind, look deep into the crowd. See all those poor little children, ragged kids, running barefoot. See the dogs, mangy and diseased, their bony ribs showing. See the soldiers! Sure, they're soldiers. Uniforms stiff with dirt, bodies bent with fatigue; underpaid, underfed, undertrained . . . but they're soldiers. They've got a fort up there on the hill. And they've got a cannon. You should see where the soldiers' families live . . . well, you shouldn't, really, because today you're here for fun, and that would depress you.

Get along to the bull fights, it's almost three. They start at three. You'll have no trouble finding the bull ring today, a mile and a half beyond the town. Just keep in line, follow the traffic, out the Avenida de la Revolución. That building down on the left, with the windmill on it? The Filigrana. No, it's not a place where you can stop for dinner later, though it does look attractive. More than some of the places. It's not a place for eating. It's a cat-house. It's the only one that survives, since Caliente. That's where the sailors go, from San Diego. The poor sailors, why blame it all on them? That's where movie stars from Hollywood go sometimes, too.

Keep on, that's right . . . straight ahead. There's the bull ring now. You can hardly see it for the dust, just the top, with its yellow flags flying. When the bull ring was first

5

built, it looked like a great copper penny shining in the sun, but one winter weathered it to a dull dark brown. It's only wood. High as a three-story house, and round. There now, you can see it better. Hundreds of cars, gaily colored posters, band music from inside, people hurrying.

"Park your car, mister? Only fifteen cents."

Sure, park it near the bull ring. Don't leave it on the road. That's right, lock it, too. You're nobody's fool. You've heard about Mexicans.

You don't mind the dust now, because you are part of the crowd, and you love a crowd. You fall into it eagerly, headed toward the entrance. What's that peculiar smell? It's a smell you'll find all over Mexico. After a while you get to like it. The smell of charcoal burning. A Mexican woman keeps her enchiladas warm, stirs up the embers. Are you hungry? Want an enchilada now? She's selling them. Afraid of ptomaine poisoning? That's what Americans always say . . . "Went to Tijuana, got sick from that Mexican junk I ate!" They're usually lying—it's usually too much of what they drank.

A Mexican kid tags close at your heels. "Buy a souvenir, lady . . . please buy a souvenir."

Two sticks, two feet long, covered with pink paper flowers. Points at the ends, sharp points. What are they, little boy?

"They *banderillas*. They use in bull fight. Like this!"

He rises on his toes, slim little body curved back, poises the sticks for thrusting, one in each hand. "They throw at bull when he charges. Fifty cents most times. Only one quarter for *you*, señorita."

He called you señorita—*so* cute—so you buy them.

6

Near the entrance, a group of excited people push, jostle, stand on tiptoes to see over each other. What's that? What's the attraction? What *luck*—it's a movie star! Fred Astaire, with his hat on, signing autographs. His wife with him, and Randy Scott. You see—*everybody* comes to the bull fights. You weren't sure before . . . spend the money? . . . drive so far? But *now* aren't you glad you came?

Klaus Eckert took the hand of his darling, and held it tight.

"Tired to stand, Jennifer?"

"No, I'm fine. Are you?"

They were a young man and a girl standing apart from the others. Both attractive, of about the same height and age, and with a look of belonging to each other. But something odd in their attitude. Around them excitement whirled; people shouted, ran, bumped into each other, pressed in line for tickets. But these two did not move, showed no intention of moving. Even the little white dog at their feet seemed stationary. On the girl's face there was a patient expression. On the man's, an expression of keenest enjoyment.

"Jen, are you sorry we not go in? Because we can go yet, if you want it so." He spoke with a heavy German accent.

"It doesn't matter for me. I only thought for *you* . . . it would be a change."

"This is change for me. It is wonderful. It is like . . . how can I say you . . . like when a man in jail is, and the guard leaves him out to see a movie. To see people again, how they are like. How they talk and dress and enjoy themselves. It tells to him that there is a fine world going

7

on someplace—and he feels better to see it so. When he goes back, it gives to him courage, and he can wait for the world a little longer now. Jennifer—see that little American boy! Look, he has an autogram."

"The word is autograph, darling."

"See how he looks on his face. So proud. He thinks how much he can get for it, I bet . . . to trade it with another boy maybe."

"I think it's a shame to put such little boys in long pants. When you were little, did—"

"Jen, look now. He's showing it to his mamma. And she shows it to the papa." Klaus grinned. "Isn't it wonderful? They come to Mexico for to see a bull fight, and look what they get—an autogram from Fred Astaire! That makes a success for their day. For a week I bet they talk about it. Oh, what a beautiful simple life those people live. Over there." His head nodded northward, and now there was envy in his voice, envy and yearning. "City streets for to walk on. Nice neighbors to talk with. Clean movie houses to go to. A nice car, I bet. A great big refrigerator. A good radio. . . ."

"All on the installment plan!"

"Yes, but they *have* them, don't they? In America everybody has everything."

"Klaus, look at me." Her eyes filled with apology and promise. "Klaus, *you're* going to get a new radio."

"I don't mean that." He held her hand tighter, pulled her a little closer. "The radio . . . what's that? I am not of that just jealous. Of everything! The simpleness of their life. Look now, Jen . . . the boy's papa . . . at the ticket window. Counting his change. He doesn't want to get crooked. See how cautious he is. Oh, I love that face."

"What face?"

"The papa's face."

"What's there to love about it?"

"For you, nothing. For me . . . I can't explain. I love even the mamma's face."

"Oh, you just love Americans, that's all." Her voice was a little impatient now. "I do wish you could learn to say 'American' right. Your accent is awful."

"To stand here and look on them. This is more interesting than in there seeing a bull fight. Jen, you know what I could do? When I see an American I could just go up and kiss him for pleasure!"

"That would be cute."

"You don't understand." Her levity, when he was serious —and he usually was, these days—always hurt him.

"Yes, I do. I'm sorry. It's just—your exuberance. It makes me afraid sometimes."

"Do you think maybe someday I'll look and be like an American, too?"

"Of course, dear. If you'll work on your accent. It's so awfully German. I wish you had a French one instead."

"Why? Because it's more cuter? I think it's sissy. For a man, anyway."

"No, I didn't mean that. But when the war comes, so people in America won't hate you."

He turned and looked at her in little-boy wonder: "Why will they hate me?"

"Oh, like during the last war . . . all the Americans hated Germans, even the ones who had been in the country for

9

a long time. They lost their jobs, got put in jail, grocers wouldn't sell to them. People pushed them off the trolley cars. Klaus—all Americans *aren't* good. At least they are not *always* good."

He looked away. "Please, Jen . . . let me enjoy myself, will you?"

His eyes fell on a group of young people racing in a long crack-the-whip line, holding hands, toward the entrance. He smiled again. The girls, college age, wore socks. Funny—and wonderful—the things they did in America. How healthy they looked. How well fed. How free of troubles.

Gradually the crowd thinned. People went in, climbed the stairs, got seated. The parade music started. Oh's and Ah's from the crowd in the stands. Klaus and Jennifer Eckert moved closer to the fence, listened, watched the last people go through. Soon only the vendors were left, and the refreshment-stand people, all Mexicans.

"Come on," said Klaus. "We can go now. Come, Schnucki." The dog stretched, got up, followed eagerly.

They were small figures on a big landscape, threading their way through the parking lot, out to the open field that led across to the road on the other side, the Ensenada road. Eight miles over the hills it led to the ocean, and then south along the ocean, sixty miles, to the bay town of Ensenada. A road that the Eckerts had traveled often, because that was where the consul was. Down there, their past, present, and future lay between the manilla covers of a filing folder, tucked away in the consul's office somewhere. As they stood there by the road, waiting for a truck to pass, they looked consul-ward. As far as they could see, everything brown

. . . brown hills, grass, trees, dried by the summer sun. Quiet . . . no life stirred, just the truck rounding the bend.

Jennifer, feeling the quiet, looked back toward the bull ring, where flags waved, people shrieked. Where lithe figures moved quickly, throwing things, flashing steel—and a strong animal poured red. There! The first bull must have gone down, for once again the band began its frantic playing.

"Come on, Jennifer."

They crossed the road, entered the driveway that, for them, led home.

Six bungalows there, all identical, lined up in two rows of three each, and facing each other. A driveway led up the center, and on further up the hill to the large ranch house above. At the entrance to the drive, a wooden archway, with a sign, COLONIA GOMEZ.

On the steps of the first bungalow to the left, Casa Number One, Irmgard sat. Irmgard, with her strong brown arms, her heavy straight blonde hair . . . her eyes too small, her mouth too hard . . . her dress too tight across her big round breasts. Irmgard sat there, picking at the polish on her finger nails. Her eyes passed over Jennifer's face, and lighted on Klaus.

"Wie geht's? Warum bist Du nicht an die Stierkaempfen gegangen?"

Klaus stopped to speak to her. Jennifer walked on. A few moments later, at the steps of Casa Number Three, the last bungalow on the left, he caught up with her. "Why did you go? You look cross."

"Why does she always speak German to you? She does it on purpose . . . so I'll feel left out."

"She only asked to me about the bull fights."

"I don't care what she says. It's the way she looks at you, as though I weren't around. She could at least pretend she likes me."

"Germans don't know how to pretend. They are not so good as diplomats."

The door of Casa Number Two, next door, opened, and Omah stood there. A little old lady, sixty-three, fragile and tiny, not more than a hundred pounds. Dressed today in her best black taffeta, her silver-white hair combed sedately in a high knot. Pale blue eyes blinking in the sunlight.

"Klaus . . . Jennifer . . . *kommen Sie herein, bitte*. For coffee and cake, *ja?*"

Klaus bounded so quickly up the steps that Jennifer felt a little twinge of jealousy. Coffee and cake in the middle of the afternoon . . . why couldn't she remember it? . . . Germans liked it. Good homemade cake. Oh, Klaus, I do let you down, don't I? But I'll learn, you'll see.

"How nice you look, Omah!"

"This dress, I am having it now since eight years. In Germany, my friends very jealous. Everything there *Ersatz* now. No more silk as this. Come in now . . . I was hoping . . . the cloth is laid, everything ready."

Coffee and cake, a ritual. No handing around of cups and plates in the living room, for balancing on knees. A fresh tablecloth in the dining room. Places laid, flowers in the center, the coffeepot brought on . . . only aluminum, but scrubbed to silver shininess. One plate of cake, another of sugar cookies.

"*Setzen Sie sich, bitte*." Omah was happy, having guests.

They sat down.

12

"The cake is not *so* good," said Omah apologetically. "If I had sweet butter, it would be better. This salt butter *nicht* good for baking."

"Jen could bring you some from the other side—couldn't you, Jen?"

"You have sweet butter in America?"

"Of course." Jennifer laughed. "We have everything. I'll bring you some the next time I come down."

In spite of the sun in the window, and Omah's festive air, the place depressed her. The bungalow was exactly the same as Casa Number Three. The rooms laid out in the same way—the small living room, the smaller dining room separated from the living room by the four-foot china cabinets. The bedroom and bath off the narrow hall behind the living room, the kitchen opening off the dining room. And throughout, the tan plaster walls. It was exactly the same as Casa Three, yet there was something, some presence that made the place forlorn. Searching for it, Jennifer finally discovered what it was. The pictures on the china cabinets.

She counted fifteen on the two cabinets, and knew there were more in the bedroom. All of the same four people— Omah's deceased husband, Herr Osler; Omah's daughter, Lola; Lola's American husband, Bill; and their daughter, Evelyn. Small pictures, big pictures, snapshots, and a few tinted ones in fancy frames. There were photographs of Lola when she was a little girl, taken in Germany . . . but the more recent ones of her, and the ones of Evelyn and Bill all bore the name of a photographer in Sacramento, California. What depressed Jennifer was that these latter three people, so conspicuously there in image, were never there in person.

"Omah . . . have you heard from your daughter lately?"

Omah looked up brightly. "*Ja* . . . just this *morgen* a letter comes."

"On Sunday?"

The lie-guilt spread over the old woman's face.

Klaus caught his wife's eyes, shook his head. "The cake is *fabelhaft*," he said through a mouthful—and Jennifer hastily changed the subject.

Later, Klaus went out. He'd be back in a little while, he said, excusing himself. Jennifer, in the midst of clearing off the dishes, thought it was strange of him to leave her when her time here was so short. She frowned, feeling lonely.

Klaus strolled to the end of the drive. Then, well out of the window's vision, began running.

He arrived at the entrance to the bull ring, breathless and warm.

The ticket sellers, the ticket takers, had all gone in now to watch the bull fight. Klaus pushed the gate open, walked through. As he hurried up the steep wooden steps, the noise and excitement of the ring burst upon him pleasantly. He heard a soft padding behind him, felt something touch his leg.

"Schnucki, go home!"

She wagged appealingly. He had no time to bother with her. "*Ach*, all right, but stay close."

From the top of the steps all was confusion. A blaze of color, movement, sound. Klaus looked for the bull. Saw him on his knees, struggling up, the hilt of a long sword showing. A stream of pink saliva like a glistening cobweb swinging from his mouth. The crowd called, "*Carnicero*

14

. . . butcher!" The boy matador moved close to the plunging bull, reached to pull the sword out.

Klaus moved along the upper platform, looking for Chato. He found him not far from the entrance. A dusty derby clamped down over his dark Mexican face, and over his shoulder a small Japanese parasol. Other parasols, as yet unsold, folded under his arm.

"Chato! Have they had the special attraction?"

"No. It come last. What you care?"

"This the fifth bull?"

"*Si* . . . and no good!"

"Chato, you hold Schnucki for me?"

Klaus gathered the white fluff in one arm and transferred it to Chato. Then he was gone.

He headed toward the steps that led down front. A roar told him the bull was down again. There was the matador bowing. The gate at the far side of the ring opened, and the mule team raced out as the band played furiously. Red plumes bobbing, harnesses jingling. A moment's silence, as the driver hooked the bull on . . . then round and round the ring the bells jingled, the plumes bowed some more . . . dust swirled . . . then the team was gone, leaving only a rosy path where the hunk of bull had traveled.

A man stepped out into the ring.

"And now, Ladies and Gentlemen! The big attraction of the day—"

There were no seats down front. Klaus stooped down, sat on the steps. He noticed his shoes. His best. They'd be ruined in this dust. What would the bull be like, he wondered. Would they put a dart in him to make him mad?

15

"Today we are offering one thousand pesos to the public!"

One thousand pesos, at five to a dollar . . . two hundred dollars. Enough to buy lots of things.

"In a moment we will let the bull out . . . one thousand pesos attached to his horns. . . ."

A new dress for you, Jennifer . . . and a negligee. Something real cute to wear, like you've never had. Not just a bathrobe. Something silky and elegant . . . soft. Oh, and new tires for the car. Absolutely new tires for the car. The rent paid up . . . and then maybe if there's some left over, a new radio for me. Not really important, but just if there *is* some left over, I mean.

The announcer's voice shouted on. Klaus didn't have to listen. He had seen the announcement, had read it eagerly over and over for a week. At last the announcer finished. A bellow and a bang behind the far gate.

"And now, Ladies and Gentlemen, here comes the bull!"

As Klaus rushed toward the fence, he was chagrined to find that a number of other men were moving with him. He had imagined there might be eight or ten daring enou 1 to get into the ring with the bull, but there were that m y already in the ring, and another ten or twelve, to his r ht and left, tumbling over the fence with him. Not Ameri ans as he had hoped—because he wouldn't have feared Ame ican competition. These were mostly men he knew. Bartenders, truck drivers, storekeepers from the town. All Mexicans— and Mexicans know about bulls. He sensed defeat even before he had begun.

He felt stupid, inept. His eyes found the bull, standing directly in the center, head down, the packet of pesos plainly visible on his horns. And behind the horns, well back, two long red paper streamers, which meant they had put a dagger in after all.

Next to Klaus, a man took off his shirt, stepped forward, waved it at the bull. To draw the bull out, to try his temper.

The bull charged, and the little group of men was no longer a group . . . quickly scattered. The bull ran to the fence and turned. Came forward, head up, sniffing. Stood still.

Behind him, Klaus heard the sound of the crowd, indistinct, jumbled . . . an old and familiar sound to him, and suddenly he was no longer at loose ends. He felt at home, knew what to do now . . . remembered his days as a boxer. When the bell rings, get up off your ass, you bastard . . . get out of your corner and move in.

He ran directly toward the bull, poised an instant, danced a little to the left. The bull began to follow. Klaus changed his direction, went around the bull to the right. Before the bull could reverse his lumbering body, Klaus reached for the tail, grabbed it in both hands.

The next moment was a blank. His arms felt jerked out of his shoulders. He felt the sting of the tail in his hands. His hands burned . . . like the burn a sliding rope gives. But it was all feel and no sight. The world went by at a dizzy pace. His feet touched something now and then. There was a sharp hurt in his ankles, and the dull burn in his hands, but in between—where were his legs? He couldn't feel his legs. Were they leaping, flying, dragging, running?

After a while he could see a little more clearly. The bull began to slow. That was the fence whirling around him. The fence, and dark objects, and a little white speck. What

17

was that? There it was again. The white speck had a sound to it, like Schnucki's barking. Now he knew where his legs and knees were—they dragged in the sand. He was down, but still hanging on. Close to his head he could hear the bull's hoofs, feel them pounding.

Klaus found his feet again, and now he used them to better advantage. Ran stiff-legged and dug his feet deep into the sand. Things slowed, steadied, became almost still.

It was Schnucki who barked at his heels . . . that's why the crowd was laughing. Or were they laughing at him? He must look ridiculous, flying around like a tin can on a cat's tail. But let them laugh. Let them laugh themselves to death. A thousand pesos. Jennifer, in silk. A radio, maybe.

"Klaus, you want me help?"

It was Chato, blanched almost white, there with the group of startled men. He came over, careful to keep well behind the bull. "Klaus, you crazy!"

"Shut up and take the tail!"

Klaus waited until the Mexican's hands were firmly around the animal's tail. Then he slid forward along the bull's belly, reached a quick arm around the horns. There, they had him!

With his free hand, Klaus fumbled at the money. It was real money all right, but *Donnerwetter!* how it was wired on. A dozen wires, each criss-crossed over the other, so tight he couldn't even get a finger under one of them.

Now that the bull was still, the others closed in, eager hands grabbing, clawing, scratching. Klaus was deluged with hands, finger nails, spit, Mexican curses. He couldn't even see where his own hand was, but it still felt the money . . . the other arm still around the horns. Someone stepped

18

on his foot, someone heavy. Then the bull moved under the pressure of twenty straining bodies, stepped a little to the side, and Klaus's foot was free again.

"Here, I got knife," said a voice at his ear. "You cut wire."

"Chato . . . get back . . . hold him!"

It was too late. The bull lurched. Men went flying. Men laughed, yelled, groaned, swore at the bull. One of them kicked him in the testicles.

From the stands it was spectacular. Out of that jumble of men came the bull, and still on his horns that same bull-dog that had first pursued him . . . lost for a while in the swarm of men, but when the others were scared off, still hanging on. Laughter quickly died, and the place rang with approval.

Again Klaus dug his feet into the sand, tried to stop the bull. The bull tossed his head. Klaus bobbed like a sawdust dummy. Then the bull tore in a straight low line, gathering momentum, running with purpose.

Someone had opened the gate.

Klaus saw it in time. His weight on the left side of the bull's head was swerving the bull to the left. Klaus saw the fence directly in front, the gate to the right. Harder letting go than holding on. His arm so long over the bull's horns— like lifting a weight to straighten it.

The sawdust dummy rolled over and over, hit the fence. The gate closed. The bull was gone.

The stands were emptying, people streaming toward the exits. The band played a few bars, stopped, packed up its instruments.

It was cold on the sand, because the sun had gone. Klaus

19

moved, must get up. Schnucki's cold nose touched his face. Chato leaned over him, helped him up.

"You all right, Klaus?"

Once up, he forgot how badly he felt. Only angry now. He looked toward the Judge's box, saw that it was empty. He turned toward the gate where the bull had gone out, lifted the lock, and walked through.

Chato ran after him. "No use make complaints, Klaus. No use!"

Inside where the bull pens were it was dark and damp, smelled of blood. The bodies of five bulls hung by ropes on high hooks, and near the bodies a barefoot Mexican waded in wet, with red feet.

"What you want?"

"Where's the bull, with the money on it?"

The Mexican shrugged, and pointed.

The bull leaned against the side of his stall, head down, his eyes still confused, frightened. There were marks on his head where the wires had cut, but the money was gone.

"See, Klaus, I tell you was no use. Come on. Go home."

They left by a side door and trudged across the field in silence, toward the Colonia Gomez. To the right, the cars made their way out of the parking space, threaded three lanes deep back toward the town.

"Chato, I don't want for my wife to see me. Can I wash in your place? Go up the back way?"

"Sure, my place. But I no sure I got towel or soap. But come on, we see—"

Chato's shack was up behind the ranch house. It was dark inside, only one small window. Klaus stumbled against something and there was the sound of glass rolling.

"What's that?"

"Those my bottles. *Cuidado*, Klaus. This way."

When Klaus's eyes accustomed themselves to the darkness —empty bottles everywhere he looked. Two trunks piled high with them in the center of the room. Bottles in boxes against the walls. In the corners. Peeking out from under the cot. Bottles on shelves. Coca-Cola bottles, whiskey bottles, pop bottles, milk bottles, champagne bottles.

"Twenty thousand!" Chato said proudly. "For the most little I get two cents apiece. Me *rich*, Klaus."

Klaus smiled, turned on the faucet, began to wash.

Most of the cars go right back after the bull fights. But some linger to shop, drink, and eat. By ten though, in the darkness, the town is emptying; a few late cars straggle down the main street in the direction of the border. All around, Tijuana makes a last pitiful effort to detain its priceless tourists. The bands in the cafés play noisily. Outside the Midnight Follies a loudspeaker blares "Cucaracha" . . . across the street, "Beer Barrel Polka." Blue, red, and yellow bulbs, strung across the street, blink poor enticement. Mexican girls click along on high heels, twittering musically. Mexican men give it up, sit in the cafés, and play dominos as the last excitement streams northward.

The border looks different at night, as you approach it from the Tijuana bridge. More formidable, lighted up like that. In the daytime you hardly notice the high steel gate stretching across the wide road, but now there are flood lights from above, and there is no missing it. The gate, on rollers, and in sections, has been slid back at either side to allow the passage of cars . . . on the left into Mexico, on the right out of it. It slides back from the fences on either side. The border fence . . . hundreds and hundreds of miles of it. When the traffic back into the United States had been its heaviest, right after the bull fights, the gate had been pushed back to allow four lanes of cars. Now, at ten o'clock, the opening had been narrowed to allow only one line.

At the gate the Eckerts stood talking to Immigration Inspector Whitie Marshall. Driving around, nothing else to do . . . they had decided to stop and see Whitie, keep him company. Whitie liked the two, was always glad to talk to them.

"What are you so quiet for tonight, Klaus? Cat got your tongue?"

"What that means, Jennifer?"

"It means, can't you talk? Has the cat got your tongue?"

"Why would the cat got it?"

Whitie laughed. "That's right, young man. I don't see no sense to it either, but it's a saying." Headlights bore down on them. "Excuse me now, here comes some more customers. Whoa there, mister!"

The driver looked surprised, whoaed. The same papa— with mamma and the kid in the back seat—that Klaus and Jennifer had watched at the bull ring.

Whitie peered into the car. "Don't you see that sign?" he asked pleasantly. "You have to stop. What's your nationality, please?"

The sight of a uniform always muddled papa. "Why I— I'm United States. That is, American. Don't I *look* American?"

"It's not what you *look*," smiled the Inspector. "It's where you were born."

22

The wife's voice sprang out of the back seat, taking charge. "He was born in Xenia, Ohio."

Whitie craned into the back, around a basket and two sombreros, as big as garden umbrellas. "And were you born in the United States, too?"

"That's right. In Holland, Michigan. My people were Dutch. My father—"

Whitie spotted the kid, interrupted: "And this little tyke here?"

"Oh, him!" Papa was suddenly inspired to be jovial. "He's just a little something we picked up!"

"Now just a minute." The Inspector had clearly lost his patience. Voice and face unsmiled. "This little boy—where was he born?"

"In Chicago. But when he was three years old we—"

"Thank you. That will be all. You may go on now."

The car moved ahead. Inspector Marshall shook his head. "It's a pity—when you ask people a simple question, they have to make a Professor Quiz out of it."

"Not a simple question," Klaus corrected. "The most important question in life—and they giggle and make jokes. When an American crosses a border so easy like that, he should get down on his knees and say for it thanks! And he thinks he is having troubles, I bet! Look!"

The car had been stopped again, fifty feet further on, in front of the Immigration Building. This time by a Customs Inspector.

"Good evening, folks. What did you bring from Mexico?"

"Just hats . . . this basket."

"Will you unlock the luggage compartment, please?"

23

Papa crawled out and around to the back, muttering. Opened the compartment.

"Thank you. You can close it now. Do you have any liquor with you?"

"Just a bottle of Scotch."

"You're not allowed to bring liquor across."

"Since when? Last time I was down here we were allowed to bring one bottle apiece."

"There's a new law."

"Nobody told *me* about it. That Mexican that sold it to me . . . that's nerve! He didn't tell me anything!"

"Maybe he thought you were going to drink it over on his side. Anyway, you can't expect Mexicans to keep Americans informed about their laws. You'll have to leave the bottle here—or try to take it back. If you leave it, it will be auctioned off for charity later."

"Fat chance I'd have of getting my money back—here, take it!"

A few feet further on a state traffic officer halted the car, asked to see the driver's license. The license had expired. Papa was told to get it renewed within five days, present it at court, or pay a fine.

The officer sank back into the darkness. Papa drove ahead, furious, fermenting. "Come to Mexico for a nice day . . . what happens. Ask us questions like we were criminals, search my car, take my liquor away. Give me a ticket. Hell's bells, what's this country coming to anyway?"

Klaus looked after the departing car, saw the taillight disappear around the curve, headed up that golden Highway 101. Had he heard them, there in the car, wailing over the small inconveniences that had occurred, he would have

24

laughed. Those lucky, lucky people. How easy for them . . . so free to come and go. They had crossed a border without showing a single paper, and in less than ten minutes. What did they know about troubles? Doors shut in their faces, the bars down, the gate closed? For some people it takes years to cross a border.

"Whitie, some day I'm going to cross easy like that, so quick . . . when I have my papers. Ask me what nationality I am . . . I've been practicing."

Whitie put his arm around the young man's shoulder. "Oh, you can't say it right yet."

"Yes, I can. Try me."

It was an old game. They went through it at every meeting.

"All right. What nationality are you, mister?"

"Amurrican!"

Jennifer and Whitie laughed.

"Why are you laughing for?" A forced grin to hide his hurt. "Didn't I say it good?"

"It's A-mer-i-can, dear. Not 'Amurrican.'"

"Take it easy, son. Another couple months and you'll have it down pat."

Another couple of months. Sounds little. But in another couple of months he'd be crazy. Suddenly he looked tired, worn. A pain reminded him of the afternoon's battle.

"Klaus, you look all in. Whitie, I think I'd better take him home. It's late. Good night, Whitie."

"Good night, kids. I'll be turning in myself pretty soon."

They got into their car. As they swung around toward town, Klaus looked back, through the gate, up Highway

101. He had a funny sound in his voice; he always did when he said it. *"Gute nacht, America."*

He looked at his wife, and already felt miserable. In less than twelve hours, she would be traveling up that road too, alone, and away from him.

2

ON a frosty March morning in 1939, Duwid Lankowski, Jew, entered the American Express office in Warsaw, Poland, said that he would like to go to Ensenada, Mexico. He was a small, slight man, about forty, round-shouldered from long years at a piano. This morning, troubled and nervous.

The trip seemed easy to arrange at first. Mr. Lankowski could sail to New York, then cross the United States, and enter the Baja California peninsula at the Tijuana-San Ysidro border. Go from there by bus, south to Ensenada.

Duwid Lankowski listened to the young man, who fortunately spoke Polish as well as he did, glanced around uneasily, sidled around to the other side of the desk, further away from the other customers. "I—I am afraid that is not possible. I have no American visa."

"But you can get one quite easily. A transit visa, permitting you to pass through—"

"I have tried." The Jew spoke with such dull finality that the agent looked surprised. Duwid Lankowski, composer, well known, rich—not permitted even a transit visa!

"But you have a Mexican visa, of course?"

"Of course." Mexican visas were fairly easy to get. Duwid

27

drew two small cards from his pocket. One for himself, one for his wife, Blima.

"Then you can go direct to Mexico, land at Vera Cruz on the east coast. From there by train to Mexico City. But from there, Mr. Lankowski, I am afraid there are difficulties. First of all, you must ask the Mexican government for special permission to go to Baja California."

"I do not understand."

"Neither do I exactly—but as it is a free state, and so close to the United States, I suppose there are border complications. There used to be a great many spies and smugglers in that section. At any rate that is the situation. You will have to get permission in Mexico City—when you get there."

The agent consulted a reference book, then continued: "I am afraid there are more difficulties. There is no train connecting Mexico with Baja California. There *is* a train to Los Angeles, which crosses the border at Nogales. But if you get off the train there you would still have to cross the border to get to Baja California. There is no road on the Mexican side. I am afraid—"

"Yes, yes, I know. If I *had* the visa—but I haven't." The Jew's embarrassment was painful. As a result he became abrupt and cross. "I have told you my situation, now will you please just tell me how I can get there. There must be some way!"

Eventually, the agent worked it out. From Mexico City there was a bus to Acapulco on the west coast of Mexico. From there Mr. Lankowski would have to arrange his own passage north, by boat, to Ensenada. There were a few Mexican boats which made the trip now and then, small tubs, fishing vessels mostly. Larger boats also stopped at

Acapulco, but from there went directly to San Pedro, in California.

"Very well." Duwid placed his personal card on the desk. "Will you please arrange as much of the trip as possible, for myself and my wife? Telephone me and let me know the cost. Thank you. Good day."

At the door he stopped, turned back. "We—we would like to make it as soon as possible." He tried to smile, tried to make his voice sound eager.

Conjecture and curiosity in the office after Lankowski had gone. No one could understand it. Why should anyone want to go to Ensenada, Mexico? Halfway across the world, as difficult as heaven to get to. And when you did get there, what was the attraction?

It was an unfortunate series of events which had led up to Duwid's call that morning and to the strange trip he was planning.

Three months before he had begun to fear for his future in Europe. His music banned in Germany, his last two operettas returned from Vienna, his contract with a Hungarian picture company canceled. He wrote to a friend, Moritz Lester, once Leshewski, and now a well-known movie director in Hollywood, and told him of his problems. Lester wrote back that Hollywood was the place for Duwid and he must come at once. "There is only one thing I must warn you about," Moritz wrote. "To get an immigration visa into the United States is difficult right now, and you may have to wait many months for a quota number. It would be better for you to come over on a visitor's visa. Then, once you are here, I can help you arrange your permanent papers."

Duwid and Blima went to the American consulate in Warsaw, applied for temporary visas. In their applications they had to give references, list properties, and state their reasons for going to America. They signed the applications under oath, returned home to make preparations for their journey.

A week later, Duwid and Blima stood before a vice-consul's desk and received their visas, stamped firmly in their Polish passports. On their faces a reflected glow, as they faced their new world and saw it ablaze with opportunity.

"I thank you much," Duwid began, his heart overflowing, his English not quite adequate. "It was kind to arrange it so, but tell me, please, there is a small thing I do not understand."

"I will be glad to help you."

"This visa is for six months. But what must I do to get another one when I am working? To who do I ask for more longer? Must I ask it in the United States, when I am already there?"

The American's face tensed. Oh, so much unpleasantness. What a job. The happy faces in front of him, so few. He spoke with dread, fearing the answer: "You are planning to stay permanently?"

"Oh, yes!" Duwid was smiling. "We make plans to live there."

"May I have your passport, please?"

The vice-consul thumbed through the first few pages, found the page where the Open Sesame to America was, laid the book out flat at that page on the desk. He reached in a drawer and picked up a rubber stamp. Planted it firmly over the visa. Duwid heard the sound, could not see the mark it made. This consul, so nice, perhaps he was arranging an extension now.

The consul turned to Blima. "And yours? May I have yours, please?"

He lifted the passport out of her still hands, turned the pages, repeated his action. Then he picked up another stamp, moistened it on a pad of red ink, and applied it to both the visas. He handed the passports back.

Blima looked down at the visa, stood like stone, her brown eyes glassy. Staring horrified at the large square-blocked word, INVALID, and at the heavy red lines, criss-crossing the length of the page.

"Our visas! Look!"

Duwid was no longer smiling. Quaking, clutching at the vice-consul's arm. "Our visas! What you do? What you do? Oh, explain me, please!"

It was only after the interpreter had been called in that they were finally made to understand. "Attempted fraud" . . . sworn statements in their applications that they were going to America as tourists, not to seek work, not to stay, but to return to Poland at the end of six months. The consul had no choice. Printed words in a book that had to be followed: "No consular officer is permitted to grant a tourist visa, when he has reason to suspect that the foreigner intends to reside in the United States permanently." He had to cancel the visas.

Duwid, wailing and moaning, his wife sobbing quietly. Their so-close dream, a fading mirage.

"I am sorry, Mr. Lankowski, but don't you understand? These laws have to be. So many foreigners try to overstay their temporary visas. Checking up, deportation . . . it is all very expensive . . . one of our worst problems."

Words, just words, to the Lankowskis.

"Please, then, please!" Blima reached far across the desk, appealed with outstretched hands. "Can we not ask for the other visas then? The longer ones? The forever ones?"

They could ask. That was about all. Duwid and Blima no longer had any illusions. There were thousands of Polish requests for quota numbers, there in that very consulate, ahead of them. In view of what had happened they could not expect their turn to come around very quickly.

Again Duwid wrote to Moritz, and Moritz answered that if Duwid were closer he could help . . . get an American lawyer to take up his case in Washington. He suggested the Lankowskis come to Ensenada, near to Hollywood, where there was an American consul, and have their case transferred there.

Twenty-two days on a German freighter to Vera Cruz. A day by train to Mexico City. Two weeks in Mexico City before they could obtain permission to enter Baja California. From Mexico City, two days by bus to Acapulco. In Acapulco Blima became ill, vomited daily, a pain around her heart. She pretended it was the climate. They missed one boat, waited two weeks for the next. Nine miserable days aboard, with ten Mexican fellow passengers, and they arrived at last in Ensenada.

As they sailed into the Ensenada Bay, Blima and Duwid stood at the rail, and the beauty of the scene eased their tension. The smooth curve of the beach, the golden mountains as far as they could see. The sky a perfect blue, bunched with whipped-cream clouds. To the left as they

32

faced shoreward, a few small buildings along the bay, puffing lazy smoke. The fish canneries. To the right, a large magnificent hotel, rimmed around with palms.

"Look," said Blima. "That hotel . . . it is like Europe. At least we are lucky to have money . . . that will be something we can enjoy. We will stay there. We'll have a room facing the sea. To look at the sea always calms you, Duwid. And we won't have to wait long, I am sure of it. Lawyers in American can fix everything."

There was no dock. There were only two other small boats, sailboats, in the bay. The larger boat anchored in the center and after a while a launch came out, bringing immigration officials. When they saw the canceled American visas in the Polish passports they talked among themselves. Duwid and Blima, miserable, looked away. Why must it be left in there? Why couldn't the visas have been torn out? Every time they had to show their passports, embarrassment and shame.

At the small shipping office, near the canneries, a customs official who spoke English told them that it would be an hour before their luggage would be brought in. Duwid and Blima set out toward the hotel to arrange accommodations.

The driveway up into the hotel was blocked off. Words on a sign they couldn't understand. They went around the barricade, proceeded further. At the rear entrance to the hotel they stopped, saw that the door was barred. Above the door, a red flag.

A Mexican lying under a tree raised himself against his elbow . . . shook his head. There was a rifle beside him. "*Cerrado!*" he said.

33

They went back to the main street of the town. There was another flag down the street, more inviting. Vivid red, white, and blue, flying above a small one-story frame building: Consulate of the United States of America. It was to enter this particular door that they had traveled from one hemisphere to another.

Blima, after her first sad experience, could never face another American consul without trembling. But Duwid was even more distraught, and it was she who had to do the talking.

She told him their story, broke down now and then with nervous tears, finally finished. "There, that is all. We want to ask you now, will you please be so kind and help us apply again for to live there?"

The consul rose. He was a harassed-looking man, fifty or so. He had listened to the long account without a change of expression. Always the same attitude of polite attention. When Blima had cried, he had looked away, waited calmly for her to finish with her tears, and continue. Consul training. All consuls wear the same expression on their faces—so that immigrants have coined the phrase, "consul face," using it in the same way as "poker face."

In a way their coldness is a kindness. It would be cruel to give people false hopes, a premature promise of friendliness and refuge.

"I will write the consul in Warsaw, and ask him to send your file. I'm sorry, I can't do anything until then. When you find a place to live, please let me have your address."

"Can—can you not tell us a place? The big hotel here . . . it is closed. We want only some place, clean please, and perhaps a little cheerful."

34

The consul hesitated. He was not supposed to make recommendations, but the two before him, so worn from a long hard journey, clawed at his sympathy.

"If you will speak to my secretary, outside, I believe she can help you."

The young American woman, discovering that the Lankowskis knew only a little Spanish, suggested they try to find a place in Tijuana. "It's at the border and more people speak English there. Also, there are other Europeans . . . a little colony . . . you might feel more at home." She wrote a name on a card: Colonia Gomez.

They went out into the white glare of the Ensenada street, so quiet, so empty. It was hot noon and the town was sleeping. Back to the shipping office.

The customs official was asleep on one of their trunks. Blima spoke softly, "*Señor* . . . *Señor*," and looked shyly at Duwid for approval because she was speaking Spanish.

The mustache twitched, and the Mexican got up. "Well, you like Mexico?"

"We like it," Duwid said.

"You try go United States?"

"Yes. We apply for papers."

"You got money to stay long time in Mexico?"

"We have for six months. We hope to come into the United States before then."

The Mexican shook his head. "You not get in then. Two years here. You stay two years here, then they give you papers. No before."

Blima spoke to her husband in Polish. "Don't listen to him. He's just trying to frighten us. Don't listen, Duwid."

35

Duwid approached the taller Mexican, looked up into his face. "Explain me what you say."

Duwid, so desperate and so tense that the Mexican backed away.

"Is not *my* law!"

"Explain me!" Duwid repeated fiercely. It was a phrase he was to say often in his new life.

"Well, you come from Europe to Mexico . . . *si?* From Mexico you apply United States . . . *si?*"

Duwid nodded, and the Mexican shrugged. "Well, the American law it say, man from Europe, who come to Mexico, to come to United States, he have to be in Mexico first for two years!"

Blima went to the window, stood looking out. Duwid followed, slipped his arm around her. "It's not true, Blima. I know it is not true. Be still now. If it were true, don't you think that someone would have warned us?"

"Missus . . ." The Mexican shuffled across the bare floor, touched Blima's hand. "Missus . . . don't blame *me*. They make the law up there, on the States side. Missus, no cry now. Mexico not so bad. Mexico glad to have you . . . Mexico hope you stay long time."

He looked around, feeling guilty, wishing for something to divert her. There were geraniums growing outside against the window. He leaned out, picked one, laid it on her arm.

Too moved to think or speak in anything but Polish, Blima murmured *"Dzię kuję"*—a pathetic thank you.

3

KLAUS had gone in to Tacuba's to look at the silk lounging robes from China. Twenty dollars apiece. Idiotic to even think of them, but he couldn't help himself. When he was lonely for Jennifer, it was a comfort to at least pretend he could buy her something, plan giving it to her.

A robe, for example. He knew precisely how he would present it, projected the exact scene in his mind. Turn the bed down, have the robe laid out there when she came in, beside her pajamas. When she arrived late at night they usually had dinner. Something he had fixed. Often it was a dinner spoiled by the delay, often he was cross and weary with hunger, but on her homecoming nights he refused to eat until she got there.

Jennifer would come in. They would kiss. He would scold her for not getting there sooner, suggest: "Why don't you undress before you eat—put on your night clothes, for comfort?"—so she would be sure to go into the bedroom first. He would stand behind her, watch her expression in the mirror. Then, when she saw the robe and rushed into his arms, pretend to be embarrassed: "I told that girl not to leave her things lying around. She is so careless!" Laughter, more kisses, excitement. Jen slipping out of her clothes to try it on. Klaus, you shouldn't have done it. How did you buy it? What with? How much? Oh, Klaus, isn't it beautiful?

But one thing—Jennifer must be more careful with this than with her other clothes. She must keep it hung up neatly in the closet. Not thrown over a chair. Not wear it in the kitchen. Jen, so American-careless. That's why she never had anything. Americans didn't care about *things*, got tired of them quickly. The least little worn, throw it away. Even presents. That was one thing he couldn't understand. A present was sacred. You always took care of it, kept it always, unless of course you got hungry. Really hungry, the third day. Then it was permissible to try to borrow on it, and if you couldn't borrow, to sell it. For hunger you could do things like that, but only for hunger.

"Klaus, I *said* can I help you?" It was Stella, one of the salesgirls. Klaus often talked to her because she had gone to school in San Diego, spoke English like an American.

"Stella, will you try this one? The pink one? You're not so tall like my wife, but I can have the idea."

"You're going to buy it for her?"

"I'd like to."

Stella put it on. The robe dragged on the floor. Klaus lifted it quickly, peeved as though he had already bought it. "Hold it up, don't make it dirty!"

The girl stepped before the full-length mirror, turned slowly. Turning, her eyes watching Klaus. Smiling prettily.

Klaus looked at the robe, didn't see the smile. It was always there for him, but he never saw it.

"It will look more better on my wife," he said finally.

"Oh, yes, I know. Your wife, your wife. That's all you talk about!"

38

Klaus wasn't listening. He couldn't buy the robe; he was only fooling himself. "I wish I had a job. I wish I could work."

"Did you write to Mexico City about it?"

Klaus nodded.

Poor boy. Stella felt sorry for him. Whenever she kneeled before the Virgin she remembered to say a prayer for him. She never prayed that he would get his American papers— if he did, she might never see him again. But she did ask the Virgin to put in a good word for him at the Immigration Department in Mexico City so he could get his working permission.

"Maybe I won't have a job anymore myself." Soft voice, hoping for sympathy. "If the Americans put through that twenty-four-hour law, we'll all be out of jobs."

"They wouldn't do that."

"Yes, they will. The merchants in San Diego and Los Angeles—they think we take away their business. They don't stop to think how much we buy over there . . . furniture, cars, radios. You know no American is going to stay twenty-four hours down here just to take back merchandise. When they make that a law, we'll be through, that's all."

"Turn around again, Stella."

"Klaus, it's really nice. So soft. Feel!" She put out her arm. He ran his hand over the sleeve.

"Stella, will you put it someplace for me? Hide it? So no one else can buy it?"

"How many things have I already put away for you like that? And you never buy anything!"

"When I get some money I will."

39

He watched her fold the robe, wrap it in tissue paper. She found a place for it, behind some boxes, way back on a shelf.

On his way again, Klaus stopped in front of the Foreign Club to say hello to Josephina and her baby. Josephina was the donkey belonging to José, one of the photographers. Three days before she had had her baby, and was already back in harness, her straw hat with the two holes set down over her ears, to keep out the sun; her offspring tottering beside her.

It was quite an offspring, striped like a zebra. Painted that way by José. Only the people in the town knew it, and would keep it a secret because José planned to sell it to an American. An American would pay all sorts of money for an oddity like that. When Josephina had foaled the last time, José had done the same thing. He had told an American movie star he wanted fifty pesos for the zebra-donkey. The actor understood him to say dollars, paid him fifty dollars, believing the odd animal would be worth many times that much in publicity. Then when it rained a week later, José kept out of sight, spent the next few days at home in case he should have an irate caller from Hollywood. José had not yet found a way to make the stripes waterproof.

Klaus spent ten minutes talking to José, patting the donkeys, then moved on. Only ten o'clock in the morning, and where to go now? It was always like this, every day, over and over, trying to fill the hours. He stopped in at the post office, was told that the postman, Julio, had already left with the mail for the Colonia Gomez.

"*Qué húbole*, Klaus!"

It was the Mexican, Grandotte, a big, sullen man, with a

mean, lined face, who owned one of the marriage and divorce offices in the town. Standing there in the doorway, he had put out his foot and purposely tripped the young German. Any bodily attack always infuriated Klaus, partly because of his days as a boxer, partly just because he was German.

"Klaus, you get letter from Europe, you give me stamp?" Grandotte asked in a manner that was not so much asking as demanding.

"I told you. I give always my stamps to Mr. Klabec."

"I collect, too. You give *me* next time, huh?"

"I give to Mr. Klabec because he is immigrant like me. He doesn't have much to do. I give him the stamps because it makes him happy."

"I like stamps, too."

"But you have a business. You have much things to do!"

"You give *me* stamp next time or you have troubles." Grandotte turned and waved to a motorcycle policeman as he passed. "I have lotta friends here," he said, nodding in the direction of the policeman. "They do me favors. You give me stamp next time or maybe you have something wrong. Traffic ticket maybe. I not say exactly, but something."

Grandotte, in spite of his largeness and unusual height, had short arms. The perfect gun length, and the right arm especially had a habit of always hanging close around his hip. As though to remind Klaus that he meant business, he placed his right hand on his gun holster, felt of the flap fastening.

Klaus saw the gesture and smiled. These Mexicans with their guns. He recalled one of his first impressions of Mexico, on the train from Vera Cruz with Jennifer. A pleasant Mexican family in the seats across the way. A large burly man with his wife, his mother, and four children. The man had been so patient, so gentle, running constantly for water, allowing his wife to sleep on his shoulder, taking the children out to the observation platform. But every time he moved you could see the bulge of his guns, one under his arm, one on his hip, and it had seemed so ludicrous. Later, Klaus had even seen guns on a dance floor in Mexico City. But he had never seen them in action, and he had the feeling that they were just props. And anyway, what were guns against fists? Klaus believed in fists.

Now he looked toward Grandotte's gun, and smiled as though he were smiling at a boy with a toy. Patronizingly.

"What you laugh at?" Grandotte asked suspiciously.

Klaus held his hands in front of him, casually closed them, closed them hard, opened them again, rubbed them together, put them back in his pockets.

"Nothing," he said.

Klaus had never owned a gun, never shot one, knew little of its lightning. As a boy he had had a quick, bad temper, and his father, fearing that one day the temper would get him into trouble, had made him promise: never to carry a knife or gun, never to touch one. And it had been easy to keep the promise, because he never had need of such things. At fifteen he had gone out into the world to battle with his fists, and they had done very well for him. Fight managers made good use of his temper . . . a faster and wilder variety than that found in most German fighters . . . and when he was seventeen, in Belgium, he had become European lightweight champion. Now he couldn't fight any

42

more, not professionally. He was old. He was almost thirty.

But the habit of years isn't easily forgotten . . . how nice it sounds and feels to have your fist go home. Klaus wished now that he could push it into Grandotte's unpleasant face. It wasn't the gun which stopped him. The only fear he had was of the vile dirty jail, where Grandotte would certainly see that he landed. The jail, and Jennifer. Jennifer had never seen him fight, said she never wanted to. Or to hear of it, even. And she had made him promise not to.

Grandotte didn't like the look on the German's face. "Listen," he said. "Next time you give me stamps, see! And remember, through Julio, I keep count. I know when you get European letter."

"Little stamp gangster," Klaus said to himself in German, and walked away.

He started home, feeling out of sorts. Out of place, alone, his body shrieking for activity. His spirit depressed by the life around him. Yesterday, the unfairness of the stunt in the bull ring. José's trick, today, with the donkey. The shops with the gloom of the proposed twenty-four-hour law already sinking down over them. Grandotte with his threats, wielding a policeman as a club. He could do it, too; Klaus knew how easily Grandotte could get the police to make trouble for him.

How strange it all was. In Germany, if a policeman arrested you without reason, you could press charges yourself. In Germany, if a prize was offered, someone received it. In Germany, if you painted a donkey, people wouldn't stand for it. Too much paint, and the donkey would die.

Oh, maybe it wasn't so in Germany now. He didn't know

what was Germany now. But it was like that before. It would be like that in America, anyway. Things orderly and fair.

Involuntarily, as he walked, he turned his head back, and looked northward.

Julio, the postman, usually arrived between ten and eleven. He enjoyed calling at the Colonia Gomez, because he had only to step inside the arch, blow his feeble little whistle, and instantly he was the center of attention, the objective of a frantic rush from the bungalows. Usually a representative from the house on the hill dashed down, too; most often it was Mady Weiss, the child who with her parents boarded at the Gomezes'.

This morning after the bull fight Irmgard was first out, in a pink cotton bathrobe. Julio was attracted by the robust blondness of the German girl and loved to prolong his brief contact with her. Coyly he hid a letter behind his back—which she snatched away crossly, hurrying back into her house to read. It was typical of the immigrants that they ran away to secluded corners to read their mail—they so often received bad news, and like animals they preferred to endure bad moments by themselves.

"*Nada para tu*," Julio addressed the small Mady. The child refused to be turned away so quickly. She stayed close to the Mexican, peered into the mail bag. She was a thin, nervous child with deep-set eyes, and unnatural dark rings under them. Children in America waited for the postman to bring them Lone Ranger buttons, pictures of Mickey Mouse, Gene Autry, and Shirley Temple. Mady Weiss waited and

44

prayed for a letter from the consul, telling her parents that they could have their quota numbers.

Klaus came up the drive, and joined the group around the mailman. Mr. Klabec, Mrs. Klabec, Mr. and Mrs. Lankowski, Siegfried, and Mady. Omah waited eagerly from her steps. There was a letter from her daughter and Klaus took it over to her. She reached for the letter with a quaking hand, went inside.

Irmgard had reappeared with hers. It was very short; it hadn't taken her long to read it. "Dear Irmgard: I am sorry I can't get down this weekend. I have been very busy, but I will try to make it next week. Hope you are getting along all right. Best of luck, Tom." It was typewritten, even the signature; postmarked Los Angeles, it had been mailed three days before.

"You, Julio. *Por qué ce brief no esta aqui antes . . . Sabada?*" Her mixture of bad Spanish, German, and English was unintelligible, but he recognized the usual complaint: why was the service so bad, why hadn't the letter arrived sooner? He shrugged, smiled.

Klaus saw the letter in Irmgard's hand. "Since when do they write love letters on typing machines?"

She gave him a hurt, pained look, and he felt sorry.

She was cross and miserable. If the letter had arrived on Saturday, as it was intended to arrive, she might have avoided the long Sunday waiting. All day she had sat on the steps, watching every car as it came from the intersection.

There was no mail for the Lankowskis, nothing for Siegfried, and only a General Electric catalogue for Mr. Klabec.

45

There was a letter for Klaus, from the Immigration Department in Mexico City.

He walked up the hill to the ranch house to find Mrs. Gomez. He understood a little Spanish, but the formal phraseology of a departmental letter was too difficult. He found a few negative words, however, which made him fearful.

He was not much surprised when Mrs. Gomez translated. In answer to his most recent request, he had again been denied the right to work in Mexico.

He had found Mrs. Gomez in the kitchen preparing a breakfast tray for Mrs. Weiss. Mrs. Gomez was shapeless and short, with her hair worn in a long bob, Hollywood style, permanented at the ends. She had the Mexican penchant for bright colors and jewelry, often wore little red flowers or bows in her hair, sometimes a rhinestone buckle taken off an old shoe. She had spent her life on the border and spoke English well. Before she married, she had been one of the cashiers at Caliente, in the spa, and it was her dream that when Caliente reopened, when there was another president, that they might turn the present Colonia Gomez into a fashionable guest-ranch resort. There would be a garden, umbrellas and tables, ping pong and tennis, the bungalows repainted. A bar in the main ranch house, and more rooms added. Good stiff prices. And of course she'd turn out the immigrants then. But for now, she had to put up with them to keep going.

Individually, they were not bad, but as a group they were not the most desirable tenants. Rent days it made her sick to see the looks on their faces. Handing over thirty dollars as though they parted with a fortune. She knew for a fact—

because her brother worked in the bank—that the Lankow-skis had several thousand pesos. The Klabecs, too; but after every rent day they were sunk in depression. Mr. Klabec had said once, "To see our money going and not to know if ever we will have more—it is like to lose blood." She understood they were nervous and frightened, but it was their problem, not hers, and she hated to be so close to it.

Mrs. Osler, or Omah, as they called her, was the worst problem. Her rent came in dribbles, whenever her daughter in Sacramento could send her five or ten dollars. What disturbed Mrs. Gomez most was that if the daughter ever stopped sending money, she couldn't turn an old lady out. Not a real old lady like that. Siegfried—he depended, too, on money from relatives. But Siegfried was a Jew; Mrs. Gomez wouldn't have to worry about him. Then, there was Irmgard; but she could get along, too. Attractive and young. Besides, Mrs. Gomez believed the story that the German girl always told her: that one day soon her American was coming down to marry her. Then, as the wife of an American citizen, she would get into the States right away.

"Klaus, how is it that you don't get your papers?" Klaus, already in Tijuana for three months—and Europeans, married to Americans, were usually put on the preference-quota list, and seldom had more than a month or two to wait. "You're married to an American—why don't they let you in?"

She saw that he was upset, jittery.

"You know the two-year law!" he answered quickly. "We came from Europe direct to Mexico. We didn't know about the law. Now we're caught from it."

"You can get around it. There was a Spaniard here once.

47

When he got his quota number he went to Panama and came in from there. That's what the Lankowskis plan to do."

"We don't have money now for a trip such as that."

"But have they told you that you *can* have a visa?"

"Not yet." He was restless, started nervously for the door.

"Klaus—don't go. I know it upsets you to talk about it. I'm sorry. Have you had breakfast?"

"No, thank you, I am not hungry."

"But you have to have something."

"Later." He paused a moment, stood looking down at the breakfast tray. "You take very much trouble for Mrs. Weiss, don't you?"

"Oh, I don't mind fixing the tray, but I won't take it in. I let Mady take it in. If I go in with it, Mrs. Weiss makes me sit down and tells me how sad she is—and then I can't get any work done for a half hour. Her husband isn't like that at all—I like him. He's good company. He makes me laugh. Klaus, maybe you can tell me something. Have you ever heard of a company in Austria called Vicki Recordings?"

"No. Why?"

"Mr. Weiss says he has some money coming from them. For some singing records he made. He showed us the contracts. The last payment was supposed to be made July first. You see— Well, Mr. Weiss is a week behind on his bill. But sometimes it takes a long time for the mail to come from Europe, doesn't it?"

It was a long moment before Klaus answered. Money from Austria? Mrs. Gomez must be a little behind on her

48

current events . . . getting money out of Austria offered the same problem as obtaining money from Germany. Germany and Austria were one and the same thing now. Then he saw that she was so eager to believe what Hans Weiss had promised, that he hadn't the heart to discourage her.

"Yes, long time, sometimes," he answered finally.

"Well, I'm sure they're a good risk. I hope the money comes pretty soon though. I'd feel a little better."

Klaus left, wandered out to the front. Mady came rushing up the hill, seized his hand.

"Klaus, after a while will you play belotte with me? I have to take the tray to mother first. Then will you? We haven't played for three days. *Please*, Klaus."

He was glad she had asked him. He sat on the steps to wait for her. A grown man, eager to play cards with a kid. That's the way things got in Tijuana.

He sat there thinking about Mrs. Gomez and the Weisses. Money from Vienna! But he was glad he had kept quiet. Immigrants should stick together, even when they didn't like each other. Mrs. Weiss was all right in her way. Mady, he loved. But Hans Weiss he disliked intensely.

The Weiss trio had come to Tijuana via the most-traveled route, southward from Hollywood on Highway 101, pushed out of the United States by expiring tourist visas. They were an odd threesome. Mrs. Weiss, a Russian, once well-known on the Paris stage as Maria Orloff. Mady, her child by a former marriage to a Frenchman. Hans Weiss, an Austrian, and half Jew. A fine singer. But he had lost his place with the Viennese opera when Hitler annexed Austria, and eventually the Weiss family had arrived in Hollywood to try its luck in pictures.

49

Hans and Maria would have the occupants of the Colonia Gomez believe that production in Hollywood was practically at a standstill, awaiting their return. But Jennifer Eckert, around at the studios in the natural course of her work, had found out otherwise, and of course she had told Klaus. They were the only two who really knew what had happened.

What had happened was this. Hans had been tested several places, and turned down. He was young, and he photographed well enough, and his voice was beautiful, but they just weren't making musicals. As for Maria, she had tried that old disdain-tactic, "I'm not interested in pictures," only she was an unfortunate one who got stuck with it. No one was interested in even trying to talk her out of it.

Through Mady, however, they did have one faint promise of fame to come. An agent arranged for her to appear at a benefit for Jewish refugees. She was neither Jewish nor a refugee (only her step-father could lay claim to that), but the agent presented her as such. Dressed in an ill-fitting blue serge dress, with her hair plaited in tight braids, Mady sang in Russian, French, and English—and brought the house down.

That was their last night in Hollywood. The next day, just as the talent scouts began to call for interviews, there was another call. An officer from the Department of Immigration and Naturalization, telling them that their visas had expired and asking them to leave within twenty-four hours. Fate beckoning with a fine gold finger one moment but pointing the way out the next.

Klaus remembered the day they had arrived in Tijuana. He remembered because he and Jennifer had had a quarrel

50

because of them. The Weisses had settled themselves as boarders in the ranch house on the hill, and then that same afternoon, Hans Weiss had come to the door of Casa Three, had asked to borrow the car to drive to Ensenada and see the consul. And Klaus had said no.

After he had gone, Jennifer was furious. Said Klaus was cruel and mean and hard. "Their first day here, they ask us a favor and you turn them down. Suppose people treated you that way?"

He had tried to explain to her. Jennifer was smart, and she was wonderful, and she was all those things, but she hadn't been around the world as much as he had. And she hadn't been to Vienna. Hans Weiss was a certain type of Viennese that Klaus knew very well; he had recognized him the minute he talked to him. Mr. Weiss would use their car, use their gasoline, kiss Jennifer's hand, make a fuss over her, but that would be all. If the gas tank had been empty, Klaus would have loaned the car, but he had just filled it—and were they so rich that they could afford to treat people to a trip to Ensenada?

"Oh, Klaus," she had said crossly. "You know if they had used our gasoline, they would pay for it!"

Well, she had seen. In the end she had had to admit he was right. It had been quite a story in the colony for a while. Mr. Weiss had borrowed the Gomez car, had returned it without a speck of gasoline in it, had hardly said a thank you. Mr. Gomez was angry, and to show his guest that car trips were not part of the ranch service, he had made a special item of the gasoline on the first week's bill.

Sitting there on the steps, and thinking of these past things, Klaus heard the door open behind him, and some eau de cologne came out. Even before turning, he knew who that was. Hans. Always excellently dressed and groomed, even for a morning in Tijuana. Closely shaved, and his dark hair sleeked back in the hope of suppressing the Jewish curl he had inherited from his father. Hans had black eyes, and upturned lashes, pert like a girl's. A mouth so small that Klaus often wondered how he could sing, how he could get the notes out.

They greeted each other in German, and Hans sat down to read a newspaper.

Klaus glanced casually at the paper, then sat forward eagerly. "Herr Weiss, is that an *American* paper?"

"Yes," Hans nodded. "The Los Angeles paper. I'm going to have one every day now. I found a man who would deliver it."

Klaus's eyes filled with sudden envy. "How much?"

"I don't know. Mr. Gomez said he would put it on the bill."

Of course. The bill. Something else for the bill. Always extras on the bill every week. Klaus knew, because Mrs. Gomez had told him—she, poor fool, thrilled to have guests who spent with a free hand. Wine, beer, extra chicken dinners, and rent for the piano—because Hans had said he couldn't live without a piano. And now another extra, a daily paper on the bill.

That was like Hans, to get all he could while the credit was still good. Klaus felt resentful. Hungering for a newspaper himself. Too provident to buy one, too German-stubborn to ask the Austrian for a piece of his. Damn it. Why were some people so adept at enjoying all the pleasures of life without paying for them?

"Herr Weiss, I was just thinking . . . in Vienna . . . the way a man would come into a café and spend the whole afternoon over a five-cent cup of coffee—and at the same time read all the free newspapers in the place." He flushed a little, because this had been on his mind, but he had not meant to say it.

"Of course." Hans smiled. "I used to do it myself—when I was a student. I remember . . . if I had half a cup left, and it was dinner time, I would ask the waiter to save the coffee for me . . . go home and have my dinner, and return for it later. Have it heated up—and naturally with a little more added free, you know." He laughed at his little joke—because what he had said was a bit of an exaggeration, of course.

"Everyone did things like that in Vienna," he continued pleasantly. "There was one place, with music and dancing. We used to take our own sandwiches, and just order wine. Dance and enjoy the music the whole evening, and it never cost us very much, that way. Ah, dear Vienna . . . city of love." He laid the paper on his knee, leaned back, and looked handsomely nostalgic. "Now it must be like a bed, stripped of its pillows and silk—no longer a pretty place to make love."

Klaus stood up, spat in the red dust near the steps. This Austrian. Try to make him feel uncomfortable, and what happens? He twists it into an opportunity for wit and charm. He didn't feel like being charmed this morning, and started away.

"Tell Mady I'll play cards with her this afternoon. I have to go to the store now."

"Herr Eckert, when I finish with the paper, you may have it, if you like."

"No, thanks. I have my own ordered, too. I'll pick it up when I'm in town later."

Now why had he said that? His own ordered! It was a lie. True, he often went to the Jap's place in town for a glass of milk late in the afternoon, and read the paper there. It was an uninviting restaurant near the jail, but Klaus went there because the Jap usually left his American newspaper spread out on the counter. He could look at it while he sipped a five-cent glass of milk. Thinking of it, he realized that it was the same sort of sponging he had criticized in the Viennese cafés. It made him feel uncomfortable inside, and annoyed with himself.

What kind of a person had he become, anyway? Sitting at a Jap's counter, reading a borrowed newspaper? Times had certainly changed. Years ago, making lots of money, spending it gloriously. And now hanging onto a nickel as though it were gold.

Still, he had his reasons, and they were good. It wasn't that the paper cost so much, only five cents if you bought it in town—probably ten, delivered. They could certainly afford that. But it was a matter of discipline. Not making any money now, not knowing when he would be allowed to. And the thrill in having a paper every day, not to be compared with the pride in not buying one at all. When Jennifer came home, to be able to say: "Look, Jen . . . remember how much money I had when you left? Two dollars and fifty-four cents. Well, here it is! I only charged some cheese, bread, soup, and some dog food at Berendo's. Oh, yes, I went to the movies, but I won that, playing

54

dominos. . . ." It made him feel that in a small way he was proving to her how badly he felt that it was she who had to earn the money now.

Sometimes Klaus won a lot playing dominos. Sometimes as much as two dollars. He had to work hard for it though, sit up all night sometimes. And it was hard to play for long hours, with everyone drinking and smoking, and not get a little thirsty himself. That was the most difficult thing—to keep his thirst from drinking up his winnings.

Reading borrowed newspapers as though they repre- sented a fortune. Working at a game as though it were a job. That was what being an immigrant had done to him. And other petty things, too—like hoarding beer in the icebox all week long. Even on the hottest day, walking around wrestling with the temptation. But it was worth it. When Jennifer came back, to remind her that there were five bottles when she left, show her five when she returned. "When you are working hard all week, I am not having any pleasures either."

Jennifer always laughed. She didn't quite understand. Sometimes she scolded. Said he was getting fanatic on the subject.

4

ON Thursday there was a large Buick parked at the entrance to the drive, and a middle-aged man in a baggy suit standing at the door of Casa Number Three, knocking.

He introduced himself. Gave Klaus a card. Vernon Steele, lawyer, Ogden Building, San Diego. He said he had heard that Mr. Eckert had immigration difficulties. One of the Mexicans at the border had told him. Immigration cases were Mr. Steele's specialty. He thought he might be of service.

Klaus asked him in.

"I'll be quite frank with you," Mr. Steele began at once, settling himself on the couch. "Immigration cases require a very special handling. They are all a question of pulling wires. You understand what I mean by pulling wires?"

Klaus nodded, flushed. "I may not speak so good English, but I understand pretty good most everything."

"Good. Well, what I mean to say is: Washington has its hands full these days . . . the Jewish refugee problem. Thousands and thousands of cases. And a case can stay at the bottom of the pile for years—unless you get someone to get in there for you, get it out and put it on top. Now I don't want to beat around the bush. I don't pretend that I can do that myself. But I do have one of those wires I spoke

56

of, a wire I can pull. I've pulled it before, and it worked. Did you hear about that German writer who was here last year . . . deported from the United States?"

Klaus hadn't heard.

"Well, I handled that case." Mr. Steele saw that he now had the young German's rapt attention, and he slowed up a little. Took his time. Began to weave his spell. "This German came over the Canadian border to the States illegally. Slipped in . . . impatient, you know . . . couldn't wait for a visa. They put him in jail and tried to deport him back to Germany. Couldn't do that, though. A Jew, see . . . and there's an international law that you can't make a person go back to his own country if he doesn't want to go because of political differences. They had to deport him somewhere though, so they deported him down here.

"Well, sir, he applied for an immigration visa and was refused. Now you must admit it wasn't an easy case after all that. You must admit it, huh?"

Klaus nodded.

"But sixty days after I took over his case he was in. Now how do you like that!"

Mr. Steele allowed an expression of pride to alight briefly on his face, then reached into his pocket and withdrew a letter which he unfolded. He tapped the letter.

"Yes, sir, in sixty days I had the man across the line . . . and through this friend of mine here. Just take a look at that signature. E. J. is a very powerful politician; you must have heard of him. He's my contact in Washington. He's my 'wire.' Now what do you think of that? Go ahead, read the letter. So you'll see I'm not making any claims I can't substantiate."

The letter was addressed "Dear Vernon," and friendly in tone. In it, E. J. asked for a detailed report on the immigration case they had discussed, as he was leaving for Washington in a week or so and would be glad to see what he could do.

Klaus didn't read it very carefully. His own problem already stirring so violently in his mind. He felt a nervous flush, as though a pressure had been put upon him, and he was as yet uncertain whether to give in to it or not.

"Now, of course, I have no idea what your trouble is," Mr. Steele continued, retrieving the letter. "But I assume there is trouble, because I understand you are married to an American, and in that case you should have your papers. Let me ask you something. Has the Labor Department passed her petition in your behalf?"

"Yes." Klaus's voice seemed to come from far away.

"How long ago?"

The young man cleared his throat, spoke with difficulty. "A long time ago."

"Then what's holding up your visa? No need to be embarrassed. Speak up. Talking to a lawyer is like talking to a doctor. You don't have to be afraid. Just explain the whole situation."

"But—well, you see my wife's isn't here now. We usually talk things like this together. I don't know as she would want to take a lawyer. How much you charged for the other case?"

Mr. Steele smiled benignly. "You'll think I'm lying—I only charged three hundred dollars!"

"I don't think that's so little."

"To get into America! To get out of this hole!" Now

58

Mr. Steele sounded disdainful. "Why, I know some lawyers who would have charged three thousand. But I only charged that because I really didn't have much to do on the case. Like I've just showed you—that letter—I did it through my friend. He and I used to go to school together. Now, if you want, I can tell you about another case, too, that I handled. A Mexican. He got his border pass taken away from him because they caught him on the Mann Act. He got mixed up with some woman in El Paso, and—"

"Will you excuse me one moment, please?"

Klaus went to the kitchen, drank some water. The pain was back in his head again. Always that same pain whenever he thought about his troubles.

The window was open. Mady stood outside. "Klaus, when are we going to play cards?"

"After a while. Soon, Mady."

He shut the window, came back into the living room, and shut the windows there. He even closed the small windows above the couch. Mr. Steele watched him, realized that the story was coming now, sat back and lighted a cigarette. You had to be careful how you handled foreigners, not push them too much. And especially this boy. He was serious, tense . . . he gave the impression of strength, and a great deal of pride. Not the usual groveling, tell-me-how-please immigrant that he most often ran across.

"Now tell me, what does the consul in Ensenada say about your case?"

Klaus took a big breath. "He—he says I'll never get in at all."

There, it felt better, to have said it finally. "Mr. Steele, do you have a cigarette?"

59

"Yes, of course." The older man offered him one. Klaus put the cigarette in his mouth, ignored the matches, just held the cigarette there. Stared out the window. "They say I—I committed perjury."

The lawyer made a sound which brought Klaus's attention away from the window at once. He saw that the sound had been a laugh. Mr. Steele was laughing and looking relieved. "You and God knows how many other people in the world! Perjury? Is that all? I was afraid for a moment you were going to tell me you had tuberculosis. Now if that was your trouble, then it really would be difficult. Or if you had syphilis, or anything like that. Any kind of contagious disease—and then you're really in a spot. You'd never get in then. Where did it happen?"

"In Nice. At least that is where they *say* it happened."

"Now look, suppose you give me all the facts now . . . why you were in France . . . what you did there. You know, start from the beginning."

"I lived in France mostly, since seven or eight years," he began with difficulty, picking his words carefully. "I used to box. And after that I was in the racing business. You know, car racing. I had two Mercedes, but they both burned up. And you can't insure cars like that—and so I lost a lot of money, and I was broke after a while. But I didn't want to go to Germany back. No family any more . . . and I hadn't served my military service. When they called me I didn't go, and after that it was too late to go. They put you eighteen months in concentration camp for evading. So then I met my wife, and—"

"Wait a minute. When was that?" The lawyer drew paper and pencil from his pocket, began taking notes.

"1938, in Paris. She came on a holiday to see her sister. Her sister worked for an American magazine in Paris and I was a friend with her, and through her I met my wife and fall in love with her. But I didn't know very sure. That's because I am German, and I get ideas slow, but once I get them they are a strong idea and stay in my mind always. So after she went back to America I began writing her. I wanted to see her more than anything in the world, and I told her I was coming to America so soon as I could have the opportunity. After a while I had a chance to go and race in the Vanderbilt cup races in New York, so that was when I went to the consulate in Paris and applied for a visa."

"I thought you said the perjury occurred in Nice?"

"No, now wait. I tell you now about the first time I applied. In Paris. They said I would have to apply from Germany because I was a German citizen, and they couldn't give me a visa in Paris. I did not have much money, and no regular job, and I think that's why they said I would have to go to Germany back. Well, so I went. But I was there only half a day, and already the authorities they were looking for me for military service so I had to leave again quick. Back to France. A lot of weeks went by, and my wife couldn't understand it. She was writing all the times why I not come to America like I promised."

"She wasn't your wife then?"

"No, I know." Klaus shook his head impatiently, his nervousness increasing. "But it was like she was my wife, and like I was already married with her. I couldn't think on anyone else. And after a while, it was like a maniac, all the time thinking on her. I was in Nice then, working in a

61

picture. Stunt work. And one day I was walking on the street, and I saw an American flag, and I knew it was a consulate . . . and the next thing I was inside asking for a visa.

"They asked lots of questions. They asked to me had I ever applied for a visa before? And I told them no. You see . . . I must explain that I had some money then, which I could show to them, so I thought sure then they would give me a visa. After a while, the secretary from the consul laid a card on the consul's desk. He looked at it and said, 'What about your application in Paris?' Fool I was. They have records all over the world, in all the consulates . . . every application ever made is always written down. . . ."

"But did you sign anything in Nice? Did you fill out an application?"

"Yes, when I went in, right at first. A girl there . . . she gave to me an application, and the question was in there, too—about did I ever get refused a visa. I wrote down 'no'—because I really *hadn't* been refused a visa, not formally. In Paris they never gave to me a written refusal. They only told to me to go to Germany, and I would get my visa there. . . ."

"Now wait a minute. In the consulate at Nice . . . did anyone administer an oath?"

"What's that?"

"When you signed the application, did they make you raise your right hand, and swear you had stated the truth?"

"No."

Mr. Steele shrugged. "Then where was the perjury?"

"That is what I try to say! There was no perjury . . . but they say I *admitted* I did perjury!"

Klaus got up and began to walk around. The air in the

62

room was stuffy now, and blue with Mr. Steele's constant smoking. A large fly buzzed, annoyingly loud. Klaus picked up a newspaper and went after it. He smashed it on the sill, shoveled it onto the paper and took it to the kitchen, threw it in the trash box.

"Look, Mr. Steele," he said when he came back. "It is hard for me to talk so long in English . . . and about this. I don't think I can say some more now. I have such a funny feeling in me. I feel it is all without hope. I think maybe it would be more better to let my wife explain you."

"As you like, but I'm a busy man, and I may not get over again very soon. To tell you the truth, my boy, I don't see what you're so upset about. So far, I can't see any real difficulties. I wish you'd at least explain why it was they denied you . . . so I can help you!"

"All right." Klaus straddled a chair. "I'll try. I wish my wife was here, though."

He rubbed his hand across his eyes, tried to draw the events from his muddled mind in the order of their happening.

"That day in Nice they said I made a lie . . . I told the consul I never applied before, and they found out I did. So I left. They said I could come back for a complete examination, but I didn't go back because I was scared then.

"I don't know. . . . I went back to Paris. And after a long while, it was Christmas, and my wife came to France and I told her. I told her everything . . . the wrong I did to tell the consul in Nice I had never applied for a visa. She said it wouldn't matter. She said after we were married and I applied for an immigration visa, and explained to them how anxious I was to see her and come to America, and that

I was half crazy with my dream—they would understand, and give me a visa, and we could go back and live in America. She said everything would be all right—only it was an important thing for to tell the Paris consul everything when I applied this time . . . about the mistake in Nice and all. And I must admit it.

"So we got married and then we both went to the Paris consul together. There was a very nice man saw me first, and looked at our marriage license and listened to the story. He was a vice-consul, I guess. He took my other papers, too, my birth certificate, and the record from the police department in my home city that I had a good reputation and had never done a wrong. He said they would have to be in English translated, and to come back in three days. He also gave my wife an application to fill out for the Labor Department . . . how much money she made, and that she would be responsible for me in America until I could find work, and that she was an American citizen, and where she was born, and so far.

"Well, three days later we went back, and they said they would have to wait to do something until the Labor Department passed the application from my wife.

"That took five weeks, and we were very happy anyway those times, because not anybody said there was going to be any trouble, and everything looked fine.

"Then we had a letter from the Labor Department that it was all right with my wife's application, and I could apply on the non-quota list, as husband of an American citizen. That same day we went to the consulate back, and I was sure that in a day or two we could sail for New York.

"But now another consul wanted to see me and I could see the way he talked that something was wrong and I got scared. He asked to me how long I had known my wife, and where we met with each other. How long we were planning to be married, and things like that, and I knew he thought I just married with her to get to the United States quick, and that made me mad. It made me mad because it was for love for her I made a lie to the consul in Nice, and not for anything else. Then he said, very sarcastic: 'I can see you have lived in France so long that you think you can use love as an excuse for anything.' And he asked me again, very loud, about what I wrote on my application in Nice. That question about ever being denied a visa.

"I told him I wrote 'no,' and explained that I really hadn't been denied . . . that in Paris they had only told me to go to Germany to get my visa. But he didn't want to listen. He only got up real quick, and said: 'All right. That's fine. That's all I want to know.' He wanted to get me out, and I went . . . because I was afraid if I was staying I would say something. I was shaking and all hot inside, because I could see he still thought I married with my wife just to get into the United States.

"Well . . . my wife, Jennifer, she was waiting for me outside, and I told her I wanted to go to the hotel back. We walked, but after a while I couldn't walk any more. And we took a taxi. In the taxi I was sick. I told my wife it was my stomach . . . it was weak from all the fights I had. But it was because I was afraid what would happen, and it made me sick, that's all.

"The next day we went to the consul again, and Jennifer with me. We had to wait a long time outside, sitting on the bench, and while we waited I had to go to the men's room. And in there I was sick again. Everything sour inside me. When I came back my wife wasn't there, and the secretary said she was inside with the consul.

"When I went in she was white in her face. She couldn't talk. She just looked at me and cried. The consul, he just sat and watched her, and said, 'I'm sorry, Mrs. Eckert.'

"My wife cried so hard, I couldn't think on anything else. I never saw a girl cry like that. Sobbing, real soft, not loud, but soft like it hurt, and like she was crying inside more than out. And I couldn't help her, for I was gagging and sick again myself."

Klaus became silent, looked up and was surprised to see Mr. Steele sitting there. He had forgotten Mr. Steele. Forgotten everything except that miserable moment there in the consul's office.

"What was the basis of the denial?" Mr. Steele asked gently.

"I remember it from heart." Klaus spoke with the dead calm of a judge delivering sentence: "No American consul could issue a visa to me because I had admitted committing perjury in the consulate at Nice, France. 'Perjury has been found by the courts to be a crime involving moral turpitude, and a alien who has committed perjury, or admits committing perjury, is inadmissible under the immigration laws'—and so are murderers, crooks, jail birds, and so far."

"A lot of nonsense!" Mr. Steele said encouragingly. "I can't see that you committed perjury. If there wasn't any oath administered, then there was no perjury."

"I don't know . . . I don't know," Klaus murmured forlornly. "We went back and back, and the consul kept saying his hands were tied. He kept saying I admitted perjury, and there was nothing he could do. He said we could not ask him an immigration law to break. His hands were tied. Even the president could not the law break. Law, law . . . they talked about law and tied hands till we were crazy.

"I think, after a week or two—every day going back and back, and my wife crying all the times—I think after a while the consul saw how much we loved each other and he was maybe a little sorry. But hands tied.

"We asked what we could do? Where he expected us to go? Not possible for me to take my wife to Germany. Not possible for her to live and work other place but America. So what we were to do? He said my wife could appeal to Washington. That's all he would say."

"And so then you came to Mexico?"

Klaus nodded. "I had money for the trip, but not much left over. My wife didn't have money either, so she had to go to work back. And we came here, so we could see each other a little, and she could work during the week times in Hollywood."

"Mr. Eckert, all I can say is that you should have had someone working on your case long before this," Mr. Steele said, shaking his head.

"You think there is hope?"

"All the hope in the world!"

He rose, took the floor now for himself, began pacing up and down, an indication that he was ready to go into action.

"Your wife has appealed to Washington, I suppose, to ask for a new application?"

"All the time. She writes and I write, and they always make the same answer, quoting about how I am guilty, and was already denied. You see, Mr. Steele, if I could work here, so my wife could stay with me, and I could make for her money, I would not care so bad. But to have her up there, and me here, and not able to do something! It's so hard. Working permission, working permission. All over, the world so strict now. A foreigner can't work anywhere now. Oh, Mr. Steele, I think to be an immigrant is the lowest thing in the world."

For a moment he seemed so tragic that even Mr. Steele was touched. But sympathy wasn't the right mood. Cheer, cheer, that's what he must give him. He placed a congratulatory slap on the young shoulders.

"My boy, your troubles are over! Not a thing to worry about! You just stop brooding now. Suppose you talk it over with your wife. And then if you want me to work on the case we'll go to see the consul together. That's the first step. He doesn't tell you all the angles, because he's not supposed to. But I guess I can make him open up! We'll find out if they do suspect this is one of those immigration marriages. There are a lot of them these days, and the consuls have to be careful. Maybe that's standing in your way. Anyway, we'll see. And then I'll get E. J. into action, and we'll have you in, in no time. I wouldn't charge you much . . . only what I charged the other German I was telling you about."

"But for me to pay after when I'm in?" Klaus asked hopefully.

"No . . . a hundred and fifty now, and a hundred and fifty when you get your papers. How's that? That's only fair. I'll need some expense money. I'll have to go to Ensenada with you . . . that takes a day of my time. And

68

then I'll have to go to Los Angeles to see my friend . . . he's up there now. And then—"

"But, Mr. Steele. We don't have money extra. My wife writes for movie magazines. Not for any one magazine. No regular salary. She writes for as many as she can. But it was hard at first, since we came from Europe . . . sometimes the magazines accept articles and then don't pay for them until months."

"Well, yes . . . I appreciate your position." Mr. Steele seemed thoughtful for a moment, and his neglected cigarette ash spilled on his vest. "I'll tell you what I'll do . . ." with renewed cheerfulness. "Perhaps I could start on the case with a first payment of seventy-five dollars. That would be easier for you, wouldn't it?"

"I'm not sure we can pay that even, but I will ask her."

"Good. Fine then. And now don't you worry. Because there's nothing to worry about. The minute you put the case in my hands, you'll see how quickly things progress. If everything you have told me is the truth."

"It's true, every word," Klaus answered solemnly.

"Then fine, fine! Talk it over with your wife, and tell her to phone me at my office. Good-by."

They shook hands. Klaus wanted to go with him to the car, but Mr. Steele begged him not to bother . . . darted down the driveway quickly . . . and in a moment Klaus heard the car start away.

It was funny, how once outside on the driveway, Mr. Steele had seemed in such a hurry to escape. But then Klaus shrugged and dismissed the thought. Mr. Steele was a busy man, and he had already kept him more than an hour. He had a right to hurry away.

69

All the rest of that day Klaus felt new confidence, a glow of exhilaration. Mr. Steele was going to help him, and he would soon be in America.

He tried not to think of the seventy-five dollars.

At five minutes before seven that evening, Klaus entered the small building near the Tijuana bridge which housed the telephone company; also the electric light company. The windows to the left, where the subscribers paid their bills, were all closed now. Klaus hurried past them and up the bare rickety steps. There were two public phone booths at the head of the stairs, which accounted for the street door being left open during the night.

He ignored the booths and went to a door beyond, opened it and looked in upon the switchboard room. Lupe, the evening operator, was just coming on duty, and as she settled herself at the board, smiled and said hello. One of her best customers. No need to ask him what number he wanted. She glanced at the clock: "You want me to wait until seven?"

Of course. It was cheaper after seven.

He went outside and paced up and down the hall.

Eventually, through the thin partition, he heard her calling the American operator. He stepped into the booth, took up the receiver. So much to say tonight, so much to tell Jennifer . . . he'd have to talk fast. "Lupe, don't forget to warn me at three minutes."

There was a moment's pause. "Klaus, there's no answer."

"There must be. She always waits, right at seven."

"But tonight isn't your night to call."

"She'll be there. Try again."

The operator kept trying but there was no answer either at seven-five, seven-ten, or seven-fifteen. Lupe grew a little impatient. "I can't keep putting it through every few minutes. She's probably out for the evening."

"She can't be. Unless—well, unless she had to go to a preview."

"I'll try once more and if she doesn't answer now, you'd better come back and try later."

He could hear the long muffled rings at the other end of the wire. Unanswered.

"All right . . . I'll come back."

"Not mad, are you?" she taunted. "Can't expect a wife to sit home all the time. Not in Hollywood."

Klaus put the receiver down quickly. He wasn't mad. Only hurt and disappointed.

Outside, he walked around. Into the Palacio for a while, and watched them play billiards. Then across the street into one of the many family relation bureaus, where shadows in the window told him that something was going on. The sign outside: Advice on Legal Matters. Marriages and Divorces Quickly Arranged.

Inside, a drunken American couple were being married. They stood before a dirt-littered desk, listened to the judge as he read in Spanish. Pepe del Rio, who owned the place, and who was also acting as witness, nudged them, told them to say "*Si.*"

"*Si, si,*" they said, and giggled.

And now Pepe asked the groom for thirty dollars for arranging everything.

The American complained, said he had understood it was fifteen.

71

Pepe explained. It was fifteen in the daytime, but this was after hours, and the judge had to be paid double.

"Oh, hell," said the groom. "What's the use of arguing." He smiled inebriatedly at his wife. "What's thirty dollars when you only get married once every couple of years! Isn't that right, Baby?"

"Sure," said Baby. "Honey, I'm thirsty. And I've got a sinking spell."

"Sure, must drink right away and celebrate." He saw Klaus now, brought him into focus. "Hey, you . . . where can we go around here for a little fun?"

"Yes." Baby also turned to Klaus. "Somewhere where it's nice. Know a place?"

Klaus pointed north. "Over there. That's the only nice place."

Pepe stepped forward, glared. He knew what Klaus meant —over there, back across the border, the States side. He turned to Baby. "Don't pay him no attention. There's a place called The Rendezvous Spot. Right down the street. Music and dancing, good liquor." Pepe had a part interest in the place.

"Thanks. We'll try it."

At the door, Klaus stepped aside to allow them to pass. The bride paused, looked at him closely. "What's the matter with you, long face? You look like you need a drink, too. Want to come along with us?"

"Thank you."

She looked perplexed. "What do you mean, 'thank you' —and you shake your head no! Thank you yes, or thank you no?"

"Come on," said her husband. "Can't you see the guy's a foreigner? Baby!" He suddenly grabbed her. "Baby, you know what? I forgot to kiss you!"

He gave her a resounding kiss.

"Excuse me, please." Klaus pushed them gently to the side, went out, down the steps and across the street into the telephone building.

Marriages that didn't matter, easy marriages, drunken marriages. Americans such fine people, but they did have funny ideas about marriage sometimes. Yet people like that had the right to be together, to live together all the time, while he and Jennifer had only a half-marriage like this. He felt depressed. More than ever he longed to talk to her.

But again there was no answer. Eight-fifteen, and she was still out. He began to be a little worried.

He walked some more, and arrived aimlessly at the Sentor Cinema. He stood outside looking at the stills. An old picture, a picture about the north woods, with Kent Taylor. He bought a ticket for eighty centavos and went in.

Several Mexican girls clustered around the door, giggling and chewing gum, and smelling of perfume. Not a cheap smell as you might expect. Most of the girls worked in the shops where the best French perfumes were sold; always a sample bottle or a free spray somewhere. Good expensive odors there at the door of the Sentor. So that when you smelled them you looked around for a smart woman in furs, wearing jewelry and with her hair done elegantly. Instead, all you saw was the long black coarse hair hanging to the shoulders. Crooked seams, run-over heels, bright-colored imitation silk dresses that sold for fifteen pesos. Pink nail polish, and thick lipstick. But the eyes of the girls bright with expectation. Sometimes a pretty smile. Nice round arms. Bodies eager for excitement and a little luxury, but doomed for a life in a shack on a Tijuana mud street, and every year a baby.

It was a little while, thinking of Jennifer and wondering, before Klaus really began to see the picture. It was the smell of the place which most quickly brought him back to the moment. The peculiar odor of Mexican cigarettes, the strong sulphur of Mexican matches, the oranges, the candy, the garlic, perfume by Schiaparelli, Lanvin, Chanel . . . and, as a basic motif for this movie house bouquet, the musty acrid odor of the place itself which meant only one thing . . . rats.

If lice smell too, there was also the smell of lice.

After a while he got used to the smells, but a second annoyance was the constant giggling. The pictures, though English-speaking, were shown with printed subtitles in Spanish. The subtitles were naturally shorter than the spoken dialogue—with the result that the Mexicans, following the subtitles, always got the point quicker than Klaus—and their laughter often drowned what the characters were saying. This frenzied him. Worried about Jennifer, and nervous anyway, he sat first on one haunch, then on the other; moved several times to get away from bothersome neighbors.

The third move, he found himself sitting next to Irmgard.

She was not alone. There was an arm around her shoulder. She squirmed and got out from under the arm as Klaus sat down. The arm belonged to Manuel, one of the young boys

74

from the beer company. His hair long and sleekly polished, his face pale and pasty. He wore a large gold wristwatch and a Mexican jade ring . . . a blue silk shirt. He was flashy looking in his way, considered very handsome.

Irmgard pretended that she hadn't seen Klaus. But when Manuel put his hand on her knee, she put it away. The Mexican became annoyed, put his arm again around her shoulder, pulled her nearer.

"Don't be bashful on my account," Klaus whispered in German.

"Oh, hello, Klaus." She tried to appear indifferent, casual, watched the screen for a moment. Then she leaned toward him, said in her deep throaty voice, almost whining, "A girl has to have some fun . . . go out sometimes."

"Why apologize? What is it to me?"

Manuel leaned forward, looked at Klaus, nodded a cool hello. He knew that Klaus also lived at the Colonia Gomez. They were speaking secretly together in German. He didn't like it. He reached for Irmgard's hand and brought it firmly to his knee.

Irmgard jerked away, gave him a hard push. Quickly she stood up, brushed past Klaus, and out up the aisle.

Manuel shrugged, touched his head and muttered something in Spanish.

Klaus tried to forget Irmgard. But he knew how long the walk home was, how dreary and dark the road—and the way the cars drove along that road, like mad, in the evening. But if he went after her, to take her home, he'd have to walk all the way back later, to phone Jennifer.

"Why don't you go get her?" he asked the Mexican.

"To hell with her. I get her later. Now, I see movie."
Klaus got up and went out.

He caught up with her near the ice house. She was walking quickly, off to the side of the road in the deep darkness. She turned at the sound of footsteps, recognized him, and waited.

They fell into step, walked on, for a moment no word between them. Then, "He *asked* if I would go to the movies. I mean, I just didn't meet him there. Don't think that!"

"I'm not thinking anything about it. I just want to see you home."

"Why?"

"I don't know. It must be the way I was brought up."

He hadn't intended that to have any special meaning, but she interpreted it as disapproval, perhaps because she was critical of herself. She had been well brought up, too. Dreams and ideals once. But if Klaus hadn't sat beside her in the Sentor, she was certain, before many hours had passed, to have been mixed up in a cheap kissing scuffle with Manuel. And she hated Manuel. Hated his kind. But—

"Klaus, a girl has to have some life. Left here to rot like this, I nearly go crazy."

"I know. It's the American, Tom. Is that it?"

"Yes." For a few steps she was silent with her unhappiness. "Bringing me all this way, and then forgetting me. I don't know what I've done to deserve this. It isn't as though he weren't in love with me first. I know he was. Until he got back home. Even then, in the beginning, he used to come down every weekend. Then every two weeks. Then every month. Now he won't come any more at all."

"Maybe he will. . . ." Klaus suggested.

"No. Why do you say that? You always say the truth. You always see and say things as they are. That's the trouble with you. Always blunt and out with it. Don't you start getting American now, saying what you don't mean, just to be kind. Keep on saying the truth."

"The truth. Yes, I always say the truth," he said ironically, thinking of the perjury.

Irmgard sighed. "I know he won't come down any more. Perhaps I don't seem so attractive in this setting as I did in Berlin. It's hard for love to last across a border. For a while it's romantic and exciting. After a while, it's only a hardship. The long trip down, the nuisance . . . and maybe he started to feel sorry for me, trapped here. When you start feeling sorry for someone, you don't like to see them any more. But I tried to be gay when he was here. Tried to make him think it was all all right. Tried not to need too much money."

"He still sends you money?"

"Now and then."

"He's married?"

She turned quickly. They had slowed to almost a standstill . . . in front of an open doorway, light streaming out. Inside a radio blaring. "How do you know? But I swear to you, Klaus . . . I thought he was divorced. He told me he was. But he told me that with a California divorce you have to wait a year until it becomes final and you can get married again. So that's why I came back with him. He said the divorce would be final this month. Maybe it is, I don't

77

know. Maybe he's free right this minute, but anyway he writes letters like ice now. He's found someone else, I suppose. Or maybe he's gone back to his wife. That's why I *must* get into the States . . . have to get in and get him back. I can't hold a man so far away. No one can. A whole world away. Only a hundred and fifty miles, but it *is* a world . . . you know that, don't you, Klaus? But if I were there, I'd get him back. You'd see, I would!"

"Irmgard . . . why don't you go back to Germany? You'll find somebody else."

"I don't want anybody else. I want him. It's foolish, but I can't help it. I tell you, if I only had money for a lawyer, I'm sure I could get in. But to get a good one, that takes lots of money."

"You think a lawyer really helps?"

"Of course. Everyone says so. The Lankowskis have a lawyer. That friend of theirs, the director . . . he got them a lawyer. Some one big, in Hollywood."

"But the Lankowskis are still here."

"But at least they have a hope now. They think they'll get the first quota number available . . . Poland doesn't have very many quota numbers . . . but the lawyer says . . ." Irmgard wasn't very interested in the Lankowskis, and they slipped away from her mind. "Oh, Klaus, I'm lonely."

"Irmgard, when you get home, why don't you go in and see Omah? She's lonely, too."

"Omah! Old woman." Irmgard shook her head. "What do I want to see her for? That constant hopeful talk of hers drives me mad . . . when she gets into America . . . when she gets into America. She talks and talks about it! Her daughter, her nice son-in-law, her little granddaughter.

78

What a nice place they have in Sacramento . . . with a garden. Sacramento is the capital of the state. Lola belongs to a bridge club . . . her husband makes sixty dollars a week . . . in another two years Lola will be an American citizen . . . on and on. Oh, she's so old . . . talks like all old people. I want to see young people, be with people who smile and laugh. People like I used to be. I'm so young myself, Klaus. I'm only twenty-three. I want to dance and go riding in a car. In an open car with Tom."

They had come to a café near the intersection, not far from the bungalows. Hot summer night . . . and the windows and doors wide open. A three-piece orchestra inside, but nobody dancing. Too hot to dance. Five or six men at the bar, one or two girls. Irmgard hung back, looking in.

"Klaus, let's go in there. Let's dance. Just once, Klaus. It wouldn't cost much. You can just order a beer, and I won't order anything. And we could dance. Just once, Klaus."

"What you want isn't to dance," he said with tender knowledge. "You just want somebody's arms around you. Come on now . . . home. We can't go in there anyway. That's where the boys take the tarts."

"Klaus, please . . . or I'll go in alone."

"Go ahead." And he walked on.

After a while, he heard her footsteps behind him.

He kept walking, kept ahead, but always listening. He turned in the driveway, walked to the front of Casa Number Three. He stood waiting, until he heard the door of Casa Number One bang loudly.

It was a long way back to town, to call Jennifer. Almost three miles to the telephone company. He was tired. Doing

79

nothing all day and he was tired . . . always makes a man tired not to do anything. He unlocked the door, let Schnucki out, and they started back together.

It was hot, and it was quiet. He walked slowly, threw sticks for Schnucki. Lovable animal. A female was always best. Stayed close, really walked with you—not always off peeing on bushes. A funny-looking dog, but he loved her. A nose like a Spitz, body of a terrier. But bright intelligent eyes, alert ears—and on her hind legs a ruff of hair that looked like a child's starched white party dress.

A car came along and stopped. It was one of the salesmen from Honold's offering a ride.

Nice of him. Lots of people in the town nice like that.

"Just been down to Ensenada looking at ranch," said the Mexican, as they drove on. "I got to find something to do, if they put the twenty-four-hour law through. I got three kids. I gotta make money somehow. I think little ranch maybe."

"The Mexican government won't let the Americans put that law through," Klaus assured him.

The other snorted. "The Mexican government, what they care about us? In Mexico City, they no think of Tijuana, way up here. And what chance Tijuana got against American stores and big capital? Americans, they make up petition now. Get all the stores in San Diego and Los Angeles to sign it. Then they put it through in Washington. What they care if we got nothing else to live from? Who care about Tijuana? Mexico don't care. America don't care. We just nobody's people." He sighed. "No use talk about it even."

He went several blocks out of his way, took Klaus directly to the telephone company.

80

This time, and at last, Jennifer was home.

She said she had come in about a quarter after eight. There had been a preview at RKO. They had invited the press to cocktails and supper first. She had gone because it meant a free meal, and she hadn't expected Klaus to call. She had skipped out after eating, had come straight home. If she could get her story on Tyrone Power okayed in the morning, she would be down tomorrow.

The explanation reassured him; he had been so afraid that something might have happened to her. Always afraid of that.

"Any news from Washington, Jen?"

"Not a word."

"You sure? You're not keeping things from me?"

"No, darling."

"Jennifer, a Mr. Steele came to see me today, a lawyer from San Diego. He says the case isn't bad. He can help me. But it would cost three hundred dollars. Only seventy-five first, though, to get started."

"Then we ought to do it."

"You really think so?"

"Yes, I do! We'll talk it all over tomorrow."

"Your three minutes is up—" Lupe broke in.

"Good-by, darling!"

"Jen—bring me some pumpernickel!"

When he arrived home, he was itching. He always itched after the movies. But the gas tank was empty, and he couldn't find a quarter to put into it, so it was impossible to heat bath water. He sponged off with cold, went to bed. Schnucki crawled under the bed, slept under him.

5

THE route from Jennifer's one-room apartment in Hollywood to Casa Number Three was a hundred and thirty-eight miles. For a girl going home, four long distressing hours.

Past six o'clock before she could get away. Drop Tyrone Power into the mail box . . . the article at last okayed, and off to the magazine. Hope to God they take it.

Stop and get the car filled with gas and oil. Old car, uses lots of oil. Have the tires checked, too.

"Miss, there's a leak in the rear left."

Sure, she knows it. Been driving it that way for weeks. Forget it. It'll get her there. Clean the windshield good. Sunset soon, and it's hard to see in the late sun's light.

At last she's off. The clutch slips and through the heavy evening traffic down Western, constant stops and starts and near collisions. Could go faster on Crenshaw, but there's a Jewish delicatessen on Western, down near Washington . . . and the best pumpernickel Jennifer had found.

The shop has a wonderful smell. Good liverwurst, cheese, and salami. Have some of that, and that, and that. Oh, and eggs, too, because the eggs in Tijuana aren't very fresh. And the sweet, unsalted butter for Omah, and an extra loaf of pumpernickel for her, too. But can't get a loaf for Omah, and not for the others: Europeans like it so much. All right. "Make it five of the pumpernickel, please"—Omah, the Lankowskis, the Klabecs, and Irmgard. They would pay her; they were always careful about such things. No bread for the Weisses though. Oh, that's mean. Of course, a loaf for them. "I've changed my mind. Make it six altogether. And I'll take the Liederkranz, too." High; thirty-one cents. But take it anyway. Klaus likes cheese, and that Mexican jack cheese at Berendo's isn't fit for eating.

There goes two dollars practically. A couple of things in a sack and it's already two dollars. Two dollars at the delicatessen, two-fifty for gas and oil. Life so expensive, and behind on the rent in Hollywood. Oh, well, don't worry. The check in her billfold, just arrived today. But no, the check was for the lawyer. Seventy-five dollars from Macfadden Publications for "The Girl Richard Greene Left Behind" by Jennifer Eckert, for a lawyer named Steele, to get Klaus into America.

Come on now, step a bit. Got to make Long Beach in an hour. The light just turned red, but slip through anyway. Won't do it again, promise. Too dangerous . . . five dollars for a ticket. Heck, forgot to get milk. Klaus won't drink Mexican milk. And he must drink milk. Give him strength, build him up. Silly—that's the trouble with him now: too much strength and no place to put it. But milk is good anyway, good for teeth and bones.

Hot and sticky, take off the suit coat. Already thirsty. Forget being thirsty, keep going. So many cars. Men going home from work. Lucky men. Drive home, nice dinner waiting, kids around. Sit down, listen to the radio. Go to bed. Get up, go to work. Come home the next evening.

Always men and women together every night. Must be wonderful.

That's better now, the traffic behind. The long clear stretch into Long Beach. To the left the oil wells, high up against the evening sky. Each one topped with a red light, warning for airplanes. Bunches and bunches of oil wells sticking up there, crowded tight, looking like black pins in a pincushion hill. The sky deep red and blue behind. Beautiful. Getting closer now. The smell of oil lying over Long Beach. The ocean mist beginning. The mist and the oil smell mingling.

Through Long Beach, twenty minutes late on her schedule. After Long Beach, straight along the ocean. Got to make up time. But the windshield misty. Getting cool, put on the coat again. Getting hungry. Smoke a cigarette, stave off the hunger for a while. Maybe a coke pretty soon. At the next town, have the windshield wiped, and treat herself to a coke at the filling station.

"Hello, would you mind—"

"Sure. Foggy tonight, isn't it?"

The nice cheery boys at the gas stations. Wiping so swiftly and surely, as though they liked wiping.

"Let me have a coke, please. Here. Here's the money. I want to take it with me."

She had handed him a quarter and he brought her fifteen cents change.

"How come? I never pay more than two cents for the bottle!"

"My boss says I got to get five."

"Gyp. *I* can't get more than two cents on the bottle when I turn it in."

84

"I know, but boss's orders. Why don't you drink it here, and leave the bottle . . ."

"Wait." She flushed, a little embarrassed—counting pennies a new practice of the last few months. But why should she make a present of three cents to a great big gasoline company? She hopped out and opened the luggage compartment. A picnic at the beach several weeks before, and if she remembered rightly, Coca-Cola along.

"Here—" She held up an empty bottle, smiled. "I guess I'll fool you."

"That's all right with me, lady. Here's your nickel. Good night."

The young man watched her away. A pretty girl like that hard up for pennies. Too bad. He'd be glad to buy her a dinner any time.

Jennifer drove with the bottle between her knees, lifting it for a sip every now and then. Tried to make it last until Oceanside.

On that long lonely stretch into Oceanside, pressing the car at fifty—and the car complaining. Grumbling in every old joint. A high ridge in the center of the road, and dangerous, but Jennifer not heeding. The wind whistling. Tires screeching on the curves. Slow up, you fool. Slow up.

But can't slow. Nearing nine now, and she knows that Klaus has been waiting since eight. At eight he starts hanging around the window, running to the door. Back and forth, to and from the kitchen. Pour the water off the potatoes, dry them out, keep them warm. Keep things from burning. Klaus with a dish towel around him for an apron. Worrying, always so anxious. Why isn't she here? Something must have happened.

85

So many stops. That's what takes so long. Another quart of oil. Get that leaking tire filled up again. The windshield wiped. Have to stop again, too, for the milk. Oh, it's a nuisance.

Really hungry now. And her leg is cramped. Try the left foot on the gas pedal. Long legs, and the space too small. Hate sitting still for so long. But at last—coming into San Diego. The landing fields. A plane coming in. Like a will-o'-the-wisp blinking against the sky.

Crawl slowly down the wide boulevard . . . cops. Past the airplane factories, working night shifts. War pretty soon and business booming. On to the ball park, near the docks. Lighted up; hundreds of cars outside. Wish Klaus could see a ball game . . . he'd like it, so typically American. Sailors on the street. San Diego—sailors' town. Stop your whistling, boys. No use trying to attract Jennifer. No eyes for a sailor. She's got a man of her own, and he's waiting.

Through the town. Turn right; still 101. The last turn. From then on, shoot home.

The last few miles, the longest. Past Chula Vista. Past the fork in the road that leads to Coronado. On up the hill. Eyes so tired, fanny so sore, sitting so still all that long distance. But soon be there. Soon be home again. Why doesn't the car go faster? Faster, faster, up this last hill. Grip the wheel tight, because you're tired now, and not thinking very clearly. Faster, fool. A wife driving through the night to be in her husband's arms. The law between them, and only the thin thread of luck allowing them to come together. A blown-out tire. A drunken driver. Who knows when it will happen? Who cares? Who thinks about such things—except Klaus, when he's waiting. Just to be together.

There, the top of the hill, and Tijuana off there in the valley. Dim lights. Cozy, sort of.

From the top of the hill, that first homecoming glimpse, Jennifer never felt any hate for the place. No matter what it was, it was home. And at such moments she always thought of the town as Aunt Jean. That's what the name meant: Tia Juana . . . Aunt Jean. Coming home to Aunt Jean. It had warmth, thinking of it that way.

One more curve and she could see the border. The border had a prison atmosphere. Cold steel fences. Gates. High flood lights. Uniforms. Police car parked in front of the State Patrol office. Motorcycles.

Entering Mexico on the right, a sign, *ALTO:* STOP.

A dark Mexican face peered at her from the low steps of the Mexican Immigration Building. They all knew her, and usually the dark face only nodded, said, *"Pase, señorita."* But tonight there was a new dark face, and it came over to the car, looked at the sack on the seat.

"Just groceries. *Provisiones,*" Jennifer told him.

He fumbled in the top of the sack, felt bread, drew it out. *"No se permite pasar, señorita."*

"It's only bread. It's for my husband. He lives here."

The officer prodded still deeper into the bag, extracted a second loaf.

Jennifer seized the sack, pulled it close beside her, her anger crackling. Nobody had ever stopped her for anything before. "Give me back my bread!"

"Pan . . . no permiso." Gravely he turned, took the

bread into the little office, laid it on the desk. He waved to her to go on.

She drove fiercely past the park to the bridge, across the narrow bridge, around the lamppost, into the town. Nervous tears. Fury inside her, and fume. Oh, Klaus . . . will I *ever* get there!

Dark the road, past the town, and dipping like a roller coaster. The car sliding off into the dirt, and back on the road again finally. There ahead, the bull ring. Black against a starry sky. There, the arch. Turn fast, watch out for that rock at the entrance.

The colony all dark, except for a light under the curtains in Casa Number Three. Of course a light there, and thank heaven for it. He waits. He is always waiting. He is there, from one week to the other—just for her.

The door opens and his body blocks the light.

Oh, Klaus. Oh, my darling. At last I'm home!

"It made me so mad . . . just took the bread and laid it on the desk, and waved to me to go on! Tomorrow, if I take Chato back with me to translate, don't you think I can get it back?" She was angry all over again, telling of the happening at the border. And it annoyed her a little that Klaus wasn't outraged, too.

"It's a law, Jennifer, to protect the bakers here," he said easily. "No bread into Baja California."

"Yes, but if it is a law, it's just for the Mexicans . . . so they won't run across and buy American bread. It hasn't anything to do with us!"

"It is best anyway for you to stay quiet."

"Why? Why should I keep quiet?" she asked indignantly.

"Because you're a foreigner here, and foreigners should always stay quiet. If they complaints have, they should only to whisper them. I know. I've been a foreigner so many places."

"But I'm an American!"

He shook his head, smiled indulgently. "That remembers me—when we were in France how you always spoke of Frenchmen as foreigners! In any country an American thinks the other people is always the foreigner. But, darling, whether you like it or no, you are a foreigner here, and no country likes them very much."

"I'm squelched. I'm sorry." Her arm went around him: "Come on now, let's eat. I started being hungry way back in Laguna."

The difficult thing about the evenings when Jennifer came home was that she was tired when she got there. For her, the end of a long hard week. For Klaus, it was a beginning. All the week long waiting for this. Living for this moment. Questions to ask, things to tell. Eager to make every second count before that misery-Monday when she would leave him again.

At the table, both of them past the hungry-point, neither eating very much. But Klaus craving news. "What did the apartment lady say when you told to her not possible to pay the rent now?"

Jennifer's eyes heavy and begging for sleep. "She said it would be all right."

"And?"

"She said it would be all right. That's all."

"But did you tell to her how expensive it is to keep two homes, like we have to do?"

"Yes, dear, I told her." Jennifer tried to be patient, but these little questions, when she was tired, were aggravating. Like a curtain flapping when you're trying to sleep. Hard for her to realize that he was eager to know every word she spoke while she was away, every place she went, everything she did. She could never quite get it into her mind that she was living for two these days. That he had no life except in her.

"Jennifer, your apartment . . . what's it like exactly? I try to imagine, so I can really see you there. But like the bed in the wall . . . I can't hardly see that. I never saw a bed in the wall. Couldn't you for me a picture draw?"

"Sometime I will . . . really, darling. But I'm so tired now. Don't you want to see the check? It's in my bag, on the china cabinet. I can't move, I'm so tired."

He rose eagerly, brought the handbag back, began to empty it. "Jennifer, what's this card?"

"That? Oh, it's for the Brown Derby. Half price card. The publicity agent sent it to me."

"What does it mean?"

She sighed wearily. "Oh, it's nothing. All the press people get them. Just means you can go there and pay only half price."

"But why?"

"So we'll mention the Brown Derby in our articles."

"That's nice." He looked fondly at the card. "We'll go there when I get in, won't we?"

"Uh-huh. Klaus, the check is in the billfold."

It seemed unbelievable to her that he could be so interested in the contents of her handbag. To her, these things just routine. But to him symbols of American life, and fascinating. He found another card.

"What's this?"

"My Hays office card. For the new quarter. They send one every three months. To show I'm an established writer. If I didn't have a card like that, the studios wouldn't arrange interviews."

"Why?"

A gesture of impatience: "Oh, Klaus!" Then quickly she felt sorry, smoothed the edge of her tone, and hastened to explain. "You see, there are a lot of people who would just like the chance to see a movie star and talk with one. So sometimes they go to the publicity department at the studios and say they're writers and want an interview. But then maybe they never write the article at all, or can't write . . . and see, that just takes up the star's time."

"So?"

"So that's why you have to have a card from the Hays office!"

"Please, Jennifer, I just want to know. Don't be mad. Why for from the Hays office?"

"Because the Hays office investigates and knows whether we really write and sell articles or not."

"You mean they give you interviews at the studio, just because you have a Hays card?"

"No, you have to have an assignment, too. From the magazine. You get your assignment first, and then you get the interview."

He shook his head, still didn't quite understand.

"Klaus, darling . . . let's go to bed."

91

"All right." Then at that moment he found the check, surprised that it was for only seventy-five dollars. "I thought they paid you a hundred, Jen."

"They do usually . . . for articles on the biggest stars. But not this time."

"Seventy-five dollars . . . it's wonderful anyway." He looked at it for a long time. "You really think we should give it to the lawyer?"

"Well, I'd like to see him and talk to him first. But we must begin and do *something*. We can't just go on trusting to luck any more. . . ."

Outside in the eleven o'clock quiet there were foot sounds on the driveway. Schnucki, on the floor under the couch, woof-woofed half-heartedly. No use making too big a noise. It was only Siegfried.

"Come in, Siegfried."

Siegfried bowed apologetically to Jennifer. There was always a tinge of apology in everything he did. She tried to smile cheerily, because to her he seemed the most lonely and forlorn of the whole colony. That questing look in his eyes . . . worse now since he had broken his glasses. His face even more tense, more searching. Siegfried, son of Abraham, looking for the land which had been promised him two thousand years before. Tonight his face panicky with fright. He looked ridiculous, about to cry.

"It's *mein pass*," he said tragically. "I have it lost again!"

Jennifer turned away, tempted to laugh. They had been through this so many times before; Siegfried, their forty-year-old problem child. Klaus went at once to the door. "All right, Siegfried . . . let's go look for it."

Across the drive, to Casa Number Six. Klaus walking

92

quickly, duty bound, anxious to get back. Siegfried pattering beside him, wailing softly.

Inside, Klaus switched on all the lights, began searching systematically. They spoke in German now.

"So sorry I must always bother you, Klaus."

"It's no bother . . . only I don't understand why you just don't carry your passport with you. Why you have to hide it all the time. I always carry mine."

"But you're young—and strong. If someone tries to rob you, you can fight. With me, it's different."

"Who do you think is going to steal your passport? Who would want it?"

"A man in Germany once—he offered me 5,000 marks for it. He was going to change the picture. There are people who do that."

"That was Germany. Nobody would want it here. Nobody could use it. Anyway, I wish you could learn to remember where you hide it."

He looked in the living room first; in the upholstery of the couch, behind the pictures, under the rug, in the china cabinets, places where Siegfried had hidden it before. Then in the bedroom.

"I don't think you understand, Klaus. If I lose this passport, I'll never get another one. They won't give them out any more, to Jews."

Klaus looked under the bed. His hand fumbled against a pile of soiled clothes, felt something hard and flat. He drew it out—the mottled dark-brown German Reichspass.

Murmuring his thanks, Siegfried grabbed the thin little book eagerly, pressed it tenderly to his lips.

When Klaus returned, Jennifer was already in bed, and

93

the bedroom dark. He called to her, but she didn't answer. He turned out the lights in the living room, fumbled through to the bedroom, undressed in the dark.

He stood for a while at the window. In the distance, in the hills, a coyote mourned. Close by a donkey brayed. Then from the river, the sound of the water pump beginning. That horrible pump. He always heard it. Every night. Monotonous rhythm. Over and over, that pong-pong-pong-pong. Never slower, never faster, never softer, never louder. Pong-pong-pong-pong, drumming in his skull.

"Jennifer!" This time his voice beseeched an answer.

"Yes, Klaus."

"You weren't asleep . . . why did you make pretend?"

"I was asleep, darling. Almost. I heard you come in, but . . ."

"Turn this way. Let me feel your eyes. You were crying?"

"Of course not. Why should I cry?" His fingers across her eyelids. "Satisfied?"

"No. Sometimes people cry with dry eyes."

"Do you ever?"

He ignored that, lay very still beside her. "Jennifer, don't you want to hug?"

"Of course I do." She moved close to him, their bodies fusing.

"Jennifer, what do you think on, nights, when you go to bed in Hollywood?"

"So sleepy, dear," she whispered.

"Do you think on the times when we can always sleep together?"

"Uh-huh."

94

"And the nice home we're going to have? Jennifer?"

"Yes."

"Please don't go to sleep now. Let's talk a little. All week I wait just to talk, and . . . oh, but poor darling . . . you're tired. The long trip. I wish I could take it on your place. I wish I could do all the things that for you a nuisance are. Wish I could work, and make the money. I wish—"

"Klaus . . . I saw one little house . . . awfully nice . . . it was for rent. . . ." Then her voice whispered away.

"Yes? Go on . . ."

"A little white fence around it."

"Did it have trees and flowers?"

"Uh-huh . . ."

He waited eagerly for more. But now she began to breathe heavily, regularly. She had slipped away from him. Cruel to call her back. He hugged her tighter, put his lips against her shoulder.

He was still awake an hour later when the pipes began. There was a loud sucking sound through the house, a long deep groan throughout the plumbing. That meant the water was going off. The town's water supply was very low, and every now and then there was no water at all . . . for hours, days sometimes.

Klaus rose, and went to the bathroom. If he hurried he might get a tubful. He turned the water on. It ran slowly, without spirit. He heard Omah up, next door. Saw lights across the way at the Lankowskis'.

He thought of the tremendous Rodriguez dam, only eight miles away. A beautiful dam, the highest Ambursen-type dam in the world, costing millions of pesos. There it was, big enough to supply water for twenty towns, and yet

95

here he was in the middle of the night hoping to catch a dribble of water. Aqueducts from the dam carrying the water only six miles. No money to lay them any further. A great project unfinished. Inefficiency, waste. His German thoroughness disapproved.

The water in the tub, rust-colored. Dirty. Nobody ever drank it, of course. Even the poorest Mexicans scraped up pennies for bottled water, for drinking and cooking. But you had to have it for the toilet and washing.

Only two inches on the bottom of the tub. All he could get. The pipes gave a final shudder and were silent. No need to turn off the tap even. They'd know when the water came on. The same loud discord of the pipes all over again.

He was glad that it happened, grateful for the noise, because now when he came back to bed, Jennifer was awake—and reaching out to him in the way that he wanted her to.

6

IN Casa Number Five, Ani Klabec heard the warning click of the alarm apparatus on the clock, hastily released the alarm before it could go off, and bounded up. That she should even set an alarm—in this timeless Mexican void—was something that her husband, Emil, would never understand.

But Ani was an amazing woman. She deluded herself, for her own peace of mind, into believing that the days were short, that there were many things to do, and she must crowd them in. It pleased her to get up early. She considered herself the leader of the colony, and leaders should always rise early. It gave her a sense of superiority to fling up her window blinds and see that the blinds in the other bungalows were still down. She . . . so active and industrious . . . while the other lazy souls slept.

Open the front door wide, toss the rugs on the front porch. Her first important act every morning. Just leave them there now, and sweep them later. She could have tossed them on the back porch, which was the proper place for sweeping . . . but she knew they would be unnoticed there, and Ani never missed an opportunity to impress her housekeeping prowess upon the community.

Go to the kitchen, put on the coffee, light the oven to heat rolls, and then dress in the bathroom.

She was a tall, slender woman, with a sharp handsome face. She was Jewish, but carried herself so erectly, and used makeup so effectively to reduce the prominence of her nose, that she looked less Jewish than she was.

Years ago she had liked her Jewish blood, knew that her good business sense and Jewish ways were responsible for the success of her gentile husband. Like most inventors, he was shy and introverted, and never would have amounted to anything if it hadn't been for her. It was she who had made him one of the wealthiest men in Czechoslovakia. But the blood that had brought them up ultimately pushed them out—and she hated it now. Of course, it might still be of use in Hollywood, and that's why she had led Emil there. She saw no reason why he couldn't work into the picture industry, somewhere in the technical end, working on new cameras or films.

Like the Weisses, they had already spent several months in Hollywood on visitors' visas, and even in that short time the place had already set its stamp on Ani. This morning she put on a cotton print dirndl which she had made for herself, copied from one she had seen in a shop on Hollywood Boulevard. There had been some material left over, which she had fashioned into a babushka. She put this on now . . . told herself that it was excellent protection for her hair when she dusted . . . but aside from its practical purpose, was really fascinated with the effect it created. Truthfully, Ani was much too tall and too far in her thirties for such girlish styles, but she didn't see it that way.

"Come on now, Emil. Get up! I want to get through

with breakfast, so I can get at my cleaning. No time to lose!" In the first morning hours she permitted herself and Emil, too, to speak in Czechoslovakian.

Emil turned over, groaned. Knew there was time to lose . . . weeks and months of it . . . maybe years. But he got up anyway. Quite used to moving when, and however, she directed. He shuffled into the bathroom. Emil was round-shouldered, and always shuffled. Because of it people said he looked more Jewish than Ani.

Waiting for Emil and the breakfast to reach the ready point, Ani moved about the bungalow, smiling over her treasures. The bungalow was the pleasantest one in the colony—because of those treasures. There were several pieces of bright Mexican pottery in the china cabinets. She had bought them the first week in Tijuana, not to be used here, of course, but to be put away and saved for later, when they had their new home. There were two small chairs, Mexican-made, the seats and backs of decorated leather, which she had also bought. Not to be sat upon now; also to be saved for Hollywood. A heavy bold-blue Indian serape which lay folded now, over the back of the couch—but to be hung on the wall of a sunroom eventually. And on the porch there were cactus plants, the beginning of a cactus garden which she would later transplant to the home she was counting on, in Hollywood.

These things which were "for Hollywood" she treated with extraordinary care. To already have them, even so few things, made her believe that she had taken a first important step up Highway 101.

After breakfast was finally over, Ani said: "Now, Emil, if you will, please dear . . . I'd like you to go to the store."

She said it every morning, just as though it were a fresh thought. It wasn't, though. It was part of her planned routine for him. Give him his breakfast, then send him to the store. The walk does him good. While he is at the store, do the dishes, heat the water for his bath. Then after he has had his bath, send him out to the garage to work on his inventions. While he fusses around in the garage, clean the house, do some baking. Then the hour before lunch, call him in, get out the English books, study until lunch. That's the way. Keep the day going. Fill it full. Keep things on schedule. After lunch . . . well, after lunch was when the day began to fall apart. But between now and then she would try to think of something. For now, she must make out her store list.

"Emil, what would you like for lunch?"

"Please don't ask me. You know I don't like to be asked. I never know what I want to eat. Just tell me what to get and I'll get it."

She thought a minute, chewed the pencil. "There was something I read about in *Good Housekeeping*. Boston Baked Beans, it was called. Very American. I might try that."

She found the magazine, turned to the recipe. "Old Fashioned Baked Beans." The phrase "Old Fashioned" disturbed her, discouraged her. What was the use of learning to cook something American if it was already old-fashioned? Ani wanted to be strictly up-to-the-minute American. Next to it was a "New Way of Preparing Lamb with Pineapple Sauce," and she decided on that.

While Ani worked on her list, Emil observed that Mrs. Eckert must have arrived the night before . . . her car

tucked into shed Number Three, behind the Klabec bungalow. The observation gave him pleasure, something to look
forward to. Emil liked Jennifer, talked to her at every opportunity. He respected her opinion (American) very much,
and always consulted her about the inventions on which he
was working.

Emil had a philosophy, and because of the philosophy he
was less intense and nervous about this exile than the other
immigrants. He believed that if America was to take him
under her roof, and become his hostess, then, like a good
guest, he must take his hostess a gift—some invention that
he could present to America, free. Naturally he wished to
make the gift useful and original . . . and it was because
of this that he had to consult Jennifer so often. Hard to
find something that America didn't already have. But Emil
persevered. He knew he would find something one day,
and when he had his gift ready it was his firm belief that
Providence would then present him with his quota number.

"I wonder what Mrs. Eckert will think of my new foot-
warmer? I wish she'd get up . . . I'd like to talk to her."

Ani looked over toward Casa Three. Not a sign of life
around the place. She shook her head disapprovingly.
"You'd think she'd get up and take care of her husband and
her house. If she's an example, no wonder there are so
many divorces in America. It's just shameful the way she
leaves that poor man to shift for himself!"

"Oh, now, I don't know. Don't forget she has to work in
Hollywood."

"It doesn't make any difference. She's here part of the
week and she should take care of him better. She never
thinks to leave something for him in the ice box when she

goes back—and he hardly eats a thing all week long. Why shouldn't she fix a roast before she goes? And his clothes! If you had to run around like he does, I'd never forgive myself. Holes in his socks, buttons off his shirts. Sometimes I don't think she irons his shirts at all, just presses them under a mattress!"

"Well, she's young. She still thinks she's going to do greater things than cook and sew. You don't understand her, Ani. . . ."

"Oh, yes, I do. She's what they call a 'career girl' in America. Career girls!"

Emil smiled at her sweetly, laid his hand on her arm. "You've been my 'career girl,'" he said softly. "Without you, I never would have been anything. Remember, Ani, when we were first married?"

He was really a dear man, so often sweet like that. Ani unbristled, forget Mrs. Eckert for a moment, looked fondly at her husband.

"All that money we had . . . it was due to you. Emil Klabec, a millionaire!" He smiled and sighed. "I never quite got used to it."

Her tenderness abated, and she looked hard and sharp again. "It's a good thing you didn't get used to it! None of it ever meant very much to *you*, I know that. Sometimes I think you are even happy here, as long as you have your work out there in that old garage."

"I am happy because you take care of me so nicely," hoping to please her, and knowing that it would. "It's like it was way back in the beginning . . . just the two of us in a little house . . . you doing the housework . . . getting along on practically nothing. Remember, Ani?"

"Well, maybe you like to think about it, but I don't! To go through all we did to get up, and then to find ourselves at the bottom again!" She suddenly rose. "Here, Emil, the list. Go to the store now."

On the way to the store he did think about it. For him, it *was* like it had been in the beginning, and he received, now and then, a sort of sentimental pleasure from it. But it wasn't the same for her, and he knew it only too well. In the last years, Ani had had a taste of wealth and ease. He watched her sometimes, saw her eyes grow feverish as she talked of the clothes and jewels and cars she used to have, and it embarrassed him. As a poor Jewish girl she had seemed to him adorable. As a successful Jewish woman she had been a delightful and entertaining partner. But as an embittered Jewess, robbed of her world and her wealth, she disturbed him. Always bragging about the things she had once had, forever belittling someone or something, intensely greedy and jealous. But he was too mild and too kind to think of criticizing her. He remained quiet, knowing that no matter what happened he loved her.

A half hour later he returned from the store, laid the grocery sacks on the kitchen table, headed quickly for the door, when the question he was dreading stopped him.

"What did Mrs. Berendo give you for a *pilón*, Emil?"

He fumbled, looked unhappy. "Ani, I'm sorry. I didn't ask her for one. Please don't make me. I always feel so self-conscious. . . ."

"Absurd. That's the trouble with you—you never speak up for what's coming to you. *We* didn't make the custom, did we? We didn't start it. Now you just go right back and tell Mrs. Berendo you forgot the *pilón*. Go on now."

Emil stood looking at his shoes, resentful and stubborn. That damn *pilón* business. A custom in Mexico for the storekeeper to give something free, whenever a customer made a large purchase—a bit of candy or fruit, or any small thing—to show that the merchant appreciates the patronage. Mrs. Berendo usually gave Emil something, without being reminded, but today she had evidently forgotten and he had been too shy to ask for it.

"Go on now, Emil. And *don't* let her give you another one of those fly swatters. Maybe you can get her to give you a piece of chocolate; it will be nice after lunch. And on the way, if Mrs. Lankowski is up, tell her—"

"She's not up yet. Her blinds are still down, too."

"That lazy Pole. Lying in bed all morning, lying around on her couch all day . . . she ought to get up and put her bedding and rugs out on the line. They haven't been out for a week! Emil, what are you standing around for?" She had the broom in her hand, and playfully swept him out.

Berendo's was more than just a grocery store. Gas station, butcher shop, poultry market, confectionery shop, magazine stand, combined. Mrs. Berendo, its proprietor, was jolly and fat, so fat that she had difficulty getting around. She sat all day in a big rocking chair in the corner, always smoking, and directed operations from there. She had three sons, half Indian, thin and dark with straight hair and straight eyelashes. They were unschooled, spoke no English, and were not allowed to touch the money—but fortunately their thinness allowed them to dart in and out and around behind counters where their mother could not go.

Mrs. Berendo saw Mr. Klabec returning, and was not surprised. She had purposely avoided giving him a *pilón* just to see if his Jewess wife would send him back. And here he was, looking so sad about it, that Mrs. Berendo's waistline quivered with silent subterranean laughter. Even now, as his eyes wandered nervously around the shop, she diabolically refused to help him out.

"Forget to buy something?" she asked, her voice light and lilting, not a bit fat. "Maybe you did not buy butter, maybe you forget that?"

"No."

"Potatoes, maybe?"

"No." He moved over to the candy counter. "Mrs. Berendo, I think a piece of candy I will have. That one there." He pointed to an Oh Henry! bar.

She leaned forward, peered into the case to see where he pointed, then ordered one of her sons to wait upon him.

Emil took the candy bar, tried to speak, but couldn't. He extracted fifty centavos from his pocket and reached it to Mrs. Berendo.

She laughed and rocked, waved her hand at him. "*Andale!* I know what you come for. Your wife, she sent you for *pilón, si?* She never forgets *pilón*, not her. Well, go on, take it. And here—" she reached into the onion bin near her chair, picked up a large brown onion. "Here, this is for her, too. She no buy onions for week, and one onion in the house, it is always useful."

Emil blushed, returned the coin to his pocket, carried the gifts in his hand. "Thank you very much, Mrs. Berendo."

Immensely relieved, he started home. As he turned the corner he saw Mady in the archway. She ran up to him. He saw her eyes devour the candy in his hand.

He knew it would displease Ani, but he couldn't help himself. "Here," he said. "It is for you. Take it."

Mady's eyes brightened, and she undid the wrapper at once, offered him a part of the candy.

"I do not want of it, thank you."

"Oh, please, a bite. Please, Mr. Klabec!" And then she broke off a piece, put it in his hand. Sticky and melting. He plopped it into his mouth; it was the easiest way to get rid of it.

"Jennifer is here," Mady announced as they walked nearer to the bungalows.

"Yes, I know. I am wishing to see her to show her my new invention."

"May I see it, Mr. Klabec?"

It was a temptation. He led her off to Garage Five . . . all of them lined up together at the rear of bungalows Four to Six . . . and was soon engrossed in showing the child how this new invention would work. It was intended to be a new kind of foot-warmer. It could be used in automobiles, on camping trips, or just in bed on cold nights. It was an oblong piece of sponge, about the size of a brick. The sponge was to be heated by a chemical. When the sponge was moistened with the chemical, sprinkled from a small can, it would grow warm, the degree of its warmth, and the duration of it, depending on the amount of chemical used.

"Put some on and let me feel it," Mady begged.

But Emil couldn't do that. He hadn't perfected the chemical yet. It was still too strong, and would burn her hand.

"But do you not think this will be good for America?" he asked. "In parts of America it is very cold in winter, not like always in California, no?"

"It's for America?"

"Yes, it is like so, Mady—" and he tried to explain his gift theory to her. As he talked, the child stared at him, caught by his intensity, the deep seriousness of his voice, but not quite following. All she understood was that Emil intended to give something free to America, and she immediately thought of Mrs. Klabec, who didn't seem like the kind to ever give anything to anybody.

"But what does Mrs. Klabec say about that? Did she say you could?" she asked seriously.

Emil was nonplused. "Why, I—I do not know. I—"

At that moment Ani was at the door calling him to his bath. He put his things away and hurried into the house.

Ani was annoyed: Emil's bath was already getting cold, and when it cost all that money to heat a bath, he should have more respect for one, not hang around talking nonsense to a child.

"Where's the chocolate, Emil?"

"I'm sorry, Ani. I gave it to Mady. She just looked it out of my hand. But I have something else. Mrs. Berendo sent you this," and timidly he showed her the onion.

"Emil Klabec, you have chocolate on your mouth!"

He wiped his mouth guiltily. "I had a taste of it, that's all."

"If the Weisses can afford to board here like hotel people, they can afford to buy chocolate for Mady themselves! I don't want to sound petty, but you know how I like chocolate. And yet I never buy any, because it's an extravagance, and you know how careful we have to be. Mustn't spend money for anything that isn't important."

At the moment, as she railed, she was dusting the "Hollywood" chairs. Emil watched her and looked at the chairs—had it been important to buy *them*, he wondered. Well, perhaps, for her, the chairs were important. People in exile had strange needs . . . and there was certainly no reason to bring it up now anyway. He took his scolding in good grace, went on into the bathroom.

Ani opened the side window which looked toward Casa Four, where the Lankowskis still slept. She opened it with a bang, then shook out her dust cloth. She called loudly to Emil, "There's some new soap on the basin," but in the main directed her voice next door.

There! She hoped that would wake up those lazy Poles.

For most of the immigrants the day's beginning was always the most difficult part of the day. The realization of the long hours to come before darkness fell and eyes grew heavy and you could go to sleep again. The object of existence at the Colonia Gomez was to wait for time to pass until life could begin again.

The day's beginning always depressed Blima Lankowski, but this morning, as she woke, there was also a dread added to the dejection. A pregnant woman may hide her pregnancy for so long, and then one day she realizes there is no longer any hope of hiding it. Imagination perhaps, but there seems to be an overnight bulge, and a heaviness that was not there yesterday.

Blima, as she lay there with just the sheet over her, felt her husband's eyes close and examining. She let him look, made no effort to move. The moment that she had dreamed of for eight years, desired and yearned for, was here finally, but no longer precious.

"Duwid, we are going to have a baby."

There was no response, so she touched his arm, shook him slightly. "Did you hear me, Duwid . . . more troubles for you. Oh, I'm so sorry. Please don't blame me. Say something, Duwid."

"When will it be?"

"After Christmas, perhaps the first of January. . . ."

He lay very quiet for a moment, then quickly sat up, his dark eyes blinking with excitement.

"Blima, we must plan something. You're sure? You couldn't be mistaken?"

His eagerness gave her hope. "Very sure, dear. Over three months already."

"But why didn't you tell me sooner?"

His cheer and optimism took the cramp out of her heart, and she drew her arm over her eyes to hide her happiness. Then she heard him mumbling something about the consul . . . pregnant . . . consul . . . maybe do something.

Her happiness stood still. "Duwid, what are you trying to say?"

"That perhaps because of you, a baby coming, they may have pity and give us our visas a little sooner."

"Oh." Her arm went over her eyes again, but for a different kind of hiding. His visa, his visa . . . all Duwid could think of these days. The musician she had been so proud of. The man she had loved and who had loved her. What had happened to them? Once in Europe, Blima had heard a saying: that a man is made up of three parts—body, soul, and papers. Duwid was only one-third alive now, living only for his papers.

"Then you think—it might help—to have the baby?" She

tried to keep her voice unemotional, as though she spoke of commodities.

He got up, hurriedly began to dress. "I am sure of it. You must go to a doctor, get his report—on paper—and I will take it to the consul, so he can forward it to the State Department. Let's hurry, Blima . . . and I will see if I can borrow a car."

Then he saw her quivering lips and body. He stood staring. His mask melted, and for the first time in weeks, Blima saw the gentle face of her husband. "Blima, oh, I am so sorry. My dear Blima, my dear wife." He gathered her in his arms. "Why, we've waited for a child all our life! Oh, please forgive me! I'm half mad lately. Do you feel all right? Do you have any pain? Tell me, Blima."

"There isn't any pain. I'm all right. I feel better now. Move away, Duwid, please, or I'll cry."

Duwid left her finally, went into the bathroom to shave.

Blima stood before the open closet door, choosing a dress to wear to the doctor's. In her heart she doubted that the baby would get them into America . . . felt that the poor thing was doomed to be born in exile.

There were several light summer dresses but their bright colors seemed inappropriate now. She pushed them aside, reached for a dark one.

From now on, Blima would wear black, in mourning for her child.

That weekend, Jennifer stayed longer than usual. She would go back late Monday afternoon, stop in San Diego on the way and see the lawyer.

Monday was a magnificent morning, bright and warm,

and with a provocative light wind. The wind had drawn Klaus, Emil, and Mady to the near by hill. The two men had made a kite for the child several weeks before, but there had been no wind to fly it. This morning, with the first breath of breeze, they hastened out to soar it on its maiden voyage.

Jennifer, elbow deep in suds at the washtub in the little pantry off the kitchen, watched them through the window. They looked as if they were having fun, and the sight thrilled her. She could also look off to the right, where the clotheslines were, and where the ladies Klabec and Lankowski were already hanging up their wash. There was a pleasant picture in that, too, she thought. Oh, the whole scene was beautiful this morning. The breeze gave movement to the panorama, made the grass, the trees, and the sky alert and lively.

Washing was good. Jennifer hadn't had much experience with it in the past, but it was a physical joy, relief from thoughts. The soap so clean-smelling. The water so warm. Her knuckles all red, and a little peeled, from scrubbing. But it was good, really good. Her back ached nicely, her face steamed. She could feel the hair around her face, all damp and curly. The tub leaked a little and there was a shallow pool at her feet. But no nuisance; she was prepared for it, wearing only old huaraches. They oozed water and squeaked; the water tickled her toes, made her giggle. She felt wonderful this morning. It was the kind of day for which God should be congratulated. Nice work, God, for turning out such a gorgeous morning. She couldn't think exactly why she was so happy . . . the beauty of the day, partly, but mostly, in the attic of her mind, the thought that a lawyer had said he could get Klaus in, absolutely, positively, surely—and this afternoon she was going to see him about it.

A sudden thought occurred to her, remembering Omah, and she hurried next door. Omah was sick and had been in bed since Saturday.

"Where's your laundry, Omah? I have some beautiful suds, and—"

But Omah stubbornly denied that she had anything to wash, wouldn't let Jennifer be bothered.

"But it's no bother. I love it."

Omah watched her radiant face, and smiled. "You are very pretty this morning, *Kindchen*. There is nothing so *shoen* as a bride about her housework. When she is first married she moves so, like you, with a happy smile. Later, it goes different."

Jennifer sat on the edge of the bed, turned serious. "Omah, I worry about you. You're so pale. Klaus says we ought to get you a doctor."

"Say to Klaus that when I have sickness, I will ask for a doctor. For now there is nothing . . . I am only maybe a little tired. No, go on, Jennifer . . . and please give to me the cards as you go out."

Jennifer laid the pack of cards beside her. Every day Omah read her own fortune in the cards . . . and sometimes Jennifer thought that it was the cards that kept the old woman hanging on, and kept her cheerful, because the fortune always came out the same way. The cards always said that Omah would get into America.

There was a shrill sound outside, and Omah's eyes brightened: "Jennifer, will you look? I think it is perhaps the letter carrier."

"No, Omah . . . it's too early. When he comes, though, I'll tell you. It was probably only someone whistling for Schnucki."

"Schnucki. . . ." Omah's voice smiled. "I have not seen her for so long, perhaps you would her send to me for company?"

Jennifer called from the door, and the dog came in gladly, bounded on the old woman's bed. Thin hands stroked her. "Any fleas today? Jennifer, would you be so kind . . . two little pans of water? One with soap in it, and a towel?"

The girl filled the pans, brought them to the bedside. She knew what was coming, and for a moment stayed to watch. Omah had two pleasures in Tijuana; telling her cards, the first—and ridding Schnucki of fleas, the other.

She was an expert flea-catcher, worked with a practiced hand, and put so much relish into the work that it was comical to watch her. A definite routine, which she followed exactly. When the flea was spied, hold the dog's hair apart with one hand, dab the index finger of the other hand against the tongue, then flop it over the flea. The flea sticks to the moisture, is lifted off. Then with a vicious gleam, Omah cracks the flea between her thumb and index finger, flicks the cracked flea into the pan of water. "So!" she announces triumphantly. Before tackling another, she washes her hand in the other pan of water, so that her finger will be clean when it again touches her tongue.

"Look, Omah . . . do you mind my asking—why can't you just wet your finger in the pan of water? Why always wet it with your tongue?"

Omah shook her head, seemed to despair of Jennifer's intelligence.

"It is not the same that way. The moisture from the tongue is more sticky than just water. See how fine it works . . . look, I have another! Fleas!" she exclaimed disgustedly. "Did you know, Jennifer . . . the last years in Germany, fleas are so seldom, that the scientific laboratories pay for them money? Think only what this Fräulein Schnucki would be worth, if we sent her to Germany in a package! And if a Mexican went from here, he could make travel expenses!" Omah chuckled at her little joke, but somehow the chuckle was so old and so faint that it depressed Jennifer a little.

But back at the washtub she soon revived. Too gay-spirited this morning to let any depression grip her for very long.

Irmgard passed the door on her way to the washlines. Jennifer called out to her: "Hey, Irmgard! Don't you dare use up all the lines . . . have to leave me some space somewhere!"

Irmgard went on without turning. It was possible she hadn't heard.

At the clotheslines Ani Klabec, in her usual bossy way, was advising Blima on prenatal care. They had all heard about the baby by this time, and Ani felt that it was wrong for Blima to do such heavy work now. Why shouldn't she get her husband to help with the washing?

"Because," Blima said softly, "my husband is a musician. His hands are to him important. Not good to have hands always in water." She said it with a shy pride. She loved Duwid's fine white hands, gloried in their nimble beauty at the piano. Not only would she not ask him to help her with the housework; she would not permit him to do so.

"He doesn't use his hands so much lately!" Irmgard voiced this airy opinion in the midst of clothespinning a few pitiful worn and torn cotton underthings. "I never hear him playing any more."

Ani turned toward her, undertook Blima's defense. "You know why? Because you play so often your victrola. He cannot work with a noise like that."

Irmgard looked away, shrugging.

"If you had something beside Mexican records, it might not be so bad," Ani continued, "but Mr. Lankowski does not like Mexican music. I am not understanding either why you buy them."

"Because they are the only ones I can get here! And they are cheap. They are old ones, already used. I don't like Mexican music either. But I can't stand the quiet sometimes . . . I hate everything Mexican!" she added vehemently.

Blima suddenly thought of that day in the Ensenada shipping office, the geranium in her hand. "You should not say such a thing, Irmgard. Mexico has given to us hospitality. We should be grateful."

"Grateful! Why? We spend money here, don't we? We don't take anything from Mexico. Of course, Mexico is glad to have us!"

The three fell silent for a moment. Faintly from Casa Three, they heard Jennifer singing.

"Her!" Irmgard spat.

"Why do you like her so little?" Ani asked.

"Oh, she is so superior. Just because she's free to run back and forth across the border. She acts like as if she was Miss

America . . . Mrs. *God!* I hate her. Always has what she wants. All Americans are spoiled. Life is so easy for them. I hate her because she doesn't understand what is it like for us, on the outside, looking in. She is so awful cheerful!"

"Mrs. Eckert has troubles also," Blima said thoughtfully. "Only she has not had them so long like us. And also, Americans are very strong against trouble."

"What does she know about trouble? She can cross the line, can't she? Trouble. That makes me laugh."

There was quick silence as Jennifer appeared on the back steps of her bungalow, and set down a heavy pail.

Klaus saw her from the hill, and came running. "Jennifer, you promised not to wash today. I could do it tomorrow after you went."

Jennifer laughed, corrected his English, and told him to hush up. "Here, just take one end of this sheet, and help me with the wringing. These sheets are heavy."

He reached for the pail. "Look, watch," he said.

One by one, between his strong hands, he turned the four sheets into small Niagaras. Jennifer watched, and buzzed with admiration. Saw the plain pure pleasure on his face . . . so thrilled when he could be of help. "Maybe I can rent myself out to housewives in America!" he smiled proudly.

"That's enough now! Leave them a little wet, or there won't be any need to put them on the line. I'll get them up, and then maybe we can go for a walk. Go on back, now. Is the kite fun?"

"Sort of. Hurry, Jen."

A moment later, Jennifer took long joyous steps to the clotheslines, her high spirits radiating in a broad smile.

"Good morning, good morning . . . how are you, everybody? Say, you didn't leave me much space!"

"Oh," said Blima, "I am sorry. I—"

"No, no . . . I'm just fooling. Really. There's plenty of room. I can always double up. I was only kidding . . . feel so good this morning. I don't know why!"

She stood on tiptoe to reach the line. The wind in her hair, in her blouse, against her skirt, and blowing the fresh cool laundry damp against her face. The wind cool. The sun hot. The filled lines flapping. The sound, movement, and feel, jolly and exhilarating.

"Isn't it just *glorious* today?"

"What is?" Irmgard asked sharply.

"The sun! The wind! I love the wind!"

"The wind, yes." Irmgard frowned. "Yes, but wait until it turns a little and comes down from the hills. They tell me it won't be so glorious then. Dust all over the place. Dust and dust and dust—until it rains. Then only mud. Late in September, and all through October, sometimes November. Dust storms all the time. Maybe you won't find it so thrilling then!"

Then suddenly she added mockery to her bitterness. "Oh, but I forgot, didn't I? You won't be here then. An American citizen always gets her husband in . . . you won't have to wait so long like we. You'll soon be saying good-by. *You*'ll just remember it here as a sweet little spot in Mexico where you spent your honeymoon!"

Jennifer stared, her happiness deflated now by the sharp prick of Irmgard's malevolence. "Oh, Irmgard, *please!* Please don't talk like that."

Jennifer felt the hate, and it hurt. She turned frantically

toward the two older women, but saw on their faces something of the same accusation that was there on Irmgard's.

"Oh, I'm so sorry. I forget. You're all so tired of it here. But I am, too. And please believe me—I don't know when Klaus will get in. There's something that we have to overcome first, like you—" she nodded toward Blima. "But look—" her eyes wandered off toward the hills and the fields. "It really *is* beautiful here. Look over there. All around. Sometimes I don't see it right myself. But we shouldn't be like that. It really *is* beautiful, if we can only get to see it that way."

Irmgard pointed to the garbage dump, a stone's throw away. Ugly death-trap. "I suppose *that* is nice to look at? And that junk over there?" She pointed up toward Chato's shack where there was a wreckage pile, parts of old cars . . . and near that another conglomeration of rusty fenders, chassis, wheels, car seats, strewn across one angle of the hill to form a fence. "I suppose *that* is pretty? That's what *I* see when I look around!"

Ani Klabec had been standing a little apart from the group. Now she took a step toward Blima and Irmgard, as though to align herself with them; the three immigrants lined up against the American.

"You see, Jennifer, it is easy for you to see the pretty parts, because you are here only two or three days and then you can go away again. But for us it is different, and about human nature it is a strange thing. To say to a person that they *must* do a thing, like we must sit here and wait, makes it full of hate, and no pleasure anywhere. We are so busy all the times looking off across the border, on to the States side, where life is lovely and free, and we are so

118

wishing we were there also that it is not possible to see if it is nice here."

She paused for a moment, then sighed: "But maybe it is something no person can understand, unless they are in it also themself."

Jennifer searched for some argument to cheer them, but could find none. She turned away, began hanging her clothes, working automatically, all pleasure gone.

Something nobody could understand unless . . .

She thought of Klaus. How little she really understood what he was suffering. How small the understanding she gave. She was in this trouble, too, but only partly, not like he was. She had only the mental turmoil and strain . . . he had to face it physically as well.

She tried to imagine what it must be like, and oddly, she thought of the bathroom door. That darn door, the way it got stuck all the time. Always when she was inside, and trying to get out. How she'd push and pull, shake and bang. She remembered how quickly she always got mad, hot with anger and rage, burning with frustration, nerves shrieking for release. The hellish door. The handle turns, the door gives a little at the bottom. Almost opens, but no. Push, pull, bear down, pull up. Frenzied mad. Stamp feet, yell. Yell loud. She always did. Yell because the damn door *should* open and won't.

To be at a border, and to have the gate stuck. It must be like the torment of the bathroom door. Rage and frustration. Helplessness. But magnified a hundred, a thousand, a million times, of course.

A towel dropped in the dirt. Jennifer let it lie and hurried to find Klaus.

7

KLAUS waited at Berendo's for Jennifer to telephone from San Diego, after she had seen the lawyer. He was eager and excited, so that the cheerlessness of her tone in her first few words struck him sharply. "Well, I paid him. He says he'll pick you up tomorrow morning and you can go to the consul together."

"Is something wrong?"

"No. Why?"

"You sound funny."

"I was just a little disappointed. But he's all right, I guess. Only he didn't seem very prosperous. And you didn't tell me he was so messy-looking."

"I did. I told you he had spots on his vest. Jen, you better come back, so we can talk it."

"No, it's going to be all right. I already gave him the check."

"You're sad. You're worried about the money."

"No. Just over-eager. Nervous, I guess. Oh, I don't know what's the matter with me. Excuse me, darling."

There was a pause, Jennifer feeling angry with herself. She had meant to control her fears and hadn't been able to. Since morning, at the clotheslines, she had known they must do something, and do it quickly, and even in Mr.

120

Steele's office she had been quite certain of what she wanted to do. They had to start some action, impossible to go on like this, bound to become bitter and twisted eventually, like the others. Quite prepared to give Mr. Steele the check, and get things started. And his enthusiastic talk had encouraged her.

It was only after she had left the office that she began to be doubtful, and ask herself questions. What was that peculiar atmosphere in the office? Why were the desks so empty-looking? Why only that one secretary at the phone taking messages? Why no law books around? Why no names on the outer door? And a most important why: Why hadn't she thought to inquire about Mr. Steele first? She could have asked Whitie at the border.

"Jennifer, listen to me. When I get in I will make money so fast—that one day we will laugh for just seventy-five dollars."

"Oh, I *know*. Of course. I've just gotten jittery lately, and a miser, that's all. And anyway I'll have another check soon. For Fred MacMurray. Next week, maybe. Nothing to worry about. If Mr. Steele only accomplishes something." Her voice began to take on its old spirit. "Be sure and wear a clean shirt, darling. Isn't there one that you had washed at the Chinaman's? Don't wear one I pressed. You've got to look nice when you see the consul."

The next morning Klaus spent an hour getting ready. Washed his hair. Worked on his nails. Shined his shoes. Sponged his best dark suit, and pressed it. Dressed at last, he felt very elegant, like in the old days. Dark suit, white shirt, dark tie, black shoes. It made him feel good, like a human again. All dressed up, ready to go someplace.

But after a while he began to be nervous, walked round and round the house. Stopped once before the mirror, and looked at himself close, noticed that the tiny scars, one above each eye, were beginning to come out. They always showed up, faintly white, when he was excited, angry, or tired. The only marks he carried from his years of boxing. Of course, there were other hurts inside, and he was conscious of them too when he was nervous. His stomach cramped and tense, an old ache throbbing again high in his ribs.

He tried to sit calmly by the open window in the living room. Turned the clock to the wall. But knew it was past ten anyway, as Julio's whistle announced his arrival. Klaus stayed still, not wanting to go out. The *Immigranten* would want to know why he was dressed up; he didn't want to talk about it.

Mady was standing near the window, apart from the others, her back to the mailman. Klaus watched her . . . her eyes closed, her little hands made into tense little fists. "Please, God," she whispered, "please God send us a quota number so Mamma and Hans and me can go to the United States and I can become another Shirley Temple, only better. Please, God. Please."

But there was no letter for her parents, and she went sorrowfully up the hill.

At eleven, Klaus changed into old shoes and trousers, walked to Berendo's, and telephoned Mr. Steele.

Mr. Steele was home ill. He had left a message in case Mr. Eckert called: he would be over tomorrow.

Home again, Klaus put away his good clothes, hung the shirt on a hanger, very carefully, to save it for Wednesday.

Wednesday came. The shirt was again worn for a few empty, waiting hours, again put away. By Thursday it had lost its freshness, began to look like something Jennifer had ironed.

Klaus showed wear, too. Fidget lines around his eyes and mouth. Ugly red razor marks under his chin. His skin, unaccustomed to daily close shaves, burned and stung. But he would dress and wait once more. He had the feeling that if and when the lawyer did show up, he would seize him by his dirty vest-front, and punch him in the nose.

Klaus was still waiting at noon. At a few minutes past twelve he turned on the radio and tried to get a quiz contest on KFI. It was a program he often tried to get, had heard it once or twice and found it a wonderful experience. Wonderful—because he could answer the questions more quickly and more accurately than most of the contestants could. That was German schooling for you; facts once learned, never forgotten. He knew more about American history, for example, than the average American. To be able to beat Americans, in their own language, at one of their own games—it gave him a feeling of pride and superiority. It was a rare feeling. An exile who sits on a country's back doorstep, like a beggar waiting to be let in, has need of such a feeling now and then.

This morning, the third of his waiting, he felt the need stronger than ever, and worked frantically at the radio. It was six years old, a cabinet model, only five tubes, and loaned to them by Mrs. Gomez, who had frankly admitted that it was not much good as a radio, but as a piece of furniture it would help fill up the room. On the States side, somewhere in the east, the radio might have worked rather well, but in Tijuana its case was practically hopeless. Station MLMS was in Tijuana, and so strong that it came through at every point of the dial. No Mexican radio commission law to restrict its power, and MLMS was a loud blare all over the western states, stronger than any of the American stations, bragging that it could be heard to Denver on the east, and as far north as Seattle. Such a sturdy station that Klaus had even heard it on the telephone wires when he was phoning.

Not only was the station annoying because of its dial-wide blasts. A further aggravation was that MLMS was not very particular about its advertisers. Any advertiser who had been turned down by the American radio chains could find a ready spot there; MLMS abounded with patent medicines, cure-alls, oil leases, friendship clubs, marriage bureaus, horoscopes, numberscopes, and psychic advice on personal problems. Klaus hated the station, felt it was a torture invented especially for him, to deprive him of hearing good American programs.

All he could hear this noontime was "your favorite singing cowboy, Billy Border, singing from MLMS, the border station."

Klaus kicked the radio, silenced it. He moved it into the center of the room, unscrewed the back, lifted out the tubes, began to take the whole thing apart. He laid the screws in little piles on the rug, in the order in which they came out, hoping he'd remember how to put them back again. There must be some way to cut out MLMS. Soon he had the entire apparatus in pieces and sections on the floor. His hands were dirty, and his face, too, where he had rubbed it. There was a dark smudge on his collar, where he had loosened his tie.

When Mr. Steele arrived, Klaus still sat turk-fashion, staring dolefully at the mess before him. He looked so muddled and so forlorn, all mussed up there in his good clothes, that Mr. Steele laughed.

"Well! What are you up to now, my boy?"

Klaus did not like Mr. Steele to call him "his boy." He did not like anything about Mr. Steele, especially not his jollity, but he was too wrung out to do anything about it. He got up.

"Mr. Steele," he said, "you don't know how terrible it is to be waiting for someone."

"Oh, yes, I do. But it wasn't my fault. Can't blame a man for being sick. But I'm here now, feeling fit as a fiddle. Are you ready to go?"

Klaus gave him a withering look, went in to wash and change.

In the bathroom, he argued with himself that Mr. Steele had been sick, and it was true, you couldn't blame anyone for that. He argued further that Mr. Steele was really a very nice man, and he was going to help him. Mr. Steele knew all the ropes, and all the wires, and he was going to have him in, in no time. By the time they left, Klaus had succeeded in convincing himself that Mr. Steele was his Saint George, out to slay the dragon.

Thirty miles down the road, Mr. Steele suggested that they stop at Half-Way House and have a drink.

Gray-blue eyes flooded with an honest, childish surprise. "Have a drink when I am a consul to see? No, no . . . please not, Mr. Steele."

"Nonsense."

Half-Way House was a small adobe-brick square, without windows, on the ocean side of the road, and now Mr. Steele drew up to it.

"It won't take a minute, and I don't mind telling you I could use one. I've been a pretty sick man, you know."

Klaus looked at Mr. Steele with microscopic intensity, noticed a vague breathless quivering of mouth and hands, a pinkish tinge to the eyes that he had not noticed before.

"Come on," Mr. Steele urged. "At least, have a beer."

Klaus followed him into the dank darkness of the place, not to have a beer, but to keep an eye on Saint George. He knew now what his sickness had been for three days.

Mr. Steele ordered a double whiskey sour, reached for it avidly, emptied it in a few greedy gulps, said he felt much better already, and thought he'd have just one more.

"No," said Klaus firmly, and laid his hand heavily on the older man's arm.

"Now, now, my boy, we'll go in just a minute. My, you're tense today. You're a funny boy . . . sort of temperamental, aren't you? What's the matter . . . dontcha think I can hold my liquor?"

"Mr. Steele, I want to go now." He spoke plainly, not very loud, but the lawyer sensed a danger signal.

"Okay, sure." He pocket-fished for some change, paid for the drink, and followed Klaus to the car.

The one drink had made a noticeable change in Mr. Steele. Loosened him up, made him silly. Grinning silly. His glasses had slipped down over his nose. He drove indifferently, talked constantly with little self-satisfied chuckles interspersed. "I don't understand you, my boy. Why you're so afraid to see a consul. Unless maybe there's something you didn't tell me about your case. . . ."

Klaus sat at the far side of the seat, staring out the window.

"But no, I think you told me the truth, and you know, I'm a pretty good judge of character. Yes, sir. That's my training, judging people. I've had lots of experience. Did I tell you I was in the consular service myself once?"

Klaus turned quickly, stared at him.

"Yes, sir . . . too bad I wasn't the consul when you applied, eh, boy? Things might have been different for you."

"Different . . . but more expensive, is that what you mean?"

"No, no, I don't mean anything of the kind." Mr. Steele seemed to realize that he had talked too much and shut up now.

So. Mr. Steele was an ex-consul. Probably kicked out for drinking and taking bribes. And this was the Saint George to whom he had entrusted his future.

Klaus felt sick with disappointment. In Europe he wouldn't have felt sick; he would have been angry. In Europe he would have canceled the agreement, and demanded his seventy-five dollars. He would have gotten it too, by force, if necessary. But that was before he had immigration difficulties. Now his troubles had changed him, made him fearful, dreading to discard even the smallest hope, and there was still a hope that through his "wire" Mr. Steele might be able to do something. And a chance, too, that as an enemy Mr. Steele might be dangerous.

All the rest of the trip Klaus wished for Jennifer, wished he could talk it over with her. Absurd, how helpless he felt without her. Absurd how this trouble had taken the fight and fury out of him. Like a trapped animal, afraid to budge, fearing that one little move might make the hurt worse.

When they arrived at last at Ensenada, at the consulate, the secretary, Miss Allbright, had a smile for Klaus, but her greeting for Mr. Steele was cold and indifferent.

"You've missed the consul. He's in Los Angeles today. He won't be back till morning. You should have telephoned first."

Klaus felt vastly relieved, and hurried out.

Outside, on the sidewalk, Mr. Steele shrugged. "Well, we may just as well stay over and see him in the morning, and tonight we can have some fun. There's an auto court down near the water. We can put up there, and then tonight we can go to Rosita's place. It's quite a place! You'll like it. Good-looking girls. And Rosita is an old friend of mine. She'll take care of us. Why do you look at me so funny? Think I'm too old to enjoy that sort of thing now and then?" Mr. Steele laughed self-consciously. "I should say not. I can still hold up my end, all right! Where are you going? Let's leave the car here and get something to eat and a drink, first."

Klaus moved away toward the car, got in. Mr. Steele presumed that perhaps this foreigner hadn't understood the evening pleasures he had been outlining. He followed him, began again about Rosita.

"Get in," Klaus ordered. "We're going. I don't want to stay here."

"Don't you want me to see the consul for you?"

"No."

"Well, for God's sake, what's eating you?"

Klaus managed to control himself, but he was shaking. "Mr. Steele, you don't understand. To come down here about my papers, and to hope I get things straightened out, that's the most important thing for me. And for my wife. And I don't think you understand that. I'd like to get back to Tijuana, and if it's all right with you, I want to drive, because then we get there more quicker."

"Sure . . . but you're certainly a funny guy. Go ahead, move over."

Klaus moved behind the wheel, and Mr. Steele got in.

"I still think maybe if we had a drink, maybe you'd relax, and then—"

Further words were impossible. Mr. Steele leaned back, braced his feet. The car shot down the dusty street, people and animals scattering. Klaus took the first curve up the hill and onto the main highway at full speed.

For the first five miles Mr. Steele feared for his life. Then he saw there was no danger. The car well in control, Klaus driving expertly. Mr. Steele remembered that once the German had been a racer. Eventually he was at ease, and went to sleep.

Still asleep when they drew up before the Colonia Gomez. Head hanging, mouth open. Flabby-faced old fool. Klaus banged the door to wake him.

"Here already? My, my. That was a fast trip. Next time we go down, I'll let you drive both ways."

Klaus wondered if there would be a next time. He had the

feeling that this was the last they would ever see or hear of Mr. Steele.

After that Jennifer phoned and wrote and stopped to see him several times. He was always out, never replied to her letters. Then she heard that his regular office was in El Paso. She wrote there, but there was no answer. Whitie told her that Mr. Steele had once been warned to keep away from the immigrants in Tijuana.

After a few weeks, they gave it up.

The check for the Richard Greene interview, which Jennifer had worked on for two weeks, wet the gullet of Mr. Steele, and served no other practical purpose.

8

LATE in August Tibor Szolnay came to Tijuana.

He came with his pipe between his teeth, with his fine English riding boots, and his blue and green and yellow sport coats, and his turtleneck sweaters, and his quick easy laugh, and his beautiful brown eyes, and his hair the color of molasses, long and curly over his collar . . . and his big handsome body, and his ungodly appetite. And he came with laziness. And languor. And conceit. And above all, a weakness for women.

But with only thirteen dollars in his pocket.

He arrived by neither of the routes which the immigrants had traveled. Neither the water route from the south which the Lankowskis, the Eckerts, and Irmgard had taken. Nor Highway 101 from the north, over which the Klabecs, the Weisses, and Omah had been forced because of expiring visas. Tibor came in by taxi, along the Criminal Trail. This is a wandering dirt path squirming its way over the mountains on the Mexican side of the border. Referred to as the Criminal Trail because the only people who ever use it are those who have no permission to cross the border and use the better road on the States side, or for reasons of their own prefer not to.

Tibor had begun the taxi trip the evening before, at

Mexicali, where he had just stepped off the northbound plane from Mexico City. He had started off, riding properly in the back seat, as befits a gentleman, but that was before he realized the trip's perils. The sheer bluffs, the short turns, the meager headlights so ineffective against the black night. And most frightening, the driver's oranges. The Mexican had a sack beside him. He ate a good many oranges. He liked oranges. He ate as he drove, skinning the orange with one hand and his teeth, while the other hand rested lightly on the shimmying steering wheel.

After watching this for some time, Tibor moved up front to help peel the oranges, so the Mexican could pay more attention to his driving. Tibor also figured that the front would be easier to jump from. And twice he did jump, sure that the car was bound for a precipice. This caused the driver to laugh. He had never had such a scary passenger.

But with daylight the going was easier, and from then on Tibor relaxed. Now at ten in the morning they were nearing the end of their journey. The car came down out of the mountains, turned on to the road that led past the bull ring, followed it north, the back way into Tijuana.

Tibor ordered the driver to stop. Got out and into the back seat again. He put on his sport jacket and the soft felt hat which had been lying there, snapped the brim of his hat at that becoming angle he knew so well, set his pipe between his teeth, crossed one leg over the other (they were booted and breeched for riding), and leaned back comfortably.

"Now drive me to the best hotel."

He had heard that Tijuana was a dump, but Tibor believed that a good entrance was always important anywhere.

They drew up before the Hotel Golondrina, a dingy two-story building on the Avenida de la Revolución.

"Not here. I told you a *good* hotel."

"Is good!" the Mexican assured him. "Is very good. Is best. *You* see!"

Two kids hopped on the running board. "Shine shoes, mister? Buy Mexican cigarettes?"

It had not been worth the effort, tired as he was, getting into the back seat for just a kid reception. "Tell the manager to come out."

The driver went inside. Reappeared with a waiter.

"Manager not here. You want room . . . I fix."

"First, I want to phone long distance."

"No got pay phone here. Best go telephone company."

The taxi moved on. Past the importers' shops, shop girls standing in the doorways. Porters leaning on brooms in the café entrances. Even in the morning the town tired, and with an air of waiting. Past the lamppost at the end of the avenue, where the road turned right to the bridge, and just before the bridge the driver stopped at the telephone company.

The girls at the desks and behind the pay windows looked up and quickened with interest as Tibor clumped in, walking hard and heavy in his boots. He noticed their interest, smiled and stepped back a little as two girls raced to the window to take care of him. He took his pipe out of his mouth to give his smile a better chance, pretended to be flustered by the attention.

"All I want, *right now*"—and he gaily emphasized the latter two words—"is to use a telephone."

The girls giggled and directed him upstairs to a booth.

133

Tibor stepped into the booth, gave the operator a Hollywood number and asked her to reverse the charges.

Hollywood numbers are always of interest to the girls at the switchboard, but the operator who took Tibor's call that day heard little to satisfy her curiosity—and her curiosity was very keen when a butler answered at the Hollywood end, and when the customer at this end asked for Miss Hiller. Tasha Hiller! the operator immediately thought. Tasha Hiller, the movie star!

But then, disappointment. Because when Miss Hiller came to the phone, the conversation was no longer in English. A strange-sounding language, with a sort of oriental tone to it. But not oriental. It sort of sounded like talking to horses, too . . . lots of whoa, hee, whoa, hee, whoa-whoa-whoa's in it. Then she realized it must be Hungarian, because that was what Miss Hiller was supposed to be. There were, however, a few words the operator recognized as they talked . . . Mexico City . . . Tijuana . . . London.

The tone of the conversation she understood very well. The man was excited, had a demanding note to his voice. And Miss Hiller, the lovely Miss Hiller, was excited, too. Only she sounded a little fearful. And she kept talking about somebody whose name was Monty. Monty, Monty . . . it occurred over and over. Then on an angry note, the conversation ended.

The operator disconnected the wires, turned to the other telephone girl.

"Guess who I just had on the line! Tasha Hiller."

"No! Really? What did she say?"

The first girl laughed. "I think she said—no!" Then there were some signals, and she got busy.

Tibor stood on the steps of the telephone building, wondering what he should do now. He was not particularly disturbed about the conversation. He knew that Tasha would be all right. She'd come down. She'd bring the money. She'd take care of everything. In Mexico City he had been far away and easy to forget. But the thought that he was now only a few hours away would soon begin its work on her. And he'd keep phoning and wiring. It would work out. But it might take time. And he would have to go easy on his money. Might be better to go to the best hotel. Better not risk any hotel. Might get stuck, and hotels have a way of hanging on to luggage.

"Hey, driver. I've changed my mind about the hotel. Take me to a boarding house, or an auto court somewhere."

And so it was that Tibor Szolnay arrived at the Colonia Gomez.

When he drove up to the ranch house, Mr. Gomez was on the front porch arguing with Siegfried about the fifteen dollars which Siegfried still owed on the present month's rent. He was not in a good mood. He had just had the same argument with Mr. Weiss, and he was ruing the day that he had ever let the first immigrant in.

Tibor tumbled out of the taxi and strolled over. "Good morning!"

Mr. Gomez took a quick look at the taxi, saw that it was from Mexicali.

135

"No!" he exclaimed abruptly. "No rooms for immigrants."

Tibor laughed. "I beg your pardon. What makes you think I am an immigrant? Immigrant to where, anyway?"

Due to six months with a Hollywood coach, and several years in London, Tibor spoke English with an almost native fluidity . . . but there was still a trace of Hungarian accent. Mr. Gomez heard that accent and persisted along the lines of his original hunch.

"You waiting to get into the United States?"

"No."

"You got papers to go to the United States?"

"No, I—"

"Good-by then!" Mr. Gomez turned and walked away, went into the house and banged the door.

Tibor looked at Siegfried and laughed. "Nice friendly fellow!"

"Ja," said Siegfried wanly.

Behind them, Irmgard had come up the hill. She stood by the open door of the taxi looking in at the luggage. It was beautiful luggage, and it was plastered with stickers from all over the world, and from many of the world's best hotels. And it made her heart ache just to look at them. The lucky people who could go places like that . . . go and go and move about in the world.

When Tibor saw a woman, a new woman, a young woman, there was a rigmarole which he always went through. He lighted his pipe. Not because it was symbolic of the lighting of an inner fire in him—though the two fires usually did light at the same time—but because it gave him an opportunity to meet her eyes across the flicker of a flame, and as he puff-puff-puffed, to lower his eyes and reveal his extraordinary lashes, then to lift them and glance at her, lower and lift again, and his mouth in a sort of kissing motion at the pipe stem, and his eyes dancing with the fire of the match . . . and well, he just knew that he looked most attractive that way. Also there was a leisureliness about it. Lighting a pipe when he came face to face with a woman for the first time gave her a chance to observe him fully. Gave him a chance to observe her, too—and make up his mind.

Irmgard, looking at the luggage and wondering why anyone who could go to all those places would ever come here, turned and looked at Tibor.

"Hello," Tibor said. And he lighted his pipe.

He saw a girl whom he immediately felt was rather prim and tense. Serious type. But then as the examination continued, he saw that her heavy eyelids were continuously half down over her eyes, and that under the pupils there was an unusual amount of white showing. He had read somewhere that this was a sign of hidden sex and sensuality, and he had been casually looking for the mark ever since. He saw, furthermore, that her skin was nice, that her hair was pretty, though badly fixed. He saw that she was a little stocky, but she carried her breasts nice and high. And above all he saw that she was *unanimated*, and this pleased him. He was a little tired of girls of Tasha's type . . . every restless, nervous, excited movement of face and body an invitation to bed. They were too easy. He felt instinctively that he might like to know somebody like this for a change. Somebody dignified. Somebody on whom he could test his seduction-skill. Somebody who would be sure to resist him.

Really resist, physically. Push and scratch and pull away. Yes, amusing, and a variation—because tantalizing bedroom battles were something at which he didn't often have a chance.

There . . . the pipe was glowing, and Tibor Szolnay had made up his mind.

"I'm looking for a room. You don't know where I can get one near here, do you?"

"Did Mr. Gomez say—"

"Mr. Gomez said no. I don't know why."

Suddenly Siegfried spoke to Irmgard in German. His little eyes were very bright, and he seemed eager and concerned. She listened a moment, nodded and turned back to Tibor.

"Siegfried says you can move in with him if you like. He has one of the bungalows and there is room for two people. There is a couch in the living room which opens into a bed, and he says you could have that and pay him a dollar a day."

"Well . . . that's very nice!" But he looked at Siegfried a little dubiously.

"Oh, he is not doing it to be nice. It will help him out. He owes money on the rent. But Siegfried is really very easy to get along with. And he speaks English when he's not scared. Don't you, Siegfried?"

Siegfried was scared now, and hung his head. Then, because he knew the stranger's gaze was critical, he felt drawn to stand up and make as good a showing as possible. Once standing, he wished he had stayed sitting down. Tibor's great height dwarfed him.

"All right," Tibor decided. "I'll try it for a day or two."

He smiled at Irmgard. "Maybe you'll help me get settled?"

"No, I am busy now. I am going to write a letter. Good-by, I will see you later. Siegfried will take care of you. He will be happy to have you here."

He watched her as she walked off down the hill toward her own bungalow, admiring that stiff, straight, still way she walked. He liked the cold way she had treated him. Knew that it would all work out just as he expected.

It was typical of Tibor that he didn't even think to inquire if she were married.

Tibor's decision to share Casa Six with Siegfried had made Siegfried one of the happiest little men on earth, and he could have stood on his tiptoes and hugged Mr. Szolnay. Not merely because of the rent help, but because he would have a friend now, and companionship. Someone big and wonderful to fill his lonely little house. Someone to talk to. Someone to go to the movies with. Someone to sit with at table. The meals were going to be different now . . . linger at the table, and smoke and talk.

There was one thought paramount in his mind all that day. Fortune had brought him a friend, and now he must make this friend comfortable so that he would never, never want to go away. He must do everything to make Mr. Szolnay happy.

And he tried. He gave Mr. Szolnay the big closet in his bedroom, transferred his own meager things to the smaller one in the hall. Hung them on hooks. Gave Mr. Szolnay all the hangers. Then he went up the hill to get extra bedding for the couch, and he thought that when evening came he would even make up the couch bed for Mr. Szolnay. And after he had come down from the hill, he cleared his papers and letters out of the desk in the living room, so that Mr. Szolnay could use it for a dresser . . . put his hairbrush and comb there, and his shaving kit. And he moved the floor lamp near the couch so Mr. Szolnay could read in bed at night if he wanted to. Then he went to the store to get things for lunch. He would buy the lunch today and fix it . . . just because it was Mr. Szolnay's first day here . . . but he knew that for the future they would make some arrangement about food. Divide the cost, take turns preparing it. And an arrangement too about splitting up the housework. Oh, many things to plan for later, but one very special little plan for now, too. After lunch, and after they had talked and talked and got to know all about each other —more than just each other's names, which was all they knew now—*then* Siegfried would take Mr. Szolnay around to all the bungalows and introduce him. That would be such a pleasure, give him a chance to bask in an important light at last: "Look, people, at what *I've* brought to the colony!"

But this fond hope was the first one blighted.

When Siegfried returned from the store he saw that Tibor was stretched out naked across the front porch, and talking with Hans and Maria who were sitting on the steps. Not completely naked, but he might as well have been, because that white wool triangle around his loins wasn't much of anything.

"Thought I'd work at my tan a little," Tibor told him in answer to his look of surprise.

The porch was small, and Mr. Szolnay covered most of it, and Siegfried thought that was why it seemed so indecent. It was one thing to see a naked body on a great expanse of beach, but another to see one like this, right out there on a doorstep, right there so close to the drive, where nobody could miss it. And it was such a startling body . . . so boldly sculptured, Siegfried thought. The Weisses wouldn't be shocked, of course . . . Siegfried had always considered them a little Bohemian. But he could imagine what Ani Klabec must be thinking now (and he could see her peeking from behind her curtain!). And Mrs. Lankowski; she'd be shocked to death. He really felt he should tell him to cover himself up.

"Move," Tibor said. "You're in my sun."

"Do you not want to eat?" Siegfried asked anxiously.

"I never refuse food," Tibor laughed. "Call me when it's ready."

Siegfried carefully stepped over him and went into the house. So disappointed. And a little resentful. He felt that Tibor had let him down—yes, and in *such* a way—and in so doing had introduced himself.

But still another disappointment was in store. Later, when they sat down to lunch, Tibor looked at the teapot and scoffed. "Who wants tea? Isn't there any beer in the house?"

Siegfried said there was no beer, but he offered to go across the drive and see if he could borrow a bottle from Klaus. He explained that you couldn't buy beer at the grocery store. You had to go all the way into town for it, to the brewery.

But Klaus wasn't home. Siegfried looked all over for him. Even went up the hill to Chato's shack, but he wasn't there either. It took him quite a while, and when he came back

141

to report his failure, he found that Tibor had already finished his lunch, and was dressing to go into town.

Shyly, Siegfried asked if he might go along.

Tibor said no. He didn't know when he'd be back. He wanted to look the town over.

"You come back for supper?"

"Don't wait for me. Just save me something and leave it in the kitchen."

After Tibor had gone, Siegfried dumped the contents of his own plate back into the pans. Maybe he'd feel like eating a little later. But for now he wasn't hungry.

Tibor lit his pipe several more times during the balance of the day, and in the process of so doing forgot all about Irmgard. The pipe glowed and burned particularly fiercely when he met Molita. And at nine in the evening he arrived home with her. That is, she brought him home in her green wreck of a car. The car was parked outside now, and Tibor was leaning against the car-door saying good-by.

Siegfried had been waiting all day with wife-like anxiety, and now he peered from the window.

"Well, so long," Tibor was saying. "I'll see you tomorrow." Then he patted Molita's cheek, chucked her under the breast, and the girl laughed and drove away.

When Tibor came in he went right to the kitchen. Siegfried fluttered after him. Siegfried was hungry, too . . . he had been waiting dinner for two hours.

"Don't bother to put things on the table," Tibor advised him. "I'll just grab something in a hurry. I'm tired and want to get to bed."

He saw two overly browned pieces of veal—cold now, lying in the frying pan. He ate one.

"It's good cold."

Then he reached for the second.

Siegfried started to tell him that the second piece was his, but then he realized that Mr. Szolnay thought he had already had his dinner and if Mr. Szolnay was really hungry, he'd better have it.

"There is beer now!" Siegfried announced proudly.

"Good. Bring it out."

Tibor drank the beer, and finished up the veal, and three cheese sandwiches which Siegfried made for him, and half a box of cookies. Then he went into the bedroom.

Siegfried ran after him, and reached for the couch bedding which was lying on the bedroom chair. He told Mr. Szolnay to get undressed, and he would fix the couch for him.

"Don't bother. Fix the couch for yourself."

For a moment Siegfried didn't understand. He stared, unbelieving, as Mr. Szolnay strode to the bed, and ripped the bedding back. He gathered blankets and sheets, pulled the cases from the pillows, swept the whole bundle into his arms, and calmly dumped it upon Siegfried.

"Here, these are yours. Now go on. I want some privacy for a change. You bustle around like my mother."

He held the door open, and there was no doubt what Mr. Szolnay had in mind now.

With the bedding heaped upon him, Siegfried moved dolefully into the dim little hall, stepped on a dragging sheet, and stumbled. The door banged shut behind him. The key turned in the lock.

So disconsolate. So tired of being pushed out of every-

143

where. Out all over the world, and now even out of his own exile bed. Oh, well. Jew. What could he expect.

"Oh, Siegfried!"

"Yes?"

"I forgot to tell you. Make yourself scarce tomorrow afternoon. From two on. I have a friend coming to see me. Know what I mean?"

Yes, Siegfried understood—and it was the final sad note of his day. The day which had started out so beautifully, and had held so much promise. He was hurt, deeply hurt, and disappointed—and he decided that from now on he would pay no attention to Mr. Szolnay. Mr. Szolnay seemed to have no wish for his company. He was going to cast him out to receive a female Mexican. He had already cast him out of his own bed. Well, from now on Siegfried would not raise one finger to help, comfort, or feed him!

When he opened the couch, dust. He coughed and sneezed. What the mattress needed was a good sweeping, but he had left the broom in the bedroom when he cleaned the closet that morning, and he had no desire to disturb Mr. Szolnay now. He patted and spanked and cleaned the mattress as best he could.

He first made the bed with the head up under the rear of the couch, but when he crawled in, it was like lying under a cliff which might fall on him at any moment. He rearranged the bedding, tried lying with his head at the bottom, but that put too much weight on the extension, and the bed tipped backwards, floorwards, most uncomfortably.

Eventually Siegfried sought sleep, lying crosswise on the bed, and he was so short that he did not hang over.

Irmgard often wished that there were some way to put her mind to sleep, and leave it sleeping until she got her quota number. Because it was her mind that gave her the most trouble. It was filled with the wildest sort of pictures. She was naturally fictive, and her imagination, stimulated by loneliness, had made a horror chamber of her brain.

That evening as she tried to sleep, the pictures in her mind were radium-painted, and stood out in the darkness with brutal clarity. There were three pictures mainly which played over and over as though spliced together on a continuous projection machine.

The first was rather hopeful, compared to the others. In it she saw herself sneaking into the United States. This opening scene was a little vague, because she didn't know exactly how it would be done. But somehow she crossed the Tijuana river, hopped the fence, crept through the fields, hitch-hiked to San Diego, and from there took a bus to Los Angeles. There she found Tom Ainsworth. There, by throwing herself at his feet, and by threatening to turn herself over to the police and then at her deportation hearing to reveal how miserably he had treated her—by such threats and appeals, she succeeded in forcing him to marry her. That reel ended rather happily, because after the marriage she slipped back into Mexico, and was then privileged to apply for preference quota as wife of an American citizen.

The second picture was more melodramatic, and inspired by bitterness. In this, she also slipped into the United States, but the climax here was that she killed Tom Ainsworth. He had said he would have nothing to do with her. He had laughed. He had said that he was happily married, or at least happily in love. Occasionally Irmgard played the last half of this picture over, and instead of killing Tom she killed the person who had come between them. But there was always a shot somewhere, and pandemonium, and a montage of police, jail, hysterics, tragedy.

The third midnight movie was the worst. It was ironical, and it was defeatist. She saw herself at last receiving her quota number . . . years hence. She saw herself entering the States, aged and wearied by the long waiting, no longer young or attractive. When Tom saw her, he turned from her in disgust. The finale to this one was swift and clear-cut. She killed herself. Leaving a note in which she blamed the United States government for her suicide.

This version was taken up almost entirely with the writing of that last letter. In it, she would include facts and figures gleaned from research libraries on the large proportion of one- and two-generation Americans in the United States. She would show how it was Europe's blood which had contributed so much to the progress of the United States. She would show, in general, that the United States had no reason to be snooty about admitting her, or any other German, or anybody, for that matter. But she found that she had to do a great deal of scratching-out and erasing before she could ever get the letter finished, because there were other things—other facts and figures—which went through her mind and confused her. The large number of unemployed in America being the main disturbance.

This letter followed her around even in the daytime. The suicide note that she could never quite write to her own satisfaction.

Tonight as she lay there, weak because of the scenes which she had just viewed, she tried to conjure up scenes from the past. Tried to replace the uncertain frightening future she had just looked at with remembered things—hoping to find in them a calm and peace. But these remembered things were disturbing too, because she could only think of Tom. Their first meeting. Their thrilling courtship. The places they had gone, and the things they had done. And how bright and gay and dashing he had been. And how he had seemed so carefree. So cocky. So American. So sure of himself and his world. And how that had appealed to her.

And then she thought, too, of the times that they had made love.

She tried to thrust this thought away, because it was a torture swelling inside her. She tried to force it out, by the simple device of talking to herself, half aloud, of practical everyday things. The things she must do tomorrow.

Tomorrow I must remember to get a mousetrap at Berendo's, because I am sure there are mice in the house. Wonder if Schnucki would get them, if I lock her in here for a while. No, Klaus said he tried to get her after the ones over there. But she wasn't interested. He had success with the traps though. What is it you're supposed to put in them . . . something better than cheese. Oh, yes, a little piece of burnt bacon. And tomorrow, let's see. Tomorrow I must go to the office of the Lotería Nacional. Take my ticket and see if I have won anything. They'll have the reports from Mexico City. Yesterday's drawing. I'd better win something pretty soon. Not much money left, and I haven't heard from Tom for weeks now. Not since that night I talked to Klaus. Won't hear any more, either. Tom is—

Oh, Tom, Tom . . . there she was with Tom again.

But just think of him sensibly now. Wonder if Tom will

147

let me starve. He knows I can't exist much longer on that last money he sent me. What will I do? How will I ever get a lawyer now? Who will ever help me? Wish I knew somebody rich, even a rich Mexican. I'd even go to bed with him if it would help me to get to Tom. I'd go to bed, do anything, steal even, to get to Tom. But who is there to steal from here? Who has money in this place? Who ever comes to this town any more?

I wonder what Mr. Szolnay is doing here? He told Maria . . . waiting for money that somebody owes him. I wonder if he is. I wonder if I could make him fall in love with me. If a man is really in love with you, you can get him to help you. Trick him, if you have to. Tell him you're pregnant. Tell him you have to have money for an operation. Tell him anything, but drag it out of him somehow.

I wonder if I could get him. Better wait to try until his money comes, though. No, too late then. Going to London, he says. Too late then, anyway, to say about a baby. Rather, too early. I wonder. Yes, it would be all right with him. He is even rather attractive. I could do it. I will do it.

And then, thinking about it, she began to see Tibor, she realized, much too clearly. She saw his soft brown eyes, and his big handsome frame, and the broad shoulders, and the curly tannish hair.

"He needs a haircut," she said aloud, and fiercely, because she felt she had to find something wrong with him. "He looks silly. Like a chorus boy in Berlin."

But she went on remembering the way his eyes had twinkled at her as he lit his pipe. . . .

"He's conceited."

And the fullness of his mouth. . . .

148

"He's a weakling. You can tell it to look at him. Lazy and weak and spoiled."

And his strong sturdy legs in their handsome boots. Nice to see somebody in nice clothes for a change. . . .

"He looks stupid, and false. Bet he can't go back to the United States because they kicked him out!"

Wonder if I could ask him in here. Wonder if Ani would talk. . . .

"Oh, Tom! I'm only doing it for you. I have to try every possible way to get to you. And this might help a little."

But somehow, no matter how she tried, right now, she couldn't call up the face of Tom.

It was another face and body with which she wrestled now, tossing and turning, and fighting it off.

9

UP the drive, in Casa Three, Jennifer had returned home, and as she was getting ready for bed, she was also thinking of that same face and figure—but as she thought about it, it made her laugh. Tibor Szolnay here with them in Tijuana! She didn't know Tibor. She had never met him. But she had seen him many times around Hollywood, on the sets and at previews and in restaurants, always strutting, always showing off—and he amused her. He had tried to get into pictures, was always bothering producers and directors— but he had made the mistake of trying to tie himself up with Tasha Hiller. Monty Arno was Tasha's man. And Monty was Tasha's producer. And Monty was just about king-pin in Hollywood. And there was a rumor that Monty had blackballed him at all the studios. But Jennifer didn't believe that. She believed that Tibor had ruined his own chances. At least, there was a particular set of words which people always used in connection with him. Pest. Plague. Idiot. Fool. Poseur. Bluff. Table-hopper. Gate-crasher. The kind who never picked up the check anywhere. He did sign a personal check though, once, when he shouldn't have, and it was because of that that Mr. Szolnay had left for Mexico City in a hurry, with deportation officers close behind him. Still, and nevertheless, and for some reason, people always laughed when his name was mentioned. Tibor Szolnay? Oh, yes, I know him. Ha-ha.

"Did he have his boots on—and his pipe?"

Klaus was already in bed, lying with his arms behind his head, gazing up at the ceiling-cluster of three jaundiced 25-watt bulbs. He had a faraway, dreamy expression on his face, and Jennifer noticed that every now and then he was struggling not to smile. As though there were some happy secret inside him.

"Klaus! What's the matter with you? You aren't paying any attention to me at all. I asked you if he was wearing boots."

"Who?"

"Tibor."

This gained his attention. He frowned. "How comes you call him by his first name? You say you do not know him."

"I don't. It's just a habit. All interviewers do it. Makes us sound like we really know people. 'I was talking to Clark the other day, and Clark said, and Tyrone said . . .' Not that I want to know Tibor, or let anybody think I do! I'm not even going to let *him* know I ever heard of him. What did Maria think of him?"

"She put some more of that stuff on her hair to make it more blonder."

"No! Oh, that's wonderful. And Ani?"

"She invited us for a *kaffeeklatsch* Sunday. So she can invite him, I suppose."

"I'll bet he's going to make a difference around here. He *is* attractive. Didn't you think so?"

"I didn't see him."

"You didn't see him?"

"No, he only came this morning. He has only been here one day."

"Well, where were you all day?"

"Jennifer, I wish you would hurry to bed so we can get to sleep." He was again looking at the ceiling, with that same peculiar expression which had been on his face all evening.

Jennifer switched out the light, got into bed. "I never heard you begging to go to sleep before. You're the one who always wants to talk. Are you tired?"

"No, but I want to go to sleep."

She sighed. "You're funny, honey."

Then she could feel that he wasn't trying to sleep at all. He was still lying with his arms up, staring into the darkness.

"Klaus, if you didn't see Tibor, how did you know about everything?"

"When I came home I talked to Maria. And then Siegfried came over for to get beer."

"I can't understand where you were all day," she mused.

There was no answer, so after a while, she said, "Good night, dear."

"Good night. Jennifer?"

"Yes."

"How did it go this week?"

"Terrible. I only had one interview and it was a flop. Eva Barnow tried to work me in in the midst of a cocktail party, so you can imagine what kind of a story I got. Oh, she came outside in the library and talked to me for a while. But such drivel. All her silly little triumphs and problems which are supposed to be of such news to the world—and they don't amount to a damn really."

"I am glad you had such a bad week. I mean—well, if you got a chance not to do any interviews any more, you would be glad, won't you?"

"I *will* have a chance some day, darling. Some day, after we get things worked out. I'll just stay home and write some real stories."

"That's what I mean. You would not miss running around the studios? All that?"

"I'd be *glad* to miss it. It's—oh, I don't know, but hanging around stars, begging for crumbs for stories . . . it makes me feel like such a parasite sometimes."

"That is not why I do not like it for you. What I do not like to think—is you sitting there, so good and fine, and saying yes, yes, yes, to people—like Eva Barnow—who are not worth the little finger of you."

"Oh, well. Some of them are."

"Would you like to stay all the times with me here? Until I get in? Do you think you could stand it maybe?"

She heard a tense note in his voice. Thought it was leading up to that old argument that they had been through time and time again: why wasn't it possible for Jennifer to write her articles here in Tijuana? Why did she have to go to Hollywood to do it? Why couldn't she go up there just one day a week to get the interviews and then do the stories when she came back? And she had explained so often that though it seemed possible to the average observer, to somebody who didn't know the business, that it just wasn't feasible. The way interview appointments were so often broken at the last minute, or postponed from one day to the next. And the need to be close to a telephone. Even when she was actually writing a story, to have to be able to call the publicity department and check on names and dates and places that she found she had to use. And then getting the story back to the studio, for okay, and following through, and checking up, and the necessity of being on hand to make corrections.

"Klaus, do we have to go through all that again? Can't we just be grateful that I don't have a job in a department store, for example. Suppose I had to work Saturdays, and be on the job early Monday morning?"

"No, we are not going to argue." But strangely, no sadness. Actually a contentment in his words.

"Klaus, are you smiling? Is there something you're keeping from me? What are you thinking about?"

"Oh, Jennifer!" he wailed in a mixture of joy and anguish. "Let's go to sleep . . . quick . . . or I am going to tell you! Please, and I do not want to tell, because I want so much to make it for you a surprise!"

She sat up quickly. "A surprise! What kind? What does it have to do with? What have you been doing?"

"Oh, I want to tell you so much, but I don't want to! *Please*, Jennifer, let me have for you a surprise. So I can know I planned it all myself."

She knew that it would mean a lot to him. "All right," she agreed quickly. "I promise not to ask one word, and if you start to tell me, I'll make you stop."

"That's nice." He seemed relieved. "But if I talk about it in my sleep?" he joked.

"I won't listen."

"Then good night, Muschi."

154

"Good night."

"If you get up real close to me, maybe you can hear it in my mind anyway."

She cuddled close, listened. But minutes passed, and after a while all she could hear was his slow sleep-breathing against her ear.

Siegfried rose early that next morning. He put his bed away, fixed and ate his breakfast, then washed his teacup and saucer, and the egg plate, swept the living room, wiped a rag around the bathroom basin, felt that this was his share of the work, then left for the day.

About nine, Tibor awoke and he was hungry. When he saw that Siegfried was gone he prowled around the kitchen, found some eggs and bread, but the coffee tin was empty. He put on his mulberry satin dressing robe and went across the drive and knocked at Casa Three. Klaus came to the door in his pajamas.

Under any other circumstances Klaus would have been curious and interested to meet Mr. Szolnay, but just now he had been dreaming, and in his dream he was in America, and he had a job, and he had just presented Jennifer with a silver typewriter with her name on it. He didn't want to disturb his dream, tried to hang on to it, keep it going. Vaguely he saw a smiling mulberry mountain and dimly he heard a cheery voice.

"Good morning! Sorry to bother you, but could I borrow some coffee?"

Klaus nodded, headed for the kitchen and Tibor followed him.

"I'm staying across the way. My name is Tibor Szolnay."

155

Klaus gave him no encouragement. He found the coffee can, opened it, then reached for a cup.

"Don't bother going to all that trouble! Just put some in my hand." Tibor held out both hands, shaped them like a bowl, and Klaus began to pour into them.

They were very large hands. And as Tibor didn't say when to stop, the can was more than half empty by the time the hands began to overflow.

"Thanks. Thanks very much."

On his way out, Tibor stumbled over a rug near the door, and most of the coffee spilled.

"Damn. Oh, well. I still have enough left for a cup or two! Thanks again. Good-by."

Klaus didn't answer. He went to get the dust pan and the broom. He swept up the coffee, so Jennifer wouldn't have to do it, then went back to bed—where she was still sleeping—turned over, and hurried back to America, he hoped.

Tibor, in many respects, had an amiable disposition. At least, he could always smile and look complacent in difficult situations. (And it was this which had really caused Hollywood to laugh about him.) He was particularly agreeable when anyone ever threatened to slug him, or when he was publicly insulted. In fact, whenever any disagreeableness loomed on the horizon, Tibor always managed to walk out and avoid things nicely. And so, because of his natural-born geniality, the coldness and indifference which Klaus Eckert had shown him this morning, didn't disturb his equanimity.

It did, however, make him thoughtful. It made him think —as he took his sunbath a little later—that it would be wise for him to be his most charming self during the time he was forced to stay around here. To put himself out, even—and make all these people anxious to have him around. Anxious most of all to have him around at dinner. Or at lunch and breakfast. If he worked it right, he wouldn't have to spend a penny of his thirteen dollars. After all, there were six bungalows, and the ranch house up on the hill. He ought to be able to manage that. A bungalow-meal each day of the week, and the ranch house on Sunday.

The Jew was a natural, of course. Tibor could see that he had already taken a great fancy to him. And that was fine. But he wouldn't bear down on him too hard. If the subject of food-money came up, Tibor would tell him not to count him in on the food bills, would say that he was going to eat out. But he would, of course, pick up what he could around the house. (And pay him for the rent when Tasha came down.) A shame the Jew didn't drink coffee. Oh, well, it had worked out all right this morning. And tomorrow he'd try another bungalow. And so on. And with a handful a day (careful not to spill it again), in a week's time he'd soon have enough coffee to last a month. But, of course, he wasn't going to stay here for that long.

Tibor was glad he was only waiting for Tasha to warm up, and not for a quota number like these chumps here. He had heard about them in town. A bunch of worn-out immigrants waiting to get into the United States. Some of them waiting six months already. Well, if they thought it was so wonderful in the United States, let them wait. They'd soon find out. The States was a place very much over-rated, especially in connection with its purported democracy and freedom. Democracy. Why, the States was alive with dictators. Only instead of wearing uniforms the

157

American dictators wore a hundred-and-seventy-five-dollar suits and silk shirts and diamond rings on their little fingers and sat behind desks with lots of buttons on them. Look at what had happened to him! Look at the way he had been treated. Had they played fair with him? Given him a chance? No. Just because he happened to go around with Tasha. Just because one of those dictators couldn't stand the competition—he had pushed one of those buttons and had had him thrown out. That check business was a lot of baloney. He could have covered the check if he had had time, but Monty saw to it that he didn't have time, all right. Well, to hell with them all.

As he was lying there, thinking, a little girl came by. She stood there staring at him. He hated children, but he thought he'd better speak to her. Because she probably belonged to somebody around here, and maybe Mamma could cook. They talked for a while and when he said that yes, he could play cards, she seemed very happy, and she said she would like to play right now except Mrs. Gomez had sent her to Berendo's and she would be busy for a while.

And so because of Berendo's, whatever that was, Tibor was again fortunately alone, and he could think some more. He thought now of how agreeably everything was going to work out, once he got to London. There was a need in English pictures for a man of his type. Not a single English actor with a body like his. Look at Leslie Howard. All the men like that. Yes, they'd welcome him. He'd get to be a big star; then have Hollywood crying for him to come back. Maybe when he got to London, he'd even take some acting lessons, like Tasha advised. Seemed sort of a waste of time, though. What does the public care about acting? The public wants personalities.

It was a shame he had to waste time here in Tijuana. Pictures in London really in need of him, and here he was, four thousand dollars away. Not as fares go. But all those debts he still owed over there. Three hundred pounds to that last tailor he had gone to. A hundred pounds at the Forsythe Club. And several other small sums here and there. And he knew that he'd never get back into England unless he paid them.

About one-thirty, and when the Jew still hadn't come back, Tibor began to get hungry. Some very delicious smells floated from the kitchen of Casa Five . . . where the Klabecs lived. He had met them briefly yesterday, along with the Weisses on the front porch.

He went inside and dressed, put on pearl-gray slacks and an orange sweater, admired himself in the mirror—turtlenecks certainly did do something for him. Then he presented himself at the Klabec door.

He was, as he was soon unhappily to realize, too late for lunch. They had lunched early in Casa Five, so that Ani could do some baking. It was the baking fragrance that had so tantalized him. And now Ani was just putting the finishing touches on the cake which would be for Sunday.

When she saw Tibor at the door, she was agog, and fell all over herself, getting to the door to let him in.

"Sorry to bother you," Tibor said. "But it's that Jew! Do you know where he could have gone?"

This reference to one of her race did not hurt Ani. It vastly pleased her. Because of course Mr. Szolnay wouldn't have spoken in that fashion had he recognized that Ani was Jewish.

"Please come in, Mr. Szolnay! Emil!" She turned and spoke sharply to her husband, to bring his head out of his stamp book where it had been buried the last hour.

"How do you do. Welcome!" said Emil.

"Mr. Szolnay, I am very glad you came in. I was sending my husband to ask you, you come to coffee tomorrow afternoon? See, I am a cake having!"

"Well, I don't know!" Tibor pretended to be thoughtful. "I may have other things to do." Then he smiled waggishly. "But of course, it might help me make up my mind if I had a sample of that cake!"

And so it was that Ani Klabec did something very much against her principles. She cut a cake while it was still warm and before the icing had set. Emil watched her and marveled. It was something which *he* had never been able to get her to do.

Tibor sat there smacking his lips over the cake, making the appropriate and necessary compliments which would lead up to a second piece, but at that moment Molita arrived. She stopped in front of Casa Six, and blew the horn.

Tibor rose. "Excuse me, but I have to go now." Then he saw that Mrs. Klabec was looking out at Molita, and her expression somewhat prudish and suspicious.

"I have a Spanish lesson now," Tibor explained.

After Tibor had gone, Ani retained her place at the window. She saw them laughing and talking there at the car. Then she saw them go in. She didn't think that it was a Spanish lesson at all.

A moment later the girl was back in the car again, driving

away. That was odd. Then Ani ducked behind the curtain, as she saw Tibor leave the house too.

The only time which Tibor ever knocked on a door was the first time he entered it. Now he burst into Casa Five.

"Hello! I came back for that second piece of cake!"

This nonplused Ani even more than the strange hurried departure of the Spanish teacher, because she didn't remember that a second piece had been mentioned. But goaded by his enthusiastic smile she brought it out.

Emil looked up from his album. "You did have your Spanish lesson so quick?" he asked with surprising temerity.

"No. She wanted too much. I didn't talk to her about rates the other evening."

Tibor thought that he had gotten away with it, but then he saw the unlaughed laughter in Emil's nice gray eyes. His own eyes answered back, and suddenly they both burst into guffaws.

This annoyed Ani very much. It occurred to her now that there was something about Tibor which might be a bad influence on Emil. Then as she heard Tibor whisper something about the Filigrana, and as they both laughed again, she was sure of it. After all, Emil was not so old that he couldn't be led astray—and with a young gay-blade like this around, no telling where he might be led off to.

It was, in reality, an absurd thought, but Ani seized it with vigor, because it would give her something new to stew about, and another excuse to keep an even closer eye on Emil. And after all, none knew better than she how dreary and boring the days were here, and she was fully conscious of the fact, too, that they *had* been married a long time.

After Tibor had finished his fourth piece of cake, Ani was glad and relieved to at last shut the door on him. In these last twenty minutes he had lost his fascination for her.

Ani returned to her native language, and to her usual faultfinding self. "Such a pig! He's ruined the cake and spoiled the party tomorrow! *Four* pieces. It'll never go around now."

"But maybe he was hungry," Emil suggested, merely in an effort to be kind. "And besides you know what good cake you make, Ani."

She glared. "Emil Klabec, don't you dare take up with him! I don't want to see you get friendly with him. I don't want you to even speak to him from now on."

"Why, Ani!"

"You know what I mean. Don't give me that innocent look. You know the way you whispered and joked . . . probably planning to go that place, I bet!"

Emil got up from his chair. He knew that the best thing to do at this moment, with Ani in this mood, was to pretend that nature was calling, and retreat to the bathroom with a book.

It wasn't practical, after all, to keep the surprise from Jennifer any longer, because late that same afternoon the wire fencing arrived.

The delivery man appeared at the door, and when Jennifer saw the rolls of fencing there in the truck, she tried to make him understand in her inadequate Spanish that he must have the wrong place.

"No. No!" he insisted.

Finally, she went to call Klaus from the back steps. Klaus

beamed. Hurried through the house, then as she watched him, and for her benefit, he put on an officious and important air. Reached for the delivery receipt. Signed it with a great flourish. Ordered the Mexican to drive around to Garage Three and put the wiring in there. Then he said to Jennifer,

"Excuse me, madame, but I am *very* busy," and walked out of the door to follow the truck, his head high, whistling jauntily.

So she knew, of course, that this had something to do with the surprise, and she hurried after him.

"Klaus, what *is* it?"

"I will give to you fifteen chances."

"Oh, don't make me guess. Please. I *hate* to guess."

"Guess!" he persisted.

When they arrived at the garage, Klaus stood back on his heels, tucked his thumbs under imaginary suspenders, watched the unloading.

"Please, Klaus . . . *tell* me!"

"Sh-h-h." He pointed to the Mexican, and whispered, "Do not ask questions now while he is here . . . in case perhaps he understands English."

"Oh, you're just trying to make it sound more mysterious." But anyway she stayed quiet until the Mexican left. "Now!"

Behind them a voice said, "Is the wood here, too? You are ready yet?" and Jennifer turned and saw Duwid.

"Hello, Mr. Lankowski. Klaus has a surprise and he won't tell me."

Klaus was gazing at the wire, immersed in pride.

"No, Duwid," he said, "I am not going to buy new wood.

163

Old wood will be all right. I have been finding some. Signs and things, and parts of old houses and things. Chato is keeping it for me behind his shack."

Jennifer tugged at his arm. "Klaus Eckert, if you don't stop standing there so know-it-all, and not telling me, I'll scream."

But Klaus was enjoying his importance, and he was pleased now to see that Blima and Irmgard were joining them, too.

Blima smiled in a happy, congratulatory way. "Well, Klaus, you begin soon, huh?"

Jennifer's eyes flashed with pretended indignance. "I suppose everybody knows about this but me?"

"All right." Klaus felt it had gone far enough. He took hold of her arms, gazed into her eyes, became very serious. "Jennifer, it is for you, so you can stay with me all the times while we are waiting. And you can write. The things you want to write. And you don't have to go any more to the interviews . . . like I told you last night."

"But *what*, darling? *What's* for me? What are you doing?"

"Jennifer . . ." and then suddenly there was such glory and pride on his face that it was wondrous and exquisite. But a little pathetic, too, because of course he got his words more mixed up than usual, as he always did in moments of excitement.

"Jennifer, I am going to chickens raise and sell the eggs, and the chickens too which don't make eggs!"

There followed a hush, broken only by Jennifer's sobbing.

Nobody could understand. Not even Klaus. He held her

against his shoulder, laughed awkwardly. "Jennifer . . . Mushi . . . what is the matter?"

Her head ached, her heart ached, her eyes were swollen and red, and for a moment there was no voice in her throat. His dear, sweet, drawn face, all lighted up like that as she had never seen it before . . . because he thought he could go into the chicken business, and end their separations that way! Something so ironical about it. Klaus, who once had everything that a lusty ambitious young man could want. Klaus with his medals, and the remembered hail of the crowds in his ears. And Klaus who dreamed of the time in America when he could start again somehow, somewhere, in some other field, and again climb to the top. And now, in this measly exile scouring the country for old wood, to build chicken coops, to raise chickens. How would he know what to do about chickens? How could he know the pitfalls of that precarious business? Probably intending to start with a couple of hens and a rooster, and believing that in a short time they would need no other income. . . . Oh, it was a wonderful thought, but so impractical. And she hated to see him counting on it so much.

"Don't you see, Jennifer . . . it will be very easy. I am going to get chickens from a ranch down the road. I will have to pay for half of them, but I have the money. I have been saving it from dominos. And some of them I can get on credit, and then pay the man back with eggs. I went to see him yesterday."

"Oh, I know . . . I guess that sounds all right . . . but will the Mexican government let you start a business?"

"No. But they are not going to know. Mr. Gomez is going to say that it is his business. He was very nice. He is like a friend and he won't tell. He says if I put the coops out there in the field, far from the house, it will be all right. He is going to pretend like I am just helping him out with it."

This made her feel better. She began to smile. She looked around at Blima and Duwid and Irmgard and she saw that they thought it was a very fine plan . . . and well, maybe it would work out. Not well enough to permit her to give up her work. She had no illusions about that. But it would give him something to do. A chance to earn a few dollars anyway. She slipped into his arms, hugged him, told him she was proud of him.

"And *all* of us will be helping to build the places for the chickens," Duwid announced sweetly—but with the vague colorless sound to his voice that was there all the time lately. "Emil is helping. And Siegfried. And Hans also. We will ask him to help. And *him* also." Duwid pointed to Tibor who had just now joined the group.

"Yes, but *not* you!" Blima appealed, moving closer to her husband, and looking at his hands. Then she turned apologetically to the others. "You will forgive him if he does not work? Please. But I will help in his place."

"What's going on here?" Tibor wanted to know.

"Can we tell him?" Irmgard asked.

Klaus couldn't resist the temptation, the chance to hear again the wonder of his plans. He nodded.

"Klaus is going into the chicken business. Only we must not say anything about it to Mexicans."

"Swell! That's fine. When are you starting? What kind of chickens are you getting?"

Klaus looked doubtful. "I am not so sure." Then he

brightened. "But they will be *good* chickens, all right!" And everybody laughed.

"There you go, already trying to get customers. Well, I wish you luck!"

They all began to walk back toward the drive. Tibor fell into step with Irmgard.

"It would be nice if you offer to help, too," she suggested. "When he starts to build the coops, I mean."

"Sure, if I'm here. I intend to!"

As the little group rounded the corner of Casa Six, Grandotte drove up, skidded close to them and stopped. Then laughed because he had frightened them.

"Hey, German, I looking for you."

At that moment, Tibor laid his hand on Klaus's shoulder, wanting to impress them all with what a fine co-operative fellow he was. "Look, you can count on me to help you with your business. I'm not much good with a hammer, but I can wield a brush. Maybe you can put me in charge of the painting?"

Klaus stepped on his foot, glared furiously.

Tibor was confused. This German was just a natural cross patch. No wonder he had been so cool this morning.

Irmgard stepped up, seemed disturbed. Everybody seemed upset. "Come, Mr. Szolnay. You like to go for a walk?"

Feeling that these were very strange people here in the colony, Tibor turned and followed Irmgard.

"I'm sorry, Grandotte," Klaus said hurriedly. "But like I told you, I give my stamps to Mr. Klabec."

The Mexican jerked his head in Tibor's direction. "What business *he* talking about?"

Klaus was panicky and his face showed it. "Nothing."

167

"Look you, I not so dumb. What you do here? You build something? You do something here you not supposed, *I* see, all right!"

"Mr. Gomez is building some chicken coops, that is all."

"He go in chicken business?"

"Yes."

"What *you* do with it?"

"I am going to help."

"He need help?"

"Yes."

"Chato no help?"

"Chato already has enough to do. He has a job in the morning now, cleaning up, at Tacuba's."

"Good. I have friend who wants job. I guess I go see Mr. Gomez. Mr. Gomez good friend to me, too. I ask him. You get stamps, German, from Mr. Klabec, give to me, and I see you tomorrow."

After the Mexican had driven away, up the hill to the ranch house, Jennifer and Klaus went into Casa Three.

"Klaus, *don't* look like that. If Mr. Gomez said he wouldn't tell, he won't. He'll take care of it. It's going to be all right. Now just wait and see. Come on, let's have a glass of beer. Let's not think about it."

"That damn Hungarian!"

"Now look, there's no use blaming anybody, when no harm has been done, even. Besides he didn't know. He didn't realize Grandotte was a Mexican. Or maybe he forgot."

"To Grandotte. He would say something in front of him."

"Well, he would have seen it eventually anyway. But please now, don't think about it. Mr. Gomez will tell him

168

the same thing you did. It's going to be all right. He'll just say that he doesn't want to hire anybody. He'll say that you have nothing to do, and so why shouldn't you help him? Somebody's got to go around and sell the eggs, and deliver them."

"It would not mind so much if later Grandotte finds out. After it is going. But now he will hang around all the times sticking his nose in. I know. He hates me."

"That's silly. He doesn't hate you. Why should he?"

"I told you, Jennifer, some people just do not like foreigners. And once I did bad to tell him I was those years a European champion. He thinks I have conceit because of it. And because he is big and I am more little he likes to play like he is the cat and I am the mouse, and on purpose he tries to tease me out of the corner."

"Well, you'll see. It will work out."

At that moment Grandotte passed. They waited until he had disappeared, then hurried out and up the hill.

Somehow what Mr. Gomez had to say reminded Jennifer of the talk she had heard from consuls. Mr. Gomez's English was not so splendid, he used none of the fine words that she had heard either in the Paris or Ensenada consulates, but the tone was the same, and the politeness, and the formal sympathy.

"No can do. Sorry." That was the gist of it.

He explained: Grandotte seemed to think that the chicken venture was Klaus's. He had advised that if it were, then Klaus must get a permit to go into business (even an American would have to do that). And to get a permit he must agree to employ a Mexican. And if he employed a Mexican he had better get one who was a union man. And if he got a union man, he would not be able to fire him without giving him three months' salary.

"So you want to do that, Klaus?"

"Mr. Gomez, how can I? I have no money to employ anyone. I cannot understand. You did not tell to him that it was going to be *your* business?"

"Yes. And maybe he believed me. Maybe. But he says then I have no right to let you help, because that means you take work from a Mexican. And if you help, he says he'll make complaint about it. I think best to let it go now. I do not want to have trouble with him or the union. It is too bad, but you see how it is here."

Yes, they could see. They turned away and started off. Then Mr. Gomez had an afterthought, "Klaus, you can still have a few chickens if you like . . . for you and your wife, even if you can't sell them. I still give you place out there to keep them. Why not you do that? That will be nice, huh?"

Klaus nodded. "Thank you, but I not think so." He felt that somehow Mr. Gomez had missed the point.

They started back for the house. Jennifer walking close beside him. Watching his profile. Wondering if he were angry now, and bitter, and full of hate. Wondering what was in his face.

"Klaus, look at me."

He turned, and her eyes searched him. But saw nothing. Only emptiness. And the retreat of a dream.

When two people have the same basic plan in mind, it is only natural to expect that a merger will occur.

In the case of Irmgard and Tibor, then, it was not surprising that they did get together. Only surprising in the way that it came about. And that it happened so soon.

It began with Irmgard's suggestion that they go for a walk. It was a nice time to walk. Getting sunset. The sun dropping down behind the bull ring, and soon the one circle would blot out the other. But that, as she explained, was not why she had led him away from the colony. It was because of Klaus, and his chicken plan, and the problem of a foreigner trying to make money in Mexico without capital, and without government permission. And because Tibor had made the mistake of talking about it in the presence of Grandotte.

Tibor seemed properly regretful.

Irmgard had set the pace of their walk, and that pace was fast. Long strong steps. And Tibor, being lazy, had no wish to move around in such a hurry.

"Wait a minute." He stood still, looked at her, and smiled. "You're walking like a Hitler maiden on the march!"

"Oh, I am sorry. Perhaps you do not like to walk?"

"No. Not very much," he answered honestly.

She slowed down. "We will only walk anyway to that fence up there and then come back. How is that?"

"Suits me. Go on. I didn't mean to interrupt you."

Irmgard had no remembrance of what she had been saying, but she went on talking anyway. She talked fast, and she began to walk rather fast again too, without realizing it—but trying so desperately hard to hide the wish in her mind—and to divert Tibor's attention away from the flush on her cheeks and the fever which she felt must be in her eyes, because it was so white-hot in her body. She was wishing, and couldn't help it, for Tibor. She had forgotten everything for the moment about Tom. No longer even struggled to believe that it was because of him that she wanted to do it. Deep down in her heart, and as far as sentiment was concerned, it was true that her every dream led to him. But this present clamor in her blood, she knew, had nothing to do with dreams.

And the worst of it was that she was discouraged. She could see that Tibor had no interest in her at all. He walked along beside her, chewing on a leaf, thoughtful. But she didn't want him thoughtful. She wanted response. Oh, it was her own fault, she guessed. How could she expect him to respond when she was so dull? So stiff and formal. But the trouble was she didn't know how to flirt any more. She had forgotten all the cute little things to say and do, the gestures to make, the ways to entice. Oh, if she could only unbend, be different, be bright and exciting. But so long in Tijuana. So alone in Tijuana. She had forgotten how. Here she was, just prattling stupidly of the people in the colony, and not able to make herself *personal* at all. And yet all the time, underneath, so conscious of Tibor.

Eventually she did try to direct at least one remark to him. Knew she had been silly to keep talking of all the others. She must get around to talking about him somehow.

"Why are you so quiet? What are you thinking of?"

"Me?" he smiled.

It amused him that she had asked, because his thoughts in the last few minutes had gone like this:

As she talked, he had watched her quizzically, charmed all over again by her passiveness, and wondering exactly how he should go about matters. Pondered the thought of approaching her physically. Not grab her in his arms, or try to kiss her. Nothing like that, not now. Because once he started in that way, he wanted to finish it. But there were other smaller ways. Those slight brushings against each other, as two people walked. And then too, the little contact-opportunities that a man can invent, those interruptions of time and thought. "Wait. Stop. There's something on your hair." She pauses. He pauses. His body close to hers. His hand touches her hair, lingers a moment, picks off an imagined leaf. Oh, lots of little things like that, and Tibor knew them all. And he knew too that once the first contact was made, the other small contacts followed in natural course.

But did he want to intrigue her this way? The electricity manner, as he often termed it in his mind. There was another method which he also favored. The conversational approach, through a careful choice of suggestive subject matter. Some girls roused even easier that way. He wondered. Thought it all over for many minutes. Feeling quite like an epicurean who turns several sauces over in his mind, trying to decide which would best suit his taste at this particular moment. Then suddenly he remembered the scene he had first envisioned when he first saw her . . . the girl who wouldn't want to, and the man who would insist. That was it. No leading up to it at all. Not now, anyway. Later.

He had just reached his decision when she asked him about his thoughts.

"Well, I was just thinking that maybe I'll come by and see you this evening."

They had, by now, reached the back door of Casa One.

Irmgard took her key out of her pocket. "Very well."

173

She tried to make her voice sound indifferent. And succeeded. "I will look for you."

Then each went their separate ways to wait for night-darkness.

The night was all that was necessary, of course. The night and proximity.

But when it was night and when they were close, they were both shocked. He, by the wild passion with which she accepted him. She, by her own aftermath tears which she couldn't stop.

Crying and telling Tibor about Tom. Crying because she was a waif left on a doorstep, because she was frightened about her future, because there was no one who cared, because she didn't know how she was going to live from now. And pouring it all out to Tibor, knowing that it was the last thing in the world she should have done but unable to control herself. Of course, she could never expect him to help her now, couldn't hope that he'd fall in love. So foolish to tell him of her troubles, and her heartache for Tom.

And all the while she cried and talked, Tibor watched her, and tried to be sweet, and tried to say some nice things, but underneath still thinking of the shock she had given him. The amazing surprise-passion hidden in that placid-seeming body.

He felt drawn to compliment her, because she had really been magnificent. And in forming his compliment, he also wanted to comfort her a little.

"Don't worry. At least, you won't ever have to starve. Not with a talent like yours. You could always get along somehow."

174

She gasped and he was afraid she was going to cry again.

"Please don't. I'm just . . . well, just trying to tell you that you're wonderful."

She smiled then. Even laughed. Didn't realize that it was a thought she was to remember and mull many times during the next few months.

When Tibor returned home, he was soon sleeping the sleep of the innocent. Untroubled by dreams. Completely unmindful of the fact that in two short days, and in his awkward, blundering way, he had brought dream's-end to Klaus, concern to Ani, torment to Irmgard, and had banished Siegfried from his house.

10

NOW that there was no longer even the slightest hope of ever hearing from lawyer Steele, and now that there was an end to the poor little chicken business even before it had begun—Klaus and Jennifer, on Monday, decided to see the consul.

When they were dressed and ready in the car, Klaus drove up to Omah's rear bedroom window, called out to her,

"Omah, are you all right?"

"*Danke schoen*, yes." But her voice thin and weak.

"Maybe she'd like us to bring her something," Jennifer suggested. "Fish maybe. They have good fish down there."

"Omah? Is there something you like for us to bring? We go to Ensenada now."

After a moment, her voice came out to them, tolling dismally.

"*Ja*. You can bring for me a quota number, please."

"Oh, Klaus!" Jennifer hid her face against his arm. "The way she said that."

"Don't let her know. Say something for to cheer her."

But there wasn't much to say, no way to really answer. They called good-by, said they would try to bring a surprise and drove off.

Everyone in the colony knew why Omah's immigration problem was so serious. It had nothing to do with the consul in Ensenada; unfortunately he didn't give out the quota numbers. These are handed out by the American consuls general in the various countries, and as Omah was German, her number had to come from the American consul general in Berlin. The Ensenada consul had written several times in her behalf, but he was handicapped in obtaining any special consideration for her. Her daughter was not yet an American citizen, so Omah had to apply for the regular non-preference quota. And her age, in this respect, was against her. Naturally she couldn't be expected to support herself; she might become a public charge. And the tragedy was that her American son-in-law had refused to submit an affidavit guaranteeing that he would take care of her. Nothing for her to do then but wait, and hope that her turn would come eventually.

The thought of Omah, and the misery of all the waiting and longing which they all had to go through, clung to Klaus and Jennifer the long sixty-some miles to Ensenada.

But when they arrived at the consulate, Miss Allbright met them with a smile and the news that there was a new consul now. Mr. Smedley.

After Miss Allbright had left them alone, to wait for Mr. Smedley, Klaus seized Jennifer and kissed her. His eyes bright, his face transformed with hope.

"A new consul! Know what that means? New luck for us! A new person always likes to make things straight . . . clear out old things. Like a proverb we have in Germany. . . ."

"New brooms? Yes, we have it, too. Well, I hope you're

right." But she watched him closely. So intent and confident that she feared for him.

"Jen, ask me what nationality I am. Like Whitie at the border."

"Oh, you're such a child!"

"But I have a feeling. I feel now we have a chance maybe."

He began to pace the small waiting room, talking to himself, clasping and reclasping his hands excitedly. He was grinning. Then abruptly he stopped in front of her, and thrust out his hand.

"Amurrican? Put it there!"

This was an old game, too, and she laughed. Put her hand in his. He shook it hard. Sat down beside her.

"Know where I learned that? There is a place in Paris. Harry's Bar. A real American bar. I was going there all the times, when I was trying to come to America to see you, and Harry's American Bar was so close as I could get. Always Americans there, and there was one man—he was drunk from morning and night. All he ever saw of France was that place, and it really wasn't France at all. But every time a customer came in, he walked up and put his hand out, and shouted, 'Amurrican? Put it there!' He thought I was American and did it to me. That's why I went there all the times. I liked that!"

"Klaus, sh-h-h."

Jennifer pointed to the consul's door. It had opened slightly and a young Mexican could be seen sitting near the desk talking with the consul. The consul wasn't visible, but by leaning forward Klaus and Jennifer could hear what was being said.

Bit by bit they understood that the boy was applying for

a year's visa to enter the United States as a visitor. He lived in Saint Thomas, a small town to the south. The consul asked what proof he could offer that he would return to his home at the end of a year. Did the boy have a job? No. Own property? No. Well, then, Mr. Smedley didn't think he could have a visa, because the United States didn't like to give temporary visas to aliens who had no roots in their own country. He made a suggestion; that the boy work for a year or two, in order to show an investment of time and money—then at the end of that time, come and see him again about the visa.

Chairs scraped back, and they rose. "Good-by then," said the consul, "and I'll look forward to seeing you in a year or so."

The casual way in which he referred to a year's time chilled the Eckerts. Okay, toots, see you in a year or two. A year, a whole long miserable year, like it was half hour, this afternoon, tomorrow. Jennifer and Klaus drew close to each other like frightened children.

Mr. Smedley stood in the doorway. "Won't you come in now, please?"

He seemed kindly. Short and plump, and eyeglasses. Jennifer seated herself in the chair near the desk. Mr. Smedley drew one from a far corner, brought it up to the desk, too, for Klaus.

"So you won't feel out of things," he smiled.

"Oh, thank you," Klaus murmured nervously.

The warm hospitality made him suspicious. Maybe the consul didn't know of the terrible thing which had happened. Anxious to immediately uncover the ugly truth, he blurted out,

"They have said to me I am a perjurer and cannot have my visa."

"Yes, I know." Mr. Smedley polished his eyeglasses. "And I sympathize with you very much"—but as he said these latter words, he turned and directed his eyes toward Jennifer. "What are you planning to do, Mrs. Eckert?"

"To do?" Jennifer asked breathlessly.

"Yes. Are you planning to stay on here? Will the Mexican government permit you to reside here permanently?"

"Mr. Smedley!"

What he had said so took her breath that it was a moment before she could go on. Then she rushed into it frantically.

"Mr. Smedley, we still have hopes that my husband *will* get in! He didn't mean to commit perjury. Surely anyone can understand how it happened. So anxious to see me again, and—"

"Unfortunately, Mrs. Eckert, in these technical matters, there is no allowance for extenuating circumstances."

Klaus turned to Jennifer, his eyes begging for an explanation. Here it was, beginning all over again, more of that technical language that he couldn't understand.

"But there must be something we can do!" Jennifer urged, her voice mounting. "They can't give us a life punishment like this—just for a lie. Even when a man is tried for murder, and convicted, he can ask for another trial, go to a higher court somewhere!"

"Mrs. Eckert, in immigration cases, there is no higher court than a consul's office. Only a consul has the right to issue a visa, and the law says that a man admitting perjury, or convicted of perjury, is inadmissible. A consul must respect that law. Now let me ask your husband something . . . Mr. Eckert, you did admit, didn't you, that you intended to deceive the consul in Nice when you told him that you had never applied for a visa?"

At that moment, looking at the distress on her husband's face, Jennifer wanted to rush to him, take him away, blot out the whole miserable pain, just run away and forget it. But she knew it was something they couldn't forget. It was their life.

"Mr. Smedley," Klaus began. "I told to the consul a lie. But the intention I did not have. It just happened so quick, like I was dazed, and only thinking on one thing . . . to get to America."

"But you also signed an application, in which you stated the same thing. Did you sign that application under oath?"

"No, there was no oath."

There was a long pause while Mr. Smedley referred to the Eckert file lying there before him. He glanced at several pages, closed the file. Leaned back, tapped a pencil against the desk.

Jennifer realized that he had no intention of revealing what he had read there. She guessed, though, that the consul in Nice reported that an oath had been administered. All applications were supposed to be made under oath, and if there had been no oath given, as Klaus claimed, then it was the consul's error—and a consul couldn't be expected to admit his own mistake.

"If they had asked me to swear," Klaus said earnestly, "I would remember, and also if they had made me to swear, I wouldn't have made the lie."

Mr. Smedley weighed this a moment, then again gave his attention to Jennifer.

"Mrs. Eckert, I would like to help you, but you can appreciate my position. One consul has already denied a visa, and the case has been closed. I can't even accept another application from your husband, unless Washington gives me permission."

"But that's what I write and ask them for all the time!" Jennifer despaired. "Nobody listens to us. I don't know what to do. Where to turn. *Who* to appeal to!"

As she talked she thought she saw genuine concern on his face, had the feeling that she was closer to help than she had ever been before.

"We thought perhaps a lawyer might help, but we had bad luck with the first try, and now we don't have enough money for another one. Mr. Smedley, please tell me one thing . . . do you think it might help if I went to Washington and saw someone there?"

"I wouldn't like to advise you on a trip like that. It would be costly for you, and I don't know that it would help. Of course . . ."

He frowned and paused.

Jennifer determined that she would not break into that pause for anything. Just wait. Not say one word. Maybe now at last they were going to get a clue. She leaned forward, watched him fervently.

"Of course," he said finally, "that's up to you."

It was all over now. This was an American consulate, of course, and Jennifer was an American citizen, and she knew that she had the right to sit there as long as she wanted, and so long as she behaved herself, nobody could throw her out. But she didn't see any point in staying. Mr. Smedley was polite; he even seemed interested . . . but she knew that what he had said was true. As far as he was concerned, the case was closed.

She looked at Klaus, indicated that they should leave. They moved and rose, said their good-bys, and their thanks. Then awkwardly, as an afterthought, shook hands.

Klaus put his arm around her as they walked to the car. Helped her in. Got in and sat beside her. Reached for her hand. Held it there on his knee. Stared into nothingness.

"Jennifer?"

"Yes, dear."

"Maybe someday I will have the courage to go from you away, and take all your troubles with me."

She didn't answer. It was too horrible to answer. She could stand most anything except hearing him talk like that. But it brought her to a decision.

"Klaus, I am going back in there. You wait here."

She dashed from the car, and flew up the walk.

Once inside, she knocked briefly on Mr. Smedley's door, then walked in.

"Mr. Smedley, I have to talk to you some more. You have to help me."

She came directly to the desk, leaned across it, her eyes full, but as she spoke her voice was steady, unemotional, factual.

"Mr. Smedley, I love my husband. Just now he said he'd better go away because he's brought me so much trouble. He thinks about it all the time . . . I know he does. And in one way I can't expect him to hang around a border forever, just because he loves me. He's a man, and a man has to have work, and a purpose in life. But I tell you now, if he ever goes away, I'll never forgive myself, or you, or anybody who has ever had anything to do with it. And I say that you *do* have something to do with it . . . because I know there must be some way we can work things out, if you'd only tell me. I know you're not supposed to ever tell anything to anybody, but you must! Please! What should I do? Should I get a good lawyer? Is that right? Do you think that's the thing? Will that help?"

He rose and came around to her side of the desk. "Do you have money for a big lawyer?"

"No, but I'll get it . . . somehow . . . if you tell me that's the only chance. Or do you think I should go to Washington? *Please*, what is the best thing to do?"

"Before you do anything, isn't there anyone in Washington who can follow through on this case for you? Someone who is in close touch with the department and can speak to them on your behalf?"

"I don't know anyone there."

"It doesn't have to be somebody you know. Somebody who could represent you."

"Represent me?" Then suddenly she knew what he meant.

"Mrs. Eckert, you appreciate my position. Your husband has admitted perjury, and according to the law, anyone who has done that is inadmissible under the Immigration Act of—"

"Thank you, Mr. Smedley. Thank you. I've heard it so often though. You don't need to go on. But thank you for being so nice!"

She grabbed his hand, shook it warmly and hurried out.

Out the door, and down the walk, back to the car. Kissed Klaus. "Darling, I think we've found it . . . someone who can help! I don't know why I never thought of it before. It's my Congressman!"

11

IT was now the first week in September, and Hitler marched into Poland.

Hans Weiss brought Blima the news, and in his manner a trace of gloating and exultation. Now another country would suffer as his Austria had. Now the world would see! Now maybe the world would do something about it!

Blima did not care for Hans Weiss, and she particularly did not like his attitude this morning. She asked him to leave. She was glad that Duwid had not been there to hear him. Poland was no longer their home. Their hearts were elsewhere now, but the news was nevertheless tragic. She was rugged, and she could stand it. But she was afraid of what it might do to him.

On Hans' heels, she went from one bungalow to another, and begged the immigrants please not to talk of the war in front of Duwid. Duwid was frail, she explained. Duwid was not in the best of health. Everyone knew what she was trying to say—that Duwid, in a mild way now and then, was out of his mind a little.

But they loved Blima Lankowski around the Colonia Gomez. She was so sweet and quiet and she never made any trouble in the community—so they respected her wish. And it was because of this that there was so little talk of the happenings abroad those first days.

At least openly. But there was, of course, a great deal of private tension. Klaus, particularly, managed to work himself into a fever-pitch, shaking and banging at his radio, in an effort to get American news releases but hearing only Jim Mora who urged him to join Dr. Burt's friendship club, or to send a dollar for ten tap-dancing lessons. And as he shook and banged, Hans and Emil and Siegfried and Irmgard running in and out, anxious to know what luck he was having.

On Sunday though, when they learned that England had declared war on Germany, all talk and outer excitement ceased. Because it was then that a dozen unanswered questions marched up and down in their minds. After that, not so much concerned with the future of nations, pondering only the effect of the war upon themselves. The questions in most of their minds summing up to one important one: Would it mean a longer time to wait for quota numbers, or less?

Then one morning, they thought they found the answer. Mr. Mueller drove by. He was one of the German immigrants living in Ensenada, and waiting for his quota number there. He said that the war was the greatest thing that could have happened for them, and that he and his wife were getting ready to leave at once.

"You mean, leave for Germany?" Hans asked.

"No! We expect to get our quota numbers . . . for the States! Don't you see what the war means? It's very easy to figure it out. With the war going on, all the borders are closed . . . Germany, Austria, Czechoslovakia, Poland.

Nobody can get out now so that gives us a chance. Think of all the thousands in those countries who must have been applying for numbers and trying to leave for the United States. But now they can't go . . . so all those numbers are available for us! I think we'll all be out of here within a month!"

Klaus walked away from the intent little group there around the Mueller car, left them talking. Their hopes soaring. Their voices fervent. For their sakes, he hoped it was true. But it saddened him, and pierced him with envy. He couldn't help wishing that his problem were as simple as theirs. At least they knew that one day it would come. One day, if they could hold out long enough, that letter from the consul saying that their number had been reached. If he only knew that! If he could only count on it. Then he felt that he could wait, a year, even two. But not to know. Not to know if he would *ever* get in.

Then he thought of Omah . . . thought perhaps it would be nice to tell her what Mueller had said. She was so sick these days, and it might give her something to hope for again.

He told her, and sunrise burst upon her face.

"I knew it! I knew it! Klaus, I am going to pack at once."

She tried to get out of her bed, but he forced her back.

"I wouldn't do that, Omah. Wait a while. It's not certain yet. It's just one man's opinion. The consul hasn't said anything about it."

"But I believe it!" she maintained stubbornly. "I told my cards again just this morning, and they say I am going to get in very soon now. This must be the way! If you won't let me get up, then you'll have to pack for me. Now just stand up on that chair there, and get those suitcases down from the shelf."

To humor her, he did. He ranged them around on the chairs, and dispatched her packing orders as she gave them.

"That heavy coat on the bottom of the big black case first, then pack my shoes around it. But the brown shoes, with the broken shoelace, leave those out, Klaus. They're the most comfortable to travel in." And so on, until the closet and the drawers were emptied, except for the few things that she said she would wear for the trip. Then, stating that she wished to be neat when she arrived at her daughter's, she sent Klaus to Berendo's to buy her a new pair of shoelaces.

That night she was so full of anticipation that she couldn't sleep. Klaus heard her coughing and tossing, even from next door. He couldn't stand it. He couldn't sleep either. He got up and walked a half a mile down the road to Dr. Pareira's, brought back a sleeping powder which he insisted that she take.

Secretly, the others in the colony held the same high hopes as Omah did, but they were afraid to even talk about it, and made their little preparations stealthily.

Then a few days later, Hans received a note from Mr. Mueller, saying that he had just talked with the consul. In his last communication from Berlin, Mr. Smedley had been advised that it would be six or eight months before any of the Tijuana Germans could receive quota numbers. "But, of course, that report was made before the war," Mr. Mueller had added, "and I still think the war is going to make a difference." But somehow there was no confidence in Mr. Mueller's words.

Hopes fell. Fever abated.

After that, most of the immigrants settled down to a normal existence.

All except Omah . . . who still kept her suitcases packed and ready for closing.

One late afternoon, Irmgard sat by Omah's bedside, scarcely listening to the old woman's drone, as she talked of days far in the past. The girl found it strange that Omah at her age could remember so vividly the events of her youth when she could hardly remember things of five or six years ago. It always seems strange to young people. But the old, as they live out life's circle, toward the end come near to the starting point, and the beginning is seen as though it were yesterday.

For three days now, Omah had lain in a kind of stupor. The mattress of her bed skinny and skimpily padded like herself, and the old bones and old springs groaned alike, complaining fitfully of their association. The old woman quite helpless. No strength to even reach for a glass of water. Dr. Pareira had said there was nothing to do. She was just burned out inside. She must not be exposed to any excitement, and someone should always be there to look after her. The immigrants had agreed to take turns sitting with her.

"Did I tell you, Irmgard, that my Walter was a dancing teacher when I first met him? Such an aesthetic man, so mild and sweet. The kindest man I ever knew. The way he loved music and paintings. . . ."

Irmgard nodded, trying to conceal her boredom. It would come now, the story of Walter going away to the war. She had already heard it four or five times and now Omah began it again. How Walter had gone away, and then one day a year later, a carriage drew up to the house. A fine carriage, and a fierce-looking man with a great black beard got out. He wore the heavy spiked Prussian helmet, with the long flowing veils. A tremendous cape around his shoulders, sweeping majestically, falling to the ground. He walked so boldly, his cape furling, sword clinking. Little Lola and Willie, only children then, were scared. When he approached them, they ran away, shrieking.

And Omah admitted that even she had failed to recognize him at first. But it was he, her Walter. The man who had gone away so meek and mild, and who had returned a warlord terror. He had come in, sat in her parlor. Sat on the edge of a chair, while she served him coffee. Talked in a strange, gruff voice. Afterwards had taken her to bed in a rough, strange way—and she had never seen him again. For years after that, Omah always thought of that bedtime with shame, as though she had committed adultery with a man she didn't know.

She didn't tell all of this to Irmgard, not the latter part, but it went its slow way through her mind. And after a while she began to talk of the years after the war, the occupation. How she had worked in a hotel where English officers were quartered, and how she hated them, and how her son had died because of them. An English officer kicked him down the stairs. Limp like a stocking when she picked him up. His head hanging, bobbing around like something on a broken hinge.

"Omah, *don't* talk about that now!" Irmgard said crossly, shivering.

It had begun to be windy out. The darkness coming early. Cold, dismal fall. Irmgard went to the window, pulled the shade, lighted the light.

"That's right . . . not talk about it . . . I still had Lola. That's what I told myself then. Don't think about it. Lola is left. I still have Lola. But they took her away from me too . . . those same English. They made a fuss over her and spoiled her. Even as a little thing, that day when she rushed to me, proud because one of the soldiers had taught her her first word of English. It was a dirty word but she didn't know, and she ran around telling it to everyone. And the officers laughed . . . loved to laugh at Lola saying bad words, and they taught her more of them. . . ."

And then Omah went on to tell how Lola was never content with the simple routine of German life after the soldiers went away. Not pleased with the young Germans she knew as she grew older. Germans so sober-faced. So serious and grim in those days, always talking of hunger, and the time to come when bellies would be full again. Lola hated talk about hunger. Hated all talk. Looked and listened only for laughter. The English had laughed a lot and had been so cheery. She remembered them as the only pleasure she ever knew, so of course when she grew up she married an Englishman. But he had died, and now Omah said that it had been a relief to her. He died on a trip to America with Lola, and Lola had stayed on in the United States and eventually she had married an American.

" 'One day we'll send for you, mother. One day we'll send for you,' that's what she kept writing," Omah said. "But I got tired of waiting, and I sold my house and went to surprise her. To Sacramento. Sacramento is a lovely town,

Irmgard. You'd like it there. It's not a big town, but it's the capital of the state, and the country around it is very pretty. Bill . . . that's Lola's husband . . . was ill. I didn't see much of him . . . but it didn't matter. Nice to be with Lola again, and to know my grandchild. Her name is Evelyn. Lola said I could always live with them. She fixed a room for me. But after a while I had to leave, because of my visa. They put me on a Greyhound bus. It was very comfortable. They gave me a nice white pillow. . . ."

Her voice died away, and for a moment Irmgard thought she had gone to sleep. But Omah wasn't sleeping. She was only trying to remember Sacramento. The three months she had spent there, a little hazy. Bill hadn't seemed very cordial, but then he was sick, and sickness always puts a man in a bad humor. Omah remembered the room very well, though. Her room. All her future to be lived there. She saw herself as she would be soon, sitting there, knitting or crocheting, telling stories to Evelyn, teaching her German. Sometimes she would go downstairs and cook a special German dish for her. Bake pumpernickel for her. Terrible, this white bread that children in America always ate. How were they ever to have strength in their teeth and gums? Look at Lola's teeth . . . so beautiful . . . because she always ate dark bread as a child.

"Irmgard!"

"Yes. . . ." Wearily the girl turned back from the door, where she had tiptoed.

"Irmgard, please get a pen and some paper, and write a letter for me. I should have impressed Lola with it while I was there, but I'm afraid I didn't. Evelyn must have dark bread . . . I want to tell her."

Irmgard went into the living room to look for writing materials. She saw that a car was outside, pulled up close to Casa Six. The car a black Ford. The top down, white tires gleaming in the darkness. California license plates. Intuitively she knew that the car was there because of Tibor—and panic gripped her. She went out quickly.

The blinds in Casa Six were down. Irmgard slipped around to the side, in the narrow passageway between Six and Five, where the windows were low. She pressed close to the wall, peeking under a blind, a slit wide enough to see through.

Tibor was talking to a girl. A girl wearing trousers, and a man's coat, and a white scarf at her neck. A thin little white face that seemed vaguely familiar, with great large circles under her eyes, and curly bangs far down over her forehead. She sat on the couch with one leg tucked under her. Tibor stood in front of her, looking down, talking excitedly. Irmgard tried hard to hear what he was saying, but heard only that aggravating sound of a voice without words.

Seeing Tibor as though in a silent movie, seeing him without the effect of words and sounds, and there in that bad lighting, the lights a dull yellow glare, emphasizing the gray dreariness of the room, Irmgard was shocked to realize how different he looked now. No longer the same man who had come to Tijuana in August. Gone his dash and swagger. Still thoughtless and conceited—that still showed on his face —but otherwise not the same at all. Seedy. Thin. Slumped. Unshaved. His clothes dirty and baggy. Having the look of a man who needs to be washed and pressed all over. Yet as Irmgard realized this, it made her glad. His state now more akin to hers. Poverty and defeat bringing him closer. One starveling grateful to have another with whom to spend the hours.

The girl didn't appear to be much interested. She kept shrugging, and swinging her leg. But then once she reached out, took the cigarette from Tibor's hand, smoked it, put it back. The small intimacy of it jostled Irmgard's heart. She hated her. Then she saw Tibor grab the girl and pull her to her feet, engulfing her with himself. The girl struggled, pushed away, and laughed. Said something, and picked up her hat.

Tibor lifted his coat from the chair and put it on. They both went to the door. Irmgard became one with the wall, and held her breath.

Steps on the porch and on the drive. Bodies settling in the car. A whir. The car backed around . . . down the drive, Tibor driving, turned and headed toward town.

A few minutes later, Irmgard was knocking at Chato's shack. She found him, half drunk, sitting among his bottles.

"Chato, quick! Drive me to town in your truck. Please! It is very important."

He held a tequila bottle toward her. "Is good. Is fine. Is my *comida!*" he laughed. "Have! I share with you!"

She pushed the bottle away, dragged him to his feet.

"Please, Chato, please."

Pulling and begging, she managed to get him out into the darkness, to where his forlorn little truck stood. A goat was sitting in the front behind the wheel. Chato pointed to it and laughed.

"See, no use! Somebody already drive truck." But he

leaned over, picked up a stone, threw it at the goat, and the goat bounded out.

As they rumbled down the drive, Irmgard pressed far back under the hood, so she wouldn't be seen in case anyone came out.

"Where you go, Miss Irmgard?"

"You just drive, and don't ask questions."

As they neared the town, Irmgard scanned the streets. Then on the main avenue, she saw that the car was parked in front of the Hotel Golondrina.

"Stop here, Chato. Don't park. Just let me off."

He slowed up. "Me go too?"

"No." She hopped out, and disappeared into the hotel lobby.

From there, Irmgard could see into the dining room. Tibor and the girl sitting in a far corner.

She wondered what she'd do now. Wondered why she had even come here. Just compelled to follow and spy. Female instinct. Then she saw the girl get up, leave the table, stop and speak to a waiter in the center of the room. The waiter pointed to the doorway where Irmgard was standing. She stepped to the side, saw there was a ladies' room behind her. She dropped into a chair and waited.

The girl didn't enter the rest room. At the door, she stopped, looked back, darted to the side, and up to the desk clerk.

"Call me a taxi, please. I want to go to the airport in San Diego." A slight accent as she spoke. She spoke like Tibor.

"Taxis not allowed to cross the border on business. Maybe I get someone else take you. But at the border, no tell them you pay for the ride. You pretend you are friend."

"That's all right, but I have to go quickly."

"You American citizen?"

"I have my papers. Now hurry, please."

The Mexican went into a back room. While the girl waited she lighted a cigarette nervously, walked by Irmgard very close, peeked into the dining room, then came back to the desk.

In a moment the desk clerk returned with another Mexican.

"He take you for five dollars."

"Let's go."

Irmgard followed them to the sidewalk. The Mexican's car parked just behind the Ford. The girl started to get into the back seat, but the Mexican insisted she get in front.

"Until after we pass the border."

Then they were gone, and Irmgard felt better. Eased and almost happy. She couldn't understand about the car still standing there. Couldn't understand any of it. But it didn't matter. Only that the girl had gone.

Now that the tension had worn off, the sudden realization that she was cold. No coat, and the night windy and autumn-cold. Tibor would be getting nervous soon, start looking for the girl. He might come out. Better not run into him here.

Irmgard crossed over to the other side of the street, and started home.

Tibor sat at the table waiting for Tasha to come back, and wondering if he had been right to be so tough with her. But he had had to be. In a bad spot like this, he had to let her know how desperate he was. No beating around the bush. Five thousand dollars. It was what he needed. What he had to have. And she'd have to get it for him. Somehow. In spite of that business manager. Business manager, hell . . . Tibor didn't believe she even had one. And if she did, then things had come to a pretty pass when a star had to get permission from some hireling to spend her own money. Of course, the business manager might not be Tasha's hireling. Monty's hireling. That was more like it. More of that button-pushing that went on in the United States. She could get around those things though, if she wanted to.

So different though. Tasha had been different. That's what he couldn't understand. Cold and sober. And serious. Just because she was working in a picture again, taking herself big, talking "career" again. "Big chance this time . . . best part I ever had . . . real drama . . . important time in my life, Tibor . . . first really good picture in six months . . . and a wonderful leading man. From the stage . . . Dory Hollister. . . ."

Thinking it over, Tibor decided he knew what the main trouble was. The thing that was the danger with all women. Stay away from them too long, and they get cold. Cold for you and hot for somebody else. That was the trouble. Hollister. But he'd fix that. Given time and a chance. He'd remind her of how it had been before, and how it was going to be again. She could come and visit him in London. Maybe do a picture with him over there, after he got going. Better order some drinks now. That would help. Tasha with a drink in her was always easy.

"Waiter!"

"Yes, sir."

"Two martinis."

But if she were really cold for him now, Tibor puzzled, then why had she come down here? She had been so odd there in the bungalow. Looked at him so strangely.

"What's happened to you, Tibor? You look so different."

How did she expect him to look? Most of his clothes sold now. (The way the damned colony had ganged up on him and made him pay Siegfried!) Only a few dollars in his pocket. Did Tasha think that razor blades, manicures, and such grew on trees? In a way, good that she saw him like this. Make her realize how frantic he was . . . so frantic he'd do anything, even keep her here, like he had told her, until she got someone to bring the money down. Oh, he hadn't really meant that. Not necessary to do anything like that. Tasha would be all right. She'd break down. Just acting coy for a change, wanted to be wooed. What was five thousand dollars to her? And as he had explained to her, it was no risk. He only wanted it as a loan. He would pay it back when he got to be a big star in London.

The waiter returned and set the drinks on the table. Tibor tasted his drink.

Five more minutes passed, and he went out into the hall.

"Did you see a girl in slacks?"

"She left ten minutes ago."

"Left?"

"Yes."

Tibor knew that this was impossible. He had the car key in his pocket. He had been driving. He had put it in his pocket when they got out. He felt for it. Yes, it was still there. But if she had a second key—?

He hurried out to the street. Came back.

"You must be wrong. Her car is still there."

199

"No, señor. She go all right. I sent her in a car to San Diego."

Shocked, not able to think, anxious to avoid the eyes of the clerk who seemed to enjoy his discomfort, Tibor returned to the sidewalk, stood looking at the car.

The waiter came out from the dining room and tapped him on the arm.

"The dinner she is ready a long time."

"Cancel it. Never mind."

"No cancer!" His Mexican temper sharp in his tone. "You go, I call police. I know you. You live in Colonia Gomez."

Meekly Tibor followed him back to the dining room.

He sat down at the table again. The waiter, calm and genial once more, put the soup before him.

Tibor stared at it, pushed it away, and tried to think.

Gradually he was able to face it. Tasha had run out on him. Had no intention of helping him. Never did have. At first thought, he believed that she had left the car, only in order to avoid a good-by scene. But now he realized that there was more to it than that. Tasha was tired of having him chase her around with telegrams and phone calls. Maybe it had become embarrassing because of Monty or Hollister. He was too close to her. Tasha had left him the car because she knew he could sell it, and it would bring money enough for him to get away. Anywhere. She didn't care. So long as he went farther from her.

Well, goddamn her.

He emptied his own martini with one gulp, emptied the second one, then reached for the soup, drew it toward him.

By the time he finished his soup, he felt warmed and relaxed. Anger went away. So Tasha thought that Tijuana was too close. She hoped he would leave. That made him snort. Did she think he wouldn't? Buried in an out-of-the-way place like this. He'd go, all right. Get out of this hell-hole. Tomorrow. Had to get back into circulation again. That's what he had to do. Sell the car and go back to Mexico City. He'd even drive there, if there was any road. Mexico City would be all right. Lots of rich travelers there now, since the war. In Mexico City he'd find a rich woman . . . marry her. Not take any more chances. Get married, go to London. Go any place he liked then. Marry a rich American, and he could probably even go back to the States. If he wanted to. If she were rich enough, she could get him back. That's what he was going to do . . . get married. What he should have done a long time before!

And so, having made his decision, and seeing the future as rosy once again, Tibor regained his old self-assurance. What was past was past. Just check it up to "experience." He had learned his lesson.

A delightful aroma brought him back to the present. The waiter was placing a fine steak before him.

"Bring me the other one, too—the one she ordered. If I have to pay for it, might as well eat it."

After Tibor had cleaned up everything, and even Tasha's dessert along with his, he paid his bill, then leaned back and asked the waiter,

"I have a Ford coupé to sell. Convertible. It's only a year old. In good condition. I want six hundred dollars for it. Know anybody who would be interested?"

"Cash?"

"Sure, cash. That's why I make it so cheap."

The waiter laughed. "You find somebody who has six

hundred dollars cash here, you lucky. Nobody that rich here. After the races start maybe. Then lotsa people work. You wait, then sell maybe for cash. Not now."

"What races?"

"Caliente track she open soon. Three weeks I think. Horses already come down. Things better here then."

"That's too long. I've got to sell it right away."

"Why for you not have raffle?" the Mexican asked. "Good fun, raffle. Mexicans like raffles. Like to gamble. Always have plenty raffles in Mexico. I sell diamond ring like that!"

"How do you mean?"

"See, you go to printer, and he makes little cards with numbers on, and you sell for ten, maybe twenty pesos piece, or dollars, how you like, and everybody sign his name for number, and when you sell much tickets, you have raffle and draw tickets out of box. You get money. Somebody get car. Very easy . . . no? But must get good Mexican hold raffle money. Like me, I do through drug store. Drug store sell tickets, see. And I give drug store little money for do. You get somebody like that. Mrs. Berendo, maybe. She help. I tell you, you sell tickets like that, you get money for car more quick than sell it. I tell you!"

"I'm afraid it would take too long. Have to sell too many tickets. And I have to have cash, and quick."

"Okay, but I know! You no find cash. *You* see, mister."

"Thanks, anyway."

And to show his deep gratitude, Tibor tossed him a dime for a tip.

Out in the night again, Tibor looked at the car, and it occurred to him that he would hurry home and show it to the immigrants. Make them envious. Not tell them that he was going to sell it. Just say that it had been sent down as part of the debt which was owed him, and that he had been promised the rest of the money soon. Maybe that would make them look upon him differently. So stingy and mean to him all the time lately, except Irmgard. All the others always closing him out of everything. Doors only half-opened when he approached, candy boxes closed and cakes covered up when he was around, curtains drawn when they ate. He saw these things. Now it was his turn to be mean. Give them their medicine. Just let any one of them ask for a ride or a lift into town!

A few minutes later, Tibor drove through the archway, blowing his horn loud and insistently. Childishly disappointed when only the Klabecs and Irmgard came out. The Eckerts and the Lankowskis were at the movies. Siegfried was up on the hill with the Weisses playing cards. Ani seemed to think the car was nice, but didn't say nearly enough to suit Tibor.

He motioned to Irmgard. "Want to take a ride? Come on."

She slipped into the car, her face shining and grateful.

"Yes, it is a nice night for a ride, now that the moon is getting up," Ani said.

A hint in her voice—and at least that was some satisfaction for Tibor. He ignored her. He started the car and drove off with Irmgard. Not particularly anxious to take her driving, but to spite Ani.

They drove out toward Agua Caliente, the palms along the road rustling their dry leaves, whispering and gossiping in their windy way. The road to the hotel was blocked off, but the road up to the left to the track, usually closed, was open now—and Tibor turned up there.

They came to the top of the hill where the grandstand and the clubhouse are, drove on past it to the right, where the road leads back to the stables, but that section was closed, and a guard stood by.

Tibor backed the car around, halted it—for now a truck was lumbering up the hill, a heavy truck, a big van carrying horses, and they had to wait until it passed.

They watched while the guard opened the gate and let the truck through. The neighing and stamping of the horses in that quiet open panorama had a pleasant sound, and something of contentment spread through Irmgard.

Sitting there next to Tibor, with only the night over their heads, the nice gleam of shiny metal around her, and the breathing of the engine. It was the dream she had often pictured. Riding in an open car with Tom. It wasn't Tom. But it was somebody, and it was good to be with somebody. And it was good to get out and away from the Colonia Gomez.

The moon was beautiful, striding boldly up a windy blue-clouded sky. The wind stirred the shrubbery, brought them sweet close smells, and the pungent far-smells of the stables.

"Tibor, couldn't we drive some more, and fast now? Into the wind. Down toward the ocean. Go fast, like"—she didn't know quite how to explain it—"like we were *going* someplace!" she said finally.

"Yes, sure." He was surprised to discover that he was feeling quite agreeable.

They went back and passed the colony again, to get on the ocean road. Then speeded gloriously. And as they drove,

Tibor was conscious of an odd pleasure. It had partly to do with looking at Irmgard. Her face turned up to the sky. That face usually so still and sullen, but the nostrils dilating now, and the mouth a little open, grasping at the wind and the beauty. Strange, that a girl could get such a kick out of an automobile ride.

Then he noticed something about the car which he had overlooked. He leaned forward, turned a button.

As the music sprang out, Irmgard clutched his arm.

"Oh, Tibor! How wonderful!"

He smiled, leaned back with a lofty air, indifferently watched the road.

"And an American station, too! Tibor, it must be a very *good* radio!"

Wasn't she a simple thing, he thought. So thrilled. But somehow it pleased him.

In fact, he was finding that all in all the ride was rather pleasant. A little hard to realize, of course, because what was a car to him, when he had had so many? He had always had things in one way or another, ever since he could remember. First from his father until he had cut him off, then from other people—a parade of eager women mostly—but it didn't matter. Until lately he had always been used to things. Yet now, he was enjoying a pleasant sensation: a steering wheel, power in his hands and under his foot, speed, the night, a girl beside him. Not a girl he cared anything about. But just the same, pleasant. Only an hour before he had had all his plans wrecked by Tasha, had been upset about that. And now. Oh, well, things were inexplicable.

Eventually they approached the Beach Hotel, dark and dead-looking.

"Tibor, let's drive in there, so we can go out front and look at the ocean."

"If you like."

He parked the car in the driveway, and when they had walked around to the front of the hotel, they saw that there was a light in the big dining room after all. The light filtered out through dirty windows. Irmgard walked up to one of them, wrote her name in the window dust, and laughed. She laughed awkwardly, because she wasn't used to laughing, and the sound startled her.

She walked over and stood near Tibor, and together they watched the sea. Listened to the great sound of it. But it was hard to tell whether it was the wind or the water that they heard. The wind swept sand up from the beach, and stung their faces.

Irmgard watched him, wondered if he were thinking about the girl who had gone away. She wished he would come very close to her, put his arms around her, kiss her. Not in any exciting way. Just kiss her. Nice. As though he really liked her.

"If you don't think it's too cold," Tibor said, "we can go down to the beach. There won't be anybody there."

She knew what he meant.

They walked a little to the left and looked for the stairs that led down to it.

When they started back, later, far off to the east, there was a line of orange-red flame sweeping over the mountains. Fire in the hills, and wind pushing it.

Irmgard sighed. "They said there would be fires, and

after that dust. I always hoped I'd never be here for the fall, but it's fall now, I guess."

Tibor was thinking of Mexico City, and didn't answer.

Returning to the colony, they saw that Jennifer's car was parked in the driveway, and everybody was outside. The Klabecs and the Lankowskis standing in front of Omah's lighted bungalow. Chato and Siegfried sitting on the steps. Mady and Hans rushing down from the hill.

"It's Omah!" Blima told them ominously.

Irmgard tried to go in, but Dr. Pareira met her at the door, pushed her back, told her to ask the others, please, to be more quiet.

Inside, in the bedroom, Jennifer sat by the bed, Klaus standing close behind her.

"Omah dear, listen to me." Jennifer leaned far forward, spoke softly. "We telephoned your daughter, and she's coming right down. Doesn't that make you happy? You'll be all right when she gets here. You're just lonely and tired."

But the old woman gave her no answer, seemed not to hear.

"Klaus, I can't make her understand. Perhaps if you say it to her in German."

Then Omah stirred. "Jennifer!" she called—as though Jennifer were far away and would have to come running. "Jennifer! Where is Jennifer? I want to speak with her."

"I'm here, Omah." The girl put a soft pressure on her arm.

"*Gute*. I want to ask to you a question. There is something I must know. . . ."

"Yes . . . ?"

"I want for you to ask to that nice immigration man at the border . . . the American one . . . I want you to ask to him . . ." Then the strain of talking was too much and she rested a moment.

They waited, a terrified hush upon them.

"Go on, Omah . . . please."

Omah tried to raise her body, to get the air in. "I want to know. Ask him, please, when I am dead, will they let me in? Or will I need a quota number for that, too?"

There, she had asked it. And she sank back relieved.

Jennifer began to cry. "Oh, Omah, Omah."

Klaus drew her to her feet. "Come, Muschi. Outside."

Then there was Omah's voice again. "Jennifer, I will wait. I want to know. Best you send Klaus."

Klaus left Jennifer's side, went out, out through the living room, out of the house, and a moment later they could hear him go off in the car.

He drove to the border. He knew it was not just an old lady's dying fancy. Knew that she had to know. It would make it easier that way. He could understand things like that . . . he had often thought it himself . . . if he couldn't live in America, he'd like to be buried there anyway.

The border office was closed, but Whitie was on duty at the gate.

"Yes," Whitie nodded. "A body can pass the line, as long as the death wasn't due to any contagious disease. Have to get special permission though."

Klaus thanked him solemnly.

When he returned, the others had all crowded into the

208

little house, too, because the doctor had said it was close to the end, and they'd better say good-by.

They stepped aside as Klaus came through.

He leaned over Omah and took her hand. "Omah, the people at the border, they say you can cross."

She smiled, a tiny triumph on her face.

"See, Klaus. I told you. My cards. They are always right. They said I would get in!"

Klaus held her hand until the doctor took it away from him, and placed it on the thin old breast.

12

AFTER the fires in the hills, to which nobody paid any attention—there were always fires somewhere in the fall—and after the mountain trees and brush had been reduced to bare stalks, there was no longer much protection from the wind. It swept down into the Tijuana hollow, putting a brown layer over everything. Dust swirled everywhere.

The room which Maria and Hans Weiss occupied had become increasingly dirty. In the beginning, when they first came there, Mrs. Gomez had cleaned and swept every day. A fresh piece of linen on the dresser and bureau tops, flowers in the small vase by the bed, the windows washed. Early in August Hans had been able to borrow some money from a friend in Hollywood to pay up his bill, but it was eight weeks now since they had paid anything—and the room showed it. The windows were streaked, mounds of dust piled along the sills, and the floor gritty with it. Curtains sagging with dirt. The lampshade by the piano had come loose from its frame, and hung down over the arm of the lamp like a hat thrown there. The cheap window-shades were torn, and one had come off its roller altogether. Maria Weiss sat on the edge of the bed, looked around at the mess, groaned unhappily.

Outside a flock of crows squeaked and squawked; food

scarce for them now, so that they hung around the ranch animals looking for droppings. They made a frightful noise, an insistent noise, as wearing as the pong-pong-pong of the water-pump at night. Somewhere in the distance Mrs. Gomez yelled for Chato, berated him in high shrill Spanish. This unpleasant sound, added to the other, caused Maria to cover her ears and press her fingers against her throbbing temples.

She laid back against the pillow, gazed up at the stringy cobwebs hanging from the ceiling. She wished she had the energy to get up and clean the room herself, but she had no spirit for anything.

"Mamma?" It was Mady, standing cautiously in the doorway, a movie magazine in her hand. "Mamma, look what Klaus loaned me. It has a story by Jennifer in it. Would you like to see it?"

"No," said her mother.

"But, Mamma, I thought of a new game to play." She advanced slowly into the room, the fearful intruder. "It's a nice game, an acting game. I made it up."

"Well, what is it?" Maria raised herself wearily on her elbow.

The child climbed on the bed, dizzy with excitement. The mother looked at the child's hair, once so golden, but dead and strawish now, with the dust in it. Noticed that since Mady had lost her summer tan, she looked pallid and unattractive.

"First of all, Mamma, we pick out who we would like to be. See, we look through the magazine, and find somebody. Like here . . . here's a picture of Joan Bennett. I decide I am going to be her. Now you pick out somebody you want to be. Here's Fay Bainter. You could be her, and then we pretend that I am Joan, and you are my Aunt Fay, and we are going to a resort somewhere and I am going to try to get a rich young man to marry. And the game is that we have lots of clothes, and now we decide what we are going to wear, and where we'll go to show off and try to get somebody. Do you understand? And now, see, we keep on looking through the magazine, to decide what clothes. See this dress?" She pointed to a picture.

"Who's that?"

"That's Lana Turner. I like that dress she's got on, so now, see, I pretend that it's my dress, and maybe I could wear it when we go to a night club. Now let's find something for you to wear. Come on, Mamma, you look too. Now remember, you're Fay Bainter."

"Why should I be Fay Bainter?" Maria frowned. "Why can't I just be me playing the part . . . me, Maria Orloff! I was more famous than she'll ever think of being."

"If you want," Mady agreed matter-of-factly. "Only I just thought maybe you were tired of being you. I know I'm awfully tired of being me. Now come on, pick out a dress."

Her joy departed. Maria had again lain back against the pillows. "Oh, Mamma, *aren't* you going to play?"

"Mady dear, go find Hans. Ask him to come here. I think he went to Mrs. Klabec's."

Dolefully the child went on her errand.

A few minutes later Hans came in, stood in the doorway, bowing in mock courtliness. He had been playing belotte with Emil, and he resented being torn away. "Madame, you sent for me? If you expect to entice me at this hour of the afternoon, you would do well to make yourself a little more attractive."

"In, and with what?" she answered bitterly. "I'm out of make-up, all my clothes need cleaning . . . and you know Mrs. Gomez won't let us charge anything on the bill any more, except our meals—if you can call a tacos a meal! Hans, I'm getting hungry. I mean really hungry, each day a little more. I'm getting scared. And the way you keep lying to Mr. Gomez . . . getting Pierre Morlet to write you those phony letters from Paris, as though he were Vicki Recordings. Oh, Hans, doesn't it worry you at all?"

He smiled. "Why should I worry when you do it so thoroughly for both of us? Maria"—he came closer to her now—"the trouble with you is that you don't know how to enjoy life. Now I've spent the loveliest day. This morning, I walked past the Filigrana and watched the whores plucking their eyebrows and the hairs out of their breasts, as they sat there in the windows—amusing and slightly exciting sight. Then from there, to the Foreign Club, where the genial manager bought me a beer, and told me a sad tale about the twenty-four-hour law, and how they've sent somebody from the Chamber of Commerce to Washington to see if he can hold it off a little. Of course, I didn't particularly care about listening to that, but I had to because of the beer. Then this afternoon, a pleasant belotte game with that nitwit Emil, who because he's thinking more of his inventions than cards always forgets to announce his extra points, and so of course I invariably beat him . . . oh, yes, and Ani Klabec even gave me a part of a candy bar. All in all a pleasant day, in spite of the atmospheric conditions.

Oh, and another thing, Schnucki listened while I sang her an aria. Now, if you would only—"

"Oh, Hans, Hans. You know you're lying. You hate it as much as I do."

He dropped his airy pose, sat down beside her. "Yes, I do. Only I don't let myself get so depressed as you do."

"But I can't stand it. I miss everything so much. I'm going crazy." She pulled him down to her, clung to him wildly. "Oh, Hans, you don't know . . ."

He pried her loose, set her back away from him. "Maria, doesn't it occur to you that this depression you're going through—it would have happened to you now, anyway, no matter where you were?"

Her eyes glassed.

"The part of life that you miss. You're not so young as you were, or so beautiful. The excitement of that wouldn't be yours any more anyway."

"Oh, you're so cruel!"

He could say those things, yes, because he was younger than she. And he had things ahead of him. She knew that in a way these months away from the world had been good for him. A fast life before, but now he was in finer singing condition than ever since she had known him. It was the difference in their ages though that wrenched her heart the most, but she knew better than to be maudlin about it.

"I know that I'm through as an actress," she said defiantly. "I know that. You don't have to remind me. I've always known it would come some day, but that's why I married you. I thought I'd have a home and a new interest in life. A woman doesn't mind losing glory if she has something to take its place."

214

"And I let you down. It was too bad, Maria." For a moment he was almost tender. "But it wasn't exactly my fault. If we could have stayed on in Vienna . . ."

"Let's not go over all that now."

"Maria. Why don't you go back? They'd let you in, I think. You and Mady. Or maybe you could go to France. I can't go now because of the war."

"Go and leave you?" The thought undermined her completely. Leave him? His youth? The only youth that she had to cling to. "I'll never leave you," she said quietly.

"Well, I offered it to you." He rose, went to the door and called Mrs. Gomez.

Mrs. Gomez did not like to be yelled at like a busboy. She came down the hall reluctantly, glowering.

"Mrs. Gomez . . . come in, won't you please?" He smiled, his eyes warm and friendly, almost admiring. "How do you feel, Mrs. Gomez?"

"Well, not so good, if you must know. The water's gone off again, and Chato forgot to fill the reserve tank. Why?"

"Because we don't feel so fine either. We're somber as broomsticks, and I thought maybe you would like to join us in a glass of champagne."

Her eyes lighted. "Oh, you have champagne?"

"No," he laughed. "Have you?"

She clouded up again, flipped her apron. "No, I have not, and there is no chance of getting any either!" Once before Mr. Weiss had sent for some champagne, and they had had to get it from the town, and it was still one of the many unpaid luxury items on the books.

"Oh, come on now, Mrs. Gomez. We're all so tense, all need cheering. I thought there might be something in the

215

house . . . wine, or even tequila. You do have tequila, don't you?" And he put his arm around her plump shoulders.

She was weakening. "Well, it's my husband's bottle. . . ."

"I hate tequila," Maria mourned from the bed.

Hans blew her a kiss. "Sorry, Maria . . . but I tried to do better!" And in a moment he and Mrs. Gomez were going arm in arm down the hall, back to the kitchen.

Maria soon heard laughter and the cheery clink of glasses. Abruptly, she knew what she wanted to do. Got up quickly and went to the closet. There was a beige suit that she had bought in Paris a long time ago. It was still a good suit, too light-weight for this weather, but she put it on anyway. Didn't care if she froze. The skirt a little long for style now, but she tucked it up around her waist, folded the waistband over. Wore a black silk blouse with it, and considered a large black straw hat to go with it. It was certainly not the season for straw, but she doubted that anyone paid much attention to mode in Tijuana. And the hat was large, that was the point. Large, and it would shade her eyes, and put the sharp lines there into shadow. She put it on, and standing far back from the mirror, she felt that she looked youthful and smart. Her figure still good. A little thin, but better that than fat these years so near to forty. There was an empty perfume bottle on the dresser. She put a few drops of water in it, swished it around, applied it to her neck and ears. Then she slipped out the side way, into the open, where the wind tore at her. She clung tightly to her hat and struggled down the hill.

She had hoped to find Tibor, but his car wasn't there. No car at all . . . it was Friday and Jennifer was due, but she hadn't arrived. All right, if she had to walk, she would. Anything, to get away.

She began the walk bravely, trudging along off to the side of the road, hanging on to her hat, and her skirt laid flat against her thighs by the wind. Feeling very self-conscious and unhappy when cars went by. Then fortunately, when she passed Berendo's, the gas-meter man was there—the one who came around to the colony every month to collect the quarters from the meters—and he offered to give her a ride.

The car was spotted and it stank, but Maria tried not to notice, sat stiff and straight, gazing forward, riding like a queen.

She asked to be let out at the bank corner. Thanked him politely. Tarried there until he was out of sight, then crossed the street and headed back toward the Foreign Club.

It was after five now, and getting dark. Lights on, inside. Several Mexicans at the bar, and a few tourists. No one at the tables. Except Maria, now. She sat down at a corner table, with a good view of the door, and ordered vermouth and seltzer.

It pleased her to sit there alone, conspicuously. She pretended not to notice anyone, but felt certain that everyone was noticing her, and that was what she wanted. It was her particular need in exile, the thing she had been without for so long. Maria Orloff, once of the Paris stage, wanted attention, longed for an audience. She regretted, of course, that the audience wasn't a little larger.

But it did grow. Two groups of Americans entered from Honold's next door. Shoppers, with packages under their arms. (Good time now to buy Christmas presents before they put through that new law.) Shoppers thirsty for a drink, before starting homeward.

Maria heard their buzzing at the bar, was sure that they were looking in her direction. Because, of course, she knew that she must look interesting and mysterious. An attractive well-dressed woman sitting there all alone, in a place like this, in a border town. She could exactly imagine what they were saying: "Wonder who that is? Wonder what a woman like that is doing here in Tijuana alone?"

And she could also imagine their conjectures. Maybe she's a spy. Or a smuggler. They caught her at the border and wouldn't let her across. No, maybe she's an actress— looks lovely enough to be one. That's it; an actress, and she's here to get border-town atmosphere for her next part.

Maria liked that "maybe," dwelled on it quite a while . . . then she thought of others. Probably they had hit upon something else now, for of course they were still talking about her. Maybe she's a rich American society woman, with a Mexican lover. A secret rendezvous.

Maybe, maybe, maybe. Fun to think about, always fun to wonder what people were saying about you.

"And, my dear!" said one of the women at the bar. "Imagine getting Shocking for only eight dollars! The same bottle is fifteen at Martin's."

Maria didn't let it upset her. That was just one of those unimaginative women who never had anything but bargains on her mind.

The waiter hovered around, looking at Maria's empty glass.

She had only one dollar in her pocket, and that a guilty one, because she had kept it hidden from Hans. She didn't dare order another drink, not knowing what they cost, and too elegant to think of asking. But she didn't want to go . . . not yet . . . this was too marvelous. She thought of all the times when she used to sit in Paris cafés. People talking about her, and pointing at her. Just like this.

"I am waiting for someone," she told the waiter, but making her voice specially rich, so that it would carry well. "I'll order when he gets here." She had, after all, decided on the fable of the rich woman waiting for her lover.

During the next fifteen minutes—for the waiter's benefit, and that of all those other people who were still watching her with so much interest—Maria glanced more and more often at the clock. Then at last when she thought it would be an anticlimax to stay longer, she allowed a delicate expression of annoyance to light her features. She followed this with an expression of quick decision, then summoned the waiter. She laid a dollar on the table, and tried not to notice the change that he gave her. Three quarters. Of course, he *would* make it quarters, so he'd be sure of a large tip. But what could she do? That's what happened when you looked affluent. She controlled her desire to pick up all of them, recovered only two.

Now she needed the remaining fifty cents for a taxi home. Not even a nickel left over to take Mady some chewing gum. She hadn't thought of taking gum before, but now that it was an impossibility, she found it a mournful fact to be dwelled upon with dramatic intensity, and near tears, as the taxi bounced her along the bumpy way home.

Maria had the taximan halt at the entrance to the colony, went the rest of the way on foot, up the hill. She was very cold in her silly little beige suit, but she didn't mind. She had had a wonderful time, and she felt alive and recharged. She slipped in the same way she had come out, threw herself on the bed, thought it all over, how pleasant it had been . . . her little escapade . . . out before the public again. Now if she could only think how to repeat the adventure soon.

Then she remembered that on Sundays from now on there'd be races at Caliente, and the thought danced merrily. The track crowded, lots of people. The call of the bugle. Riders up. Horses off to the post. People leaning against the rail, sitting at tables in the clubhouse, warming themselves with drinks at the bar. Lots of people to notice her there. Men with glasses in cases, on straps swung over their shoulders. Attractive men, who had eyes for interesting women. She'd show Hans that she was still beguiling, still a magnet. A man smiles and tips his hat. "Hello. Haven't you had any winners? Why, you poor dear lady. Better bet with me from now on. I've just won eighteen-eighty. Come on, I'll buy you a drink. Come on, into the bar."

Oh, she could just see herself. Standing there, sipping a champagne cocktail, looking so sophisticated—a little hat down over one eye, her furs slipping off her shoulders, smart gloves on her hands, the bulges where her rings were underneath. And the man simply taken with her. There, Hans should see that!

Then a stricken cry in her throat, as she lay there on the bed, and her pretty picture went smash. What furs, what gloves, what rings, what hat? What man? What race track? Nothing to wear, no way to go there. She turned over on her face, muttering and crying, miserable again.

13

KLAUS had spent the morning cleaning the house, making it nice for Jennifer's arrival in the evening. He hated housework, but there are some hates which had to be endured—and at least it meant action. Every Friday he pitched in with a will; washed windows and even slung a mop. This Friday, because it had started off as such a nice day, he had gone a step further. Bought some ten-cent polishing oil at Berendo's and had tried to put a shine on the floor where the soap and water had left its gray streaks.

About noon he had finished, and about noon the wind and the dust had started up again.

Now it was evening. Newspapers in the door cracks, and against the windows, but the dust and dirt had crept in anyway—and Klaus was furious. No such thing as a shine anywhere in the house. Everything dulled with dust. Two large napkins spread out over the table for protection, over the dishes and the silverware where he had set places for the late evening supper.

Ten o'clock, and waiting. Ten o'clock, and worried. Ten o'clock, and mad.

He sat on the couch, hugging his coat around him because there was no heat in the house and it was cold. Schnucki lay on the floor watching him. Outside the wind romped and rattled at the windows, and banged at the door —and then, when Klaus would go to the door thinking he heard Jennifer, like a kid at Hallowe'en the wind ran away and hooted and whistled at him from the darkness.

Each time he came back the dog looked up, swished her tail briefly. "Fool," she seemed to say. "I'll tell you when she's here. You just take it easy, and let me listen."

He was thinking of what a bad night it was for driving— especially through Tijuana. The streets not well lighted, the road bad. He was thinking that he should have gone to the border and met her there. After a while he decided not to think, but to do it. "Come on, Schnucki."

He put on his dark blue winter overcoat, the nice one, the one he used to wear in Paris, for evenings out . . . put it on over creaseless gray pants, and a polo shirt, and they started off.

Only a few cars on the road, the night unfriendly, and they had to walk all the long way.

At the border, Klaus stood well back, fifty yards or so away from the Mexican immigration building. His Mexican visa would expire soon, and he had no wish to remind the immigration officials that he was around. He had already written to Mexico City for an extension, but until it came he felt it was best to lie low. From where he stood, anyway, he could see and hail any car that crossed.

He waited for an entire hour. Sixty bad and troublesome thoughts. The thin tires on the car. Jennifer, such a careless driver. A ditch by the side of the road. Broken arm. Broken leg. Blood on her pretty face. His fault. His fault. Everything his fault. Jennifer, Jennifer, Jennifer. What a life for her. Deserves better. A man to take care of her. Not a man for whom she has to drive one hundred and fifty miles through the night. On bad tires. In a ditch. In a ditch. Oh, Jennifer.

Calm down now. You know you go through this every Friday night, every Monday morning. Calm down. She'll be here.

How differently he had planned it. The day they married: "I promise you we are going to have a beautiful life, my friend." Jennifer laughing because he had called her friend. She was friend. She was comrade. She was everything. She was what God had given him. God always gives people one blessing. Beauty, fame, genius, success, insight, knowledge, philosophy. To everybody He gave one good thing, or a chance at it at least. To him, He had given Jennifer.

When the hour had passed, he decided to telephone. Perhaps for some reason she hadn't left. Maybe trouble with the car.

But his pockets were empty. His money lying on the dresser.

He started back, hoping to run into somebody who would loan him a dollar.

But no somebody, no dollar. Turning in at the Colonia Gomez, Schnucki gave a little yelp, bounded ahead. Klaus saw that the car was there.

So relieved he could cry. But a man can't cry, so he got mad.

He walked slowly up the drive, entered the house, closed the door.

Jennifer was standing at the dresser in the bedroom, at the end of the short hall. Schnucki ran toward her, leapt about her. Jennifer patted the dog, then smiled and reached her arms toward Klaus.

"Next?" she asked.

But he remained standing in the middle of the living room, shedding his coat. "How did you get here? I was waiting at the border."

"Oh, darling, I'm so sorry."

She ran toward him, but his frigidity held her off as though it were hands.

"Please don't be cross. I know it was terrible waiting there, but we must have missed each other. I've been here over an hour."

He noticed her flimsy nightgown. Thought wistfully of the robe at Tacuba's. "Put on a sweater or something," he said crossly. "You will catch cold."

"No, I won't." She touched him timidly, tried to slide in under his arm. "It's not cold in here. Didn't you notice? Look, Klaus. Over there."

His eyes followed her finger. An oil heater. Not three feet from where he stood.

"Jennifer!" The look on his face as though he were gazing at beauty too bright to behold.

In reality it was an ugly black thing, second-hand, rusted, smoking a little, too. But it did give off a soft yellow glow and warmth in the room.

"Jennifer. It's *wunderbar*."

"I bought it in Hollywood, but I had to get the oil after I got here. That's how we must have missed each other. Hardly any place open, and I had to look all over. You like it?"

"*Like* it!" Still that same marveling enchantment on his face.

"I should have gotten a new wick. That's an old one in it, now."

"What's a wick?"

"The thing it burns on."

He stood there, with one arm around her, looking around the room. He realized now that the heater had given it an entirely new atmosphere. Made it almost cozy, in spite of the dirt and dust, and the wind outside. Then he saw, too, that Jennifer had removed the old dust-laden papers at the door and windows and had put fresh ones in their place, tucking them in more neatly than he had done.

"Jennifer, you are the most wonderful woman in the world and I am the most lucky man." And he pulled her tight and close, and kissed her.

And as he kissed her, she knew that she was lucky, too, for in spite of all their troubles, this was her preferred man, and in his place nobody else would ever do.

Later after they had eaten, they decided just to sit around the living room. Sit around the living room—just like any folks. Because it was cheerful there now, with the heater. The past weeks they had shivered off to bed, after food was finished. But it was different now.

Jennifer got out some old pajamas, said she thought she'd tear them up, and start crocheting a rag rug.

He watched her for a while, then suddenly he had to ask it: "I do not suppose you have heard from Washington . . . from the Congressman again?"

She raised her eyes quickly. "No. Not since that one letter. But he'll do something. He said he would. Naturally

225

he's busy now . . . that special session and everything."

She tried to go on with the rags, but her fears were making more noise than the ripping. She knew that the peace that had been upon them there for a moment had awakened the melancholia in her husband's heart. She knew what was going through his mind . . . wondering if they would ever have a real home, if they would ever really be at peace, if there ever *would* be evenings when they could just sit around, not worrying, not thinking. She knew it was in his mind, because it was in hers, too, and it frightened her.

"Want to play some checkers, Klaus?"

"You are not tired?"

"No. Not so much tonight as usual. Come on, let's play. It'll take our minds off things."

He went to the china cabinet, got out the peeling checker board which Jennifer had bought at the ten-cent store, set it up on a chair drawn between them, and they started to play.

Jennifer and Klaus playing checkers against the loud fright of their hearts—and as they played, the smoking of the oil heater putting smudges around their noses.

The next day, shortly before noon, a gray coupé arrived with prospective tenants for the colony. Not immigrants, but Americans. A boy driving . . . no, not a boy exactly. A young man really, but the size of a boy. When he got out of the car to make inquiries about a bungalow, the immigrants, standing around, saw how little he was, stared fascinated at the boots on his tiny feet.

"A midget!" Ani whispered.

"Midget, nothing!" Tibor corrected. "He's a jockey. They're all pint sizes like that."

The jockey, for such he was, overheard Tibor, scowled and yelled across at him. "You the manager here?"

Tibor laughed. He thought that was very funny.

"Hey, I'm speaking to you," the jockey reminded him with a fierce little face. He had an odd habit of squinting his eyes as he talked, jerking them open and shut, like a child learning to wink . . . and that made Tibor laugh even more. That little runt standing there, arms akimbo, making such a show of gruffness.

"Keep your didies on," Tibor advised him. "Here he comes now."

While they waited for Mr. Gomez to come down the hill, the jockey moved around to the other side of the car, where its other occupant was sitting. This was an old man. Nobody could see very much of him, because he was bundled to the gills, and even had a scarf over his head, under his hat. But it was a nice old face, and he seemed very tired.

"I don't know whether we want to live here or not," the jockey yelled at him. Yelled it loud, because the old fellow was deaf—and he looked at Tibor as he said it.

Tibor strolled over, pointed to Casa Two. "That's the only bungalow vacant, and an old lady died in there just a little while ago. Maybe you're afraid of ghosts?"

Klaus moved over from the steps of Casa Three, grabbed Tibor from the rear, swung him around.

"Hey!" Tibor exclaimed.

"You mind to your business," Klaus warned him. "That bungalow is for rent, and Mr. Gomez needs to rent it. Stop making trouble around here."

"I was only joking."

227

"Then you make jokes in another direction. No need to talk about Omah."

Jennifer stood close beside him now. "Leave him alone, Klaus." Her tone said, "He doesn't know any better."

Tibor strolled off, as Mr. Gomez joined the group.

Jennifer's eyes followed Tibor, and she felt a little sorry for him. Poor fellow . . . he couldn't help it, she guessed. Putting his foot in something every time he turned around. She felt sometimes that maybe they had been a little cruel. He was unhappy here, as they all were, restless and disappointed that it had taken so much longer to sell the raffle tickets than any of them had expected. Even though they had all turned out and sold some for him. Oh, well, they'd soon be rid of him—and he'd probably be just as glad as they were.

"Mrs. Eckert, would you please make the dog to move?"

It was Mr. Gomez, wanting to show Omah's old bungalow, and Schnucki was growling from the steps. Since Omah had gone, Schnucki lay there in front of the door most of every day.

"Here, Schnucki. Come here!"

The jockey and Mr. Gomez went in, came out a few minutes later. They stood on the steps, and the new tenant handed over thirty dollars. Mr. Gomez gave him the key, and went on back up the hill.

The boy went to the car, and opened the door. "Come on, Old Man," he yelled. "We're going to pitch tent here."

He helped his companion out of the car. "Has it got a stove?" the old man trebled. "With an oven?"

The little fellow nodded. "Sure, nice stove," he shrieked.

The boy glanced at Jennifer. She was smiling, trying to

228

make him feel welcome. "The Old Man makes good biscuits, see," he told her. "It's all he can make, but he's kind of particular about the stove."

After he had planted the old man in the house, he came back, threw open the luggage compartment, began to take out some cases and saddles.

"Can I help you?" Klaus asked.

"Sure, if you want."

They worked silently, the boy handing the things out, and Klaus carrying them into the house.

When they had emptied the car, the boy said, "Thanks. My name's Hilary Evans, but you don't need to call me that. I ain't ever called that by nobody except on the racing programs. I'm just the Kid . . . that's what everybody calls me. And him in there—he's just the Old Man."

"Your father?"

"Geez, no. We just travel together."

He threw himself down on the steps, leaned back on his elbows. "Everybody thinks he's my father, but he ain't. He don't mean nothin' at all to me really. Exceptin' once he done me a favor. Got myself cracked up—you know, 'gainst the rail, and no money to pay for the hospital, so he come across and on accounta that I gotta stick to him." He blinked his eyes some more, and then added, "He was a big shot once."

"Yes?"

"Yeah. Had lot of horses one time. Big money. Big name. But now he ain't nothin'. Just the Old Man. He's a problem kind of. It slows a guy up, having to drag him around all the time. I wish he'd die quick, but I guess he ain't gonna. Say, Missus—" He turned to Jennifer. "Guess

I'd better go get some flour and junk so's he can start baking. Is there a store around here?"

"Right down the road. Just turn the corner and go to your left a little."

The Kid rose. He had broken a twig from a bush, now slapped it against his boots, blinked his eyes, looked at Klaus.

"Well, I better get going. Wanna drive over to the store with me, buddy?"

Klaus felt quick pleasure surging to his face. Buddy. The Kid had actually called him "buddy," in the good old American way, just as though he were an American, too.

Jennifer saw his tiny thrill, understood that such things really were thrills. "Of course, he'll go with you. And Klaus, while you're there, get me some carrots. I need them for the meat pie."

They drove off in the Kid's car. Klaus felt already drawn to the Kid in a way he couldn't understand. He stole a look at him, sitting there behind the wheel, sitting high up on a cushion, like an infant. But he didn't talk like an infant. He talked tough, and had a coarse sharp little voice, and Klaus thought that maybe that was what he liked about him. He made him smile inside. The youthful face all screwed up, trying to be forceful as he spoke . . . looking grim and trying to sound brutal, because he was only twenty, and not quite a hundred pounds. Yes, he was amusing.

But there was something else, too. Something very masculine about the Kid, in spite of his doll-like size. Very alive, and lots of bright energy. And these qualities, after a diet of Emil and Duwid, and Siegfried and Hans, all of them languid with their unhappiness—these qualities appealed to him. He had been away from *men* and men's talk so long. All he ever heard here was a wailing When, When, When, like a woman's wail, and he knew that he was just as guilty as the others. But that's what waiting did to you. Vaguely, past scenes and sounds and smells went through his mind. The heavy work-sweat smell in the training gyms. The whine of a supercharger up the hill the big race day in Monte Carlo. The rough talk of the mechanics, and trainers, and all those things that he had forgotten now.

The Kid, this kid, strange as it was, somehow brought it back to him. Because the Kid was talking now of horses, and bankrolls, and guys, and dames, and pool and billiards, mudders, parlays, frame-ups, and so on. Most of what he said was a muddle to Klaus, but he got the tone of it and he liked it. It was a fresh breath to him from another world. A tough world. A man's world.

The Kid enjoyed his own talking so much, and Klaus so enjoyed listening, that after they arrived at Berendo's they just sat in the car and did some more of it.

"Aw, it's a sucker game," said the Kid, while they were still on the subject of betting. "I never bet any more. When I get rid of the Old Man maybe I will, but right now he's a responsibility. And I gotta go easy. If I get a couple a horses to ride every race-day I'll be satisfied."

"But there is only one race-day a week. Only Sunday. How can you make much here?"

"I know. It ain't the best place for a jockey to get rich . . . but well, I gotta take it like it is. If I get three horses every Sunday, and bring one of them in, I can live offa that, and save a little over. That's what I gotta do. See, I gotta get enough money to take the Old Man to Florida. That's

231

where he wants to go and I gotta get him there. Nearly freezes to death out here, the old stinker. Geez, he's a pain to me."

"It's not so cold here for freezing!"

"For you and me, it ain't. But he sure thinks it is. You oughta see him when he gets himself dressed up to go to bed at night. I'll invite you in some night to watch him, just for the laugh. Three sweaters over his pajamas, a scarf around his neck, and one over his head, then over all that he puts his overcoat. Then he climbs in. Then sometimes if there ain't enough blankets, he puts a rug on top of the bed, all over. And then through all that, I *still* hear the old guy squeaking and shivering. He thinks if he gets back to Florida it'll be different. He used to live there when he was younger and he thinks of it like it was home, see."

At that moment a car went by, stopped, backed up, pulled up next to them. Grandotte leaned out of the window.

"Hey, German! I get tired waiting for you."

"Don't bother me any more," Klaus answered.

"But I tell you get stamps from Mr. Klabec. And I mean, when I say! I be there tomorrow . . . and *you have!*" Then he started the car again and drove away.

"What the hell was he shouting off his mouth about?"

"Oh, nothing. He just doesn't like me, and he has a stamp collection. He thinks I get letters from Europe all the time. I used to, sometimes, from friends. But no more. Not since the war."

"Why didn't cha punch him in the puss?"

"I will, if I am not careful."

"What you got to be careful about? You look like you could handle him, even if he is big."

"It is something you would not understand. It is because I do not belong here."

"Where do you belong?"

Klaus tried to laugh. "I do not know myself." And then suddenly he was telling the Kid the whole story. About trying to get into America, and about how he couldn't because of the perjury that they said he did, and how he happened to be here. And he talked quite easily, and found that after all, it was a very simple thing to tell . . . when there was a friend listening.

"Geez," the Kid kept saying. "Geez, no kidding."

The story seemed to astonish him more than anything. "I can't get it through my nut," he said at last, after Klaus had finished. "Since when is it a crime to lie? And I didn't know it was so hard to get into the States. I thought they let everybody in. I knew some Eyetalians, gangsters. They let them in."

"They were just lucky. Some people don't have luck."

"And those other people over there?" The Kid jerked a thumb back toward the colony. "What did they do that keeps them out?"

"Most of them didn't do anything. They just have to wait until their turn comes."

The Kid shook his head. "Just think . . . you dying to get into America, and me all my life dying to get over there and take a squint at Europe! Only last week I was wishing I was bigger so if we get into the war . . . they'd give me a free trip over. But they won't. Not my size. Think America'll go fight you Germans?"

"I don't know. We don't talk so much about the war, in our place. It's more better to forget it."

233

They sat quietly for a while, then the Kid said the Old Man would probably be getting worried, so they'd better get the groceries.

They got out and went into the store. While the Kid was buying his things, Klaus went over to the magazine counter, looked through the movie magazines, found one of Jennifer's articles. Took it over and showed it to the Kid.

"My wife wrote that."

"Yeah? What is it?" The Kid peered close at the magazine, squinted. "She a writer?"

"Well, she doesn't call it writing. It is only about movie stars. When I get in, and get to work, she won't write about movies any more. She wants to write real stories. You know —like they have in the other magazines. That is her ambition. Sit home and write real stories."

"Why don't she do it now?"

"Because it is more easy to sell things about movie stars," Klaus said slowly. "And we have to have the money now." A shadow had spoiled his mood.

The Kid sensed that he had brought up an unwelcome subject. "Say! Wanna buy that magazine? I'll buy it for you!"

Mrs. Berendo stopped rocking, called out, "No buy magazine! Magazine *pilón*. Go on, take it. *Pilón* for you, Klaus, for bringing new customer."

Klaus thanked her, tucked the magazine under his arm.

"Here, bud, give me a lift with these groceries, will ya?"

Klaus grinned. He couldn't help it. Maybe it was foolish . . . but "Here, bud . . . hey, buddy" . . . like one American pal to another . . . it had a wonderful sound!

234

14

THE Filigrana is a somber-brown building, off on one of the sidestreets, built of brick and stone, and seeing it for the first time in innocent daytime, the place looks like a school. Almost any afternoon you'll see a bunch of kids playing and shrieking at baseball, on the open lot to the right of the Filigrana. That's the thing that throws you off. This ball diamond, for the Tijuana youth in that section, looking so much like a school playground, right smack next to the building.

But just step up to the front door, and inside. You'll see you're wrong. The place is what it is, obviously, the moment you enter. Its main foyer hung with large and flagrant oil paintings, all nude women of the old-fashioned fat and vulgar variety. To the left, a long bar; behind it, waxy Japanese barmen. Above the bar, a unique electric board, on which numbers light up, as "visitors" within the far rooms ring for service. Across from the bar, a kind of lounge where several girls sit in waiting. And behind all this, a further larger room known as the "night club" part of the place where, during the evening, customers may dance with the girls, or sit at tables and watch the girls dance with each other. The monotony occasionally relieved by solo fan dancer and castanet clickers.

Even in Tijuana's poor times, about twenty girls in the Filigrana. Girls? Hardly a one of them under thirty-five. Most of them nearer forty. Fat, dowdy, droopy. A few Mexicans, several French women, and the rest Polish or Russian Jewesses. The place has known better days, of course. When Caliente was open. When gambling was going on. They say it was a sight to see then. Beautiful girls. Really *girls*. And, as Tijuana proudly remembers: "Even plenty pretty American girls at the Filigrana then." But not now any more.

Now such a sad state of affairs that a complete summing up of the place may be best revealed in the fact that Tibor Szolnay had only visited it once. And then only for a beer. And where Tibor cannot find a female to rouse his desire, then it is only because there is a considerable lack of what it takes to arouse. He thought the place was hateful. Had a genuine fear of its grabbing, pawing women.

He had gone, that one time, hoping to find Molita, whom he had not quite forgotten. He had not found her. She had worked there at one time, he was told, but they had had to let her go. Too young. Too much competition for the other girls. She was around town somewhere, working "private" now.

After that one visit, Tibor never expected to go back. Yet, on that same Saturday which brought the Kid and the Old Man to Tijuana, there was Tibor, around five o'clock, parking his car at the left side entrance to the Filigrana, and walking back toward a rear door marked "Deliveries."

He entered a narrow dark hallway. Blinked. Tried to accustom his eyes to the dimness. At one end of the hall, a door which he hoped was the one he wanted. He knocked, and a squeaky voice from inside called, *"Pase."*

Inside, two male Japanese playing cards.

"I beg your pardon, but is one of you Mr. Huji Oro?"

"I am, *si*."

"Then I have a note for you."

Mr. Oro put down his cards, passively read the note which Tibor handed him. Then he rose, sucked his breath in through his teeth, and bowed.

"Much pleased. Much pleased. Mrs. Berendo she very fine woman. Any friend of her be fine fellow."

Tibor returned the bow. "Thank you. Then I'll state my business briefly. . . ."

He explained that he was trying to raise money to get out of Tijuana on Wednesday. On Wednesday, a boat sailing from Ensenada for Mazatlán, from where he could get a train to Mexico City—and after Wednesday's sailing, not another boat for a month. He was trying to raffle his car: a hundred and twenty tickets at five dollars apiece. Mrs. Berendo had already sold ninety tickets for him; he was now trying to dispose of the remaining thirty before the raffle on Tuesday. And Mrs. Berendo had suggested—

"That you sell here?" Mr. Oro divined.

"That's right. She said if you knew she was handling it, that—"

"What kind car?"

"You can see it from here, if you'll come to the window."

Mr. Oro moved to the window.

"It's a very good car," Tibor urged him. "Worth at least seven or eight hundred dollars."

The Japanese nodded, went back to his card table. "Okay, you go see girls. And when you through, you come back. Maybe I buy ticket, too. Maybe two, three."

"Thank you."

"You know where find girls? First hall to right. Tell 'em boss say okay."

"Thank you." But Tibor still stood there. Disturbed and hesitant. Mr. Oro had given him permission to canvass his house, but it was not particularly for this that Tibor had sought him out. What he needed most of all was Mr. Oro's protection.

"Mr. Oro, you have been very kind, but I wish you would do me another favor. Would you mind coming with me to see the girls?"

"Why?"

"Well." Tibor managed to laugh boyishly, and with the proper amount of abashment. "Well, you know how it takes a man a long time to get down the length of that hall, what with all the sales talk that each woman gives him! And I don't exactly want to be torn to pieces."

A slight flicker of amusement crinkled the lines around Mr. Oro's eyes.

"Okay, I go."

It was all just as easy, and as successful as Mrs. Berendo had said it would be. "Girls at the Filigrana, they make plenty money; they pay five dollars chance on car easy." With Mr. Oro to hold the women at bay, Tibor sold fourteen tickets there in the hallway, off which the "rooms" opened. A few of the women stood behind Mr. Oro, and tried to entice Tibor, gesturing and moving suggestively, but he pretended not to see, and they soon gave it up. Later, in the front part of the house, he sold raffle tickets to three barmen, and to three more of the girls on duty in the lounge. Mr. Oro also took three tickets.

When he left eventually, it was with a total haul of a hundred and fifteen dollars. In addition, he was also carrying seventy dollars which Mrs. Berendo had advanced to him out of the four hundred and fifty she was holding. In case the plan at the Filigrana fell through, this money was to be for his boat passage.

From the Filigrana, Tibor went directly to the garage where the Ensenada bus was usually quartered. There was no place in Tijuana where he could purchase the boat ticket, but he intended to ask the driver to arrange for his ticket for him the next time the bus went south.

The bus was not there. Still in Ensenada. It wouldn't be back until morning.

During the next hour, Tibor stopped at the cleaner's, had some spots taken off his clothes. Had his shoes shined. Went to the barber's for a shave and a shampoo, stopped at the Foreign Club for a drink, found Siegfried there and offered him one too. Unheard of. But Tibor so recklessly happy at the thought of at last getting away from Tijuana that he didn't care what he did. He even *talked* to Siegfried, which was more important to Siegfried than the drink. . . . Certainly was a shame, Siegfried thought, that just as Tibor was getting so nice to him, he had to go away.

On the way home, an hour later, rounding the curve near the ice house, Tibor saw a large billboard which he hadn't noticed before.

RACING AT CALIENTE
EVERY SUNDAY

A few yards further on, Mrs. Berendo was just closing up shop, waddling off to her car, into which she would have to be hoisted by her sons. Tibor drew up beside her.

"How you make out, Mr. Tibor? I wait for you to come, put money in safe."

"I didn't see Mr. Oro. He wasn't there. They said I'd better come back tomorrow."

"Well, Sunday very good day. After Saturday night, much money at Filigrana. Tomorrow you sell all tickets. You see! Well, *buenas noches*, Mr. Tibor!"

A new excitement in Tijuana. The opening of the races, and the town with the old Sunday blood pouring into it again, as on those few Sundays in summer when there had been the bull fights. Mexican vendors got out their trays and their little straw horses, and clustered around the entrance to the track, and the photographers moved their donkey carts out Caliente way, and set up their cameras.

Not the best season for racing, but the track owners had no choice. In the summer, no hope of competing with Hollywood Park and the other California tracks which drew so many people north from San Diego. Their only chance was winter. But the dreariness and coldness of the weather didn't make any difference to the race fans today. They rolled in from the States in family cars, in coupés, in roadsters, in busses, and loaded in taxis.

Jennifer and Klaus were there, too, because of their new neighbor, the Kid. Also just because the excitement would do them good. The fever of the place, the constant shifting of people from ticket windows to seats and back again, the surge of excitement and noise, the presence of Americans— all brought color to Klaus's face, brightness to his eyes. Jennifer watched him; she felt gratefulness for his pleasure.

They were leaning against the fence which separates the grandstand section, where they were, from the more expensive clubhouse, looking across into that restricted region; so attractive with its tables, there on the stone terrace; its bright umbrellas like multi-colored giant mushrooms. But no envy. Not wishing they were there. Just happy enough to be here at all.

Jennifer smiled as her eyes caught sight of Tibor. Strutting up and down in front of the clubhouse, looking like a million dollars. Pausing before the bookies' stand, to survey the betting odds importantly.

"Will you look at that? Tibor. Showing off, pretending he has money to bet. See him, Klaus?"

Klaus shuddered, turned away. "No! And I do not want to. Why for should I look on anything to remember me of the colony? That is why I like it here. I feel *away*. Oh, Jennifer, Muschi, isn't it beautiful?"

Jennifer gazed off into the distance. To the left, the purple mountains. To the right, rolling meadows and pasture fields. Looking away from the track, no sign of civilization within eye's scope, except the picturesque stables seen beyond the track, directly on the other side.

"Beautiful," she agreed.

"Oh, I do not mean that!" seeing where her eyes had taken her. "This, right here." He gestured toward the milling people. "That—" he pointed to a couple eating hot

241

dogs. "That—" an old man scratching his head as he pored over a racing form. "That and that and that." All homely everyday sights at any race track. "Jennifer, I get so lonesome for crowds, I cannot tell you."

"Yes, you can. I know." He had been brought up on crowds. She forgot it sometimes but remembered it now. Contact with swirling life; that's what he needed.

"When you are here, anyway, I never complain," he told her. "Right now I am so happy as any man can ever be."

His happiness lasted for perhaps five minutes.

It was nearly post time for the fourth race. The Kid was riding. They raced to the paddock to wave and wish him luck. They hurried back to find a spot at the rail near the finish post. They pushed in through the crowd, elbowing and shoving, like the rest of the people.

Klaus was pushing against a big uniform, and the uniform turned. A handsome brand-new uniform, and the badge on the cap and the one at the belt shining and bold. But the face an ugly leer of importance.

"Oh, it's you," Klaus laughed, as he recognized that face. But even Grandotte could not spoil his mood today. "Why for the fancy uniform?"

"I chief private policeman here now. I important."

"Sure, I know. But move over, will you? Let my wife in here. We have a friend riding."

"What friend you got?" the Mexican jeered. "You no got friends. They no let *you* in the United States even!"

Klaus let it pass. But he was white. "Come on, Jennifer. We find a place farther down."

"You scared, huh? I policeman. You scared now." He was rocking back on his heels, his thumbs tucked in his belt.

242

Klaus hesitated. His face went even whiter than before. Then he struck him. Grandotte sprawled back. He reached for his gun. Klaus kicked it out of his hand.

There were two other uniforms handy. They had been standing close behind Klaus, waiting just for this. They seized his arms from the rear, pinned them back.

Two minutes later he was thrown against the cement floor of the small cell under the grandstand. The door clanged shut with a steely sound. He jumped up, banged on the door, kicked and pounded with a vigor that was terrifying to the people outside. The pent-up strength of many months beating itself out there. The darkness maddened him, the locked door maddened him, the sounds of people moving about in the grandstand above were like close thunder and hurt his ears.

Angel Saravan strolled out from his office under the stairs. "What the hell is going on here?"

He had heard the fracas and had come out to find a group of curious people standing around, staring at a door against which some wild thing was banging. When people stand around they don't bet, and when people don't bet, Angel loses money. So Angel was concerned.

He turned to Grandotte. "Can't you break this up? What's the row?"

"Somebody hit me. I put him in jail."

"So what? Break up that crowd."

The pounding at the door had grown worse. Angel frowned. "God's sake, make him stop that racket!"

"He won't," said a frightened voice at his side. "Are you the manager here?"

"Not exactly." Angel jerked his head in the direction of the cell. "Does that in there belong to you?"

Jennifer nodded. "Please let him out. Please!"

Every blow at the door stung her flesh, made her quiver. Her eyes were wide and moist, and perspiration rimmed her mouth.

"Don't worry, he can't keep that up for long."

"Yes, he can. You don't know. Please make Grandotte go away, then let him out." She was almost crying.

Angel turned to Grandotte, and demanded the key. Stubbornly the Mexican shook his head. "I chief here. I send for police wagon."

"Cut it. You can't make a regular arrest here. You're only a track policeman. Come on now, do as I say, or I'll see you're fired."

Disgustedly Grandotte tossed him the key, then quickly lost himself in the crowd.

Angel turned and faced the gallery. "Look, people, I'd like to let this man out. I can't do it with all of you standing around. Move back, please."

They gave a little. Pretended to walk away. Then stood still again.

"Get away from here!" Jennifer shrieked in sudden nervous exasperation. Little wildcat, yelling.

There was laughter, giggling.

"Go on, all of you!"

Angel touched her arm. "Here now, girl, what's the matter? What's got you so frightened? He wasn't drunk, was he?"

She was unable to talk. The crying catching up with her.

"Hurt?"

244

"No." But there was no actual sound to the word. Only breath blown out through a round mouth.

"Here, you can open the door yourself."

As she worked the key in the lock: "Sh-h-h, darling, sh-h-h," she kept saying to herself. Knew he couldn't hear. But suddenly he was quiet anyway. The sound of the key had stilled him.

She opened the door. "Klaus, it's me."

He stood there with blood streaming from his nose. Women screamed.

"Are you all right?" she asked fearfully. She knew that his real hurt was one she couldn't see. The sharp pain of embarrassment hidden inside.

"I'm fine," he said coldly. But he didn't look at her. He was looking for Grandotte.

Then abruptly she was against his body, her arms around him.

He set her aside. "Where is that Mexican?"

Angel stepped forward. "Hello, I'm Angel Saravan. Grandotte's gone. Let's go into my office. You know, you made quite a racket in there!"

"I don't like to be locked up," Klaus told him succinctly.

"Don't blame you. But come on now, please. . . . I want to get that blood off your face."

Klaus, immobile for another full minute, warily scanning the crowd.

"He's not here, really. He's not going to hurt you," Angel told him.

A grim smile. "No, he is not." Klaus turned then, walked beside Jennifer, followed Angel into his office.

245

When the door was shut, there was a moment's silence. Angel sensed that between these two there was a problem more complicated than the simple facts he saw on the surface. The young man had had an argument with the track policeman, a fight, and the Mexican had locked him up. But so what? A usual race track happening. If things like that didn't happen, there would be no need for those cozy steel-and-cement cubbyholes which every race track harbored somewhere in its entrails. Yet in this there was some dramatic undercurrent he couldn't understand.

"You promised me you wouldn't," the girl scolded sadly. "Oh, Klaus, why couldn't you have held on to yourself! He had it all planned, and you did exactly what he wanted you to do. I'm frightened. What's going to happen next?"

They were quiet then, just looking at each other. Angel moved over to the wash basin, ran the cold water, soaked a towel in it. Took it back, handed it to the girl. The young man took it out of her hands, applied the towel himself. When he had cleared most of the blood from his face, he handed the towel back to Saravan.

Then at last the young man touched the girl. "Jennifer, don't be frightened. It will be all right. Only they cannot forever treat me bad because I am a foreigner and an immigrant. I am sorry. I will not do it again. I will promise you. I will keep out of his way, and if he will keep from me, it will be all right. Only it is such a sorry, Jen—we will never be able to come back to enjoy the races and the people again."

She slipped into his arms. He held her quietly.

"I can almost feel you unwind," she whispered.

He kissed her on the cheek. "Come on, Muschi. I guess we have to go home."

At the door they turned, said, "Good-by, and thank you."

Angel was pleasantly surprised . . . he was sure they had forgotten he was there.

15

TIBOR disposed of Siegfried, that evening, by taking him to the movies. For ten minutes they sat side by side in the crowded, chirping Sentor, watching an early picture of the Hardy series. Then abruptly Tibor clicked his fingers as though he had just remembered something. What he had remembered, he said, was Irmgard. He had promised to take her to the movies tonight. He'd have to go back for her.

Siegfried was dismayed; might have known something like this would spoil his evening.

"We'll probably have to sit in the back," Tibor told him. "But look for us after the show is over."

From the Sentor, Tibor drove to Funcke's gasoline station; had the car filled with gas and oil. From there he drove home, parked at the rear of Casa Six, went in the back way.

There wasn't much to pack, and it didn't take him long. When he had closed the suitcases, he placed them on the bedroom floor near to the rear window, made sure that both window and screen were unlocked. Then he went out the front door and down the drive to Casa One.

Irmgard was waiting for him. He knew she would be. And he didn't want her to wait. Hanging around, looking out the windows.

"Sorry, but the movies are off. I haven't any money. I'm broke until the raffle on Tuesday."

"You're broke?" An odd expression crossed her face.

"Not a dime."

"Oh." She hesitated a moment. "Well, come in anyway . . . please."

"For a minute maybe . . . but I want to get to bed early."

He flopped down on the couch. She came over, sat beside him. Her gaze strange, close, and solemn.

"Why do you lie to me, Tibor? You had lots of money last night. Remember when you asked for a cigarette? I looked in your coat pocket. There was something else in the pocket, too. A whole round lump of it."

"Oh, that! Sure. That was my boat money. I sent it down with the bus driver tonight . . . to Ensenada . . . to get my ticket."

"The bus didn't come back from Ensenada today."

"Oh, yeah? What makes you say that?"

"Mrs. Berendo told me. There was an accident or something. Why do you lie about that, too?"

He rose up on his elbows. "For Christ sake, what's getting into you?"

"You can't fool me, Tibor. You still have the money."

"That's what you say!"

"I know what happened. You got money from Mrs. Berendo for your boat ticket. And then you went to the races. Chato saw you, and Klaus and Jennifer. And Chato said you were cashing and winning lots of money. So now you're rich and you are going to leave. You aren't going to wait for the raffle even."

"You're crazy." He laid back and tried to get away from her eyes. But there was nowhere to look. In one direction, only the wall very close. In the other, only Irmgard blocking the room. And her eyes boring into him. "You're crazy," he repeated, because her solemnity and her silence aggravated him. "Where in the hell would I leave to? How would I get out of this dump except by boat? You know I don't have any visa."

"You could go the same way you came in," she reminded him quietly. "Over the Criminal Trail. Is that what you're planning?"

"I'm not planning anything. Why should I?"

"I've heard you say lots of times you could probably get more money for the car in Mexicali. And if you thought— well, if you thought you could get away without having any trouble with me . . ."

"What are you getting at?" He asked it crossly, but he was wary. A small fright on his face. "What the hell kind of trouble would I have with you?"

"Tibor, you have to take me with you." Her words were heavy and hung like smoke in the room. There was a long pause.

"*Have* to?" he asked finally.

"No. I don't mean that. Once I planned to tell you I was going to have a baby. But I don't have the heart for it now. I only mean that I am begging you, please—for once do a kind and good thing in your life, take me away from this place. Because I can't stand it any more."

There was something about her mood, her dead calm, that held him in a vise. If she had been hysterical and fluttery, he would have known how to handle her. A few embraces, tears calmed. But this. Sitting so still, talking so quietly.

"You were afraid of this, weren't you?" she questioned. "Afraid I'd ask you. You've dreaded it all along. Then luck brought you a chance to escape it. You should have left right from the race track, Tibor. But now, with your lies, you gave me a chance to know. I don't love you, Tibor. It's not that. Only I have to get away from here. Please take me. Whenever you go. Is it tonight, Tibor? I feel it."

There was only one thing he could think to do. "Poor Irmgard," he said. Then he put his hand on her head, drew her head toward him against his shoulder. He was not inspired to do this because of sympathy—but only because he was muddled and couldn't concentrate with her eyes upon him. Against his body, he could be rid of her for a moment. Rid of her to think.

And what he thought was that it was a damned nuisance. Irmgard suspicious. Now she would watch his every move. Make the others watchful, too. God damn it. He could lie, of course, insist that he was not leaving until Wednesday— promise to take her with him then. But it wouldn't save the situation. He *must* get away tonight, without anyone knowing. And how could he now—with her hawk eyes peering into the darkness? She had guessed wrong about the money, of course. But wrong or right, she had put him in a spot. How, now, to get out of it?

Then suddenly it seemed simple. Tell her he'd take her to Mexico City, start off with her, but leave her in Mexicali. "Irmgard, are you sure you want to go?"

"Oh, yes!" Her head bobbed up. Her eyes wide and imploring.

251

"All right. It's okay with me. But we'll have to hurry."

It was a moment before he could push her away from him. Clutching him, thanking him, assuring him that he would never be sorry.

"Now stop," he ordered, finally. "There isn't much time. Get packed."

She moved toward the door. "I want to tell Klaus and Jennifer."

"No!" He was so emphatic that she was startled. "There isn't time. I want to leave right now. So we can get to Mexicali by morning . . . sell the car and get on that morning plane. We'll have to take the plane as far as Guadalajara. It's the only way to get out of there."

"You mean—not to say good-by to anybody?" she queried slowly.

"That's right. There's nobody I want to say good-by to."

"But Tibor!"

"That's the way I feel."

"How about Mrs. Berendo? The boat money? The money she advanced?"

"I saw her. I gave it back. She's going to return all the raffle money tomorrow. Now look, if you want to hang around, you just say so. But I'm leaving. You're not the only one who has had enough of this place. I want to get out of here!"

"All right, Tibor." And she hurried to pack.

It was nine-thirty by the time they got away. Irmgard still disturbed by the secrecy of their departure. Tibor insisted on quiet . . . insisted that she bring her bags out the back way, after he had driven the car around to her rear door. She looked back toward the Eckerts'.

252

"Oh, Tibor, they'll be so hurt. It seems so awful not to say good-by."

"When you travel with me, you'll learn not to worry about other people. It slows you up. Are you ready?"

"Yes." She settled the small bag on the ledge behind the seat.

They drove swiftly for the first ten miles, until the trail began to lead them up into the mountains. It was an unpleasant night. A fine drizzle in the air. Not really rain. But threatening. Cold and damp, and pitch black. And the road twisting and curving. The earth under the tires slushy and slippery-smooth.

"Tibor, suppose it rains, and we don't get through? Maybe we should have waited until morning."

He was having difficulty with the road. "I'd appreciate it if you'd be quiet."

Irmgard began to be nervous. Not because of the bad road and the night. Now that the excitement of leaving had passed, she was beginning to think and wonder. Doubts in her mind. When Tibor had first come to her door, an hour or so before, his odd manner, his lies, had made her suspicious of the thing she feared: that if he had the chance he would try to get away without saying good-by to her. And yet even after he had agreed to take her, he had continued to be nervous and hurried. And why? He had given reasons at the time. But now it occurred to her that there must have been something else. And the only answer she could find was that Tibor had not returned the boat money to Mrs. Berendo. He had lied about that too. She should have recognized the lie, but in her own eagerness to get away she had let it slide.

253

She tried to let it slide again, now, but the thought drove along with them for miles and miles. Eventually it grew loud and bothersome in her mind.

"Tibor, there is something I have to ask. You didn't return the money to Mrs. Berendo, did you?"

The concern in her voice annoyed him, aggravated him. So puritanical and scolding. It made him feel like being cruel to her. They were far enough on their way now; he could safely be so. He told her the truth. Told it proudly.

"Of course, I didn't. I couldn't."

He could sense her disapproval. It both peeved and delighted him. It spurred him on.

"You flattered yourself that you were the reason I wanted to sneak out. A scene with you wouldn't have bothered me. I've left women crying behind me before."

"How much money did you get from her?" she asked quietly.

"Seventy dollars."

"And for seventy dollars, you would make a bad name for yourself? Be a stealer?"

"Oh, don't hand me that. It was only gambling money." Then suddenly he was tempted to tell her more. "You think I have money." He laughed nervously. "I don't. I have two dollars. I lost a hundred and eighty bucks at that damned race track."

"You lost? I don't understand."

"It's very simple." Quickly he reviewed his afternoon. Good luck on the first two races, but by the tenth and last race he was down to forty-five dollars. It was a quinella race and he thought he could recoup. Those quinellas. All you have to do is pick two horses, and if they're the first two to the finish line, you clean up. The betting somewhat like the daily double . . . a pool . . . so that sometimes it pays a couple hundred dollars. He had bought ten different combinations, put four dollars on each. Thought sure he'd get his losses back. He hadn't.

She waited until he had finished, went back and picked up what he had first said.

"A hundred and eighty dollars. Where did you get all of that?"

"I sold some tickets at the Filigrana. Be upset about it if you want. I'm not. A bunch of whores. What do I care if they don't get their money?"

"Tibor, Mrs. Berendo will have to give it back. Haven't you thought of that? All the people that you've stolen from, they'll make Mrs. Berendo pay what you've taken. And if she doesn't pay, they won't go to her store. Nobody will. She'll be ruined."

"I can't worry about that. All I know is I'd have been a chump to hang around for the raffle—get only three hundred and eighty dollars for the car. That's all that Mrs. Berendo's got left for me now. I'll sell it for much more in Mexicali."

"Unless the police catch up with you."

"They won't. They're not even going to come after me. You forget. A raffle is only a gamble, and gambling isn't legal in Mexico. Nobody will dare make a fuss!"

"Except what they'll do to Mrs. Berendo."

Tibor laughed again. He laughed over the wheel, staring ahead into the darkness.

The car careened around a sharp bend. Skidded into a hole. The tires spun ineffectually for a moment, then the car pulled out, jerked on. Tibor continued to laugh.

255

Irmgard could see that he was on edge. Nervous, obviously frightened. She was quite apart from him, though. . . . The car, the road, the trip. Thinking about poor Mrs. Berendo. Then her own misery crept into her consciousness again, and suddenly she felt a desire to be like Tibor. She wanted very much not to care. Not to think of others. Nobody had thought very much about her, so why should she worry? This, at least, was a chance to get away. Make herself cruel and selfish, just as Tibor was. Mrs. Berendo would believe that she had been in on the plan with Tibor . . . believe her to be just as dishonest as he was. They'd all think that. They'd all hate her. All of them there at the colony. "But I don't care. I don't care. I'm going to get away," she kept telling herself.

Annoyingly, past scenes came back to her. Things she hadn't thought much about at the time, but which were all too clear now. The time Jennifer had brought her pumpernickel. How sweet Blima had always been . . . (and Blima soon to have a baby). The way Mady once had said that she (Irmgard) was as beautiful as the sun. She wasn't beautiful, of course. She knew that. But her hair was like the sun sometimes, that was true. And the time Ani had brought her soup when she was sick. And Siegfried. And Klaus. The Klaus-thought hurt the most. The way she had always admired him; he'd know she was trash now.

But what good were sentiments? She fought them off. Wanted very much to believe that in escape there should never be any looking back. Tibor was quiet now, driving fiercely.

"Tibor, I've been treated so bad. Why should I care what happens? If you'll still take me to Mexico City."

"That's right. Glad you're getting on to yourself. Got a handkerchief, or something?"

"Why?"

"It's fogging up in here. Wipe the windshield on the inside."

After that, for the next few miles, there was harmony for a change. The harmony that sometimes exists between accomplices.

Then suddenly an electric thought shocked her into sitting up straight. Every sense alert and live.

"Tibor! My quota number!"

The idea swept quickly through her mind. Suppose her number would come, and in the meantime the consul should find out about this. Sneaking away under these conditions: immoral, dishonest.

"Tibor, I've got to go back, or I'll never get my visa."

"Oh, you and your goddamned visa."

"Take me back, *please*."

"Shut up. You can have your case transferred to some other consul."

"The report would be the same. I would ruin my chances. I've got to go back."

"We're not going. I can't chance it now. It's too late."

"Then stop and let me out. I'll go myself!"

"You've lost your mind."

"Let me out." Her voice had risen. She sounded panicky, wild. She reached for her luggage.

"Sit still. You can't walk from here!"

"Yes, I can. I've got to. And we're so far away, it's safe for you. It'll take me a long time back. Tibor, stop!" She had put a hand on his arm. Shook him.

He had to stop. It was dangerous to go on. He couldn't drive with her clutching him like that.

She hopped out, drew the large heavy suitcase and the small light one after her. He let her do it because he figured she was right: he could get to Mexicali long before she could walk the long miles back to Tijuana. He was safe.

"Aren't you frightened?" he asked. It was so bleak and lonely along the road. He felt a little sorry. But it was better this way. He wouldn't have to ditch her later. Be saved the bother of that.

"Good-by, Tibor."

"Good-by." And he drove on.

After he had disappeared, and when she could no longer even hear the sound of the car, standing there in the midst of that gray drizzle-fog, she realized that she was frightened, after all. There was a faint moon now, trying to reach its light to her, but the air so thick and damp that it couldn't quite get through. She felt the mountains on either side of her. Great dark staring mountains. And the high ridge of the road under her feet, moist and sloppy. But it was no good, just standing still. She had to get going. Start walking. Keep to the high ridge in the road, make her feet go forward. At least, it was downhill. That was something.

For one instant, the thought: Maybe she had been a fool. Maybe she should have gone on with Tibor. But that passed. The thought of America, and of Tom, loomed up again, and gave her courage. Odd, how she thought of him again, now. When he had been such a disappointment. But still the hope that it would turn out all right. She had waited so long, it would be silly to give up now. As she walked, his face and name again a part of her.

The air moistened her clothes. Chilled her clear through. She transferred the suitcases, back and forth, from one arm to the other. Tried to keep her ankles from turning over. Plodded on. Keep going. Keep walking. Don't think at all, except about moving.

She began to sing. A dismal little voice. Some marching song that she remembered from Germany. She didn't realize that it was the marching song of the Hitler youth. Nor did it matter.

Irmgard had walked thus for perhaps an hour—when Tibor came back down the road and picked her up.

That made her cry.

"I couldn't get through," he told her. "There was a tree across the road, and I couldn't move it. Sit quiet now. And stop crying."

But she couldn't stop. She was so cold and shivery and re-lieved. She edged closer to him. He pushed her away.

"Don't get the wrong idea. I didn't come back because of you. Not for you, or Mrs. Berendo, or anything. Just the tree, understand. Here, help me out of my coat."

"I don't want your coat, Tibor."

"You're going to take it," he stated crossly.

He made her take off hers, and put his on. "It would be nice if you got pneumonia, wouldn't it?"

She knew it wasn't a tree that had brought him back. She knew he had been scared for her. She knew, because he was so belligerent.

The raffle was held on Tuesday, as scheduled, and the car was won by Dr. Pareira's brother. Tibor had phoned down to Ensenada to reserve passage. Tuesday night he left on the bus. Three hundred and fifty dollars in his pocket. The other thirty dollars he had paid to Mrs. Gomez, for Irmgard. For her rent.

After he had gone, Emil said, "I think perhaps, if he not go away so soon, and he stay in exile here more longer, we maybe could make a more good man of him. Do you not think so, Ani?"

"He did learn to knock on doors," Ani admitted.

"And he was not so bad to me either, more lately," Siegfried offered.

And so it went, all around the group. Blima recalling how he had improved about the garbage. It made them laugh to remember how arrogant he had been at first . . . refusing to go near the garbage heap . . . how he had tried to get Mady to take his pail out for him, until Jennifer discovered him. They laughed, too, and snorted, about the coffee. That day Klaus had run into him when he was at Berendo's, and had reminded him he'd better buy some. But American coffee was expensive at Berendo's. Tibor had taken one look at the price, "Oh, no, I don't drink coffee any more. It's bad for my nerves!" Oh, what a cheapskate.

"But anyway, he got to be rather thoughtful about giving us rides into town," Maria remembered.

Yes—the trouble was, they all agreed, that he was just vain and conceited and naturally cheap—but if they could have worked on him longer, they believed they might have overcome that.

"What do you think, Irmgard? Do you say it also?"

Irmgard gulped. Her heart too full, and suddenly too lonely, to speak.

16

SITTING in the Congressman's office one November morning, Jennifer looked around at those who were waiting with her, tried to imagine what in the world they were doing in this particular office. She was so used to waiting for people—for stars mostly, on sets, in studio dining rooms, and in Dressing Room Row—that she had learned to wait graciously. Never occupied herself with tapping feet, or twiddling thumbs, but twiddled only her mind—and most often over the human life which she observed around her. In the studios, she could guess about people, and know that her guesses were usually right. That young man over there, a trade-paper space salesman . . . this young girl, a stock player. That man with the "air," a technical adviser. And so on. It was easy, because they were all familiar. But she had never been in a Congressman's office before. This morning she could get nowhere in her mind about this strange medley of people, who ranged around the room in the following order:

Next to her, an insignificant little man with a big brief case.

Beyond him, a tall boney woman, with a corsage of artificial violets on the lapel of a shiny black suit.

Across the room, a stringy-haired girl of nineteen or

twenty. A young boy with her. Both of them pale, under-fed, and poorly dressed. The boy chewed his nails. The girl slapped his hand, then in the same gesture affectionately smoothed a dangling lock back from his forehead.

On the settee next to them, two repulsive-looking men. Checkered suits, flashy stick-pins, and derbies. Large noses and drooping underlips. The nose and the lip of one on a grander scale than the nose and lip of the other—and he, obviously, the leader of the two.

Then, next to Jennifer, and by far the nicest-looking person in the room, the tall handsome boy, who had given her his chair when she entered. He was standing now near the window. Neat blue suit. High stiff white collar. Nervous. Turning his hat in his hand. As Jennifer watched, he spit on his finger, leaned down and applied the spittle to a small spot on his gleaming polished shoes. He looked up. Saw her smile. Blushed, turned away, pretended interest in the blank wall outside the window.

Jennifer was curious. Couldn't place any of them. Couldn't figure their association with the Congressman, and it bothered her. She supposed, too, that she would never know; assumed that when the Congressman was ready to see them, each in turn would disappear into the inner office to state his business.

But it was not to work out that way.

When the Congressman entered the room at long last, the tableau of those who waited came to life. Especially the young man in blue. He straightened, increased his height by two inches. Chest out. Stiff attention. His body snapped, actually made a clicking noise. Everyone turned to look at him for a moment. Then heads re-turned and faced the Congressman.

A thin little man with a thin nose, and thin brown hair—the long side-parts brushed across the top of his head to try to hide his baldness.

"Who's first?" Thin, high-pitched voice.

The giant underlip started to rise. "My name is Lemuel. I—"

But the woman with the violets sprang between them. "I'm first!" She looked toward the private office beyond; expected that the Congressman would invite her in there.

"Speak up, please, I don't have much time. I have to be out of here by twelve-thirty."

The woman glanced at the clock. It was after twelve now. Again she looked toward the private door.

"Go on, please. What is it?"

His hurried manner made her nervous. Also he had a peculiar way of leaning toward her. He was slightly deaf and his straining ear was planted dangerously close to her bosom . . . her height having at least fourteen inches the advantage of his.

"My name is Mrs. Fishbein. I'm secretary of the Neighborhood Improvement Guild."

"The *what* guild? You'll have to speak more plainly."

This only added to her confusion. The speech that she had planned drifted away.

"Oh, here." She reached in her bag and handed him a letter.

Congressman Hurlich read the letter. Told her that he appreciated the invitation, but would have to consult his calendar and write her about it. "Only a few weeks before

Congress convenes again, you know—and I'm very busy. But thank you for coming in."

After she had gone, "Next, please?"

Again the giant underlip: "Congressman, my name is—"

But this time it was the little man with the brief case who bobbed up, and superseded Mr. Lemuel.

"Joe's office sent me over with some more data on that Merton bill. It's in here." He tapped the case, thrust it in the Congressman's hand. "He told me to leave the whole thing, 'cause he says if you have something to carry it handy in, maybe *this* time you'll take it to Washington and take care of it. Not forget it like last time."

"Joe *did*, huh," the Congressman murmured.

"Yes." And so saying, the little diplomat *sans portefeuille* hastened out, leaving Mr. Hurlich to stare after him crossly.

It was now Lemuel's true turn, but suddenly he seemed not to want to avail himself of it. "Too public in here, Mr. Hurlich. I'll wait and speak wit chou privately later, if you don't mind."

The young man at the window was struggling forward. He tripped over Jennifer's chair, tripped again over a wrinkle in the rug. His face and neck crimsoned.

"I'm Emery Stanton, sir." He drew himself up tall again.

"I didn't get you."

"Emery *Stanton*, sir."

"So?"

"It's about that appointment. Don't you remember? I wrote you."

"I can't carry all my correspondence in my mind."

"About the appointment to West Point, sir."

"Oh." The Congressman smiled. Now he understood the

264

boy's exaggerated pose of "attention." He looked aloft, the
entire length of that noble young figure. "I remember now,
but you didn't send me enough recommendations. It'll take
more than an ability to look good in a uniform, you know.
I'll tell you what you do, son. Give your name to my secretary again. I'll see exactly what other letters I need and
write you."

"Thank you, sir. Good-by, sir."

The Congressman caught Jennifer's eyes . . . and he ex-
changed a smile with her. Both sharing the same thought
. . . the hope that the boy would get there. Nice boy. Shy
boy. And so eager.

For a second, it took Jennifer's mind off her own uncom-
fortableness; a respite in which she forgot to be frightened
of the moment when she would have to stand on her feet
and blurt out her heart. As Mr. Lemuel had pointed out, it
was rather public.

The stringy-haired girl arose. With dignity and calm,
walked toward the Congressman. "It's about my dad," she
began. "His name is Nicholas Bremecelli. They're going to
deport him next month . . . unless you can help me."

Jennifer's interest shot forward. The girl speaking so
simply; but underneath, a tragic undercurrent.

"Did you go to the Labor Department over in the Federal
Building?"

"Yes, sir, but they sent me to you."

"Well, what's the case?"

"Well, you see, sir, my dad is here illegal. He came here
first twenty-five years ago, with my mother. And we were
all born here. This is one of my brothers—" nodding down
at the boy. "There are six of us altogether. All American

265

citizens. But my dad never took out his papers. Neither did my mother, only it wouldn't matter about her, anyway. She's dead now. Since last year."

"Go on, please." The Congressman's voice was kind.

"Well, about the story is that my dad went back to Italy . . . while he was there, there was that Ethiopia war, remember? My dad didn't want to go to that war. He wanted to come back to us. He is a very good dad to us, I want you to understand that—and he thought maybe if he had to go to war, he might be killed. Then he couldn't take care of us. So he came back anyway."

" 'Anyway'? You mean he didn't have a visa to come back?"

"That's right." She nodded matter-of-factly. "No visa. So he sneaked in through Mexico. But a couple of years ago, they caught him and deported him back to Mexico again. He was there for more'n two years. Then when he heard Mamma died, he couldn't stand it any more, thinking how alone we were. So he came back again."

"The same way?" The Congressman asked, shock in his voice.

"Yes, sir."

"Well! Your father must know a pretty good hole in the fence!"

"Yes, he does, sir. But then you see, they caught him again. Just a couple of months ago. Now they got him locked up. And please, don't you see . . . all his trouble is only because he wanted to be a good dad to us. He's never done anything really wrong. Of course—"

She shifted from one foot to the other: "Of course, well, there *was* some other trouble."

266

"Something *else?*"

"Yes, in a way, sort of—my dad has a record against him. But he served his time! He paid his debt, like they say. And anyway, it was a long time ago, during prohibition. A liquor charge. But you can understand, can't you? He had to make a living somehow."

The Congressman looked down, put his hands in his pocket. "It's quite a case, my dear girl. What do you expect me to do?"

"Isn't there some rule, about if a man has lived in the United States for seven years, he's allowed some kind of forgiveness?"

"I don't know. Have to look into it. First, you'd better bring me some letters from people who know your father and would like to see him helped. I can't promise you any success. But I can try."

"We are very worried. Next month is awful close. And my dad is very important to us."

"Yes, I know."

"Well. Thank you then. We'll bring the letters. Goodby." She gave the boy a tug, "Come on, Nicky"—and they went out.

This recital had not only engrossed Jennifer. It encouraged her. If there was any hope for "Dad"—and the Congressman hadn't entirely washed his hands of it—then there was certainly hope for Klaus. And also the girl's sweet brave dignity had given her inspiration to speak up with the same unabashment. The girl hadn't been embarrassed—no matter what her father had done.

The Congressman was looking at Jennifer now. She rose

and stepped forward. "Congressman Hurlich, my name is Jennifer Eckert. I wrote you in Washington about my husband. He's German. I am trying to get him into the United States. He was denied a visa because they say he admitted perjury. Do you remember?"

"In Tijuana? Is that the case?"

"Yes. I'm asking for permission to have him reapply. You wrote that you would help me."

"I don't believe they'll permit it. I've already spoken to the department. I saw them just the week before I left."

"Oh, Mr. Hurlich—"

"I know it's bad news—but you must try to understand. With so many worthy cases on hand, you can't expect them to go back and reopen a case where they've already found a fraud."

"But there *isn't* any fraud . . . and worthy! My heavens, Mr. Hurlich . . . if you only knew how worthy it is. If we could only sit down, if you could give me fifteen minutes or so, and I could tell you the whole story. I'm sure you'd see then that something has to be done. There's been a dreadful mistake somewhere. . . . Couldn't you . . . ?"

He glanced at the clock. Her spirit sagged.

"I want to hear the story, really I do. I want to help. But unfortunately, I have an appointment now, and it's after office hours. Couldn't you come back next week? No, not next week. I'll be out of town. But suppose you write me a letter outlining the whole case. Have it on my desk for me when I come back. Then after I've had a chance to look it over . . ."

Jennifer tilted her head forward, fumbled at her handbag.

"Oh, now, look here!" Congressman Hurlich peeked under her hat, saw her distress. "You mustn't be upset. It won't do any good for us to talk now, anyway. I don't go back to Washington until the end of December. There'll be time to go into it thoroughly before then. Please now, you mustn't be discouraged. These things take a long time. But they usually work out."

"It's been so long already."

"Sometimes it takes years."

A new face and voice entered the picture. "Buck up, kid!" Mr. Lemuel said, close to Jennifer's ear.

Jennifer turned, stared at him vacantly. He grinned. A flabby, quivering grin. His eyes were drooling. "What did a pretty girl like you want to go and marry a furriner for, anyway?" Then he glanced at the Congressman. "That's what she gets, ain't it? When there are so many good Americans around like me and you, huh? Eh, Cap?" He winked.

Jennifer looked past him to the Congressman. "I'll write you the whole case, Mr. Hurlich. Good-by, and thank you."

She raced out. In the hallway was unable to see through her tears. Poked around blindly for the elevator button.

Following this interview, Jennifer was panicky. Oh, of course, the Congressman wanted to help. She didn't doubt that. But now she knew what brought people to Congressmen's offices. All of them wanting something, each pressing a problem upon him. She had only seen a brief half hour of it, but every day it must be like that. People asking please, please. And how could he help everybody?

In the clear thinking that followed the tears, Jennifer decided that from now on she was not going to depend on anybody. Only on herself. Finished with letters and long-distance begging, and with lawyers, and consuls. Finished, too, with really counting on the Congressman. From this moment on, she knew there was only one thing to do. Get to Washington and plead her case face to face with the controller of her destiny.

It wasn't going to be easy. Easy after she got there maybe. But to get there. It involved more than train-fare. When she went she'd have to be prepared to stay several weeks. Had to work hard and fast now. Secure new assignments. Write and sell the stories and get the checks in fast.

The whole of that afternoon she spent "covering the studios." This was the part of her work which took the most time, involved the most endurance. Chasing around to publicity departments, talking to contact people. Trying to dig up facts, or fancied facts, about the stars. Hoping to find good angles for stories. A most important part of her work, because it was from these story angles, sent off to the magazines, that the assignments eventually came.

Her work hadn't been going well the last months. She knew it. Klaus and their troubles always on her mind. Her volume falling off. There had been a time when she was known as the fan-magazine writer who sold every article she wrote. But now half of what she wrote came back. This was not only a pinch in the pocketbook, but a blot on her standing at the studios. In the past, publicity departments would serve up almost any star to her, confident that Jennifer would turn the star's time and talk into important, profitable space in some magazine. But interviews had missed fire lately. On this particular afternoon, she ran into two unpleasant reminders of it.

First at RKO: "Jennifer, what happened to that article

on Ginger Rogers? Remember? 'Ginger's Path to Freedom'?"

"*Modern Screen* sent it back."

"Have you tried it some place else? I don't like to nag you . . . but you know what trouble I had to arrange that. . . . Ginger is hard to get to. Let me know if you get it planted."

"I will."

Then later at Metro: the same thing all over again about a story on Hedy Lamarr.

There was a little more hope about this one. Jennifer had sent it off on its second trip to *Picture Screen* just a few weeks before. And they hadn't yet sent it back.

"I guess it means they're going to take it."

But when she arrived back at the apartment at dinner time, there was a large bulky envelope in the mail box. The Lamarr manuscript, and a note from the editor, attached: "I do need a story on Hedy, but for some reason, this doesn't have the stuff that fans go for. You know the kind of gush we have to give worshipers. More of that 'My God—but-she's-beautiful!' stuff. Maybe you could rewrite it; I'd be glad to see it if you do. And for heaven's sake, try to sound a little more sympathetic about her problems. . . ."

Jennifer bunched the pages under her arm, put her key in the door.

"Problems! What kind of problems can Hedy Lamarr have! 'Please God, make my legs thinner, my bust bigger.' Phooey!"

She entered the one-room-and-kitchenette, threw the manuscript at the typewriter.

Hateful apartment, because it was empty of Klaus. Hateful business, because it was phony. Hateful world, because it was hard.

Resentfully, she fixed herself cinnamon toast and tea. Resentfully undressed and put curlers in her hair. Mended a slip. Took an aspirin. A half hour later, resentfully pulled the bed down and got into it.

Picked up a magazine. An old *Good Housekeeping*. A few stories she hadn't read. Resentfully fluttered through it. But this particular resentment not born of the day or the moment. A vexation which she always felt wherever she held a general story magazine in her hand. Writers getting five hundred, a thousand, fifteen hundred dollars for stories such as she found here. And probably it didn't take them any more time or effort to write stories like that than it took her to write her silly little articles . . . running around, chasing stars . . . and all that rigmarole she had to go through to make seventy-five dollars. And, sometimes, not to make it. And further: if fiction writers had to struggle for story ideas, wasn't it a struggle for her, too, to get Hedy Lamarr to drop a publishable pearl of wisdom from her luscious, lovely lips? Oh, she wished she could think of some idea, something apart from stars . . . whip it into a story, sell it for five hundred dollars. That would get her to Washington quick. Oh, she wished, she wished.

In the hot, stuffy gas heat of the room, Jennifer dozed. The magazine spread out across her tummy. Not quite asleep and not quite awake. As she lay there, the placid voice of a stringy-haired girl came back to her. "My dad is a very good dad to us, I want you to understand that. Of course, there was some other trouble. You see, my dad has a record against him. But he is a very fine dad, and he means a lot to us."

"Poor darling—and I think that *I* have troubles." Jennifer reflected. "Suppose I had a real mess like that?"

She stirred in the bed, realized that she ought to turn off the gas. She dragged herself out and over to the radiator. Shut it off. Opened the window. Stood for a moment with the cool air on her. Funny, how she kept hearing the girl's voice. It had followed her around the room. Boy, what a story that would make. Destitute Italian family, with a dad that kept sneaking through a hole in the fence, to be near them, taking a chance against the law.

No, not that. Better, it should be the story of a strange relationship between daughter and father. On the surface, disapproving of each other, always quarreling, each claiming that the other was a peck of trouble in his life, but underneath, their hearts filled with love and pride. His last and most dangerous attempt to get back to the States, made because of her. And she at last revealing her hidden love for dad in her pathetic appeal to the Congressman.

Not bad.

She could try.

A fresh piece of paper in the typewriter, and in the upper left hand corner: "My Dad. A story by Jennifer Eckert."

The machine clacked along speedily for the first four pages. She began the story with the six kids and the mother waiting outside the Federal prison, for the release of Nicholas Bremecelli, as the law returned him to them after a two years' sentence of rum-running. It proceeded smoothly. At the end of the fourth page, Jennifer stopped typing, and read what she had written.

273

She really honest-to-goodness didn't think it was bad. At least, not very bad. But wasn't it perhaps too dreary, and not peppy enough for a popular magazine? Where was the boy and girl stuff? Just kids and a pop might not intrigue anybody. Oh, well, she'd keep on writing, see how it was turning out. As long as she wrote with good momentum, then it would be all right. It was when you stopped, and got stuck, and fumbled, that it meant there was a hole in the story.

Was it a hole now which made her go so slowly for the next two pages? No, just a few lines in a letter which lay there by the typewriter. Jennifer had caught sight of it again. "I do need a story on Hedy . . . maybe you could rewrite it . . . I'd be glad to see it. . . ."

Oh, damn, damn. A pretty sure seventy-five dollars, against "My Dad." The latter such a gamble. Such a long shot. It would need lots of polishing, going over and over. And those big magazines. Sometimes six weeks before they get around to even reading a story.

Crossly, Jennifer took "My Dad" out of the typewriter. Put "Hedy" in its place.

All the rest of the evening she worked—putting more goo into the article—making Hedy glow like alabaster, talk with the sweet moan of a Circe, walk like a dream, and laugh with the quick melodious tinkle of grace notes.

Two weeks later the story came back. The editor wrote that Jennifer had piled it on thick. A little too thick.

"Sorry, Jennifer. But let me know when you have something else. Best regards!"

274

17

ONE Saturday morning, Klaus was called to the Mexican immigration building. He went fearfully, knew that at last he was to get an answer about an extension of his Mexican visa.

He smiled, sighed a huge sigh of relief, when Señor Rosa handed him his extension. Then his smile faded.

"But it is only for two months. I asked for six!"

"Sorry, two months is most you have for now. Later maybe you get 'nother extension. New laws maybe coming out."

"New laws?"

"*Si.* New regulations for bonds."

"But I've already paid my bond. When I entered at Vera Cruz. Five hundred pesos. The government still holds that."

"I know. But maybe you have to pay more now. It is not so sure, but maybe. That is why you have for only two months. What you care? Be glad you get two months. Some people have trouble for that."

"How much more would the bond be?"

"The government in Mexico City talk now of maybe twelve thousand pesos."

"Good God! That's over two thousand dollars!"

Señor Rosa nodded. "*Si.* It's a big lot of money. But now

everybody wants to use Mexico. All the refugees from Europe. Why should Mexico be sap? Why should we let everybody in? We gonna be difficult, too."

"Yes, it is the fashion," Klaus mused wryly.

He left a few minutes later, his new visa in his pocket, but a new dread in his mind. He didn't think he ought to go straight home. Jennifer, so quick to read his face; he wanted to spare her this new worry. But good heaven, she *had* to get to Washington fast now. Two months of grace was all they had. Two months—and then two thousand dollars. The Mexican immigration officer had said it might not apply to the foreigners already there. It might only apply to the new arrivals. But still, if the latter were to be the case, why then had they refused him the six months he had asked for?

The whole thing made him sick, just thinking about it.

He hoped to find diversion. Hoped to tuck the worry back in his mind, before going home. But everywhere he went, everywhere he looked, the gloom of Tijuana itself pressed down upon him.

Poor, unfortunate Tijuana. In front of Tacuba's a new sign, written in chalk on a blackboard, and in those few words the story of the tragedy which had befallen the town just a few days before.

ALL ENGLISH PIPES REDUCED TO $5
MANY FINE FRENCH PERFUMES
ALSO REDUCED TO $5

There reductions had been made because the American twenty-four-hour law had at last gone through. Americans were now required to stay in Tijuana for a full day and night, if they wanted to take merchandise back into the States duty free . . . that is, merchandise valued above five dollars. Items that cost five, or less, could still pass the border without rigmarole. But anything above that called for duty, unless the purchaser had been in the town the required twenty-four hours. And as was apparent, there were few Americans who wished to hang around that long. They still came in droves on Sundays for the races, but when they stopped to shop on the way home, they were careful not to purchase anything valued above the duty-free amount. And few Americans showed up at all on weekdays any more.

Tragic at any time, but doubly disastrous now because it had occurred just the few weeks before Christmas. In the past Tijuana had lived for Christmas; had also lived from it. Profits during that one season enough to carry most of the stores a whole year. But now, as Klaus entered Tacuba's, it was empty of purchasers and filled only with listless salespeople.

"Hello, Stella. I was afraid maybe they fired you. I'm glad to see you're still here."

"Glad? Is anybody glad about anything?"

"I came in here, hoping to get some cheerfulness. But I guess I—"

"Go to the owner of some big American store in San Diego. They're the only ones who can be cheerful about this. They fixed us up fine."

"Oh, now, Stella. You can't blame it all on them."

"Why not? They're the ones who put that law through. We sent people to Washington to beg them not to do it.

But they ganged up on us. It just shows you what American capital can do. Even make laws for themselves."

"But there's something else you have to think on. Don't you know that in a few months Tijuana would have been in a depression, anyway?"

"How?"

"Because of the war. With boats being sunk. Pretty soon you wouldn't have any more European merchandise to sell, even. Don't you understand? Look there—" He pointed to a bolt of English woolen. "Maybe that is the last we will see on this side of the world for a long time."

"Baloney. You just say that. Trying to take the blame off the Americans. Always trying to stick up for them. You make me sick. You think they're so fine and democratic. You'll find out. It's not like you think. They're mean . . . just like anywhere where there's lots of money. Dollar signs for hearts. You wait. You'll see."

"I do wait. I wait for a long times. But there is no use to argument with me, Stella. When I love something, I love."

"Yeah. German blindness. Like the Germans love Hitler. Like you love your wife. Just love, love, love—and no seeing."

"Why you say something about my wife?"

She saw the white anger. "Oh, I don't mean anything particular. Only if she loved you like you act about her, I should think she'd stay with you more."

"It is only my fault that she is not here all the time. Because I cannot make any money. What she does now is more a meaning of love than any woman I ever heard of."

"Maybe." But Stella's face was hard. She turned away, began to apply a dust cloth to some perfume bottles.

Klaus left, more depressed than ever, and sat for a moment motionless, in the car. Then there were steps running toward him. Stella, shamefaced and apologetic.

"Oh, Klaus, I am sorry I was mean. Only we're all so upset. It's kind of like going through the same thing you are. Realizing that we have no power against a force bigger than ourselves."

"It's all right. Only I had bad news this morning, too. I got my Mexican visa. But only for two months."

"That'll be time enough, won't it? Can't Jennifer go to Washington before then?"

"As soon as we get the money. We are saving everything. We even promised not to buy Christmas presents for us."

"The robes . . . remember, Klaus? They're reduced to twelve-fifty now."

"I know. I saw them on the table. You put mine out too, didn't you?"

"I had to. Know how many months ago that was?"

"You do not have to remind me."

"Anyway, I have something for you. Maybe you can have fun out of this." She took an envelope from her pocket. "Tickets for the dance Christmas Eve."

"A dance . . . in Tijuana?"

"Yes . . . at the old gambling room, in Caliente. I can't use the tickets. . . . I have to go to my mother's. I'm sorry I didn't think of it before. There are six . . . you can give the extra four around the colony."

"How much—"

"That's all right. I don't have to pay for them. It's the Tijuana Club. We pay for it out of dues. No need to thank me even."

But he did. Thanked her smiling—then made the car leap home.

He grasped quickly at the proposed event, saw in it a chance to escape for one evening at least. He had heard that the gambling room was magnificent. He saw the whole scene. The room softly lighted. Those splendid chandeliers. Entering with Jennifer on his arm. Evening clothes again. A man out with his wife, proud of his wife. The floor smooth. The music smooth. Everything smooth and beautiful. Christmas Eve they'd live the old life again. Forget Tijuana. Its mud streets. Its filth. Its poverty. For one precious evening, release.

When he arrived home, Jennifer greeted him with the news that the Weisses had received their visas!

"But how? You mean they went to Ensenada this morning?"

No, it hadn't happened that way. Jennifer explained that the consul had stopped by on his way to San Diego. He knew how much it would mean to them, and if he waited to write, it would be Monday before they had the letter. So he had personally brought the news and the necessary papers. They could go right away . . . only had to stop at the border to see the doctor, for a new health examination. They had had one once before, but so much time between then and now, that the procedure had to be repeated.

"So that's what Duwid is looking so sad about." Jennifer and Klaus were on their own steps. Klaus looked down the way at Casa Four. Duwid sitting there with his head in his hands.

"Can you blame him? He's envious. Everybody is. But I wish you'd been here when it happened. Oh, it was wonderful to see their faces. The Weisses, I mean. I'll just never forget it. They were so happy that they had kind of an ashamed look about them—when they looked at us. It made me think—I can just hardly wait till I see you look like that, too. So relieved. So happy. So—oh, I don't know—resplendent."

"Think maybe I'd better go talk to Duwid?"

"I wish you would. He's so morose. But don't let him get you that way, too. Please, darling."

"I won't."

Klaus sat beside him on the steps of Casa Four. "Hey, Duwid. You have to cheer up, you know."

But there was no response.

"Duwid, how about going for a ride with me and Jennifer this afternoon. Duwid." Klaus touched him on the arm. "Look up here. Don't be like that."

Duwid did look up. He looked closely at Klaus. "You know, Klaus, if someone would come to me and say to me my papers I could have if only I would give a piece of my body for them . . . I would do it! I would give an arm, or a leg. I would not care. And even I would give an ear for a *pilón*."

There was a sharp cry from behind. Blima standing there, and she had heard. "Oh, no, Duwid. Do not say such things!"

"Why not?" he asked, without turning toward her. "I would even give all that just for the baby to be born over

281

there. So that the baby for one would be born free, and not ever to have troubles in life like we have had them."

Blima bent over, put her arms around him. "Duwid, my dear. Look, is there not always trouble for everybody? But trouble always comes to an end sometime. See, like the Weisses. They were unhappy, too . . . but now see, they are free again. It will be also like that for us. If we can wait a little longer."

"I will try," he said, and looked up toward the hill, where happiness burst in shouts and laughter from the windows.

Up there, in the ranch house, the Weisses were packing. Packing at fever-pitch. And in the jumble of clothes and suitcases, stopping for quick kisses and sudden happy tears, and shrieking and shouting . . . the hysteria of leaving. Mady all over the bed, and on the chairs, trying to be of help, but thinking maybe she'd be of more help just to keep out of the way.

Then, at that moment, Mrs. Gomez appeared in the doorway. "Mr. Weiss, my husband wants to see you."

"I expect he does!" Hans answered gaily. His mood fine. His smile radiant. He smacked Mrs. Gomez on the fanny as he passed.

Found Mr. Gomez in the living room. "I know—you want to see me about the bill. I don't blame you. And I'll give you an American check for the full amount. Date it ahead two or three weeks. But you won't have to worry. Once in Hollywood we'll get work, or I've got friends. I'll make it good. If I don't, you can put me in jail."

"You, in jail, will not pay me my money," Mr. Gomez reminded him.

"I know. But don't worry. I have been stuck here so long, I will not be anxious to get in prison again. You have a blank American check?"

Mr. Gomez handed him one, together with the bill.

"I'll make out the check for ten dollars more, just because you have been so good to us."

The check made out, Hans waved it to dry it. Then handed it over. "We will never forget how good you have been. If not for you, we would be on the street. We know that. And now I have to ask you for one more favor. Would you be so good maybe to drive us to the border?"

"I will drive *you* to the border," Mr. Gomez said pointedly. "You and your baby. But not your wife. I think it best Mrs. Weiss, she stay here."

Hans' fine high color instantly paled. "I don't understand you."

"I do not want to be mean, but I am only poor Mexican man, and I owe money, too. And you know you have not been so cheap to keep. You have fine tastes, all of you. I know you mean to pay, but when people are far away, it is easy to forget. So your wife stay here, to make you remember, maybe.

"You see, Mr. Weiss, there are many people America don't want. American no want paupers for one thing. If I tell them at the border that you have no money, and owe me, they not let you through. You tell Mrs. Weiss. You tell her I only make her stay until you send money for bill."

"I can't. I can't tell her that. You have no right."

"Right? A man has a right to what he is owed. You explain carefully. You tell her I put Chato to watch her all the

283

time after you go. And if she step one foot off this property, I go to Berendo's, telephone head immigration man at the border. You see what happen then. He no let her cross. Bring you back maybe, too. You explain. She smart woman. She understand."

A few minutes later, there came the sound of a loud Russian wail from the Weisses' room. "I won't. I won't. No! No!"

After a while though it died away. Hans was explaining.

The card party at Jennifer's that evening had been intended for the purpose of cheering Maria, on her first lonely evening without Mady and Hans. But, at the last moment, she sent Chato to say that she was ill and had gone to bed.

So there were, after all, only the Klabecs, the Lankowskis, and the Eckerts. The others had been invited, too, but Siegfried had preferred to play dominos in town—where he could play for money; he had become the town champion and was making his living from it. And Irmgard had gone off to the movies with the Kid.

From the first moment that they sat down—the three men on the far side of the dining table, and the three women on the side nearest to the warmth of the oil heater—it appeared that they were going to have trouble with Ani. So cantankerous tonight. Full of complaints. First it was too stuffy in the room. Then when the window was opened, it was too draughty. Then when she had worn them out on that subject (and herself too probably), she began to pick on Blima. In mean little ways. Catty fault-findings. Why did Blima always wear black? Didn't she know it wasn't becoming? And if she must wear black, at least she should use a

284

little lipstick. And why didn't Blima put more time on her English? Look at the progress that she (Ani) had made. And so on and on.

And during all this, they were trying to play poker.

Jennifer had suggested poker, as the best game for six people to play. Neither Blima or Ani had ever played it before, but they were willing to try. And Ani, of course, as in everything, was quick to catch on, but for Blima it was a struggle. Her mind slow and lumbering like her body these days. It was this slowness which finally brought about a climax between the two women.

Blima, bless her, thought she had a winning hand at last. Triumphantly, she laid down her cards. "Three Queens," she announced proudly, beaming at Duwid for approval.

"Three Queens you are crazy!" Ani told her. "Cannot you even read your cards?" And she pointed out a Jack in with the Queens. Then laid down her own hand. Three tens. They were playing with matches. She drew the pile toward her, shook her head smugly.

For Blima it was the final straw. Foolish to be upset by this, but she couldn't help it. Ani had been picking on her for so long. Her eyes brimmed, and to try to hide their brimming, she quickly excused herself from the table.

Jennifer saw what had happened, followed her into the bathroom.

"Blima dear, please . . . you mustn't let Ani upset you. Don't you know she's just cranky tonight . . . seeing Hans and Mady leave today. It made her unhappy, like all of us— only she has a different way of showing it. Come on now, please. Don't cry. Here— Why don't you bathe your face and your eyes? Freshen up. You'll feel much better."

She fussed over her, patted her, got a clean wash cloth and towel—then happened to get a look at her own face in the mirror. Around her mouth, it was all dark from the smoke of the heater.

"Look at us," she laughed. "If we aren't a sight. It's that darn old wick. We had a new one just a little while ago—but we use them up so fast."

They both washed, and combed their hair. "There now, see! You're a new woman, Blima. And no more nonsense, now. You just talk right back to Ani if she gets sassy. Oh, wait, we'd better take some Kleenex."

She gave Blima a handful. "You can keep wiping the soot off with that."

An impish look came into Blima's eyes. "Please, Jennifer, I was thinking, suppose we do not say anything to Ani about the heater?"

"You mean . . . ?"

"Yes . . . you know. Pretty soon she will be a Negro." Blima chuckled just to think of it.

"You amaze me," Jennifer said. "Come on, I'm with you."

Afterwards, Jennifer was to realize that it was the first time she had ever seen Blima have any fun. They had planned it well, by the time they returned to the table. Jennifer pulled the heater quite close to Ani, even turned it up a little. From that moment on, Blima and Jennifer wiped often at their own faces—surreptitiously—and watched with growing pleasure what the heater was doing to Ani's. The men at the far side of the table were far enough removed from the heater not to have it make any extravagant changes on their faces, though they did have a grayish, dingy color all over. But the change it made in Ani was really spectacular. The blackness started around her nose, spread to her mouth, set heavily under her eyes.

"My goodness it's getting warm in here again," Ani said, and rubbed her face, and in so doing put a beautiful smudge right up to her forehead.

At first the men couldn't understand what was happening. But every time they opened their mouths to comment, swift kicks under the table. And eventually, they caught on and were in on the joke, too. Duwid and Klaus were amused, but Emil at first was worried, and tried his best to warn Ani. But—

"Emil, what *are* you making faces at me about? I wish you'd keep your mind on your cards now. Look how Klaus is winning!"

So after a while he let it go, too. And a couple of times even he got the giggles. Because, as the evening progressed, Ani became even more arrogant, and the more arrogant she became—with that face—the more ridiculous she looked.

The evening eventually ended—after coffee and cookies. All of them at the door saying good-by. Blima squeezed Jennifer's hand hard, muttered something about the nicest evening she had ever had in Tijuana.

Jennifer believed it. At least she had never seen Blima so little-girl gay, as she was now, going home with Duwid, and laughing into the darkness.

When Ani arrived home, her mirror, of course, told her the story. And she remembered how often Blima and Jennifer had seemed to have handkerchiefs at their faces—and the amusement looks which had passed between them. She was furious.

She turned on Emil. Railed at him for letting them put her in such an undignified light (or was it dark?). But even that did not relieve her of all her indignation.

The next morning when she saw Jennifer and Blima, she was still mad. She tossed her head airily. She refused to give them a greeting.

Ani kept her silence; might have continued to do so, except that two days later Klaus gave her tickets for the Christmas Eve ball. At that point, her gratitude led her to forgive the Eckerts, and because Jennifer insisted, she also started speaking again to Blima. It was rather easy to do—because from the very moment that Ani held the dance tickets in her hand, there was really only one thing on her mind—a point of paramount issue (to her)—to be the most elegantly gowned woman at the party.

Preparations took days. First to decide on a style. As usual, magazines were her reference books. She was told by the editors of *Vogue* that strapless evening gowns were all the fashion. She was well aware that the magazine was four months old, but conferring with Jennifer, she learned that *Vogue* was always far in advance of the trend; that set her mind at ease, and she went ahead with her plans to construct something strapless.

There was no time to make an entirely new dress, but there was, in her closet, a once-magnificent silver-spangled black tulle gown, left over from the Prague days, when she had had all her clothes brought from Paris. She thought this might be adapted. She tackled it with vim and vigor. She scissored the top of the dress, at the top-of-the-bust line, bound it around at its new topline with silver ribbon.

Put a few darts under the arm, and at the back, to make it fit as skin-tight as possible. Pressed and re-pressed it, and then spent one whole day trying to brighten the silver trimming.

The dress was finally finished a few hours before the party. Ani put it on, and her face fell—because the dress did. She perceived then that she had forgotten something very important. She had counted on her bosom to hold the dress up, but alack! without inner stays and stiffening it just wouldn't stay there. It bulged, it gapped, it slid most dangerously.

She was never long at a loss for ideas, though, and she quickly dispatched Emil into town for some adhesive tape.

And thus it was that she was well plastered—but only with tape—when she arrived at the party.

She felt so elegant that it distressed her to have to arrive with the Lankowskis, and the Gomezes—in whose car they had all come. Blima looking so dull in an all-black dress, which showed the baby so plainly. Mrs. Gomez so garish in a brightly flowered velvet, which showed so plainly where Mrs. Gomez had so often sat down. "Oh, dear," Ani thought. "The company I've been forced to keep these days." She felt like a peacock in with the waddling ducks.

Her disappointment increased as she got her first glimpse of the gambling room. So this was the "magnificent" room which Klaus had said they would see. Maybe it had been beautiful once, but Klaus had forgotten to reckon with what had happened when the place was closed down by government decree. The way the Mexican workers must have moved in with hatchets and picks and greedy hands, to rob the place of its splendor. Tonight, where were those famous crystal chandeliers? Tonight, the night of the Christmas Eve ball, only naked bulbs in bare sockets all around the room, glaring and hideous.

And the floor? Unpolished. Unsmooth. Like sandpaper. "Must *be* sandpaper," Ani reflected, as she listened to the sound that the dancers made. Scrape. Scrape. Above the sound of feet she could scarcely hear the music.

But at this moment, the music must have ceased. Because the scene stopped swirling. Dancers broke away from each other. People crisscrossing back and forth over the floor, as men and boys took their partners back to their places.

"Let's sit down, too," said Mrs. Gomez.

There were chairs all around the wall. Just like at a school dance, Ani realized. And what chairs! Of plain unpainted wood. Squeaky and lopsided. Ani gently eased herself into one. She felt of its edge to be sure it would not catch her dress, and tear it.

"I'm just going to sit here all evening," Emil told her, in their native language.

"You certainly are not. If you think I'm going to be stuck here with Blima, you can have another guess. It makes me feel like 'old folks' already."

Emil smiled, looked at Blima, and then back at his wife. She understood what his look meant: Blima and Duwid were really the younger couple.

"Well!" she simpered. "Anyway, that's the way they make me feel."

Her eyes wandered around the room. Such tawdriness. The Mexican taste in clothes, to her, seemed simply awful.

"Look at that, Emil. Look at that row over there, where

all those girls are. Doesn't it just hurt your eyes to look at it?"

"Why?"

"The colors."

"They look sort of gay."

"Gay? I never saw such cheapness. Pink, blue, red, green, yellow, orange. And I bet every yard of it is imitation taffeta."

"Maybe they can't afford anything else. Don't be so hard, Ani."

Mrs. Gomez leaned out and looked down the row, interrupted the flow of language that she didn't understand.

"It's a nice party, isn't it?" she asked, her eyes shining.

"Oh, yes," said Ani. "Oh, yes. Very."

"What I like about these parties," Mrs. Gomez went on, "is that everybody comes. Fathers, mothers, children, grandchildren. See? Over there are the family groups."

She pointed to a far wall. Worn Mexican mothers, children squawking at their knees. Older men sitting and smoking and stamping cigarettes out at their feet. "It gives everybody a chance to enjoy it, even if they don't dance. Half the fun is watching, don't you think?"

Ani nodded, but stared, horrified, at the smoking. At the dead cigarette butts.

"The only trouble is, it won't last very long," Mrs. Gomez sighed. "It has to end early. They end it early every year . . . shortly after eleven . . . to give the people time to get to Christmas midnight mass. Oh! There's the music again."

Mrs. Gomez bounded up, quickly followed by her husband. They seized each other gaily, exultingly danced off.

291

Scrape, scrape . . . again.

And a whirl of startling colors like a revolving multi-colored spotlight again swept the room.

Ani leaned out, and over, toward Duwid, who was sitting on the other side of Blima, holding her hand. "How do you like the music, Duwid?"

"I do not hear it," he replied.

Ani laughed. "Lucky for you."

"Ani!" It was Emil, speaking crossly, almost a command. "Cannot you see that it is not nice to make fun? For these people here, it is their big party. For them it is good. They have never known anything else. They cannot be blamed if it is a little pathetic. Tijuana is caught in circumstances, like we too. And who are we to judge them?" Then he feared that he had gone a little far. His eyes brightened with teasing. "Just because you have a nice dress!"

She smiled, fluttered, looked down at herself. "You really like it, Emil?"

"You look lovely."

"Then let's dance." She was all sweetness and light again. "I am sorry I said what I did."

She stood up, waited for him to rise, too.

"No, please, Ani, I do not want to dance."

"Not dance? What do you mean? You always used to like to dance."

"Yes, but not now. Not tonight."

"Why not?"

"It's your dress, Ani."

"You just said you thought it was beautiful!"

"I know, but—well, I'm afraid of it."

At that she laughed. Hastily assured him that nothing

was going to happen. The tape would hold it secure. His fears were nonsense.

Against his better judgment, he allowed her to dance him off.

Perhaps it was because he was so nervous that it happened. They reached the center of the floor, were caught in a dance jam—and what Emil had greatly feared came about. He, or somebody at least, stepped on Ani's dress. Ani bleated. A painful bleat. Clutched herself about her. Looked wildly for a ladies' room. Hastily retreated to repair the damage.

A half hour later, she came back. Sulky. Hurt. Embarrassed. Relegated to a chair the rest of the evening. No hope of moving about any more. As it was, she had to keep herself puffed out to avoid the exposure that threatened momentarily. Stiffly she sat there, wishing the evening were over, wishing the Gomezes would take them home, wishing she had never left there. Turned her attention for the remaining hour of the dance to criticizing the dancers.

Irmgard, dancing by with Manuel, that cheap-looking boy from the beer company! And again dancing with other Mexican boys. Even with the gas-meter man. And just look at her. All that rouge on her cheeks. And her dress so tight. The dress, borrowed from Jennifer, and much too small for Irmgard's stocky figure. Showing everything. Simply everything. It was disgusting.

Nor did she approve of Jennifer and Klaus. "Look at them, Emil! Dancing so close." Jennifer with her eyes closed and her body sheathed tight against her husband.

"Why shouldn't they dance like that?" Emil asked. "Aren't they married?"

"All the more reason not to. Married people can wait till they get home. Married people carrying on in public. There's nothing more vulgar."

Had Ani known . . . the Eckerts were not dancing in public. They were deep in a world of their own. They saw none of the cheap, gaudy glare about them. They had seen it as they came in, had been disappointed just as Ani was, but had decided to put it away from them. This was their one night out, in all the long months that they had been in Tijuana . . . and they were going to make the most of it. And making the most meant inventing the best. And so it was that they danced in their own world . . . and in their dream they were gliding smoothly, on a smooth floor, 'neath soft lights, and to sweet music.

At eleven, the refreshments were brought out. "Here comes the champagne," Klaus whispered to his darling. "Shall I bring you a cup?"

"I don't think you'll have to bother," Jennifer told him. "It's already here"—as she reached her hand, and a waiter thrust a beer bottle into it. And in the same moment, he slung her a paper-wrapped sandwich.

Klaus and Jennifer looked at the sandwiches.

"How about taking them home to Maria and Siegfried?" Klaus suggested.

"All right, but what do we do with this?" She held up her beer bottle.

"Drink it, I guess, like it is." There were no glasses, but all around the room, people were tipping up their bottles. So Jennifer and Klaus did the same—and the beer went gurgle-gurgle down their throats.

After the eating and drinking, the place looked like a

neglected picnic park. Empty beer bottles on, and under the chairs. Oil-paper wrappings from the sandwiches fluttering across the floor.

But Jennifer and Klaus didn't see it that way. As they danced the last dance, and the papers got mixed up with their feet, Klaus sighed happily.

"I like dancing in the autumn, in the out-of-doors, don't you?"

Her eyes looked up, asked what he meant.

His grin grew. "Oh, you know how it is when you dance outside—the way the wind blows leaves against your legs?"

It was midnight now, and time for Merry Christmases.

Up on the hill, Maria waited for the Gomezes to return from church. Chato sat across from her, keeping guard, singing to himself, and drinking tequila. She was sick of his face. Seeing it the whole long evening. Suddenly she took off her shoe and threw it at him, cursing him in Russian. Then she cried. But it was a different kind of crying than she had ever done before. Because tonight it was Christmas Eve, and tonight, for very nearly the first time in her life, her tears were mother's tears and they were wept for Mady.

Down the line:

In Casa Six, Siegfried gratefully consumed the ham sandwich which Klaus had brought him.

Next door in Five, the Klabecs were gazing into a cup of cold water, into which Emil had dropped a spoonful of melted lead, hoping to find, in the shape that it took, what the next year might hold in store for them.

In Four, Blima lay on her couch, happy and content, be-

295

cause across the room, Duwid was, for the first time in months, placing his fine white hands on the ivory of the piano. The music so awkward and strained at first, but growing in beauty.

In Bungalow Three, a silly little Christmas tree, all done up in cranberries and cotton. And hearts holding hands. Because no matter how meager it was, this was, after all—for Jennifer and Klaus—their very first Christmas.

In Two. The Kid took a blanket from his own bed, laid it over the Old Man. "Here, Old Man—just on account of it's Christmas. Now shut up."

In One. Irmgard crumpled a ten-pesos note in her hand, closed her eyes, and then without further resistance, received an angry but eager Manuel. "I have to live somehow," she muttered to herself. But her words were lost in the pounding pressure of the moment.

18

ANI was no longer the first one up in the mornings, around the Colonia Gomez.

Every morning, the alarm clock in Casa Two smote the silence and knifed it in two, at precisely five o'clock. This sound was followed by the whine of the couch springs, as the Kid squirmed and struggled out of his sleep to shut the damned thing off, and at last stand upright on his slim little legs.

Sometimes he stood for five minutes, his eyes closed, swaying a bit, as he waited for the morning chill to wake him up. He counted on the shivering of his own body to at last jerk him into sensibility. This accomplished, he then fumbled in the darkness, found his clothes and dressed.

And all of this, just to make a few extra dollars a week. By going to the race track in the early morning, he could always find horses to gallop and train—and pick up some extra cash that way. By now, the Kid was just as anxious to get to Florida as the Old Man was. Not for the same reason, but because Tijuana and the Colonia Gomez had begun to bore and depress him. His friendship with Klaus had been its one saving grace. Still, he was as anxious to get away as any of them, and on this particular January morning, he figured that a get-away would be possible in another ten or twelve days.

He hurried out to the garages beyond the bungalows on the other side of the drive. Still sleepy, and damning the necessity of these morning sojourns. But he consoled himself with the thought that anyway, in another few hours, he could tumble back into bed and sleep until the Old Man had lunch ready for him at noon. It was the same consoling thought he harbored every morning, at exactly this same moment—feeling his first contact with the cold, eerie, and unpleasant dawn.

Start the car quietly, back out, swing around to the drive—and head off toward Caliente.

Was that a voice he heard? He drew up at the end of the drive. Funny, he could have sworn he heard his name. But that was ridiculous. Who would be calling him at this hour? He went on.

When he returned, a little after eight-thirty, the sun was up, but the colony was still quiet. Ani Klabec hadn't yet thrown her rugs on the front porch. The Kid returned his car to the garage.

"Now!" he thought. "Now for bed again!"

But bed was to have no part in his destiny that morning. Blima Lankowski was standing on her back porch.

"Please, Mr. Kid, I wish to speak to you."

As he came nearer, she put her hand on her lips. "Sh-h-h, if you please. I do not wish to wake my husband. It is best he sleep."

"What's the matter, Mrs. Lankowski?" It occurred to him that she looked strange this morning. Kind of white.

"Mr. Kid, I must to the hospital go. Will you take me?"

"Jeez Christ, is it here?"

"I tried to call you before."

"You mean it's been on its way since *then?*" He, could he have seen himself, was even whiter than Blima was. "Couldn't you get somebody else?"

"Who?"

It was true. There was no one else. Jennifer had the Eckert car in Hollywood. The Gomez car was in the shop.

"And you see, I mustn't wake my husband," Blima reminded him.

"But we gotta wake him. Why not? I can't take you by myself."

"No, please." Again she put her finger to her lips, imploringly. "I know what I do. For him it is all such a sadness to have the baby here . . . but after it is over, it will be all right, I know. Oh, please, Mr. Kid . . . do this for me."

"Yeah, but . . . Oh, Christ!" He was just plain scared, that was all.

And what he saw next made him even more frightened. Blima went away from him. Stepped behind the door. Her hand gripped there against the door's edge. The knuckles white—she gripped so hard. Pains. And she said she'd been having them since five. He couldn't. He couldn't take her. Suppose she had the baby right in the car!

"There!" she said, and came back again. Now she carried a little black satchel in one hand. She had drawn a big black cape over her shoulders. He saw that she was ready to go.

"Come on," she said, and began walking to the car.

What else could he do? Some gallantry that he didn't even know he possessed came to the fore. "All right. All right. Let me help you."

He got her in. She leaned back against the seat. Her eyes closed. Her face not looking like her own face at all. At least, the Kid had always remembered it as soft and round. But now thin and drawn. Sort of wet-looking all over. And so gray-pale.

"Are you sure?" he asked. "Are you sure we'll make it?" She fluttered her hand. Motioned for him to start on.

He started as smoothly as he could, let the car roll easily down the drive. Then on the main road at last, turned toward town. There his troubles began. The last weeks, the rains had ruined the road. It was about to be repaired. The detour signs and blockades were already up. He found he had to use a makeshift road off to the right. This one, too, was full of rain-holes. Had to drive in first gear. Fifteen miles an hour. The most speed he could risk, over bumps. And as it was, every time the car squeaked and seat-springs groaned, he thought it was Blima moaning. And yet when he looked at her, her lips tight together, still leaning back, her eyes closed.

"I'm sorry it takes so long," he said once. "But I'm afraid to go faster."

At last, at long years last, he was in the heart of the town, and the few people on the streets and in the shop doors made him feel better. At least, if Blima should have the baby right now—he could call for help from somebody.

"Mrs. Lankowski, I am sorry to bother you, but you'll have to tell me now . . . which way from here to the hospital? We're at the bank corner."

Blima forced her eyes open and looked around. "Oh, not here," she murmured weakly. "The hospital . . . it is back by Caliente. Oh, please, we hurry now."

300

Then she sank back, lowered her eyelids . . . returned again to that frightening stillness.

Back by Caliente! What was she talking about? Then he remembered. That white building, near the entrance to the hotel . . . it had been the Caliente Golf Club once, was the Civil Hospital now. "Geez, I made the wrong turn." But how could he have known, or thought, at the time . . . naturally he assumed the hospital was in the center of town. But what a mistake! "Back by Caliente" meant two miles back the same horrible road over which they had just crawled . . . and then another mile after that. And all those bumps and holes. Oh, they'd never make it. They just never would. He knew. He remembered his mother telling him of the surprising speed of his own birth. How she had been out at a restaurant, and had had to rush home, and didn't even have time to take her shoes off. And Blima already trying to have the baby since dawn. No, he couldn't chance it. Absolutely not—unless, of course, he could get hold of a doctor quick. A doctor could tell him if there was still time to take her back there. A doctor could tell, just by looking at her. And there *was* a doctor near, the Kid suddenly realized! Doc Hester, the immigration doctor at the border. Doc sometimes came over to the track. Once the Kid gave him a tip. Why, of course; the Doc would do him this favor! And the border was near. Only a quarter of a mile.

They arrived there quickly. The Kid parked the car just behind the border gate, on the Mexican side. Hopped out. He was on the verge of dashing across the line into the American immigration building, when the idea came. He looked at Blima. And he looked at the building. They weren't far apart . . . and the immigration building was on

American soil. Its side entrance was not much more than twenty yards away. It was the entrance that the Mexicans used when they came to see about their border passes. Nobody bothered them very much about coming in—only about coming out. And, at this moment, there was not even an officer at the gate. The officer on duty was up under the customs shed, sixty yards beyond.

"Mrs. Lankowski, do you think you could walk a little ways?"

Faint voice. "Are we here?"

"Yes, we're here," he answered—and decided to do it.

As though she were sleep-walking, she allowed him to help her out of the car, and then to pilot her slowly through the gate opening, and across toward the building.

"Hey, where are you going?" Whitie yelled from the customs shed.

"Only into the office!" the Kid called.

As they entered the office, the Kid looked quickly to the right where there was another door marked "Health Department." The door was open and, thank heavens, they were not too early. It was just nine o'clock, and through the open door, the Kid could see Doc Hester just taking off his hat and coat.

There was an officer on duty at the desk, but fortunately, at this moment, he was bent above a filing case.

The Kid set Mrs. Lankowski on her path. Gave her an ever-so-gentle shove. Scarcely more than a touch. Awkwardly, she moved ahead, dazed, right to the doctor's door.

The doctor looked up. "My God, woman!" Sprang forward to receive her sinking body in his arms.

Pandemonium from then on. The Kid sank down on a

bench near the door. He listened to it all . . . watched it
. . . with the detachment of one who watches a movie. A
movie slightly speeded up beyond the normal pace, he
thought. And decidedly one of those thriller pictures. Because suddenly the place swarmed with uniforms and badges.
Immigration officers, customs officers, and even State police-
men from the Patrol office across the road. And somebody
jiggling a telephone in haste and excitement and then a moment later—the only really clear dialogue that the Kid could
hear: "Tell the Tijuana hospital to send an ambulance.
Hurry. There's an alien in here that's going to have a baby.
They gotta come and take her away!"

And a girl leaping into the midst of things from somewhere, and going into the health department, and the door
banging. Then the door opening and banging again. And
eventually the sound of a siren, and the ambulance arriving,
and two men with a stretcher hurrying in, and then the
doctor's voice at the door:

"It's too late to move her now."

And after that, one of those long awful hushes when
there was just the clock ticking, and the pacing of feet, as
though there were a dozen expectant fathers in the room.
And this went on interminably, and the Kid thought, "If
something would only happen now . . ." and then it did.

Someone said, "Well, how the hell did she get in here?"

And they were looking at him.

And they continued to look at him.

"I—I—well, I hardly know her," the Kid said. "I don't
know nothing about it. She just lives across from me and
she asked would I bring her to the border, and so I brung
her."

Then someone laughed. That was good. Somebody was laughing.

"Well," he told himself. "After all, what can they do to me? They can't blame me for nothing. She walked in under her own steam, didn't she?"

But suppose, oh geez, suppose she dies? They could blame him for that, all right . . . for not taking her to a hospital where he should have taken her.

He had a great desire to get out, and hurry away. But he couldn't move. It was like there was glue on his pants, the way he kept sitting.

And the clock ticking.

And all those men standing around, looking at that door.

And then the door opened, and the doctor motioned for the ambulance men, and they carried the stretcher in.

Geez, why hadn't he told them something?

They came out, bearing Blima. Her face round again. That was funny. Her body thin again and her face grown fat, all in a little while. In less than an hour.

Then the girl coming out through the door, smiling and carrying a bundle, and the bundle moving and making a whimper-sound. And relief in the air. Whooping and cheering and sighing. Well, that's that. Thank God, that's that.

The ambulance drove away, back to Mexico.

"I suppose somebody'll have to face the chief about this," somebody said. "For letting an alien give birth to an American."

The Kid rose and started for the outer door. But the strain was too much for him. His legs gave away, darkness swirled. He fainted.

19

THE suitcase which Jennifer took to Washington contained, in addition to her clothes, five hard-boiled eggs, three Hersheys, notes on Ann Sheridan and Dorothy Lamour, which she had taken during recent interviews, the six pages on "My Dad," a snapshot of Klaus and Schnucki—and something else which she didn't know was there, a note from Klaus tucked into her pajamas. He had placed it there, thinking she would find it her first night on the train, when she undressed. Jennifer had neglected to mention that she was going by coach. He didn't know that it would be four days before she would have use for those pajamas.

Jennifer took along something else, though—something far more important: the firm conviction that this trip meant the last of their troubles. In the last hour before leaving, she tried to impart some of her sureness to Klaus. "I don't know how to explain it, darling—but I just know that by now God figures we have had enough."

God? What was this talk of God? So often Jennifer had said that she didn't believe in Him. Believed that there was a Deity, or a Principle, or a Something which ruled the world . . . but not a Being who had an Ear and who listened when you prayed. Klaus reminded her of that.

"Oh, I know," she admitted. "But I always just say that.

Because it's the thing smart people are supposed to say. Nobody ever admits that there is a He on a throne . . . not openly at least any more. But, in a way, deep down inside, I do think He's there, and I sort of know exactly what He's like, too."

"Then why haven't we prayed to Him more often?"

"Well, because I don't think the usual, daily kind of praying does much good."

"No?"

"No. Because if you believe that He rules the world, then you've got to believe that He knows what He's doing. Don't you?"

"Go on, Muschi. Go on."

"So—if He's working it all out according to plan, then there's not much use of us butting in."

"You believe He has a plan?"

"Sure I do. For everyone. And it's always for their eventual good, too. But of course He's got to give some kind of trouble to everybody. Just like in a story. If there isn't any conflict, it's a dull story. The same way with life. We all have to expect it. To some He gives it early. To others late. We just got ours kind of early, that's all."

"I'll say."

"Of course—" Jennifer paused an instant. "Of course, what gets me is the tricky troubles He keeps on thinking up. Everybody has something different. He certainly is original about that."

Klaus smiled. "You would not be thinking on Him as a great big story writer, would you?"

"Yes, in a way. The Supreme Plotter. That's right. That's why I say it doesn't do an awful lot of good to keep nag-

306

ging at Him. He knows how everything is going to dove-
tail and fit in at the last chapter."

"It doesn't always come out right. Sometimes people die
before they—"

"I know. But you have to realize that maybe sometimes
His characters make it difficult for Him. Get hard to handle.
And then He doesn't have time to work it out in the regular
span of life. That's why we've got the Hereafter. If there *is*
such a thing," she added lamely.

Klaus shook his head. "I don't think so. I think God gets
his people in such a mess that even He finds it hard to get
them out of it. Us, for example."

"Then that's where the praying comes in!" she exclaimed
brightly. "Sure, you've got to pray sometimes. Not so much
to beg. But just to remind Him. Maybe He's forgotten. Like
us. He stuck us off in a corner, all wound up and bound
around with our troubles. Well, that's when we have to
raise our hand and wave, and remind Him we're here . . .
and that He'd better start unraveling us." Then she put
her arms around Klaus. "I've been doing it lately," she said
softly. "I've been waving and praying. And I tell you,
Klaus . . . I really think He saw me and heard me."

"If He didn't, then He's made a terrible mistake."

He kissed her then. It was their last kiss before parting.

A few minutes later, they left for the border, stopped
on the way to pick up Stella. She was going to drive to the
San Diego station with Jennifer, bring the car back.

At the border, Jennifer whispered, "Don't kiss me again,
or I can't go."

She drove away, looked back only once . . . just before
the car rounded that first curve on Highway 101.

307

Saw him in a blur. He was standing there waving, with Schnucki in his arms. Jennifer had seen him so often like that. Klaus, at America's back gate, watching his heart go away from him.

Then he was gone; she could no longer even see him in the mirror.

"Wouldn't you rather that I drive?" Stella asked.

"No. It helps. Gives me something to think about."

But she drove automatically, and her mind still trundled its sadness.

"Stella, sometimes it just gets me down. You know the sorry way you feel when you see a poor little boy standing outside a shop, a bakery shop maybe, looking at the goodies inside. Wishing he could have some. The hungry look on his face. Makes you sick to see it. Klaus is like that when he stands back there. And he's not the only one; that's what makes it worse. It's like the whole border, on both sides, up north, too, at Canada . . . like it was a great big plate-glass window, and thousands of people pressing their noses against that window, looking at the goodies on the other side. The American goodies. Oh, it's terrible, Stella."

Stella was quiet. Jennifer glanced at her quickly. "Are you sensitive because we aren't content to live and stay in Mexico . . . even if we could . . . even if we could work there?"

"No. I don't blame anybody. In the other part of Mexico it's all right. But even I am ashamed of us here. It could be such a glorious spot. But the people are discouraged. We need help from Mexico City. We need money for roads, to develop industry. Money for law and order. Don't you think I see the difference when we cross the line, step from

Baja California into the States? I see it just as well as you do. Immediately everything changes. The grass seems greener, the trees more leafy. Everything changes from brown to green. And it isn't because God drew a line and said on this side it shall be beautiful green United States, and on that side brown, dilapidated Baja California. The difference in the people drew the line. Back there, we're lazy, because we're discouraged. We're shiftless because we're poor. Here on this side the people have a reason to water their lawns and paint their houses, and keep their fences neat."

"Never mind," Jennifer consoled her. "Some day you'll get help down there. Then the people will be different."

"I don't know. It seems like it will never come."

"It's funny . . . after Klaus and I get out of there, I bet there'll be a lot of things that we'll look back on . . . kind of homesick for. 'Cause there have been lots of nice things mixed in with the unpleasantness. Things we'll probably never catch sight of again. The way you Mexicans love flowers, for example. Always flowers, even if they're only geraniums, around even those old adobe huts. The way they stick them in tin cans in the windows. It's wonderful, really.

"And seeing an old Mexican woman doubled over a tortilla slab. It's a picture. Pounding and rolling the dough, or whatever you call it. Then sitting back on her legs, flattening those little round discs between her hands. Slap, slap, back and forth. Like playing pattycake.

"And then, too, Stella . . . the way so many of you have been nice. Wonderfully nice. Giving us rides to town. And the dance tickets you gave us, remember? And—oh, yes, when Klaus and I used to go to the beach. Almost every time we were down there, some old Mexican rancher would ride by on his horse. Stop to talk—and let us ride, too. That was fun. Galloping up and down the beach in the sand. Oh, there were lots of things. Did you ever walk along the irrigation ditches out toward the dam . . . on Sunday. On a hot summer day?"

"No. Why?"

"We did once. I'll never forget it. We came around a bend and suddenly there was a big, fat Mexican woman bathing in the ditch. She had her children with her. About four of them. And they were having a marvelous time. The children were naked. But the woman had an old white nightgown on. Only it was wet and it showed right through, and she was embarrassed. You should have seen the way she sank down into the water, and that nightgown ballooning about her. And she was laughing. You know that wonderful musical laugh of the real native woman? I tell you it was beautiful. The gay splashing. The cries of the children. That awful, hot day and the irrigation ditch so cool and shady. It's one memory I hope I never lose. Klaus said he wished he was an artist and could have painted the picture."

They drove mutely for a while. Then: "Well, we're here, Stella."

Jennifer stopped the car at the station entrance. "Thanks ever so much for coming with me."

"Don't you want me to come in?"

"No. I'd rather you'd go right back with the car. Klaus will be waiting. He'll worry. Give him my love again, will you?"

"Of course. Good-by, Jennifer."

Jennifer took the suitcase and the portable typewriter out of the car. Nodded. Smiled. Went in through the door.

For a moment, Stella gazed after her. Envious. Some people felt sorry for Jennifer, all the trouble she had to go through . . . her husband's immigration difficulties. But Stella didn't feel sorry. Would have gladly changed places. She knew that the love that Klaus and Jennifer bore each other was a great and enviable blessing. She knew that there were ties between them which nothing—not even laws or boundaries, or the whole United States Government itself— could ever sever.

In her pocket, there was a letter which Klaus had secretly asked her to mail, from the States side.

She stopped at the corner, hopped out to the mail box. Glanced once again at the envelope. It was stamped for air-mail and addressed to

The Florist
The Mayflower Hotel,
Washington, D. C.

This envelope was opened late the next day by a sweet-faced woman. It included a dollar bill, a small card, and a letter.

Tijuana, Baja California

DEAR SIRS:

Please will you send flowers for this dollar to Mrs. Klaus Eckert at the Horner Hotel, and please make them so nice as possible for this amount, and send them on Thursday which is when she will get there. I do not know for sure if I am sending this request to the right place, but it is custom for a big hotel to have a florist store, and somebody tells me that the Mayflower is a big hotel. If there is no flower store here and I am wrong, please send this to where there is one.

Sincerely yours,

K. ECKERT.

P.S. And please inclose this card which I am inclosing.

"Look here, Helen." The woman turned to her assistant. "What kind of flowers do you suppose a man thinks he can get for a dollar . . . at this time of year in Washington?" Her voice and her expression mildly disdainful.

She passed the letter along, then picked up the card which had been enclosed.

DEAR JENNIFER:
Just to leave you know I am all the times along with you on this trip—only you do not have to tell the immigration department that.

Your alien husband,

KLAUS.

"Well, we could send a half dozen short-stemmed roses," Helen was saying.

There was mistiness in the older woman's eyes. "Nonsense. We'll send two dozen of our best. And don't let me forget it! Thursday. The Horner Hotel . . . wherever that is."

Thursday. Jennifer's room was small. It was on the first floor. It had only one window. It was dark and dingy. But the roses helped to change all that.

The roses—and the letters. She found two from Klaus when she arrived, and now she lay on the bed, reading them. The first just full of yearning. But the second contained

312

news. News that made her laugh. The Klabecs had received their visas, and had left Tijuana.

It was Klaus's description of the leaving that amused her. How Emil had refused to believe it at first, because he hadn't yet finished his invention. But it was true, and they had left right then, on Tuesday. Klaus wrote about the taxi which had taken them north from the border. Loaded down like a gypsy van . . . filled with Ani's chairs and china and what-not. It would have been much simpler, of course, if they had arranged to have their things packed and shipped from Tijuana. But they didn't want to stay over even an hour for that . . . would do it later, from San Diego. And then the funny part: characteristic to the last, Ani had had a squabble with the customs man at the border, because he wouldn't let her take her cactus plants into the United States. Those plants which she had nurtured and nursed all those many months. And she had driven off, fussing and sputtering about the idiocy of American laws which wouldn't allow plants to cross the border.

The colony came back so clearly to Jennifer. She thought of its slow dissolve. First Omah had gone. Then Tibor. He had never really been one of them, but even at that, they had missed him. Then Hans Weiss, and Mady—and finally Maria, too. Hans hadn't sent all the money, only part, but Mr. Gomez had had to let Maria go, anyway. Jennifer remembered the scene: the day Blima had returned from the hospital with her baby. Maria looking at the new baby, and her own mother's heart quickening again. The way she had thrown herself at Mr. Gomez's knees. Pleading. Begging. "Please, please, let me go to my baby." So he had sent her off, relieved and glad to get rid of her. For weeks her face

313

so white and tragic. Roaming like a wraith through his house.

And now at last the Klabecs had gone, too.

Must be lonely now around the Colonia Gomez. Casa Five, empty and still. Gone, that irascible Ani. Dear to them all, in spite of her occasional bad temper and the little quarrels they had had. Jennifer, as she lay there thinking, realized that such disagreements were bound to exist between so many different nationalities, all living in the shadow of a Mexican bull ring. All of them nervous and worn, and the background itself not compatible to any of them. It was surprising that there hadn't been more trouble. She wished she could have been there to see Ani leave. Spunky, as always, right up to the end of her exile. Railing about the cactus. That would have been something to see and hear.

Jennifer got up. Leaned the letters against the vase of roses. Went down the hall to run bath water. Spunk? She'd better get a little of it for herself, she figured. Bathe away the four days of train, soak out the cramps from sleeping in a seat . . . then get out and clear up her own troubles. Right this afternoon. Every moment important.

Thursday, Friday, and Saturday passed, and Jennifer couldn't see that she was much better off than when she started.

Thursday afternoon she saw Congressman Hurlich. Had to call him off the House floor. He was kind, concerned, and helpful. He phoned Mr. Gatig at the State Department, arranged an interview for Jennifer on Friday.

On Friday, Jennifer saw Mr. Gatig. Talked to him between constant phone calls and numerous secretarial interruptions. She heard the names of more countries and nationalities than she ever realized existed. American relatives and friends, calling and writing and making inquiries, "But tell us how; where; what do we do next to get them in?"

Jennifer sat quietly, between the episodes of her own story, listened to Mr. Gatig dispatch advice, and condolences.

"I'm sorry but the Chinese quota is filled for six months ahead. . . ."

"There is no consul in Maylo Sandor. She'll have to go to some other island."

"We'll cable the general consul in Armenia, if he wants to pay for the cable."

And so on and on. Jennifer felt weak, realizing that it was through these offices that the stream really poured . . . the stream into the melting pot of America. And what a swollen churning stream it was right now, because of all the unrest elsewhere throughout the world. How small her own case seemed now . . . how tiny . . . how unimportant . . . mixed in with these thousands and thousands. And how unattractive. Klaus, a German. And Germans responsible for so much of the world's agony.

"Is he a Nazi?" It was one of the first questions Mr. Gatig had asked her.

"No, he is not."

And eventually, during a moment here and there, she had a chance to tell the whole story.

When she had finished, there was one point she wanted very much to stress, so she went back to it again. "Mr. Gatig, the main thing I feel is that when my husband and I

315

were married in Paris, the consul officers there must have had the wrong idea about our marriage. Thinking maybe that it was one of those immigration marriages . . . just so my husband could get his visa. I think that's why they put so much stress on that lie he told in Nice. Maybe they just used that to keep him out. Maybe they didn't *want* to forgive or understand it. And, of course, if they really thought our marriage was phony, I don't blame them. But I am sure we've proved now that our love is real. This whole last year in Tijuana . . . it's the only thing that has kept us together."

During the last few minutes, Jennifer felt that Mr. Gatig was watching her very closely. Poring over her words. Judging her tensely.

"Mrs. Eckert," he had said at last. "I'll be honest with you. I can't advise you a thing, until I have a chance to go over your husband's file. Suppose you come in to see me tomorrow."

That had been Friday.

On Saturday, Jennifer noticed a change in Mr. Gatig. Still noncommittal. It was still she who had to do most of the talking. But she could feel an increase in seriousness. He was very grave, gave much closer attention.

"Mrs. Eckert, what did your husband plan to do, as a business, when he tried to come to the United States?"

As was characteristic of her high hope, Jennifer changed the tense of the verbs, put them in the present. "When my husband comes in, he hopes to work at anything he can get. He says he will dig ditches if necessary. Anything to support me, and himself. But he won't have much trouble. He

316

knows everything in the sport world, you know. He used to be a boxer. He doesn't want anything more to do with that, though; he'll probably go in for skiing. He's a very good skier, and it's a sport that's growing in the United States. He could instruct, or if we can get some money together, we might open a little place of our own. You know, a skiing lodge up in the mountains. Or he could probably get work at the studios; technical advice on sport scenes . . . things like that. But why? Why should this be a problem now? The Labor Department has already passed my petition. They were satisfied that he could find work, or that at least until he did, my work could carry us along."

Mr. Gatig ignored her question, answered with one of his own, "How long did you know your husband in Paris?"

"I knew him, and we wrote back and forth, for a year before we married."

"But how long did you know him *in Paris?*"

"I was only there a month the first time. I saw him nearly every day. Then when I went back, we had to wait twenty-one days until we could be married. After we made our application. It's the French law."

"What was he doing the first time you were there? What occupation?"

"He put some money into a picture. A short . . . a sport picture. It was going to be all about the bobsled track at Saint Moritz. But that went sour. The promoter disappeared with the money. It cleaned him out. Up until then he'd had a lot of money . . . money he made boxing years before. You see, Mr. Gatig . . . you have to understand; my husband couldn't just go out and get a job in Paris. He

317

was an alien there too, and just about that time they began to close down on their working permissions. His only chance was to get work in the entertainment or sport field. Permission was easier to get for that."

"Well." Mr. Gatig made a move to get up. "I hate to make it seem as though I am putting you off. I'm sorry—but I'll have to ask you to come back and see me Monday at eleven. Can you?"

"I'll come and see you every day if you'll let me. I'm here to get something accomplished. I'll stay until I do. I've got to get this case reopened."

"I can't promise anything, but I'll speak to Mr. Beckerly. Maybe he'll see you on Monday."

"Mr. Beckerly?"

"He's the man who might be able to help you."

And so Jennifer went away. Discouraged. She felt that Mr. Gatig was just passing her along to get rid of her. Maybe he planned to pass her around among the whole force, slowly wear her out that way . . . thinking that after a while she'd get tired and go home. But she wouldn't. That's where they were wrong. She'd stay. If worse came to worse, camp on the Secretary of State's doorstep until he saw her. There was a man who could do something. And she'd heard he had a heart. She *must* get to the hearts.

She wondered if Mr. Gatig had one. He looked like he had. He had really been very nice. She had liked him. But maybe his heart was buried by files and phones, and figures and correspondence from pleading persons everywhere. She supposed so.

After Jennifer left, Mr. Gatig went in to see Mr. Beckerly. Jennifer wouldn't have doubted Mr. Gatig's heart, had she seen the kindly, worried expression on his face.

"Mr. Beckerly, do you remember the case of the German boy, Eckert, living in Paris, and now in Tijuana?"

"Vaguely."

"Well, that's a case I think you ought to listen in on. Mrs. Eckert's been in several times. I feel very sorry for her. I don't think she knows what she's up against. And she seems to be an extraordinary type of young lady. I wish you'd see her."

"Was that the case where the boy was mixed up with Briset?"

"Yes. I asked her to come in Monday, at eleven. Will you talk to her?"

"If you think I should. But it's not up to us. You'd better get somebody over from the other department. Call Terrain. They're the ones who have the objections."

Gatig went back to his own office, to arrange for Mr. Terrain to be there on Monday.

20

SUNDAY, for Jennifer, was an uneventful day, filled from morning to night with the clickety-clack-clack of her type-writer. First a long letter to Klaus, and after that, a "So Long, Sarong!" piece on Dorothy Lamour.

But three thousand miles away in Tijuana, the day was not without its happening.

The Kid came home from the track, after the fourth race, the last one he would ever run at Caliente. He packed the Old Man and their luggage in the car, then reached a hand around for good-bys.

Blima and Duwid, and Siegfried and Irmgard and Klaus. All of them out there by the car, sad, dreading to see him go.

Blima held her baby in her arms, smiled shyly at the Kid. "You know," she told him, "we have decided to call her Hilary after your own real name."

The Kid blushed. "Oh, geez, no. That's a crappy name."

"Crappy?" Blima asked. "What is that? I think it is very pretty. Hilary Lankowski. It has a nice sound. We want to call her for you. Because of you, you see, we are very near happy again."

"That is right," Duwid nodded. And it was true; on his face a new kind of peace and calm the last few weeks.

All of this embarrassed the Kid; he speeded up his departure. Pounded Siegfried. Hugged Irmgard. Pumped Klaus's hand very hard.

"Don't worry, old fellow, I'll be seeing you this summer. Right in California . . . the old home base."

"Hope so," Klaus murmured thickly.

Then the Kid and the Old Man drove away.

As always, after departures, the immigrants sat around, talking about those who had gone. They were still sitting there on the steps talking about the Kid and the Old Man, when the little gray coupé turned into the drive—and they were back!

"Don't ask questions, nobody!" the Kid warned them. "Just don't ask nothin', hear?" Then he looked at Klaus. "You can give me a hand with this old stinker again"— He nodded toward the Old Man. "Help me get him back in the house, and the things out. Only don't ask *nothin'*. I'm so mad I could spit."

He bristled. Even Klaus didn't venture to question him. But he did as the Kid suggested. He helped the Old Man out, and back into the bungalow again. Helped carry some of the luggage in.

When the car had been completely emptied, the Kid threw himself down on the steps. Shook his head back and forth. "Can you beat it?"

The others were waiting with bated breath.

"What is it?" Klaus asked. "Can't you tell us?"

"Can you beat it? And to think it had to happen to me! You know what?" He jerked a thumb back toward the house, yelled disgustedly: "That Old Man in there—*he ain't no American!*"

"No American?"

"No. Oh, geez, this is a fix now. Know how it happened? We get to the border and the guy there says, 'Where were you born?' to the Old Man, and Jesus Christ! if the Old Man doesn't say—as innocent as you please—'Montreal, Canada.'"

Siegfried laughed.

"And don't you laugh none either, see?" The Kid glared at him.

"But look," Klaus intervened. "It is not so bad. He didn't come into the United States illegally, did he? When he came from Canada, I mean?"

"Naw. He came in his mamma's arms, not even a year old. Least that's what he told the officer."

"Well then, his parents must have become citizens."

The Kid was disgusted. "Aw, his parents! What does he know about them? He ran away to be with horses."

"But doesn't he *know* about them?"

"How? He don't even know if they're dead. He knows from nothin'. That old geezer. There he is . . . an old guy that never says a word, never opens his trap . . . never even tells *me* much about his life . . . and what happens? The one time somebody in uniform happens to ask him a question, he has to open his mouth and pop out with somethin' I bet he never thought of for years. Maybe he *wasn't* even born in Canada! How can he remember?"

"Oh, it will work out. They'll investigate and find out he's all right. They'll let him back in."

"Yeah, and in the meantime? Suppose it takes months. I *told* you that old guy was nothin' but a load around my neck. Always messing up my life. And it ain't fair. Specially when he don't mean nothin' to me at all."

"No?" Klaus smiled. "Well then, why for don't you just go on to Florida? You can go and leave him here. We'll look out for him."

The Kid scuffed one boot in the dirt. Kept his face turned down.

"I'll think it over. But it'd be kind of a mean trick, don't you think? I wouldn't want to even leave a dog in a hole like this."

The immigrants looked at each other. Smiled. They knew the Kid would never leave the Old Man. They admired, adored him for it. Somehow, to them, he was what they dreamed and imagined that all Americans would be. On the surface, cocky and tough . . . but sentimental and good underneath.

Only Irmgard's smile faded sharply. A couple of words came back. "Wouldn't even leave a dog."

Yet it was the way that she had been left.

In Mr. Beckerly's office, that Monday morning, Jennifer faced three men.

Not frightened. She had faced so many important people for interviews that she had long ago conquered self-consciousness in front of strangers. In fact, she was encouraged; feeling that the more people she could get to listen to her, the better and quicker it would all be. The faces of these men were extremely serious. But nothing was going to mar her mood of confidence now.

The interview began similarly to her former interviews with Mr. Gatig alone. Mr. Beckerly asked a few questions. Jennifer got into her story; from then on she carried it along by herself. After the first five minutes, she felt that their sympathy was with her.

She told of life in Tijuana. She told of Klaus's efforts to get working permission. She tried to show how they suffered because they had to live in two separate worlds. Her tiring trips back and forth. The expense of keeping two homes. She stressed their one wish in life—to be able to live together, work together, have a home, put roots down in firm soil, begin to raise a family. Then after she had established their plight, she went back to tell of all the events which had led them into it . . . trying to show that that one lie to the consul in Nice had certainly never warranted a punishment such as they had received, and were still enduring. And then, above all and especially, she tried to make it clear that they were not bitter or disillusioned . . . that they were only at a great loss to know *why* it had happened like this.

She was surprised that her listeners let her continue right through to the end. She must have talked for fifteen or twenty minutes. Then suddenly she was talked out.

"I—well . . . well, I guess that's it. Only please, gentlemen, can't you help me?"

A hush in the room. Mr. Gatig looked at Mr. Beckerly. Mr. Beckerly looked at Mr. Terrain. "You'd better ask her some more questions, Beck," Mr. Terrain suggested.

So Mr. Beckerly began. "Mrs. Eckert, when you married . . . did you have any idea of the trouble you were going to run into?"

"No. My husband told me of what happened at Nice. I couldn't possibly imagine that any serious difficulties would come from that. I still can't imagine it. He said he lied to

324

the consul . . . foolishly . . . and that he had been 'caught.' But he wasn't lying under oath. He was just lying thoughtlessly, out of an emotional desire to see me again."

"But he filled out an application there."

"I know—and in that application he said that he had never been denied a visa. But that was his belief. He didn't really think that he *had* been denied in Paris. That first time in Paris, they just told him to go to Germany, where he was a citizen. Said he had better get it there. They didn't actually deny him a visa."

"That's true," Mr. Gatig intervened helpfully. "There was no formal refusal."

Jennifer leaned forward. "To tell you the truth, we never could understand why they didn't give him a visa, the first time in Paris. We have often talked about it. You see, he found out that other Germans in Paris got their visas there. The only thing he could think was that it was because he was so low on money."

"Hasn't it ever occurred to you that perhaps there was another reason?"

"No. If there were, I should think somebody would have told us." She looked from one face to the other, saw the men exchange glances. "Why? Was there?" she asked fearfully.

"Mrs. Eckert, in all fairness to you, I think it's time we bring this thing out on the table."

"That's what I'm hoping you'll do."

"Well then, first of all—did your husband ever mention knowing a Frenchman by the name of Briset?"

"Jean Briset? Yes. I know him, too."

325

The atmosphere had grown tense. Jennifer's heart speeded up. "Why?"

"Were he and your husband good friends?"

"I think so. At least, they were friendly. Would you tell me, please, what you're trying to find out?"

"Does Mr. Eckert ever speak of him now?"

"No. I had forgotten him myself. We had dinner with him one evening in Paris. That's the only time I ever saw him."

"What business was he in?"

"I don't remember. Oh, yes, I do. He owned a gift store. I remember now because my husband was going to take me there. Mr. Briset was supposed to have some very beautiful things from the Orient. Why?"

"When your husband first applied for a visa in Paris, he was asked to bring a letter of personal recommendation. It's the usual procedure when applicants are living in an alien country. Your husband brought a letter from Mr. Briset. The letter said they had been friends for years. It also said that—"

"Oh, Mr. Beckerly, don't drag it out. What are you trying to say?"

Mr. Beckerly stared straight into her eyes. "Jean Briset was head of one of the largest narcotic rings in France. He was also active in the United States. You didn't know that?"

On her face—complete shock. They recognized it as such. They were men who were trained in studying reactions.

"No," she said breathlessly. "I didn't know, but now I understand. You thought . . . my husband . . . was connected with him?"

326

"We're not saying that he *was* involved, Mrs. Eckert, only—"

"Let me go on from here," Mr. Terrain suggested. "Perhaps I can best explain, as long as this part is in my department. I know what you're thinking, Mrs. Eckert. Why didn't we tell your husband that it was because of that letter that he ran into difficulties? Is that right?"

Jennifer nodded.

"Well, I'll try to explain." Gravely he emphasized that they had had to be secretive. They were trying to catch Briset. Working on the case with the French authorities. Hadn't been able to arrest him in France, but about that time Briset was also planning to come to the United States, and they knew they could get something on him there. For that reason, they were anxious not to tip him off. If they had told Klaus that he was under suspicion because of this friendship they were afraid that Klaus might relay the matter back to him. And as for Klaus, the letter was brand enough. It didn't make him guilty, but it did make him a suspect. Then too, there was something else which made the authorities wary: the Frenchman had told several of his associates that he was increasing his activities in the United States, that he was sending a representative to Hollywood.

"Unfortunately, that was where your husband was bound for," Mr. Terrain pointed out.

"Oh gentlemen!" Jennifer said. "It's so silly. Not from your point of view—I know those things are serious—but from mine. If you only knew my husband!" She laughed. But not a normal laugh. "He was no more involved in a business like that than I am! Can't you see that that

327

letter—the very letter which made you suspect him—it's actually the thing which shows how innocent he was! Who would bring a letter, supposed to be a letter of recommendation, from somebody who was a narcotic dealer? Would you? Would anybody? It shows that Klaus didn't know. Mr. Briset wasn't the only Frenchman that my husband knew in Paris. He could have gotten such a letter from any one of a hundred different people. But by chance, by awful chance, he went to Mr. Briset for it. Isn't that proof that he didn't know about him?"

Jennifer saw that she had scored a point—at least, with Mr. Gatig and Mr. Beckerly. She saw their thoughtfulness, their accord with her reasoning. But Mr. Terrain remained doubtful.

"It could be that your husband knew about Briset, but *didn't* know that the authorities were on to him."

For the first time, Jennifer's control slackened, her voice louder.

"Oh, how can you go on so long suspecting somebody without investigating? Why don't you investigate my husband? Why don't you *face* Mr. Briset with the mess he's gotten my husband into?"

"Briset is dead."

"Dead?" she repeated dully.

"A few months ago. Killed himself, in New York, when he found out that we were going to arrest him."

"Then what about my husband? You said before the only reason you had to keep the case closed, was that you were afraid to investigate Klaus's part in it, because that might warn the man you wanted."

"The situation still holds. We're still rounding up some

of that crowd. You see, Mrs. Eckert, the only reason we're bringing the thing to light now is that now we've had a chance to meet you, talk to you. We're all sympathetic. We've seen what a tragedy all this has really been for you. We want to do something. We want to give you a chance now to clear it up if you can."

"Then let me phone him!"

"Telephone Mr. Eckert?"

"Yes. Right now. While we're all here. You can listen in. If we do it now, then you'll know I've had no chance to warn him . . . and you can tell a lot from his reaction. You see, if my husband had been in the same business, don't you think he'd know about Mr. Briset's death? Well, I'm going to prove to you that he doesn't. That he doesn't know anything about him . . . what business he was in, or anything. You've got to give me this chance. Oh, please. This is our future life I am begging for."

It was a long instant while she waited for an answer. Then Mr. Beckerly rose, said they would go down the hall, to the conference room. There were several extensions in there. He also asked Mr. Gatig to have one of the court stenographers come in.

In the conference room, Jennifer was suddenly frightened. Wasn't she perhaps making things worse? Staking so much on the hope that Klaus hadn't heard about the Frenchman. Suppose he had heard? Death news always got around somehow. Some friend in Paris might have written him. Still, Klaus always told her everything. It might be though, that he had meant to tell her and had just forgotten. Things like that happened sometimes—and if Klaus knew about Briset now it would only make matters more difficult.

329

For one instant she weakened, was afraid to go through with it. How unbelievable it all was, that so much heartache and confusion could result from just knowing the wrong somebody. Yet in immigration cases anything could happen. Look at the Lankowskis, all their trouble because of one innocent, but badly timed, question! People when they ask for visas, on trial socially, morally, and financially. And what irony. Klaus, her dear, sweet, good Klaus, damned as a possible menace to American morals.

"How are you going to handle the call, Mrs. Eckert? We wouldn't want you to ask anything point blank. It should be very casual. How will you explain it?"

"I'll have to think of something. . . . Perhaps . . . yes. Yes, I could do that. I have a sister in Paris. I don't hear from her very often. We're not very close. She's older, and she's lived there for so long. But I can pretend I heard from her . . . something about Mr. Briset."

It was ages, putting the call through. Jennifer heard the Tijuana operator, eventually heard Mrs. Berendo. Mrs. Berendo saying she would have to send a son to call Mr. Eckert. Then a long, long wait. Jennifer's heart was frozen.

Then Klaus shouted "Hello"—and his beloved voice released her tension.

"Hello, darling, it's me."

"I knew it was. What's the matter? What's happened? Are you all right?" His voice full of fright and worry.

Jennifer spent the whole first minute or two calming his fears. No, she hadn't been hurt. She *wasn't* sick. She was fine. No, really! Everything was going beautifully. She told him that she had already seen several men in the department

330

and she was soon going to see more. They were all being very nice, very sympathetic; it was going to work out.

"Then why do you call? I don't understand. Isn't it expensive? Why didn't you wait until night?"

"I'm upset. I have some news that worries me. A letter from Marian. Forwarded from Hollywood. I thought it would be good to talk to you. She's going to be married!"

"Marian? Good. I should think that would please you."

"It's *who* she's marrying that bothers me." Jennifer took a big breath, closed her eyes. Now it was coming. "It's Jean Briset."

His quick answer was a glorious relief. "That's not bad news. She couldn't do better. He's rich . . . good-looking. Only I don't understand how she got him." A pause. "Hello . . . Jennifer? You still there?"

"Yes, darling." She had sagged for a moment. Knew the crisis had been passed. She didn't look up at the others, just leaned further into the phone, as though the phone were Klaus, and she embracing him.

"I cannot understand why you worry," Klaus went on. "Is it because you are afraid to have another foreigner in the family? You think maybe she will have the trouble with him, like you have with me?"

"Well, I—"

"She won't. Jean comes back and forth to America, all the time. He travels everywhere. But why isn't he in the war?"

"She didn't say. Klaus, are you sure he will be a good husband for her?"

"If she can keep him. He's awfully crazy about women. Otherwise he's a good fellow. He's done for me a couple favors. You know, like he tried to help me out that first time I went to the consulate. He gave me a letter."

The pathetic irony of this was not lost to Jennifer. She looked quickly at Terrain.

"But, Klaus, wasn't he mixed up in some kind of crooked business?"

"Some of his Chinese antiques are fakes. But what of it? He gets away with it. I don't understand you, Jennifer. What you're so worried about. Didn't you really just call because you are homesick? You can admit it, because I am too. You are my home and when you are away from me, I am out in the cold and I am miserable. Are you sure you're all right?"

"Oh, yes, of course."

"Did you like the flowers?"

"I adored them. I wrote you a long letter yesterday. You ought to have it tomorrow."

"I wrote you one this morning, too. Schnucki's in heat. I wrote and asked you what I should do with her. Do you think maybe she would like some puppies?"

"Better ask *her*, hadn't you?"

"I think she would. But there's still time to decide when you come home. You think it might be soon?"

"Very soon . . ." and again Jennifer looked at Mr. Terrain. "Darling, I think our three minutes is about up."

"Didn't you ask her to warn you?"

"I forgot."

"Then let's don't let it run over. Good-by, Muschi. Try hard for us, won't you?"

"I am. I am trying every minute. Good-by, darling."

332

Jennifer put the phone down slowly. She leaned forward over the table, that great long, shiny conference table, and cried. She cried because of happiness, and exhaustion; knew that she had reached near-to-the-end of a long and wearisome journey.

"Well, no reason now why we can't at least reopen the case," Mr. Terrain said. "It doesn't mean he can have a visa. That's still up to the State Department. But our department will investigate him—we'll probably have to send a man—but if everything is as you say, there is a chance that we will withdraw our objections."

She raised her face, smiled.

"A chance is all we want, all we need," she told him gratefully.

On the way to the train that same afternoon, in a taxi, Jennifer saw some words written in stone on a great building.

THE PAST IS PROLOGUE.

The words blazed into her heart.

"What's that building?" she asked the driver.

"The Hall of Records, I think they call it. Did you enjoy your stay in Washington, miss?"

"Yes, in a way. I haven't seen much of it, though."

"You saw the Capitol at night?"

"No."

"You didn't? That's something to see. All lighted up, it looks like a big wedding cake. You saw the Lincoln Memorial?"

"No, I—"

"Not even that?"

333

"To tell you the truth I haven't seen anything. I haven't been able to see. This is the first moment that my eyes have really been open."

"You been sick?"

"In a way sort of. But I'm well now. I'll come back again sometime, when I have my husband with me. It's no fun to see things alone. When we come back together, we'll go over every square foot of the place."

"It's beautiful in the spring if you can make it then."

"I'd like to." She paused. "I'm glad anyway I saw those words back there before I left."

"What words?"

"Oh, just some words on a building."

THE PAST IS PROLOGUE. The words went through her mind again and again. It seemed to be Washington's message to her. What was past was only the beginning of the future. The future for Klaus and Jennifer was beginning now.

"I want to stop and send a telegram."

"You can do it from the station, miss."

It was three weeks before the special investigator came to Tijuana to go into the case. A whole day of questioning. But not nervous. Klaus went through it with an eagerness and a joy beautiful to see.

As the investigator left, he warned them it would be another two or three weeks before the Immigration Board at Washington would have a chance to study the testimony and arrive at a decision.

"We can wait," Klaus told him. "We can wait even a long time. It won't be hard now. Because we *know*."

334

The investigator frowned. "You can't be too sure of anything."

Klaus and Jennifer just looked at each other, smiled.

The investigator smiled, too. "Well, when you have faith like that, maybe you can be sure. I'm rooting for you anyway."

After he had gone, there were many things to plan. Not distant, doubtful plans as in the past. But close almost-any-day-now dreams. And in this kind of planning, the greatest happiness they had ever known. The first thing Klaus would eat, when he got into America. The first thing he would wear. The first thing they would do. The first place they would go. All tiny firsts, but so important. The beginning of a new world.

"I'm going to say, 'Howya Fred! Hi pal! Howya Billy!' to anybody and everybody I see on the street!" Klaus laughed. "You know, because they are going to be my fellow citizens some day."

"No, you're not," Jennifer reminded him. A big grin. "You know what you're going to say?" She thrust out her hand. "You're going to say, 'American?'"

"Put it there!" he chimed in. Ecstatically they shook hands.

Then he quickly sobered, in awe of their happiness. "Jennifer, just think. It can all be now as we planned. This time, a *really* beautiful life, my friend. Me working. You sitting home writing your stories. You can finish 'My Dad' now. No more running around the studios. . . ."

"There's one interview I still have to write."

"What's that?"

" ' "How I Brought up My Child to be a Star," by Maria Weiss as told to Jennifer Eckert.' "

"You think there's a chance?"

"Mady? Sure. I think Metro is going to sign her. I hope they do. Oh, I hope things work out for *everybody*. There's only one thing I feel terrible about. That's Irmgard."

"I know."

"I don't worry so much about Siegfried. He's taking care of himself. Or even Blima and Duwid. At least, they've had some happiness, in the baby. But suppose the consul finds out what Irmgard's doing? They'll never let her in then."

"I have warned her. But what can she do? She has to live. I can't blame her. She has to take the chance. And it is not very fair. Look at what happens all the time! An actress in Paris, or London . . . along comes a Hollywood executive on a talent search, and she can sleep with him if she wants, and maybe get a contract because of it, and they bring her to Hollywood, and no one ever thinks anything on that. They don't think on her as a prostitute. But Irmgard taking ten pesos from somebody to pay for frijoles and bread . . ."

"Couldn't we do something to help her?"

"Could we not give to her each month, the thirty dollars we have been paying for rent here? And a little more besides for food? We won't need so much money now. And I will be working soon."

"Do you think she would take it?"

"We could mail it from the States. Just put it in an envelope and address it on the typewriter. Tom always used to write her on the typewriter. She might think it is Tom."

336

"Wouldn't it be cruel to let her think that?"

"It is what she *wants* to think. It would help her. Cheer her up. Give her hope. Then after she gets her quota number, and really gets in, it won't matter any more, anyway. She will find somebody else more finer than he ever was."

"You're sweet, dear. It's what we'll do." She kissed him quickly.

With that settled, their spirits could soar again.

The great day came. The great hour. The great moment.

At the border gate, and at long last, they could cross together.

Blima, Duwid, Siegfried, Irmgard and the Kid there to say good-by.

"Please, Jennifer," Duwid said, "I have something to ask from you. When you are over there, on your side, and you say your prayers, will you say one for us, too?"

"Why of course, Duwid." Her voice thick, the tears creeping up.

"Because I sometimes think," Duwid explained, "that if you speak to God for us, and say it to Him in your nice English, then it will help. Because maybe, you see, He just doesn't understand our accent."

"Come." Klaus put his arm around Jennifer, saw that she had begun to cry. Duwid's words had pierced her spirit. He led her away to the car, which had already been passed through the gate and through customs, and with Schnucki sitting in it, was waiting at the other side.

He helped her in. "Don't be sad, Muschi. Take an example from me, or even from Schnucki. Look how happy she is."

337

"What does she know?" Jennifer mused. "For dogs, it is all the same world. What does she know about lines?"

"*I* know, though. Look at me."

"I can't," she smiled. "Your face is too bright. You dazzle me."

He started the car. Headed up Highway 101. The car went smoothly, sailing.

"Even the car goes better on this side!" Klaus exclaimed.

"Darling, we have to look back just once. We have to wave. Here, before this turn. This is the only chance."

They leaned out, waved back. Jennifer's eyes filled again as she saw Duwid's fluttering hand, remembered his last pathetic words.

"Oh, Klaus, I—"

He put his hand under her chin, drew it slowly around, turned her face forward.

"This way, Muschi. From now on, it's this way. Straight ahead."